RIDING
A CROCODILE

A Physician's Tale

PAUL KOMESAROFF

RIVER GROVE
BOOKS

Published by River Grove Books
Austin, Texas
www.greenleafbookgroup.com

Illustrations courtesy of Mirranda Burton

Distributed by River Grove Books

For ordering information or special discounts for bulk purchases, please contact River Grove Books at PO Box 91869, Austin, TX 78709, 512.891.6100.

Design and composition by Greenleaf Book Group LLC
Cover design by Greenleaf Book Group LLC
Cover images:
©iStockphoto.com/Gurzzza
©Shutterstock.com/charnsitr

Chapters 26, 55, and 80 contain quotations (at times slightly modified) from Komesaroff, P. A. *Experiments in Love and Death* (Melbourne University Press, 2008).

Publisher's Cataloging-In-Publication Data
Komesaroff, Paul A.
   Riding a crocodile : a physician's tale / Paul Komesaroff.—1st ed.
      p. : ill. ; cm.
   Issued also as an ebook.
   1. Medical personnel—Professional ethics—Fiction. 2. Widowers—Fiction. 3. Medical ethics—Fiction. I. Title.
PS3611.O447 R54 2014
813/.6

LCCN: 2013957925
Print ISBN: 978-1-938416-50-7
eBook ISBN: 978-1-938416-51-4

First Edition

For Sally, Frida, and Ilya.

A distressing feature in the life which you are about to enter, a feature which will press hardly upon the finer spirits among you and ruffle their equanimity, is the uncertainty which pertains not alone to our science and art, but to the very hopes and fears which make us men. In seeking absolute truth we aim at the unattainable, and must be content with finding broken portions. . . . Each one of us may pick up a fragment, perhaps two, and in moments when mortality weighs less heavily upon the spirit, we can, as in a vision, see the form divine, just as a great naturalist . . . can reconstruct an ideal creature from a fossil fragment.

—Sir William Osler

In its expression, in its mortality, the face before me summons me, calls for me, begs for me, as if the invisible death that must be faced by the Other, pure otherness, separated, in some way, from any whole, were my business. . . . The other man's death calls me into question, as if, by my possible future indifference, I had become the accomplice of the death to which the other, who cannot see it, is exposed; . . . as if I were devoted to the other man before being devoted to myself, or more exactly, as if I had to answer for the other's death even before being. A guiltless responsibility, whereby I am not the less open to an accusation of which no alibi, spatial or temporal, could clear me . . . a responsibility stemming from a time before my freedom—before my beginning, before any present.

—Emmanuel Levinas

CONTENTS

I LOVE YOU
YOU WILL BE MISSED
GET WELL SOON!

DRAMATIS PERSONAE

Abraham Nevski, physician and professor of medicine
Rebecca Sanderson, Abraham's registrar
Desmond Ray, ward head nurse
Ashis Narayan, resident/intern
Nic Praxotidis, Abraham's colleague and confidant
Madeleine Silverstein, Abraham's colleague and confidante
George, Carmen, Bruno, Tracey, students

Harry Krokowski, Director, Emergency Department
Allison Wong, Director of Medicine
Jonathan Bitic, Director of Surgery
Ian Moloney, respiratory physician
Frederick Tauber, Head of Neurology
Peter James, oncologist
Damien Trentino, Director of ICU
Kerri Yavuz, Director, Hospital Transplantation Service
Natalie Hermann, palliative care physician
Jeremy, night registrar
Doctor in the Emergency Department
Emily, nurse in ICU
Jenny, Abraham's secretary
Margaret Wilson, Chief Executive Officer
Colin Tyler, expert on Freedom to Choose
David Draeger, economist at Ultimate
Susanna, Freedom to Choose communication consultant

John Blair, Emergency Department registrar at Swamp Road Hospital
Carly O'Hallaran, registrar at Swamp Road Hospital
Denise Roland, Director of Nursing at Swamp Road Hospital
Nurse Jones, nurse at Swamp Road Hospital
Dr. O'Brien, consultant doctor at Swamp Road Hospital

Mordechai Nevski, Abraham's father
Esther Nevski, Abraham's mother

Various patients and their family members:

Pete Adams
Mr. Alvarez, son Diego, daughter Sofia, granddaughter and grandsons
Marina Bell
Briony Best and daughter Bree
Dorothy Camello
Jocelyn Chauchat
Betty Da Silva
Wilma Dreyfus and daughters Maggie and Josephine
Christine Fellegi
Billy Georgiannis, mother and brother George
Mrs. Gurewitz
Mr. Herbert
Mr. and Mrs. Hörök
Barry McLeod and daughter Patricia
Mrs. Newton
Quentin Prince
Kath Simpson, husband Robert and daughters Gillian, Christine, and Helen
Charlie Timmens, partner Wendy and friend Kevin
Ursula Timoshenko and husband Yevgeny
Dimitri Tzorvas
Dr. Vilgis and sister Dora
Flora Wood

Most of the action takes place at the Royal Prince John Hospital.

PART 1

WARD 3B

1.

braham Nevski was on his way to work. As usual, the train carriage was packed to capacity, with women and men of varying ages, professional and manual workers, office staff, shopkeepers, cleaners, students. Coming from different directions, going to different places, for a few minutes they shared a journey.

Although it had been two months since Abraham had last traveled this route, little had changed. There was the same erratic rocking and jerking of the train, the same torn upholstery, the same graffiti-spattered walls and ceiling. As usual, the passengers sat, if they were lucky enough to find a seat, or stood holding on to the steel poles or plastic straps, bracing themselves against the train's unpredictable changes in speed. As usual, some struggled to read newspapers or books, some listened to music through headphones, and others simply gazed into space, resignedly waiting out the journey. Today, even though it was early, the air inside was already warm.

Over the nearly twenty years he had worked at the Royal Prince John Hospital Abraham had covered the route many times. He couldn't imagine how many people he had seen come and go during this time. Large stretches of lives had passed in front of him. He had seen schoolchildren grow up and leave school and office workers grow old and retire. Although today there were many familiar faces in the carriage it was unlikely that he would exchange words with any of them. The etiquette of the public transport system prevented this.

Abraham had developed a private game to amuse himself on these journeys. Secretly adopting the role of an undercover detective, he would scrutinize his fellow passengers carefully and construct stories around what he was able to observe. He would complete a mental checklist of the facts: details of passengers' clothing, how they sat and interacted with others, their facial expressions, what they were reading, even what they said in the phone calls on which he was able to eavesdrop. He noted the fresh-looking, carefully groomed appearances of his fellow travelers in the mornings, how their hair was meticulously brushed and their clothes fresh and ironed, and how the women smelled of perfume and the men of aftershave or deodorant. In the evenings, he observed how their clothes had become crumpled and the smells had changed, how the perfume had worn off and had been replaced by a faint scent of sweat. Sometimes the scent was not so faint.

There were a few regular travelers who Abraham had decided were probably office workers. His eyes fixed on one of these, a man in late middle age with sparse graying hair and a ruddy, deeply furrowed face. Abraham often enjoyed surreptitiously watching him and inventing stories to explain his observations. Today, as usual, he went through the facts one by one. First and most obvious, the man was grossly overweight and always out of breath, even when sitting at rest. Second, he invariably carried an old leather briefcase and, regardless of the weather, dressed formally in a threadbare business suit, an old-fashioned vest, and the same stained tie. Third, he maintained a fixed expression of haughty disapproval of his fellow passengers, from time to time peering censoriously at unruly schoolchildren over the top of expensive, gold-rimmed glasses. Fourth, was the way he moved. Grasping any available fixture for support, gasping and wheezing, he would maneuver his large frame and swollen belly slowly and laboriously in a manner that indicated both pain somewhere and failing muscle power. Sometimes he teetered so precariously that Abraham feared for his safety, especially when the train jerked or lurched, but so far the man had never actually fallen. Eventually another passenger would make a seat available for him into which he would lower himself with obvious relief, never acknowledging the act of generosity but merely accepting it as if it were his entitlement. He would then sit stiff and erect, his mouth pursed with disdain, for the remainder of the journey, at least until Abraham himself alighted.

Playing his game, Abraham had concluded, after careful deliberation, that his companion had once been a wealthy businessman who had fallen on hard times. The pompous expression and formal attire showed how much he resented the humiliation associated with his decline. Abraham speculated that when the business had failed the man's marriage had broken up—or maybe it had been the other way round—and he had sunk into a depression. In the end, merely to survive he had taken a lowly job as an accountant in a government department. Now, as he was aging, his health was badly failing. His body was betraying him just as his wife had done. The problems with his heart and lungs meant that even minor chores were difficult, evoking a rising dread about the future. Sadly, he was entering old age infirm, poor, and alone. The man's life, which had once been so promising, was drawing to a joyless and disappointing close.

Abraham thought of the imaginary predicament he had constructed for the stranger and his heart filled with pity. How many of these people, he wondered, were unhappy and frustrated like this man? How many of them lived out their lives without a sense of purpose, without the promise and optimism they undoubtedly once felt in their youth? How many of them, like him, longed for companionship, for love, for intimacy? If there was something he could do to help them, what might it be?

As he continued his musings Abraham's attention was drawn to a young woman sitting not far away in a corner of the carriage. He had not noticed her at first and could not recall seeing her get on the train. He guessed that she was in her mid-twenties. He scrutinized her carefully, playing his game. She had long, flaming red hair, and although dressed in an elegantly cut shirt and slacks, nonetheless seemed slightly disheveled. Her facial features were fine and her skin pure. She was clutching a calico bag tightly on her lap, as if it contained something of importance that she sought to conceal or protect from those around her. She was wearing gold stud earrings but no other jewelry or makeup. Although in a carriage crammed with people she gave no indication of any awareness of others. She was alone, immersed in her thoughts, which were somehow connected with whatever she was guarding in the bag.

He tried to imagine what the bag might contain. Was it a message from her mother in another city relaying the news that her father or some other close relative was seriously ill? Was it a notification from her employer advising her that her services were no longer needed? Was it a letter from her boyfriend telling her that he had found someone else? Maybe it wasn't a letter at all. Perhaps it was a precious artifact, which reminded her of someone dear. Maybe it was something from her childhood. Maybe it was a gun.

Suddenly, perhaps aware of the intense gaze focused on her, the young woman stirred from her reverie and looked across at Abraham. Their eyes met and they held each other's gaze for maybe four or five seconds. As they did so Abraham felt a chill throughout his body. There was something about her that unnerved him, that captivated and compelled him.

Since Abraham's wife had died he had become increasingly aware of the power women could exercise over men and his own vulnerability to it. The young woman was certainly attractive, but this was no exercise of sexual power. She was alone, painfully alone. In her eyes was a sadness deeper than anything Abraham had ever before witnessed. There was also a beauty, a melancholy beauty. But what unnerved him was an unmistakable sense she expressed of raging anguish and frantic despair, of turmoil that was beyond contact with the outside world. She drew his interest but then rejected and dismissed his attention with a wild, resigned hopelessness.

Abraham was suddenly struck with a terrible realization: she is going to her death. He could feel it in his own body. Almost in panic he tore his gaze away. He could feel his heart beating. Sweat formed on his forehead. He felt a sense of disorientation, of falling through space, so much so that he actually threw out his hands to steady himself.

I must do something to save her, he thought, but then he quickly checked himself. What a fool he was! How absurd to think that way! This was just a game, a private game! How could he know anything so personal about a complete stranger sitting on the other side of a railway carriage with whom he had had no more than a few seconds' contact? What right did he have to impose his idle reflections on her, to intrude on her own private musings?

He forced himself to look around the carriage. There were lots of people there, no doubt just as unhappy as she was. Or maybe she wasn't unhappy at all. He could know no more about her than he could about any of dozens of other passengers in the carriage. No one else appeared to have noticed anything untoward. All continued quietly to go about their business, or lack of it.

The train was pulling into his station. What should he do? Should he go to her, offer his help, offer to calm her, to comfort her? He couldn't make up his mind. Reeling with uncertainty, he stood up. The train had now stopped and the doors had opened. He turned back toward the girl, but to his shock her seat was empty. He looked around frantically. For an instant he caught sight of her red hair as she disappeared toward the end of the platform. He did not know what he should have done, but whatever that was, the moment had now been lost.

He stepped down from the train himself into the warm, stale air of the station and set out on his own familiar route. His body knew where to take him—through the gate, up the ramp, along the streets, to the hospital. But this time was different. He felt weak and unsteady. Something about that brief moment's contact had shaken him to his core.

Why am I so affected, he asked himself. She is a stranger. I have been aware of her existence for no more than maybe ten minutes. Yet this tenuous connection has somehow exerted a hold on me. It is as if by that most elementary contact I am now tied to her. I was confronted with the need of another person to whom I felt called upon to respond, and I chose not to do so. I will never see her again. I will never know whether she was sad or happy, in love or in despair. I will never know whether my decision not to act was the right one. But I cannot escape the fact that our paths have crossed, however briefly, and as a result my life has been changed.

The young woman lingered long in Abraham's thoughts as he made his way along the street, to the hospital steps, and through its large sliding-glass doors.

2.

Inside the building, the discomfort Abraham had carried with him gradually gave way to the reassuring familiarity of the world he was entering. The air was cool and dry, with the faint staleness characteristic of hospitals everywhere. A controlled hustle and bustle had replaced the chaos of the traffic outside. People moved in all directions—striding, limping, carrying bags, pushing carts or wheelchairs; using crutches, canes, or walkers; wearing dressing gowns, white coats, or operating room garb; with grave, sad faces or beaming with optimism. Abraham loved the atmosphere. For him, it was an entire world; he had, in fact, spent nearly half his life in it. It was a world of pain and pleasure, of purpose and perplexity. There was tedium and crushing routine, but also excitement and profound satisfaction. He breathed deeply, his dark thoughts about the girl on the train now a fading memory.

"Abraham!" a voice called out. He turned to see one of the senior consultants, Madeleine Silverstein. "Hello! It's nice to have you back. We've missed you."

Everything about Madeleine suggested efficiency and decisiveness. Her black hair was cut short and she wore dark-rimmed glasses, a plain shirt, a flared, calf-length brown skirt, and sensible shoes. Her only concession to nonfunctional values was a brooch in the shape of a butterfly pinned to her shirt. She spoke in clipped sentences. "It's been busy in the hot weather. Lots of elderly people admitted with dehydration. I'm personally looking forward to the cool change. Our house has been dreadfully hot and I haven't been able to sleep for a week. How was your break?"

Abraham recognized the forced breeziness in her manner. She as much as anyone knew how hard it had been for him in the last year, with his wife's illness and death, his estrangement from his children, and the burden of caring for his aging parents. She was one of his allies in the perpetual battle with management and now just to see her made him feel secure.

"Hello, Madeleine. It's good to see you, too. The break was okay. Things get a bit easier every day. I'd better keep moving, though. I've got to get to my first handover."

"Oh, I forgot that you're taking over for me on Ward 3B today! Well, perhaps we can meet for lunch. I'll ask Nic Praxotidis to join us, too, if he can. There's lots to tell you. It's not all good news either. See you at lunchtime."

She hurried off. Abraham made his way to Ward 3B, thinking about the conversation. He was pleased to be back. He liked the patients and was looking forward to resuming clinical duties. He loved the teaching, too, often referring to it—partly to antagonize his colleagues who saw it as an onerous chore—as a "high honor." But he wondered what Madeleine had meant. No doubt he would find out soon enough.

3.

The morning ritual of handover was an old medical institution in which one carer passed the baton of care to another, explaining the triumphs and frustrations of the time just past. In the modern hospital setting it was a formalized process, marking changes of shifts of doctors, nurses, and others, ensuring continuity and consistency of care, and providing an opportunity for unresolved problems and uncertainties to be discussed with colleagues. This handover was going to be especially important for Abraham after two months away.

"Hi, Prof!" a couple of young doctors chorused as he went past.

"Hello! How are you?" he answered with feigned brightness, hoping to cover the fact that he could not remember their names. He passed through the ward into the handover room, where the proceedings were almost ready to start.

Abraham prided himself on being an old-style doctor, one who spent time with his patients and actually listened to and talked with them. This was, he thought, rare in these days of emphasis on rapid, decisive action, often linked to the use of technologies, tied to the demands of budgets and administrators, and in response to ever-increasing numbers of patients in the chronically overburdened public hospital system.

His wife used to get annoyed with the interruptions to home life from his cell phone. "You shouldn't give all your patients your cell phone number," she would say, "or else you don't always have to answer it."

"But it may be an emergency," he would reply. "And I trust my patients not to call me for frivolous reasons." She had usually not been convinced and the problem was never solved.

Although Abraham appreciated the value of the morning handover session it was the ward round that followed he really enjoyed, along with the outpatient clinics and the teaching sessions he worked into his schedule whenever time permitted. Today was going to be a long day: after handover he had the students, then a ward round, then outpatients, then a couple of research meetings, and some hospital committee or other and a teleconference or two. If he was lucky he could be out of the hospital by seven. Then there was the evening's program of reading, writing, doing email, catching up.

The small, windowless room in the center of the ward was already buzzing with activity. The night resident was there yawning, waiting to give his reports, and the other residents, the students, the nursing staff, and others were straggling in, some with a few stories about their evenings, others looking as if they had just gotten out of bed.

A young woman came up to him. "Are you Professor Nevski?" she asked. "I'm Rebecca Sanderson, your registrar. We hear you've been away on vacation. Welcome back!"

Abraham looked at her—a slim, attractive woman of about twenty-five, with shoulder-length brown hair and a disarmingly warm smile. "Hello, Rebecca. Thanks. I'm pleased to be back, too. I'm looking forward to being on the ward. How long have you been in the unit?"

"This is my fourth week."

"It can be a tough rotation. How are you finding it?"

"It was hard at first. It's the first general medical job I've done and a lot of things have been new to me. I think I'm getting the hang of it now, though. Dr. Silverstein was the consultant over the last month and she gave me a lot of support."

"Yes, Madeleine's a great teacher. Perhaps after this meeting we can go through all the patients on the ward. I have to take the students at nine o'clock. Would you be able to do a ward round at ten?"

"Yes, that'll be perfect. It'll also give us time to check up on whatever urgent things need to be done." She turned to a nervous-looking young man standing close by. "I'd like to introduce you to our intern, Ashis."

The young man smiled shyly. "Hello, Ashis," said Abraham. "I'm looking forward to working with you, too. How long have you been on the ward?"

"Hi, Prof. This is only my second week but I'm really enjoying it. There's a lot to learn!"

Abraham looked at the young man. Slightly built and neatly dressed in a shirt and tie with formal trousers; the pockets of his shirt stuffed with pens, pieces of paper, and a pager; and a stethoscope hanging round his neck, the impression he created was an agreeable one of earnestness and unassuming warmth. Abraham had an immediate sense that he would enjoy working with Ashis.

"When you're with us it's important that both of you feel fully supported," he said to the registrar and the intern. "I'll give you my cell number so you can call if there's anything you need to discuss at any time." He continued, "I think we'd better start."

"Jeremy the night registrar's over there," replied Rebecca. "Do you want me to introduce you to him?"

"No, that's okay. I know Jeremy." Then in a loud voice to the company, Abraham began. "Hello, everyone. Let's get under way. For those who don't know me, I'm Abraham Nevski. I'm taking over as the consultant on the ward for the next two months. I'm pleased to be here and looking forward to working with all of you. Jeremy, I understand that you've been covering during the night. It's nice to see you again. Can you tell us how the night went?"

"Thanks, Prof. It's good to see you, too," replied the young doctor. "The night was okay. We only had three admissions and two emergency calls, although I did have a bit of trouble with Mrs. Gurewitz, the old woman with the fitting, who kept dropping her blood pressure. Oh, and Mr. Saleh died; he was the sixty-eight-year-old man with lung cancer in bed fifteen."

The resident summarized the problems of the three new patients who had come in overnight: an elderly man with a heart attack, a woman from a nursing home with a chest infection, and a young drug user with an overdose. For each of them he stated what was known about the background, explained the immediate circumstances of the admission, and recounted the findings on physical examination. After each there was a brief discussion about what tests needed to be done and whether there were any other issues to be considered.

While the discussion was proceeding Abraham surveyed the other people in the room. These included a number of junior doctors rustling papers and consulting lists, a student sending a text message on her phone, another looking distractedly into space, a muscular looking physiotherapist, a social worker with bright lipstick, and one of the ward nurses. Ashis was taking detailed notes from the night resident's monologue. The intern had a small book in which he evidently jotted down points he had to remember and the tasks he had to complete during the day. Interns can be organized and systematic, or chaotic and always in crisis. In the latter case, the burden on the consultant was always significantly greater. Abraham felt a sense of relief that Ashis seemed to be of the more organized kind.

He also took the opportunity to observe Rebecca more closely. He now sensed a radiance that went beyond the smile. Her lips were gentle and there were small frown lines on her forehead, which he thought quite becoming. She was wearing a demure, dark-colored T-shirt and a plain skirt and had a gold chain around her neck from which was suspended a gold, heart-shaped locket. She looked athletic. Abraham speculated that she exercised regularly; maybe she ran or cycled.

The resident drew to a close. Abraham took over again. "Thanks, Jeremy. We'll wait to see what turns up today. Can anyone tell us about Mr. Saleh who died?"

"He was ours," said Rebecca. "He was a sixty-eight-year-old man who'd come with a couple of months of weight loss and coughing up blood. The chest X-ray showed a suspicious lesion in his right middle zone, and a CT-guided biopsy showed a small cell carcinoma.* We staged him, and the ultrasound showed lots of lesions in the liver. We discussed the possibility of chemo with him and his wife and son, and they were going to think about it. Mr. Saleh seemed to accept the diagnosis okay. I think he was expecting it."

Abraham reflected that in a few short, prosaic sentences the registrar had summarized what for the patient and his family had no doubt been a story of terror and despair. Coughing up blood is a frightening symptom and for almost everyone evokes the possibility of cancer. Some early cancers can be cured. Why did he delay two months before seeking help? Was he just paralyzed by fear? He was sixty-eight—still a young man by today's standards. Maybe there were many things he had still planned to do. He'll never do them now. "Why do you think he died? Was it an expected death?"

"No, we didn't expect him to die. In fact, he was still working until last week."

"Could it have been a complication of the medical tests?"

"The biopsy was on Wednesday, and we really haven't done anything else invasive to him. I mentioned the possibility of a postmortem, but the family is Muslim and they said they just wanted to bury him as quickly as possible. I wish I knew why he died."

"Probably we'll never find out."

Abraham wondered how Mr. Saleh's family was taking the death. It must be a terrible time for them. Maybe Mr. Saleh knew he was going to die. Did he say goodbye to his wife and son? Will it matter to them if he didn't? Will they blame the hospital for his death?

The meeting continued with its business. There were routine ward issues, a few patients with IV drips to be replaced, a few matters the social worker

---

* For explanations of the meanings of technical terms and abbreviations see the Glossary on pp. 363–364.

needed to discuss, reminders about the day's meetings, and the lunchtime pizza being put on by a drug company in the residents' quarters.

Already the routine was taking over. Abraham did not mind this: in fact, he enjoyed the sense that he was always in demand, always wanted by someone. As soon as the meeting ended, he leaned across the table.

"Rebecca, I have to take the students at nine. Have you got any patients who'd be good for them to see?"

"There's a great patient in bed twelve who came in with a fever. We don't know what's wrong with him yet, but he's a good historian. His name's Mr. Herbert."

"Thanks. He sounds perfect. I'll ask him if he'd be happy to see medical students. See you at ten."

4.

He went to the reception area at the center of the ward to wait. All the wards in the hospital followed the same standard design. They were laid out in two parallel corridors about fifty meters long, off which, facing outward, were the individual rooms, each accommodating one, two, or four patients. The space in between the corridors housed the various facilities required for patient care, including the clean and dirty utility rooms; offices of the head nurse and ancillary staff; meeting rooms for nurses, doctors, and patients' families; assorted rooms for storage; and the reception area itself. At one end, both corridors led to the main hospital elevator area and at the other they led either to the ward pharmacy or to the "procedure room," which was used for minor procedures or to house an occasional noisy or disruptive patient.

Abraham looked around him, as usual going through the facts he could observe one by one. Anyone entering the ward from the elevators would be presented with a long straight walkway in which, at any time of the day or night, people came and went, engaged in a variety of tasks. As elsewhere in the hospital, the area was lit with bright fluorescent lights set into a ceiling constructed of plain white fibrous panels. The light brown carpet on the floor, patterned with randomly placed, curved red and brown lines, served the purpose both of softening the effect of the straight architectural lines and hiding any stains. The walls containing the doors to the individual rooms were broken up intermittently by bathrooms, hand washing stations, and alcoves for storage of patient records, where doctors and nurses could sit to write notes, consult, and make entries on the ward computers. On the inner walls, the entry points to the various utility areas were interrupted halfway along by the reception area where the ward clerk sat with the telephones; a large board containing patient names; and various computers, printers, and fax machines. This wall contained a few art works—mainly cheap prints of Impressionist or other well-known paintings in dilapidated frames.

In addition to the severe, rectilinear layout, the harsh lighting, and the overall sense of commotion, a visitor would quickly become aware of the sounds and smells that also characterized the ward. The presence of such a large number of people inevitably produced a persistent, drumming murmur, only partly muted by the ceiling panels and the carpet. Occasional snatches of conversation merged with the incessant background hum of the air-conditioning; the inevitable beeping of pagers, cell phones, and other equipment; the sounds of doors opening and closing, water running, music from patients' televisions and radios, and frequent announcements over the loudspeaker system through which an unseen person with an expressionless voice paged staff members, asked named patients to return to their beds, or announced a medical or other emergency somewhere in the hospital.

The olfactory environment was no less richly textured than the auditory one. The enclosed, recirculated air produced a sense of controlled mustiness. As one walked around the ward this changed rapidly and unpredictably, being frequently punctuated by odors wafting from one source or other. The pungent smell of disinfectant could be mixed with the fragrance of flowers brought by visitors, and the heavy odor of overcooked food might merge with the earthier—and sometimes frankly nauseating—stench of feces and vomit.

Abraham, now half in a trance, closed his eyes to immerse himself more fully in this heady plenitude of sounds and smells. He stood there for a few seconds, alternating his concentration between one and the other, reflecting on the fact that he had once been so habituated to the hospital environment that the sensory richness was almost invisible to him. His recent personal experiences with hospitals during his wife's illness had changed that. He now seemed oddly distant from the place. He could understand how overwhelming and terrifying the assault on the senses must be for anyone entering it for the first time as a patient or relative.

His reverie was interrupted by a voice behind him. "Are you Professor Nevski?" someone asked.

Startled, he spun around. "Yes, I'm Professor Nevski," he replied, forcing a smile to hide his surprise. "You must be the students."

5.

Standing to one side of the reception area, he introduced himself to the four medical students and asked them to tell him a little about themselves. Abraham was aware that he was not good at remembering names and had therefore trained himself when he was introduced to someone to inspect them closely in search of a memorable characteristic. George had a short, ginger beard, Bruno was swarthy with thick glasses, Tracey had a clear, pale complexion and short, blonde hair, and Carmen was tall and well built, with high-heeled shoes and an awkward manner.

He led them to the patient's room, ushered them inside, and asked them to introduce themselves to the man in the bed, who as they mentioned their names acknowledged each of them in turn with a slight nod of his head.

Abraham then turned to the first student. "Now, Carmen, can you tell me what you know about Mr. Herbert?"

The student looked nonplussed. " . . . I don't know anything . . . I've only just met him."

"Look carefully and tell me what you see."

Carmen looked even more awkward. She brushed her hair nervously with her hand. "He has an IV drip in his arm?" she said, looking at Abraham pleadingly, as if this were a question he should answer.

Abraham adopted a manner that he thought was stern but kind. "What else?"

"He doesn't seem to be in any distress."

"Take your time. Start from the beginning. Look around the room, look at Mr. Herbert, and tell me carefully what you observe. Anyone else can help."

"He's a middle-aged man," said another one of the students.

"Good."

"According to the sign above his bed he was admitted yesterday," said another.

"Yes."

"Saline's being infused through the IV drip."

"He has lots of bruises over his body."

"He's very thin."

Mr. Herbert shifted uneasily.

"His face looks like it may be a bit swollen."

"Anything else? Look around the room."

"He hasn't eaten all his lunch but has left most of it on the tray in front of him."

"He has his own quilt and pillowcase . . ."

" . . . Er . . . There are lots of get-well cards on the dresser."

Silence. "That's excellent. Let me tell you what I think's happening here . . . Remember, I haven't met Mr. Herbert before, either, except to ask his permission to talk with us, so what I say may be completely wrong. But let's see how we go. I think the story may run a little like this: Mr. Herbert's a man in his fifties who's suffered from a chronic inflammatory bowel condition for many years, most likely Crohn's disease. It's been difficult to treat and has required therapy with systemic cortisone-like drugs. The illness has been complicated by diabetes and an episode of venous thrombosis, for which he receives the anticoagulant warfarin. In recent weeks he's become unwell, with tiredness, fevers, and some nosebleeds. When he was admitted he was very sick but has responded quite rapidly to antibiotic therapy. He has a close and supportive family and at least two grandchildren." Abraham turned to the patient: "How did I do, Mr. Herbert? Is any of that right?"

The patient was obviously taken aback. "You're a hundred percent right, Professor. Congratulations!"

The students were silent for a few moments. Then one of them asked haltingly, in a small voice, "How could you tell all that?"

"It was simple," said Abraham, allowing himself to gloat slightly. "It's clear that Mr. Herbert has a chronic condition that's put him in the hospital many times. He's evidently comfortable in hospitals and is so familiar with the journey here that he even knows to pack his own quilt and pillow. He's very thin, so he's probably unable to absorb nutrients from his small bowel. The most common chronic inflammatory condition of the small bowel is Crohn's disease, of which I'm sure you've heard. His face is swollen in the typical pattern caused by steroid—so-called 'cortisone'—treatment, further supporting the hypothesis that he has a chronic inflammatory condition. As a complication of the cortisone treatment he's developed diabetes, as is indicated by the sugar-free meal he's partially eaten. He's also developed the relatively rare complication of inflammatory bowel disease, venous thrombosis—that is blood clots in the veins—which have necessitated treatment with the anticoagulant warfarin. This is evident from the bruises over his body. Am I right, Mr. Herbert? He's pale, suggesting that he may be anemic. This could be due to the fact that he's been malabsorbing iron or other nutrients. However, I assume that his doctors would have been very alert to this and he would have received all the necessary supplements. This means that he may have lost some blood. However, if this is the case it wouldn't have been from his bowel, because then he wouldn't be allowed to eat, pending tests to find the source of the bleeding. Accordingly, the bleeding must have come from elsewhere, probably the nose. I wasn't sure about this, and to be honest it was really only a guess. The IV's infusing saline at a very slow rate, indicating that its main purpose is to introduce other drugs, most probably antibiotics. The possibility of an infection is increased by the immunosuppression caused by the cortisone-related treatment. This means that when he came to the ED he was probably suffering from fevers, in addition to the tiredness and lethargy related to his anemia. He's now sitting up in bed looking quite well, indicating that he's responded quickly to the treatment, which was therefore the right one. The proliferation of cards and signs around the room, which include at least two marked 'to Grandpa,' in spite of the fact that he's been here for only one day and is in the habit of coming to the hospital not infrequently, testifies to the closeness and commitment of his family support. That's right isn't it, Mr. Herbert? There you are, as I said, it was obvious."

Abraham stopped to soak up the silent admiration of the students. Still basking in his success he then invited them to question the patient closely about his condition. As they did so, he interrupted from time to time to ask why they had asked this or that question, or how they interpreted this or that answer. When they had finished he thanked the patient and ushered the students outside. They discussed what they had seen and heard. Abraham tried to sum up the lesson.

"In the time you're with me I hope to be able to show you how potent clinical reasoning can be. Don't underestimate the power of the weapons at your disposal. You have to cultivate this power but also learn to use it carefully. At a single glance—an informed, cultivated glance—you can sometimes see into someone's darkest secrets and most intense fears. Take everything into account, develop the habit of constantly posing and testing hypotheses. I know you feel a bit overwhelmed and bewildered at the moment, but you'll be surprised to learn how much you already know. Sometimes you can get into trouble by knowing too much. Be humble and discreet and take care to make use of your knowledge judiciously and with circumspection."

He was aware that he was pontificating, but on this occasion he allowed himself the indulgence. His success with the diagnosis justified this once. The sermon over, he parted from the students and made his way to the meeting with the ward staff.

6.

"Watch out!"

Abraham looked up just in time to jump aside, narrowly avoiding a large, portable X-ray machine that was rumbling along the corridor at high speed. The driver of the machine, a rough-looking hospital porter covered with tattoos, glared at Abraham as he hurtled past without slowing down.

Abraham, bewildered, looked around and tried to regain his composure. His return to work was turning out to be more of a struggle than he had anticipated—the strange feeling of aloofness, the red-headed girl, the bad news Madeleine and Nic had to tell him, and now, near disaster in the ward. He was surprised to see Rebecca and Ashis close by, evidently enjoying the scene and laughing loudly. He collected himself from his absent-minded daydream. "That's the third time that Hell's Angel's nearly run me down!" he muttered.

Abraham was suddenly aware that his appearance to the young doctors must have seemed slightly ridiculous. He pretended to smile. "Okay. I'll let it go. Do you have time to go through our patients?"

"Yes, we'd better get started," replied Rebecca. "We have fifteen patients, including the three new ones who came in overnight and excluding two who went home this morning. We'll need to talk about all of them, and there are a few I'd like you to see right away."

7.

Desmond Ray, the nurse in charge of Ward 3B, was widely regarded around the hospital as a colorful character. Flamboyant and extroverted, he alone seemed to be on first-name terms with all the members of staff, including the orderlies and maintenance workers. With his loud voice and raucous laugh, the sounds of which were familiar around the ward, he was always ready to hold forth on any topic. In addition, his often-outlandish dress was a frequent subject of conversation, a fact that he himself obviously relished. Today, he was wearing a French-style beret on his closely cropped head, positioned carefully to highlight the ring in his left ear.

Everything about Desmond irritated Abraham, who could never understand why people considered him interesting. It could not, he thought, be because of his physical stature, which was unremarkable. It couldn't be because of his exaggerated self-confidence or his penchant for brightly colored shirts. It was surely not a result of his habit of taking strong, definitive positions on contentious topics without any understanding of the complex details. Nor could it be the physical liberties he took with others, male and female, such as grabbing their hands or even throwing his arms around them, which Abraham considered inappropriate in the serious formality of the hospital setting.

Despite some grudging mutual respect, over the years they had known each other their relationship had always been frosty. Abraham acknowledged Desmond's commitment to his job and undoubted technical skills but could not restrain his impatience with the nurse's captious and histrionic manner. He knew that on the other side, Desmond recognized his intellect but was irritated by his fastidiousness, making no secret of the fact that he considered this an affectation. He suspected that the hostility between them reflected the traditional tension between nurses and doctors, even if the battle lines between feminized caring and manly technocratic potency were in this case blurred. As time passed, a mutual tolerance might have formed, at least on the basis of the many hours they had shared together in patient care. But if anything, the opposite was the case, and the more contact they had the greater was the hostility between them.

Abraham was always pleased when Desmond was on a day off or had taken a late shift, so that another nurse would have to accompany the doctors on the ward round. Typically, the four of them—Abraham, the registrar, the intern, and the nurse—together from time to time with a medical student, a physiotherapist, a social worker, a chaplain, or anyone else on the clinical team—would pass from patient to patient, discussing histories, examination findings, treatment plans, observation charts, fluid balances, drug sheets, and discharge dates. Abraham would greet the patient, and the registrar would summarize the circumstances of his or her illness, after which the two of them would proceed to ask a few questions and conduct whichever aspects of the physical examination were of particular relevance.

This often involved listening to a heart or a chest, palpating an abdomen, looking at a wound, testing a reflex, or something similar. The intern would usually observe from the end of the bed and take notes, recording the proceedings in the patient's history and compiling a list of the tasks he had to complete once the ward round was over. Following this, there was general discussion about the main issues that needed to be addressed and the most appropriate way to do so.

For the sake of the solidarity of the team, attempts were made to include everyone present in the deliberations about individual patients. Here, as far as possible, the personal tension between the head doctor and the head nurse was kept from view. Nonetheless, from time to time Abraham declined to suppress his annoyance with what he regarded as Desmond's opinionated and dogmatic views. On the occasions when overt disagreement erupted in relation to a particular matter, the hierarchical relationship—that is, Abraham's view—would prevail and ultimately determine the outcome, inevitably deepening Desmond's resentment even further. In this manner, a precarious—albeit somewhat poisonous—balance was maintained between the medical and nursing components of patient care.

8.

The four of them went quickly through the patients who had been admitted in the previous weeks and whose treatment was proceeding as planned. There was an elderly woman with heart failure, a man from a nursing home with pneumonia, and a couple of people recovering from heart attacks. There was an interesting and sad case of a patient who had developed sudden, unexplained weakness in his legs and had spent two days on the floor at home until he had managed to attract attention by draping a sheet out the window of his apartment; despite gradually recovering from the trauma of his ordeal the cause of the weakness remained a mystery. There was an elderly man with alcoholism who moved from emergency shelter to emergency shelter, accepting food from charitable organizations, and who had come to the hospital with severe pain in his hips due to osteoarthritis. He had arrived dirty and smelly. The nurses had cleaned him up and given him fresh clothes, and the doctors had prescribed strong pain medications. He remained, however, ungrateful for the care he had received and made endless loud, abusive, and insistent demands on the nursing staff. Desmond was all for throwing him out "to protect his nurses," but Abraham insisted that he be formally assessed by the hospital psychiatrist and that the social work department be asked for an opinion on options regarding accommodation.

They moved from the disaffected and disinfected vagrant to the patient in the next room. Abraham recognized him immediately from the doorway. "Billy Georgiannis," he said. "Why is he here?"

Abraham knew Billy well from previous admissions. A twenty-six-year-old man who had suffered a major brain injury following an infection when he was three years old, he was a frequent inpatient of the hospital. Abraham could see that the young man had a plastic tube emerging from his nose and was gasping for breath.

"Yes, it is Billy," replied Rebecca. "And I did want to discuss him with you. He came in with yet another chest infection. He's doing okay, even if he doesn't seem to know much about what's going. But I'm finding his mother and the rest of the family a bit trying. They're so insistent, and no matter what we do it doesn't seem to be enough. I admire their commitment but I'm wondering if they're perhaps too committed. There's a family member with him all the time; they even sleep next to him."

"His mother's devoted her entire life to him," cut in Abraham.

"It's also his father and brothers," continued Rebecca. "They have a very close family and everyone's involved."

"Do his brothers have their own families?"

"One does," replied Ashis. "He works in a bank and lives with his family about ten minutes' drive away. The other's still living at home, but Mrs. Georgiannis was saying yesterday that he's just gotten engaged."

Abraham nodded. The intern was very good at remembering the facts. "I wonder if his departure will make things more difficult for her."

It took Ashis a moment to realize he was being asked for his opinion instead of more facts and he stumbled a little in his reply. "Er, yes, and I get the impression that she's worried about the change . . . But officially she's only expressing support."

The intern looked nervous, so Abraham tried to keep his face impassive as he turned to Rebecca to ask a question to which he already knew the answer. "Was he considered for intensive care?"

"We thought of calling the ICU consultant," Rebecca began carefully, "but I knew that the person on duty was Dr. Trentino, the director. I was his resident last year, and I know that he'd never accept someone as disabled as

Billy. His attitude—which he always repeats—is that ICU is to make people better, not to keep sick people alive."

Abraham sighed. "It'd be good to talk with the family, and maybe even Billy himself, about their opinion regarding that attitude," he said. "But let's get back to Billy's present condition. What was done for him?"

As soon as he changed the subject, he could almost hear Rebecca and Ashis exhale with relief. "He was given intravenous fluids and antibiotics, and I think his infection's slowly resolving," the registrar replied, confident that she was now back on secure ground. "We've made him nil orally. However, we'll need to start feeding him soon, and I'm not sure how to do this. We've assessed his swallowing and he's definitely aspirating food and liquids into his lungs. I'm sure that if he's allowed to take food by mouth it'll just be a matter of time—and probably not very long—before he aspirates again and comes in with an even more serious pneumonia. And the episodes are getting harder and harder to treat."

"We may have some work to do here," said Abraham. "If not on this occasion, perhaps on another. Let's see him."

There were two people standing next to the patient's bed, one of whom Abraham recognized as Billy's mother. "Hello, Professor! It's so good to see you," she said in her heavy Greek accent, her deeply lined face breaking into a submissive smile. "You remember my son George?"

Abraham adopted the posture and tone of authority he knew was expected of him. To emphasize this he spoke with exaggerated precision. "Rebecca's been explaining to me what's happened. I know that Billy's come in with another chest infection but is responding to the drugs we're giving him."

"God will bless you all!" the woman responded with equally exaggerated effusiveness. "Billy will be well enough to come home soon?"

"It sounds like that'll be the case." Then in a loud voice to ensure that his attention to propriety was not missed, he turned to the patient. "Hello, Billy, how are you today?"

The young man gave an indistinct grunt and rolled his eyes. That was enough to set off a violent paroxysm of coughing. His mother and a nurse from the other side of the room came running, the mother quickly arming herself with a pile of fresh handkerchiefs and the nurse with a tube to expectorate the viscous sputum. The air was thick with sweat and stale odors. Abraham was unruffled.

"Do you mind if we listen to your chest?" This time, Billy made no movement in response. Abraham and Rebecca moved into position on opposite

sides of the bed and with some difficulty wrestled Billy to a half-sitting position. Rebecca proceeded to percuss the patient's back, thumping, in the
time-honored medical practice, with the third finger of one hand on the
third finger of the other pressed flat against the skin. Both then took out
their stethoscopes and placed them in their ears. Abraham wedged his arm
against the middle of Billy's back to allow the registrar to listen, which she
did intensely, moving the device around his chest rapidly from place to place.
When she had finished she took up a similar position from her side of the
bed, and Abraham listened with his stethoscope. As he leaned across the bed
to listen to the far side, he came close to Rebecca, who was inclining from the
other direction. He was momentarily flooded with the sweet smell of her perfume, which mixed oddly with the rank odors fixed around the patient's bed.
He finished listening and then they both gently lowered Billy to his former
position, in partial recline propped up with two pillows.

Abraham turned to the patient's mother and spoke with well-practiced
sensitivity. "Mrs. Georgiannis, we agree with what you've said, that things
are improving here rapidly. We're very pleased because when Billy came in he
was very sick. We expect that he'll need to stay here for a few more days but
if everything continues to go well we're confident that he'll be well enough to
return home toward the end of the week."

The woman's response took Abraham by surprise. "Doctor, er . . . I mean Professor," she said, her voice heavy with emotion, "please don't send Billy home yet. He needs to stay in the hospital to get better." She was pleading. "We're happy that he's safe in the hospital. We want he should stay here at least another two weeks." She averted her eyes as if to apologize for the vulnerability she had exposed.

Abraham softened his voice. "Don't worry, Mrs. Georgiannis," he said gently, "we won't send Billy home until we're all comfortable that it's safe to do so. I assure you of that. We'll talk more about it tomorrow."

The party took its leave and moved back into the bustling corridor. Outside, they continued the discussion in private. "I think we should be firm with her," the head nurse began immediately. "It's important that she gets used to the idea that when he's medically fit he'll go back home without delay. It'd be impossible to get a patient like him into a rehabilitation center, and in any case it wouldn't do him any good. If he doesn't go home we'll be stuck with him forever. As it is, he's spending too much time in the hospital. I think that we're approaching the time when we might have to ask the hard questions, like whether he has any useful quality of life anymore."

Abraham felt his jaw clench involuntarily. Desmond's self-confidence and the unproblematic way in which he saw the world offended him to the core. He breathed in deeply to answer, not knowing if he would be able to suppress a scathing response. But before the first word had a chance to escape they were joined by Billy's brother George, who had followed them out. "Please look after Billy," he said. "He's very precious to us."

He was pleading too, but his manner was not submissive. He looked Abraham directly in the eye and, before the latter could reply, went on. "It's never been easy," he said, "but we do what we have to do. Other people always have difficulty understanding how we can love him so dearly.

"We've shared many precious moments. Once when I was about fifteen I came home from school covered in mud. I'd just been mucking around with my friends but I knew Mom'd be mad if she saw how dirty I was. I came into our bedroom where Billy was propped up in bed and I took off my clothes and hid them in the corner under a pile of magazines. I turned round and saw that he was looking at me. We looked straight at each other and I knew at once that he understood exactly what I was doing. He gave the faintest smile—just a hint of a smile is all he's capable of."

George shook his head slightly. "It's moments like these that make it all worthwhile." He shrugged his shoulders. "It probably doesn't sound like much to you, but to us it's everything."

9.

"I'd like you to see Mrs. Gurewitz in bed sixteen," said Rebecca. "She's very sick and looks like she's going to die, but we don't know what the underlying problem is."

Ashis summarized the story with his usual earnestness. "Mrs. G's a ninety-year-old woman originally from Poland, Prof," he said. "She's lived alone since the death of her husband about ten years ago but has a very supportive daughter. She suffers from high blood pressure and mild cardiac failure and has apparently been managing pretty well at home despite an ongoing battle with depression." He explained how, as far as could be determined, her current illness had started about a week earlier with an epileptic seizure, following which she developed drowsiness from which she had not recovered. Her general practitioner had referred her to a neurological specialist who admitted her to St. Mary's Hospital for testing. Because her condition had continued to deteriorate he had arranged for her to be transferred to the RPJ for further assessment.

The registrar then took up the narrative. "She arrived here yesterday morning. When I examined her she was drowsy but responsive, speaking in both English and what I assume was Polish. Although she seemed to understand what I was saying to her she couldn't tell me anything about what had happened over the last few days. But she indicated clearly that she had confidence in her daughter's judgment and was happy for us to talk with her daughter and make decisions about treatment." The previous night, her conscious state had deteriorated even further. Rebecca had spoken with Madeleine Silverstein, who thought that in the absence of a proven diagnosis antibiotic therapy should be started, just in case there was a hidden infection. "Ashis and I came to see her a few minutes ago," the registrar concluded, "and now she's unrousable."

"She's obviously sick," replied Abraham, "and from what you've just told me it's quite likely that she'll die. However, we need to work through the list of possibilities in order to see what, if anything, can be done to help her."

Abraham approached the old woman lying on the bed, her face thick with age. Addressing her by name, he obtained no response, so he squeezed and rubbed her hand, again without success. Then the three of them went to work, attending to the details of the physical examination. After they had finished they retired to the computer station outside the door to scrutinize in detail the various tests she had already undergone. The whole process took about twenty minutes. While they were busy Desmond wandered off to do some things elsewhere in the ward, returning just as they were finishing.

"Well," proclaimed Abraham, not exactly triumphantly, "you're right. It's not obvious what's going on here. She's completely unresponsive now, indicating a serious brain problem. However, there's no evidence of infection, metabolic disease, drug or other toxicity, structural brain disease, or a specific neurological abnormality." He went on to list the additional tests he wanted the residents to arrange, directing that for the moment treatment with antibiotics and anticonvulsants should continue. He asked if the nurses could keep a particularly close eye out for any changes, which might shift the focus of the tests or therapies.

Desmond readily agreed to this. "I'll tell the nurses to page Ashis or Rebecca if anything happens," he said, adding, "We should talk to the daughter. I'm not completely certain about her. She's supposed to be fully involved and she was here yesterday but when we asked for her contact details she said that she was going away for a few days and would be out of cell tower range. You don't usually go for a vacation when your mother's dying in the hospital." Then he added, in a tone that was unmistakably provocative, "How long will you keep treating her?"

"At this stage," Abraham replied briskly, "I don't really know. I guess we'll just have to take each day as it comes. If there's no clinical response in a couple of days we'll certainly have to reconsider our approach." Without giving Desmond a chance to respond, to ensure that they were on his side he turned to Rebecca and Ashis. "Are you satisfied with that?" he asked.

"Yes, Prof. That sounds good," Ashis answered compliantly. "It'll be interesting to see what happens."

He could tell Desmond was seething. The group moved on with the ward round.

10.

After leaving the ward Abraham headed for his office to check the mail and make contact with his secretary to identify the many tasks that inevitably were awaiting his attention after returning from vacation. He was engrossed by the morning's activities. A new season of ward service always evoked vivid emotions and he often came away feeling simultaneously inspired and daunted.

He was proud of his office, which over the years he had made a personal haven from the hustle and bustle of the hospital life going on just outside it. Located in the busiest part of the hospital, near the ICU, it provided for him a place of tranquility he often found himself desperately needing. From the outside, it appeared to be like any of the other offices around. Inside, it resembled the drawing room of a comfortable old villa. On one side stood a desk of polished wood and in the center a couch and armchairs of dark leather. A large Persian rug that Abraham had inherited from his grandmother covered the floor, and the walls were lined with books and art works, mainly in the style of nineteenth-century landscape painting. On the desk, and on a small wooden table in the center of the room, were some artifacts Abraham had collected on his travels in Africa years before. In a cabinet in one of the corners was a CD player, a few CDs, and a bottle of good whisky that he would turn to in times of emotional stress or when he needed to sit and meditate upon a problem. This was Abraham's sanctuary, in which he would spend long hours thinking, writing, and listening to music.

He poured himself a glass from the bottle, settled into one of the armchairs, and breathed in the whisky's earthy aroma. Ashis was a smart young man, lacking in experience but eager to learn. Like all junior doctors, he possessed considerable book learning but limited ability to apply it in real-life settings. The clinic was much more complicated than was ever represented in textbooks or the classroom. Doctors—like philosophers—always sought to describe what they did in abstract terms, as if the profession of medicine could be subsumed under a few broad principles. This was often perplexing and misleading for young doctors like Ashis.

He took a sip from the glass, held it briefly in his mouth, and then allowed himself to swallow. He loved the feeling of the whisky assaulting his mouth, pushing its way down his gullet, and flooding his body with cold fire. He knew that alcoholic drinks were strictly forbidden on the hospital premises but this only added to the intensity of the experience. He closed his eyes for a few seconds, waiting for the sensations to subside.

Abraham recalled the first time he'd come across the idea that there were fixed ethical principles underlying medical practice. He had been a junior resident himself and had attended a public lecture by a famous visiting philosopher he had seen advertised in the paper. He was inexperienced then, looking for ways to rebel against social conventions and driven by a romantic idea of serving humanity. He had looked forward to acquiring the skill and the knowledge that would enable him to solve the problems of the world. When he entered medical school, however, he was surprised by what he found. Medicine was not just a collection of facts and skills, even complicated and highly respected ones. There was no single body of scientific knowledge that could be relied upon to provide the answers to the infinite array of questions that presented themselves. In talking with patients a doctor had to move seamlessly among many disciplines: from physiology and biochemistry to psychology, sociology, ethics and philosophy, economics, and religion.

But clinical practice was not just a matter of academic disciplines. Abraham found that the doctor could not remain an innocent bystander. He was himself immersed, engaged, and inevitably changed by the process. What's more, he had to negotiate the path to be taken in relation to powerful experiences—some of them shared—of hope and despair, of joy and loss, of pleasure and pain, of living and dying. The clinical relationship could not be contained by simple rules of thumb, universal principles, or algorithms for calculating or validating decisions.

While he was listening to that lecture by the famous philosopher he had realized immediately that the idea that clinical practice was based on a few, fixed ethical principles was wrong, although he understood the attraction of a set of rules that might bring the whole confusing mess under control. As his own experience developed, this conclusion was confirmed again and again: that the vast sea of suffering and sorrow through which medicine ploughs its way could not be described by a set of rational scientific principles or laws. Indeed, it was the intractability of the project, the irreducibility of suffering to reason, that for him constituted the immutable, tantalizing core of clinical practice.

Abraham's thoughts returned to Ashis. He saw his own youth in the open and generous face of the young man. He could identify personally with his optimism, his keenness, his commitment to the future. I hope, Abraham reflected, I hope that he can be protected from the dangerous traps lying ahead along the path he has chosen for himself.

He finished the whisky with a few more gulps and put the glass down. Abraham himself was no stranger to personal pain. His recent experience of the illness and death of his wife had left him profoundly shaken. Prior to that, however, he had not really understood what it meant to suffer deep grief. He had tried to listen carefully to his patients' descriptions of their illnesses—not just their physical symptoms, their pains, their weakness, and their tiredness, but also what it meant to them to be sick, the impact on their lives and on those of their families. He felt he was a sympathetic listener and that he could understand what he heard, at least enough to offer them the sense that he was an authentic witness to their suffering. He hadn't tried to pretend that he could share all their pain, but—sometimes to his colleagues' amazement—he had deliberately sought to expose himself to the experiences of those he treated. Although he did not have diabetes, he took on the task of injecting himself—with pure water—four times each day for a month, just to understand what it was like to live with such an intractable limit to one's freedom. And although he was not overweight he undertook to lose ten kilograms just to understand why, despite all the publicity and increasingly insistent public health messages, his obese patients often found it impossible even to achieve the most minimal weight loss.

It was now just a year since Stephanie's death and he had not recovered from the despair and the horror of her illness: of the moment the cancer was diagnosed, of the fear leading up to the operation, of the terrible effects on both of them of the chemotherapy, and of the slow, inexorable ebbing away of her life that had followed. In fact, he knew he would never recover. He felt her loss every day as a physical sensation of pain in his own body. He still occasionally burst into tears with no provocation, often to his own embarrassment and other people's surprise. He felt that his life was depleted, damaged by the loss. He still had his two children, Henny and Jack, of course, whom he loved dearly, and his elderly parents, who were increasingly dependent on him. But the intensity of the comradeship, the physical closeness, the preciousness of the loyalty and commitment, were now just sad memories.

Abraham would have been the last to claim that his life had been hard. He recognized that every day he came into contact with people whose suffering was much greater than his. But listening to their stories of pain made his own excruciating sense of sorrow and loneliness reverberate inside him. He hoped this made him a better doctor, more accessible and more compassionate, but he also knew the risks. He knew that to be of use to them he had to do more than simply recirculate his own experiences. He needed to allow them to make use of him in whatever ways were efficacious for the tasks they had to undertake. The project of being a doctor was a difficult one: he needed to be able to present himself as a flesh-and-blood human being, as someone capable of suffering like them, of sharing in their hopes and fears. But he also needed to maintain a distance, so that he was not *that* person, *that* individual with specific hopes and fears, aspirations and misgivings, not *that* man who has experienced these actual things. He needed to be both things simultaneously—the person who can bleed and the principle who can be shaped to the needs of another.

His mind moved to Rebecca. He thought that he would enjoy working with her. He went over the work they had done together this morning. On a couple of occasions she had picked up quite subtle physical signs that a less gifted or experienced doctor could easily have missed. If the registrar was diligent and reliable that made his own job a great deal easier. Also, he found her very agreeable personally. He liked her straightforward manner and her easiness with the patients. He had been struck by her open smile and sparkling eyes. Abraham allowed himself a moment of indulgence as he remembered brushing her arm and her sweet smell as they had examined Billy together. He savored the moment again, experiencing a quiet glow of warmth.

He deliberately turned his thoughts away from her lithe, graceful body. This is a professional relationship, he scolded himself. Her physical attractiveness should be irrelevant—no, invisible. In the dark, prefeminist past men had related to women only as sexual objects; now we are equals, as colleagues, friends, mentors, and students. My own feelings, Abraham continued to lecture himself, are irrelevant. I am, after all, twice her age. I have no doubt that while I was marveling at the curves of her breasts she barely noticed me. On the other hand, it is not possible to subtract sexuality from one's interaction with another person. Rebecca's body is who she is, not some soul or spirit or "essence," but a flesh-and-blood human being. And that's what we're dealing with in medicine, after all—people as they are, diseased, with their festering wounds and stinking pus and phlegm; with rashes and diarrhea and cacophonous, ungracious shouts of pain and dismay; with their loyalty and courage and cowardliness and greed; and their soft breasts and sweet smells and kind eyes and shining skin. That I deal with and see all these features doesn't mean—has never meant—that I'll be less professional, less punctilious about the propriety of my relationships, whether with patients, colleagues, or students. Rebecca is quite safe with me. In return, I should be able to feel free quietly to enjoy her sensual beauty. She never needs to know.

11.

"Sorry I'm late. The ward round turned out to be a long one—I guess it always is when you've just come back on the ward—and then I had to clear the backlog with my letters and email, and then I got caught up in a daydream."

"That's all right, Abe. When I saw you this morning, I could see you were in a hurry. Almost immediately after that I bumped into Nic, so I knew it had to be."

"And anyway," Nic added brightly, continuing Madeleine's sentence, "Madeleine and I expected nothing less from you, old boy, than to be ten minutes late!" He beamed with obvious pleasure. "It's good to see you after all this time. How've you been?"

Abraham, Madeleine, and Nic had been friends since medical school, and all three enjoyed the easy conversation that had been a feature of their lunchtimes together for nearly twenty years. They usually met in the hospital cafeteria, most commonly with other colleagues, and even had a favored table in a far corner of the room, in a vain attempt to create a sense of privacy.

"You might have heard that there's a meeting about Freedom to Choose that we all have to go to this afternoon. We need to chat about that," Nic added. "But first let's catch up on the gossip."

Abraham sensed the tension in Nic's voice but allowed himself to sit back to enjoy the warm familiarity of the small talk. Nic had spent his holidays at home while Madeleine had been on ward duty, which as usual had been busy on the hot days but quiet at other times.

"I've never really understood it," she reflected. "Holidays are always quiet at the hospital. If people are able to take a vacation from being sick when it's Christmas or whatever, why don't they do so all the time?"

Nic turned the conversation back to Abraham. "What about you, old boy?" he asked gently. "How was your time off? Did you manage to regroup a bit? You've had a rough time, haven't you?"

"It's true," Abraham replied candidly, "and it's still hard, but I feel better for having had the break. I just stayed at home. It's pretty lonely without Stephanie, but I guess I'll get used to it. The good thing about being alone is that you have plenty of time to think." He smiled weakly. "I'm trying to get some writing done, putting down some of my thoughts about theories of ethics. I think I've made a bit of progress."

Barely aware of his friends' presence, Abraham continued to reflect. His children were struggling to come to terms with their mother's death and had remained aloof from him, which he took almost as an allegation against him that he was somehow to blame for it, further increasing his sense of desolation. In his time of need, his own parents could offer no support. His mother, Esther, affected with Alzheimer's disease, was herself in increasing need of protection and care, and his father, as always, remained immersed in his own needs.

His father had always been a difficult character—brilliant, erratic, and exquisitely self-centered. His mother had always looked after him. Now, not only was he unable to handle her decline but the only response available to him was to become increasingly angry and aggressive, to others and to the world. Abraham had spent years pondering the question of whether his father's real problem was a psychiatric illness or just a difficult personality before coming to the conclusion that it really didn't matter what the answer was. Once, he'd been a powerful lawyer, always used to giving orders and having them obeyed. Mordechai Nevski had never accepted retirement, where people no longer respected him for his money and power. Now, at eighty-five, he was often vicious and ungrateful to carers and nurses who came to visit, often shouting at them that they were ugly or stupid and that he could not bear to have them in his house. Abraham had calculated that the average lifespan of a carer with him was five-and-a-half weeks. They all tried hard at first and were indulgent of his undoubted wit and feistiness. However, his rudeness was always unrelenting, and after a short time they declared that they were not paid to be abused, and resigned, or else they just went home one day and never returned, leaving Abraham to run around looking for a replacement.

Although he tried to offer support Abraham understood that this was likely to be a losing battle. Besides, why should he always be the one supporting others? After all, he himself had been abandoned, left to fend for himself. When he had most needed help, his children, his parents, his friends had been unable to provide him with the solace that he needed.

"It sounds like you're doing a great job as usual, old boy," Nic was commenting. "It's a tough world. Take my advice: don't grow old! If there's any way I can help, just let me know."

The conversation turned to the afternoon's meeting. Freedom to Choose was the advance directives program being promoted by the hospital CEO, or "Her Royal Highness," as Nic called her.

Abraham was surprised to hear about the meeting. "Why are we meeting about Freedom to Choose?" he asked. "I thought that we'd examined it in detail last year and our working party decided it wasn't for us."

"That's right. But she's the CEO and, like your father, she doesn't like being contradicted. It seems that when we were asked to look at it last year we weren't meant to veto it. Apparently, there's more of an agenda than appeared at the time. As I understand it, HRH is looking for ways to save money following the government's budget cuts, and she's decided that the main area where savings can be made is in care for the very elderly. That's not the only one, of course. She's also shaved money off the cleaning budget, and while you were away she cut out afternoon teas for the patients. That should save a few pennies.

"The rumor is," Nic went on, his tone reflecting Abraham's unconcealed look of repugnance, "she's going to announce today that we've joined the program and that we're expected to implement it without delay. She's asked Colin Tyler from Mountain View, who developed the scheme, to tell us about how it works."

"This sounds like another nail in the coffin of democracy at the Royal Prince John Hospital," Abraham commented curtly.

"I think it's a fait accompli, old boy, and I don't see any point in resisting it further. I know you felt pretty strongly about it last year and that you're always ready to take up a fight—we've been in a few together over the years—but it looks like this is one battle we're not going to win. Though it may turn out that one day we'll have to do something to limit care for the elderly just because it'll become too expensive, we shouldn't pretend that we're doing it for their benefit. The RPJ's not a democracy, and I dislike the CEO as much as you do, but she's the one who has the power to hire and fire staff. I don't think it's worth my job to fight this one."

"To develop a policy for the care of anyone on the sole basis of its cost is just wrong," replied Abraham. "It'll produce no benefits and only lead to uncertainty, fear, and injustice. If she wants a fight I think we should be prepared to give it to her. We've gotten rid of tougher customers than her over the last twenty-five years."

The unexpected force of Abraham's words took all three of them by surprise. Nothing more could be said. They finished their lunch in silence.

12.

At the head of the table, preparing to commence the proceedings, sat Margaret Wilson, the chief executive officer. A middle-aged woman who had come to the role of administrator after a not particularly distinguished career as a hospital pharmacist, the CEO was neither respected nor liked by the medical staff who, behind her back, could be quite unkind in their comments about everything from her administrative style to her dress sense. Indeed, although there may have been some disagreement about the former, there was almost complete unanimity that the latter was execrable, and as if to prove it, on the present occasion she was dressed in a bright yellow dress with long sleeves and lace cuffs and a low-cut bodice that highlighted her cleavage.

While waiting for everyone to take their seats the CEO adopted a fixed, forced smile, occasionally acknowledging with a nod individuals who happened to catch her eye. It was true that she could be petulant and did not like to be contradicted. But Abraham knew that the barely concealed hostility the doctors displayed toward her also reflected their lack of respect for administrators who had no personal clinical experience. Deeply ingrained in the hospital culture was a sense that while the clinical staff were committed to caring for patients, and did so at considerable personal cost, the hospital administrators were only capable of seeing monetary values, which wasn't quite fair.

The CEO cleared her throat to attract attention and brought the meeting to order. "Thank you everyone for coming," she said. "It's good to see you all. I hope that those of you who've been on vacation have had a pleasant break and didn't get too sunburnt." Abraham could not suppress an image of the CEO herself sunbathing on the beach in a bikini.

She came straight to the point. "As some of you know, we're here today to discuss the rollout of the Freedom to Choose program. I'm delighted that we were successful in our application to the government for funding support for the program. To assist with the process I've asked Dr. Colin Tyler to join us. Colin is one of the architects of Freedom to Choose and has great personal experience with the details of its implementation. He'll present the background to the project and explain in detail how it works. Before handing the meeting over to him, however, to avoid misunderstanding about the aims and expected outcomes, I think it would be helpful for me to summarize the main reasons for adopting this as a core program of the RPJ.

"The hard facts are that our society is facing a mounting crisis with respect to the funding of health care, which is already having an impact on the services that can be offered by our hospital. This crisis is, very simply, a result of the fact that medical care at the end of life has become more expensive than we can afford. The hospital board has undertaken an analysis of the increase in costs over the last twenty years. It was quite a big job, and to do it properly we obtained the services of the consultancy firm Ultimate Economic Health Solutions. Ultimate has produced a report for us called 'Health Costs at the Royal Prince John Hospital Into the Twenty-First Century.' We have a few copies available if any of you would like to read it. I've asked Mr. David Draeger, the economist at Ultimate who prepared the report, to present his main findings to you. David, thanks for coming here today."

The CEO turned to a slight, gray-looking man sitting a few seats away from her whom Abraham had not previously noticed. The man stood up, nervously shuffled a little, and began in a barely audible voice that was as colorless as his appearance. "Thanks, Margaret. I'm . . . pleased to be here . . . and Ultimate Economic Health Solutions is honored to be able to provide assistance to the great Royal Prince John Hospital."

"And, I bet, receive a fat wad of money from it," Nic muttered under his breath.

"Ultimate was asked to provide some figures on how costs had changed in both the long and shorter terms," the economist continued, "with special emphasis on the last five years. We were also asked to break down the costs in relation to different kinds of services and patients. This was quite a big job for which we had to go back through the hospital's annual reports and budget submissions to the government over the last twenty years.

"The results were striking but not unexpected. I have a few slides with the main figures, which I'll show you now . . . Here's the first one . . . It . . . arr . . . shows the national figures on the way health care costs for the whole society have grown over the last twenty years. As you can see, the total cost of health care in the country has approximately doubled over this period. As the bottom of the slide shows, it now amounts to about 9.4 percent of our gross domestic product.

"The second slide shows how costs have increased at the Royal Prince John. Your budgets have grown during this period at an average of 3 percent a year faster than the overall national figures. That doesn't sound like a lot but over ten or twenty years it makes a great difference. Essentially, what it means is that costs have been increasing faster than the total public expenditure on health, which itself has been increasing rapidly. If this continues—not for twenty years but merely for another ten—the country will be unable to pay for its health care. If it continues for merely another five the hospital will be broke."

The economist was warming to his subject and his voice was getting louder. Abraham reflected that it was rare for such a dry subject to be treated with such rhetorical force but, despite his unprepossessing appearance, there was no doubting the interest and commitment of the speaker. Abraham felt a sense of uneasiness about where the discussion was about to lead.

"The third slide examines the underlying cause of the problem," continued Draeger. "We looked at the different areas of hospital activity in an attempt to find out where the extra costs were occurring. There were two conclusions. On the one hand, there were some particular areas that had become more expensive, such as radiology, where some large investments have been needed in new machines, and nursing, where wages have increased rapidly over the last few years. There's not much we can do about these changes, and by and large they've kept pace with the overall expenditures. The most interesting results occur, however, when we look at the cost of providing care for different patient groups. The health costs of patients younger than thirty have been relatively stable or have even fallen. Between thirty and seventy-five they have increased modestly. But after seventy-five the costs increase astronomically. In fact, now about 80 percent of the costs incurred in a person's entire lifetime are incurred in the last year of life, with 55 percent in the last illness, that is, the illness from which the person actually dies."

He paused for effect. The members of the audience, uncertain of what was expected of them, fidgeted a little but remained silent. The economist moved to the peroration. "In fact, the amazing thing is that almost the entire amount of the additional costs—the costs we soon won't be able to afford—arise out of illnesses in very elderly people just before they die. We're not doctors, of course; we're economists. But it seems to us that a lot of people are coming to the hospital merely to die and are creating very large expenses in doing so. We've suggested that the hospital board look into the possibility of reducing costs in this domain of the cost structure. If, for example, it's possible to delay hospital admission in the last illness—or even to avoid it altogether—it may be possible to avert the mounting crisis facing us all.

"So this is the problem: how do we limit the utilization of health care resources by elderly people, especially in the context of the illness that's most likely to kill them? The need to do so is our conclusion, which we think is irrefutable. As economists, that is, however, as far as we can go. We cannot answer the question; that part is up to you. Thank you for your attention."

"Thank you, Mr. Draeger. We're grateful to you and Ultimate for all the work you've put in." Then, turning to the larger company, "You'll have a chance to ask questions of Mr. Draeger in a moment. Before that, however, I want to tell you how the board has responded to Ultimate's report. We were, of course, aware that there was a problem but were astounded to find that it was as serious as it's turned out to be. We accept that urgent action needs to be taken to avert financial disaster overtaking the hospital. I've personally discussed the subject with our government reps and with the CEOs of the other major hospitals in our area. The government has made it clear that with the present fiscal constraints no resources will be available for our hospital above and beyond what we would normally expect from the annual budget. The other hospitals depend heavily on us and are very nervous about the implications for them."

"We have therefore determined that we need to find ways to cut our costs. We're a public hospital and are obliged to provide certain services to the community. However, we also have to balance our budget. As CEO it's my responsibility to ensure that the hospital doesn't live beyond its means. We don't want to cut jobs, although we may have to do that. That would be difficult, because the main reason for the crisis—and I emphasize that it is a crisis—is not too many services but too much demand. What we really need to do is to find a way to reduce the number of patients who come into our hospital, and once there, we need to reduce the period of their stay here. Of course, we want to do this in the most ethical way possible.

"I have for some years been aware of the work of Dr. Colin Tyler, who is deeply committed to the extension of advance directives as a way of increasing the appropriateness of medical care in the hospital system. Colin is the originator of the Freedom to Choose program, a system for ensuring that as many people as possible have the chance to express their wishes about what kind of treatment they would wish should they find themselves facing serious illness or death. Colin has found at Mountain View that when asked, many people are very clear that if they were to become ill they would not want to receive invasive and expensive treatments—in fact, many would not want to come to the hospital at all. We therefore see the program as a means, on the one hand, to ensure that people are not subjected to unnecessary and burdensome treatments but are treated with the respect they deserve, and on the other, to reduce the overall demand on hospital services."

The last few sentences were delivered by the CEO in a torrent of words, creating the sense that she was undertaking an unpleasant task and just wanted to get it over and done with. She was clearly much less confident at this point than the speaker before her had been, but she knew she had the power, and she was using it. "As I said, we've decided to adopt Freedom to Choose. We're confident that this will provide a way to preserve the financial health of the hospital, which, of course, is necessary if we're to continue to provide the best possible health services to the community."

This was an unfortunate choice of words, Abraham thought, and the general sense of disquiet that was palpable around him seemed to confirm that others felt similarly. Nic muttered fiercely, again under his breath, "Just watch this. She's trying to dodge questions about the whole idea. She knows what she's doing!"

She went on: "I've therefore asked Dr. Tyler to talk with you today to explain the elements of the system. To many of you Colin needs no introduction, but to those who haven't met him previously, all I'll say is that he's a pioneering surgeon at Mountain View Hospital who's worked for many years to reduce the demand on hospital beds. He's well known in the media as an advocate for his system of recording advance directives, so even those of you who haven't met him in person will undoubtedly know what he looks like."

Dr. Tyler rose to speak. He was obviously an established performer and here he was on familiar territory. He had the swagger of a senior doctor and had clearly enjoyed the reference to him as a celebrity. He was conservatively dressed in a business suit, white shirt, and yellow tie. Abraham marveled at how the color yellow was suddenly very popular and made a mental note to comment to the others later how well he thought Colin Tyler's tie went with Margaret's party dress.

Tyler moved straight to his main argument. "As you've just heard, the overwhelming burden"—he stressed the word "burden"—"of the growth in health care costs in the last five years has been attributable to the over-seventy age group. This is because people are living longer and are receiving more expensive, high-tech treatments. Even ten years ago it would have been unusual to find someone over the age of seventy-five in the Intensive Care Unit. Today, in this hospital, 25 percent of all admissions to ICU are older than eighty and—surprise, surprise—the growth in ICU demand over the last ten years has been almost exactly 25 percent.

"We realized at Mountain View a couple of years ago, as you're realizing now, that this is simply unsustainable. If we're to continue running our hospitals at all we need to find ways of cutting costs. That's the bad news, but there's also some good news. As it turns out, when you ask eighty-year-olds if they want to go to the ICU and be hooked up to respirators and ventilators and have endotracheal tubes thrust down their throats and so on, guess what? They say no, they don't. For years we've been thinking that we're humane for providing ever-increasing treatment for older people. However, we're now beginning to realize that these treatments have been pushed onto them against their wishes. If you ask people whether they'd rather die quietly in their homes or would prefer to come to the hospital where the chance of surviving is increased from, say, 20 to 30 percent, they almost invariably choose to stay at home.

"Our data show that a significant proportion of elderly people who come to the hospital haven't chosen to do so but have been sent in by their doctors or families without proper consultation. That's why we devised Freedom to Choose. This is a program that, very simply, asks people to tell us how they'd prefer to die when the unthinkable but inevitable finally happens. We encourage them to sign a form that provides clear instructions about what can and can't be done, including whether they should be admitted to the hospital, when that point is reached.

"We've had the scheme operating at Mountain View for over a year. We estimate that we now have advance directives on five hundred people, the majority of which contain some statement about limiting treatment. Of course, they're free to change their minds any time they wish. There's absolutely no coercion. We think that this is an important mechanism for ensuring that the wishes of old people—previously disregarded in the interests of medical paternalism—are respected. There's a lot of support behind the program. The government has agreed to fund not only our program but also another ten in and around the city, including, I'm delighted to say, here at the RPJ."

He waited a moment before continuing. "So welcome to the Freedom to Choose community! This is a proven system for ensuring the fairness and appropriateness of medical treatment at the end of life. It allows all elderly people to choose how their journeys will end. It restores the autonomy of the patient, which has largely been replaced by the logic of technologies. And it'll help us make the changes to save the public hospital system."

Even Abraham couldn't help being impressed, although his favorable response was quickly dispelled as the doctor went on to describe some cases to show how the Freedom to Choose program worked at his hospital.

"Here's the first case. Mrs. X was a ninety-year-old woman who was admitted with pneumonia. A chest X-ray suggested that she might have an underlying lung cancer, so the doctor in Emergency ordered a CT scan."

His expression changed to one of derision. "This shows the problem we're faced with. Someone is ninety and a CT scan is being organized! The whole purpose of the Freedom to Choose program is to avoid this useless waste of resources."

Abraham was shocked by the unexpected bluntness of Tyler's comment. He sensed that others were too, although the room remained silent. Just because someone is ninety, he thought to himself, doesn't mean that we can only assume that she shouldn't have treatment. And knowledge of her underlying condition may help devise the most humane and appropriate approach to such treatment.

The second case confirmed his worst fears. "Mrs. Y was sixty-four and had advanced breast cancer. She was obviously going to die. But what did her oncologist recommend?" He paused for an answer. Again, no one said anything.

"That's right," he pronounced with a flourish. "More surgery, more chemo, more X-ray therapy. In a patient who had a life expectancy of no more than six months. Is this what we've come to? This was not respecting life or fulfilling the mission of medicine. This was technology gone mad. What this patient needed was pain relief and support in the dying process. Not expensive treatment and ICU and utilization of precious resources.

"So we swung into action. We have trained communication consultants who go to all patients coming into our hospital and consult with them to fill in a directive about how they want to die and what treatments they do or don't want. We ask them if they want to end up in ICU on a ventilator. Ninety-four percent of them say 'No.' We explain to them that CPR only works in about 5 percent of cases and ask if they want that. Eighty-two percent say 'No.' We ask them if, once diagnosed with disseminated cancer that will inevitably kill them, they'll want chemotherapy or other treatments that could prolong their lives by a few months. Only 12 percent say 'Yes.'

"In Mrs. Y's case, once we talked with her it became clear that she didn't really want the extra treatment. We notified the palliative care team and she went home the next day. What would have been a two-week stay in the hospital with a bill of $30,000 became a one-day admission that cost no more than $4,000. Mrs. Y went home and died peacefully with her family around her two weeks later."

Like the economist before him, he paused for effect. There was no response from the audience, apart from a few puzzled nods and frowns. The CEO intervened. "This is a brilliant innovation which we're pleased to implement at the Royal Prince John Hospital. I'm grateful to Dr. Tyler for sharing his scheme with us. He'll be conducting special tutorials for the first batch of interviewers, who we plan to have in operation within the next month."

Abraham shifted uncomfortably in his chair. He was aware of the unease among his colleagues sitting around him. He could see that the CEO was committed to introducing the scheme regardless of his views or anyone else's. But he couldn't hold back.

"Margaret," he said, "can we be sure that patients will not feel pressured to stay out of the hospital? Elderly, sick patients sometimes develop the impression that they're regarded as a burden by the rest of society. This is a very vulnerable group of people and it'll be easy to exploit them."

The CEO frowned and pursed her lips. "Thanks for your question, Abraham," she replied curtly. "Of course, it's important that no pressure is exerted on any patient. I have confidence in Dr. Tyler's scheme that they're careful to avoid this. Dr. Tyler, can you explain how you make sure that patients don't feel subjected to pressure?"

Tyler stood up, now looking weary. "The whole point of the program," he said, "is to give people back their autonomy. At present, it's assumed that if they're very sick or even dying they'll go to the hospital. However, as I just told you, most people would prefer to die at home. It's the present system that's overriding patients' wishes. Our communication consultants are trained to make sure that they question people carefully without exerting any pressure.

"Sometimes pressure can be subtle, and even unintended," interjected Peter James, one of the oncology consultants. "It depends on detailed knowledge and explanation about their illness, prognosis, treatment options, et cetera. Only a doctor has all this information. Also, it's part of the doctor-patient relationship to engage in discussion about what the patient wants next. I'm concerned that this may be undermined by your scheme."

"*Our* scheme," the CEO corrected him. "I wish what you say about the doctor-patient relationship were true. As fine as it sounds, we know that most doctors don't have these conversations with their patients at all. And anyway, doctors have enough to do without having to spend hours talking with patients about where they want to die. This'll free you up to do your real work."

Abraham erupted involuntarily. "Some of us think this *is* our proper job," he said. "We don't resent talking to our patients at all. In fact, we spend a lot of our time talking with them about this and many other issues—"

"Thank you for your comments, Abraham," said the CEO severely. "Management is very confident that the new system will help address the fiscal crisis of the hospital. Of course, this will not be enough in itself. We'll also need to find ways to reduce bed stays. In fact, this may turn out to be just as important as Freedom to Choose. Management has looked at this, too, and has found that there's considerable room for improvement. Everyone will be expected to pull their weight."

She looked around the room but Abraham hadn't given up. "Can you share with us your plans for reducing hospital stays?" he asked sarcastically. "I hope that management will not be patrolling the wards giving orders about what medical treatment is needed."

"Of course we won't do that!" she retorted, now with undisguised hostility. "It's a principle of our hospital that the medical staff have clinical independence. However, that doesn't mean that all of us don't also have a responsibility to work for the good of the hospital. We have, in fact, compiled a list of things that doctors and nurses can look out for that will allow them to reduce bed stays by more than one day, on average. Our analysis has shown, in the majority of cases of terminal illness, treatment is continued for at least two days after it's become clear that the patient cannot survive. This is wasteful and doesn't serve the interests of the patient. We propose that once the inevitability of death becomes apparent, treatment be scaled down or withdrawn within twelve hours. We'll be preparing a special form for 'ultimate treatment' to assist with the management of this process.

"In many other cases treatment will not change the final outcome. Everyone has to die. We're all aware of the difficulties faced by our society as the population grows older. The cost of supporting old people is killing not just our health system but other institutions, too. We need to act in a humane fashion to limit care at the end of life rather than indulging ourselves by continuing treatment after the point where it'll no longer change the outcome. If we don't, the decisions will be forced on us."

Obviously now anxious to end the meeting, the CEO continued without a pause. "I'm afraid that we've run out of time, ladies and gentlemen," she said. "We need to continue our conversation. The next step will be for you to start getting to know the Freedom to Choose program communication consultants. I wish to emphasize that we're serious about supporting this program and taking concrete steps to change the population basis we treat in the hospital. To do so we plan to introduce a new system of performance bonuses, which will reward those units that are most successful in addressing the key challenges confronting us. Every unit will be assessed in relation to the average age of the patients it admits and their length of stay. Each time these two statistics improve a bonus will be paid to your department. It will be up to the departments themselves to decide how to distribute the benefit, for example, by rewarding highly performing individuals or by sharing the bonus equally. Full details will be provided in an email to heads of department in the next few days, but I wanted you to be the first to know about it."

The announcement was greeted with a surprised silence. This time the opportunity was used to close the proceedings. "I'm sure that you all have lots of questions to discuss but we'll have to leave them until next time. I think that this has been a very productive and useful meeting. I'd like to thank Dr. Tyler for the wonderful work he's doing and for giving up his time to talk with us today. Can you please show your appreciation in the usual way?"

13.

As he and the other staff filed out of the boardroom Abraham was overcome with a mixture of anger and an intense sense of foreboding. Caring for sick people was his life; it was his central project, how he defined himself, his chief source of meaning, and his purpose. He felt in his bones that the rising emphasis on tightening budgets, cutting costs, and limiting care was going to put all that at risk. The Freedom to Choose program would be only the first step. It was enough to establish the principle that controlling health costs justified the hospital management taking over and controlling what doctors did, who they were allowed to treat, and what treatments they could use. Who could know where it would end?

As he walked through the ward area to his office he was sharply aware of the patients in the beds he was passing. Nearly all of them were elderly. Many, no doubt, were confused, afraid, in pain. Most were accompanied by relatives or friends. All were receiving some treatment or other. Freedom to Choose was a device to start denying these people treatment on account of their advanced age, because insufficient resources were allocated to the health care system.

Abraham reached his office and went inside. He was still seething as he poured himself a drink from the bottle stored in the wooden cabinet in the corner and sank into the leather couch. In his mind he could still see the forms of the CEO and her henchmen with their sneers of condescension toward the medical staff. How dare they talk about improving the care of elderly patients, he thought. As if they would know what caring was. They knew nothing about illness, with its infinite resonances of meaning and discovery, its wells of tears of pain and happiness. All they knew about was the cynicism of the hospital machine and the health care bureaucracy.

He felt weak and weary. He knew a fight was brewing but was not sure of his ability to see it through. He was not sure he had the strength and courage to take on the CEO, the hospital, the world. He'd been through so much lately, all he really wanted was some peace, some time to rest. Nic and Madeleine were right: this was a battle they couldn't win. There was no point excoriating himself on account of someone else's problem.

On the other hand, of all the people in the hospital he was the one who proclaimed most loudly the need to avoid compromising one's values. He was the one who had spent his life preaching to others about honesty and commitment. He had made much of the risks of uncritical complicity with the system, any system. And he had meant this sincerely. He had genuinely sought to avoid becoming entrapped by bureaucracy and convention. All his life he had been prepared to break rules, to crash through barriers. As a young man, swept away by the fervor of the times, he had dreamed of fighting in a revolution, of going where people had never gone before. He had longed to make a difference. At a personal level he had rejected the quest for material wealth or status. He had even agonized about the conventionality and conservatism implicit in wearing a tie.

"Be pure," he would say to his students, his junior colleagues, his children. "Be driven by values. Resist the blandishments of careerism and the consumer culture. Don't allow yourself to be compromised. Be prepared to take your life in your hands. It's only through taking risks that one comes truly to know oneself."

He had wanted extreme experience and had found it vicariously in the lives of his patients. "You don't have to climb Mt. Everest or swim the Amazon or go bungee jumping to experience the limits of experience," he would say. "You don't need to ride a crocodile. You just need to listen to the stories of people, old and young, rich and poor, triumphant or beaten, as they struggle with their pain and despair, or experience their joy and hope, and you just need to go a little way with them on their journeys."

But how pure was he himself? How much courage did he really have? How true was he to his own ideals? In spite of his supposed radicalism, his world had remained safe and protected. Despite his contempt for the trivial successes of position and power, he occupied senior, respected positions in the hospital, the university, and society. He was internationally recognized for his scientific work. Although he disparaged monetary wealth, he was well paid. However indirectly or insidiously, he was complicit in the protection of privilege and the perpetuation of inequality and injustice. In spite of his public rejection of sexual stereotyping and the representation of women as sexual objects, in his secret thoughts he still looked at women with lust. In spite of his attempts to cultivate a gentle and magnanimous exterior, he hated the CEO with a vengeance. He even wore a tie.

Here he was, at age fifty-three, supposedly at the height of his powers, a functionary of a system in which individuals were rewarded for denying care to elderly people, in the interests of rationing the society's health resources. He talked about authenticity, about values, about courage, but he knew he had never really been tested. He had never himself been called upon to act.

He was jolted out of his reverie by the phone. It was Rebecca. "Prof, we have a patient in intensive care we've been asked to see. Would you be free to go over there soon?"

14.

It often occurred to Abraham that entering the Intensive Care Unit was like what it must be to enter a spaceship. One had to negotiate a series of doors and air locks before gaining access to its rarefied interior. Once inside, it was even more like a spaceship, with computer consoles, complicated-looking equipment, and electronic beeps on all sides. The ICU staff even wore special suits covering their entire bodies, including their hair, their hands, their feet, and—if the circumstances required it—their faces. While much effort had been expended in making hospital wards less forbidding and impersonal it seemed that exactly the opposite tendency had guided the development of intensive care departments.

Abraham and Rebecca negotiated the portal to ICU. The registrar spoke quickly as they moved through its vast space. "I have to tell you about the patient we're going to see. It's an attempted suicide—very tragic. Her name's Flora Wood. She's a twenty-six-year-old teacher with no medical or psychiatric history. She made a pretty good effort to kill herself and very nearly succeeded. She threw herself under a train. She was a real mess, with internal, skeletal, and head injuries. They operated on her for hours and had to remove a kidney and amputate one of her legs. It looks like she'll survive, but only just."

"Is anything known about why she did it?" asked Abraham, listening intently.

"According to her parents, she's always been concerned about the state of the world, and in the last couple of years she's become involved with a group to help refugees. She teaches them English by getting them to recount their personal stories. Flora's parents say that in listening to these stories she'd become increasingly preoccupied and upset about the way refugees are treated in the media and by the government. They tried to convince her to reduce her involvement but had no idea she was so disturbed. The emergency workers found a note in a bag she was carrying stating that she could no longer bear the cruelty and injustice of the world. It's very sad!"

They located the cubicle they were looking for. Rebecca slid open the door and they stepped inside. Like the ICU itself, the room exuded a sense of precise, clean, technology-driven care. In the center was the bed containing the patient who, as usual, was unconscious. Arrayed around her were a number of machines and computer screens, with various tubes and cords curling backward and forward, some into the patient and some to connection ports in the walls. To one side was the nurse's station, which contained a bench with another bank of computers and a pile of charts. The staff—in this case two were present— were dressed in green or white surgical gowns with rubber gloves.

Abraham began in his usual way to review the situation. He noted the monitors for blood pressure and heart rhythm, the IV lines, and various other catheters and drain tubes. But when he came to look on the patient's face his blood froze.

"Oh no!" he cried. "It's the girl from the train!"

The others stared at him. There was no doubt that it was the young woman he had encountered that morning. Her face and her hair were unmistakable. The scene in the train flooded back to him. He saw her, with her red hair, her gold earrings, her crumpled clothes, her calico bag. He recalled her look of icy solitude, of intense, exquisite sadness and pain. He relived those seconds when their eyes had met, when he had felt the chill throughout his body, when he himself had experienced that wave of overwhelming despair and desolation that had cut into him. He was deathly pale, standing transfixed, unable to speak.

"You know her?" asked Rebecca in amazement.

Abraham felt dizzy and nauseated. "I . . . I saw her . . ." he stammered. "I saw her on the train. I was looking at her and realized she was upset about something. I tried to guess what the problem was—a game I sometimes play when I'm by myself. I knew she was in trouble. I was so worried that I even thought about going up to her to ask what the matter was. But I couldn't make up my mind to do so. By the time I'd decided, she'd gone.

"I knew she was in distress. I saw it. I could have saved her. But I did nothing."

He gazed at the face of the young woman in the hospital bed, with intravenous lines and other tubes penetrating her delicate body. She was exactly as he remembered her, except that the terrible expression of anguish that had so moved him this morning was gone. Instead, amazingly, she appeared to be at peace.

He took her hand and, continuing to gaze on her face, spoke silently to her unconscious form. Flora, he pleaded, please forgive me. I knew that you were calling out to me for help. I was maybe the last person who could have stopped you but although I heard your cry loud and clear I failed to respond. Please, please forgive me for letting you down.

He could feel the others staring at him. He tried desperately to clear his head. "It's so sad," was all he could say. He paused. Clearing his throat, he added in a thick voice, "But let's get to the medical matters. Rebecca, what contribution are we being asked to make?"

The conversation moved uneasily to the clinical issues, to the question of the patient's current condition, the longer-term physical problems she would experience as a result of her injuries, and the painstaking process of rehabilitation that would be needed. Abraham concentrated as best he could but was unable to erase from his mind the stark image of the girl's expression that very morning. He wondered about meeting her parents and what he would say to her when she finally awoke. Had she been so engrossed in her mission to kill herself that she had already renounced her bonds with the world and other people? Would she remember him as he remembered her?

PART 2

HOSPITAL BUSINESS

15.

The staff were filing into the handover room, which was as untidy and stuffy as ever. On the table was a pile of brochures marked in big letters "Freedom to Choose Program: Information for Staff." Abraham brushed them aside and set the proceedings under way.

"Hello, everyone," he said and then waited a few moments for the talking to die down. "We should get started to let the night staff get home to bed. Jeremy, do you want to go through what happened last night?" The young doctor's eyes were red from lack of sleep; his clothes were crushed and his hair awry.

"Mrs. Gurewitz in bed sixteen, who you thought might deteriorate, has been stable. I popped in to see her a couple of times but she was just sleeping. She didn't seem to be in any pain so I didn't change anything.

"There are two other new patients. I think Rebecca knows one of them—Mrs. Dreyfus. The other is Mr. Alvarez, the man I called you about briefly in the night, Prof."

"Ah, yes," replied Abraham, "the elderly man with the cerebral hemorrhage. It'd be helpful if you went through his case."

The resident continued, speaking mechanically. "Mr. Alvarez is a ninety-two-year-old man with an interesting history. He comes from Chile, in South America. He was an engineer and taught at a university. Apparently he became involved in politics and later even became a government minister. It was a radical government that was kicked out in a military coup, some time in the 1960s, I think . . ."

"The Allende government—the coup was in 1973," Abraham corrected him.

"Thanks." Abraham noticed that the resident's tone did not suggest that he was impressed with his erudition. "Anyway, according to his son, after a lot of complicated business he ended up here with his whole family. He had nothing and was forced to start again, in his fifties. He must have been pretty smart because he managed to set up a factory that still operates. I think it makes handbags or something. Actually, he's continued to run it himself until just a few months ago. Lots of members of the family work there. It sounds like they idolize him. His wife's around his age—they've been married for more than sixty years. Over the last three months he's become increasingly confused, so much so that he was actually admitted to a nursing home. He was otherwise pretty well, though, apart from atrial fibrillation, for which he's taken warfarin for years. He was sent to us from the nursing home because they were worried about his conscious state. Apparently he'd fallen over a couple of times in the last week and was found confused and semi-conscious by the staff. By the time he arrived here he was deeply unconscious, responding only to strong painful stimuli. Vital signs, however, were stable, and there was no evidence of trauma or infection. Examination of the heart, lungs, and abdomen were normal and so were routine bloods. A CT scan of the brain showed a large subdural bleed in the left parietal-occipital region with a major mass effect.

"We contacted the neurosurgeons to ask if they'd want to operate on the hemorrhage but they told us there was nothing they could do. I spoke to the family and explained that we'd offer comfort care only. They took it very badly and insisted that everything possible be done to keep him alive, including even admission to ICU. So I called the ICU reg and she said pretty much the same thing. That's when I called you, Prof, for advice about what to do."

"I said to tell them that I'd see them as soon as possible this morning. Did they settle down a bit after that?"

"Not really." It was clear from the resident's tone that quoting the authority of the professor had made no difference whatsoever. "By the time I got back to them there was the son, a daughter, and several adult grandchildren. They said they were prepared to pay for him to be transferred to a private hospital where he could be admitted to ICU. When I explained that this would be futile and that there was really nothing we could do for him they got really angry. The son even said that they'd take the hospital to court if we didn't do what they wanted. It all ended up taking up most of my night. The last conversation was only a couple of hours ago, and I asked them to go away and have some breakfast and then come back about ten o'clock to talk to you."

"Thanks, Jeremy, you've handled it well. No wonder you're looking so exhausted. We'll let you go now. Have a good sleep."

The night doctor left. The day ahead's going to be interesting, thought Abraham.

16.

Desmond provided Abraham, Rebecca, and Ashis with the latest nursing information about Mr. Alvarez. "He's woken up a bit since Jeremy last saw him," he reported. "But I'm afraid that hasn't proved to be a good thing. He's been thrashing about and screaming. The family got really upset and I had to order a couple of them out of the room to calm things down. You guys know that we've booked the interview room for a family meeting at ten, don't you?"

Abraham, Rebecca, and Ashis had a brief discussion about Mr. Alvarez's medical issues and checked his test results. Ashis, on the computer, let out a whistle. "Here's the CT scan. Wow! That hemorrhage is pretty impressive! I can see why the neurosurgeons said that palliative care was what was needed."

On the bed, tended by a nurse, was a large-framed elderly man with thickset facial features, lying quietly. Abraham asked a few questions, to which there was no response, and then beckoned to Rebecca to carry out a physical examination. She did this quickly and methodically, with the others looking on. After finishing, she summarized her findings with the usual clinical precision, concluding that the patient had evidence of a severe brain injury causing a depressed conscious state. The group then retired again to the corridor outside.

"What do you think we should tell the family?" asked Abraham.

Desmond responded without hesitation. "It's obviously a hopeless case. I think we just need to be direct. He's not going to survive, and we shouldn't do anything to prolong his death. In fact, I think that questions can be legitimately asked about why he was admitted to the hospital in the first place. He's just occupying valuable resources that we all know could be used in other ways."

As Abraham drew in his breath to answer he noticed that Desmond was looking straight at Rebecca, who returned his glance with a calm familiarity. Sensing Abraham's gaze, the registrar reddened slightly and stammered. "Er . . . I agree that we should keep him comfortable," she said, obviously trying to think of something safe to say, "but it doesn't look like he's in pain now."

Another step forward for Freedom to Choose, thought Abraham to himself, but he knew this was not the time for a fight.

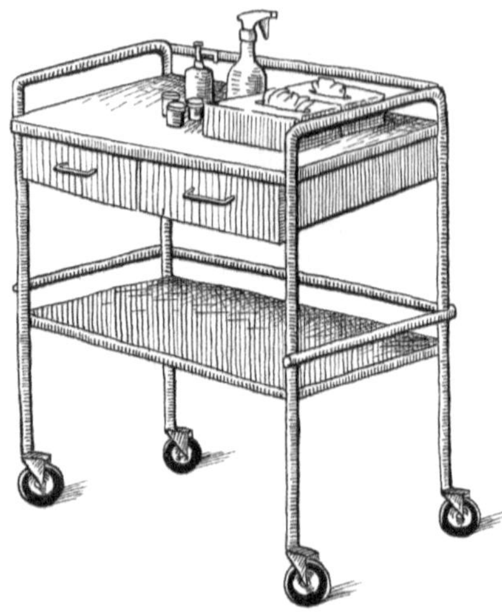

17.

The ward round ground on. They worked their way through the various patients, attending especially to those with impending procedures or operations and those who were ready to go home.

"Rebecca, how's Mrs. Gurewitz?" Abraham asked.

"She's just the same, Prof—completely unresponsive. Her blood pressure, oxygen sats, and urine output are okay; her heart and lungs are functioning normally; and there are still no localizing neurological signs, but she remains deeply unconscious, now not responding even to painful stimuli."

"How long has she been receiving the antibiotics?"

"She's had three full days' treatment, in addition to the anticonvulsants we're giving her, and there's been no evidence of any improvement."

"It sounds like, if anything, she might have deteriorated. Have our tests shown anything?"

"No, they're pretty much unchanged, too. There's no evidence of infection, and her heart, liver, and kidneys seem okay. The brain scan still isn't showing anything abnormal and the EEG just shows changes consistent with unconsciousness."

"Has anyone seen the daughter?" asked Abraham.

"Oh, yes. In spite of our original concerns she's been fully involved. She's adamant that her mom above all doesn't want to lose her independence and live in a nursing home. She feels that we shouldn't keep treating if there's really no chance of a reasonable quality of life."

Abraham nodded in agreement. "I think we have to be realistic and admit that the chance of a substantial recovery is now very low," he said formally. "If they're her wishes then we have no alternative to stopping active treatment. Let's go ahead and do it. Let's stop all her medications, except those for pain and distress, like morphine and benzodiazepines."

"What about food and water? Do we stop them, too?"

"I don't think there's any point in continuing food and hydration," Abraham replied. "If she seems to be distressed as a result of dehydration we can address that at the time, but if she remains unconscious like she is at the moment, it won't be a problem."

"How long do you think it'll take for her to die?" the registrar asked, tentatively.

"It's not possible to say exactly, Rebecca," Abraham continued in his methodical style, "but it'll be a few days. It's undoubtedly going to be a difficult time for everyone, especially her daughter. We'll have to look out for her." He turned to Ashis and Desmond, who had been listening to the conversation. "Is everyone happy with this strategy?"

"I agree that it's futile to keep treating," replied Desmond. "My nurses will continue to provide full comfort care. But we wouldn't want it to go on for too long: that wouldn't be good for anyone."

"Let's cross that bridge if we come to it. I appreciate your help and support," said Abraham insincerely.

18.

"Prof, I'm really looking forward to hearing what you think about Mrs. Dreyfus," Rebecca said. "She's the woman I admitted last night."

"What's her problem?"

"I'm not sure," replied the registrar. "She's seventy-seven and has previously been pretty well, apart from recurrent depression treated with Prozac. She lives in her own home alone and has two daughters who live some distance away—one in the city and the other in the country. It seems that she was found on the floor by a neighbor who hadn't seen her for a few days and knew where she kept the spare key. He went into her apartment and found her on the floor semi-conscious and called an ambulance."

They talked for some minutes, examining the information that had been provided by the paramedics and the hospital lab, and then entered the patient's room. Abraham studied the scene with careful concentration. He approached the woman lying unconscious on the bed. She had short, obviously dyed blonde hair, making her look markedly younger than her reported age. "Hello, Mrs. Dreyfus. My name's Abraham Nevski. I'm one of the doctors looking after you. Can you hear me?"

There was no response, so he put his face quite close to hers and spoke in a louder voice. "Mrs. Dreyfus . . . Wilma . . . I'm Dr. Nevski. We have to find out what's wrong with you. Can you please open your eyes for me?"

There was still no response. Abraham continued with the standard maneuvers. "I'm going to squeeze your hand. Please let me know if you can feel me touching you." He took one hand, looked at it very closely, and then examined the other one.

Together, the consultant and the registrar continued with the examination. They examined various parts of her body, listened to her heart and chest with their stethoscopes, palpated her abdomen, and flashed lights in her eyes, moving her from one position to another in the process. All the while Abraham talked to her as if she were wide awake, explaining every step and taking care to uncover only a part of her body at a time, as well as muttering the examination findings to Rebecca along the way. The patient herself remained completely inert throughout.

When they had finished, Abraham again spoke to the unconscious patient. "Wilma"—he was now speaking with the familiarity of someone who had just had close contact with another person's body—"Wilma, we're going outside to talk about you now. We'll come back a little later to check up on you again." Then, turning to Rebecca, "Would you like to summarize the examination findings?"

The registrar responded without hesitation, obviously familiar with the protocol. She assumed a formal, slightly stiff manner. "Mrs. Dreyfus is an elderly woman, unconscious with a Glasgow score of nine. She has an IV drip and a urinary catheter. She's febrile, tachycardic, and hypertensive. She's sweating slightly and has some rigidity in her arms. Her heart sounds are normal and her chest is clear. There's no evidence of abdominal pathology . . ." She continued to list the physical signs, emphasizing both the positive and important negative findings.

"So what do you think's going on?" asked Abraham.

Rebecca, uncomfortable to find herself at the center of Abraham's sharp gaze, could do no more than think aloud. "There's obviously a serious problem with her brain," she reasoned. "She could still have an infection, although that seems less likely now. There's no evidence of trauma or organ failure or a cancer or other metabolic problem. Another possibility is a reaction to the Prozac: that'd be unusual but would fit reasonably well with what we've found."

Abraham was pleased with the young woman's punctiliousness. "I think you're right, Rebecca. What treatment would you recommend?"

The registrar again went into a detailed description of the possibilities, which included a combination of intravenous fluids and specific drug therapies.

"You've done a good job, Rebecca," Abraham said at last, putting on a paternal smile. "We can expect things will settle within the next twenty-four hours or so. If they don't, we'll have to go back to the drawing board. It sounds like she was managing okay at home, so with a bit of luck she'll be able to return when she recovers. Did you say she had a daughter? It'll help to have a supportive family." He looked at his watch. "It's ten o'clock. We'd better hurry. It's time for the meeting with Mr. Alvarez's relatives."

19.

Desmond had arranged for the family to congregate in a room set aside for private meetings, a large, bare room lit by a bank of blazing fluorescent lights. On the table stood a small vase of wilting flowers, incongruous in this atmosphere of utilitarian, comfortless austerity. It was a room in which many grim words had been spoken.

Abraham surveyed the family—a man and woman, probably in their fifties, whom he assumed to be the patient's children, and three younger people he guessed were grandchildren. He opened the meeting with the exaggerated formality he invariably fell into on such occasions. "Before we start, I want to assure you that our first commitment is to Mr. Alvarez's care. It's always our aim to work with the family to devise the best and most appropriate approach to treatment. I shall ask Rebecca to summarize the medical facts, but may I first inquire about Mr. Alvarez's wife?"

After some peremptory introductions in which the woman identified herself as Sophia, the daughter, and the man as Diego, "his son," the latter replied to Abraham's question in a thick accent. "Our mother's English is not so good. She is not so good either. Is better she does not come here, we think . . ."

Rebecca knew what she had to do, which was to repeat the same summary that had been given to Abraham with a little less jargon. "Mr. Alvarez is a ninety-two-year-old man who's led a very remarkable and active life. He's been fit and healthy until only a few months ago when his ability to think started to decline. It became too difficult to care for him at home so he entered the Brandon Nursing Home three months ago. It seems that over the last few weeks he's been falling over and yesterday was found unconscious by the nursing home staff. They sent him here, and our tests have shown that he's suffered from a very large bleed into his brain. We've asked the specialists in the hospital if there's anything that can be done to help and they've said that surgery wouldn't be of any use and that there'd be no benefit in sending him to intensive care. Our treatment has been to stop the anticoagulant he was taking, which could have increased the chance of bleeding, and to give him some steroids to reduce brain swelling. He seems to have improved a little bit but he's still very unwell."

She stopped there. Abraham recognized how carefully she had chosen her words and once more felt pleased with the care and sensitivity she had displayed. To emphasize Rebecca's main points he added, "It's obviously a very bad thing to have a bleed into the brain. What's more, we've seen the X-rays and think in this case the bleed is a very serious one. It's important for you to recognize that. But before going on I want to make sure you understand what Rebecca said. There might be some technical language that's difficult to understand. If there is, I want you to feel free to ask us to explain. Do you have any questions?"

"Does my father have chance of recovering?" asked Sophia.

"It's possible that there'll be some degree of recovery," replied Abraham, "but your father's suffered a very serious injury that's damaged or destroyed a significant part of his brain. Under these circumstances I have to tell you that the chance of a full recovery is extremely small or nonexistent. And what's more, he's very elderly—"

"But as the doctor said"—this time the question came from one of the grandsons—"until the bleed happened he was fit and healthy, so his age shouldn't come into it."

"We're not making any judgments on the basis of his age," said Abraham, "and it's certainly in his favor that he's been so fit. But whether we like it or not, recovery is slower and harder in older people. In any case, recovery from serious strokes can take many years and requires intensive commitment and work with physiotherapy. That'll be much harder to achieve in this case than with a younger man."

"What do you think will happen?" asked Diego.

"Do you want to answer this, Rebecca?" Abraham said.

"I'll try. It's a bit too early to tell how your dad will be when the swelling in his brain settles down. It's possible that he'll never regain consciousness. It's also possible that he'll wake up but have significant disabilities, like difficulty moving or talking. He could have a further bleed, which would quite likely kill him. Or he could develop a different problem, like pneumonia, which could also make him much worse or even kill him."

"I know this is very difficult for you all," added Abraham, with practiced but genuine sincerity. "Your father and grandfather is obviously dearly beloved and it's terrible to see him in this state. Also, it's especially hard because we can't say exactly what's likely to happen. What we'd normally do in this situation is provide support and see what does happen. If there's a further bleed, decisions about what else we could do might become unnecessary. If not, at some point we may need to make a decision about the extent to which we want to continue any treatment at all."

Diego was staring at the floor. The other grandson burst out, "Doctor, we need to be very honest with you." He was talking very earnestly. "My grandfather's very precious to us. We need him. We want him alive, even if . . ." He controlled himself. "We've been reading the newspapers and we know that hospitals are doing things to cut off care for old people. We're worried that just because Grandpa's ninety-two someone's decided that his quality of life isn't good enough. We just want him to stay alive, that's all . . ."

The young man was choking on his words. The family was looking at Abraham imploringly. He tried to keep his voice even. "I understand what you say and I appreciate your concerns. It's true that there's been some public discussion about the cost to the community of the medical care of elderly people. However, in this hospital we never make decisions about care on the basis of cost or age. We have to be prudent in our use of resources, of course, but the single, dominating issue is always and only what's good for the patient. I give you my word, absolutely and unconditionally, that decisions about Mr. Alvarez won't be made primarily on the basis of cost considerations and that care won't be withdrawn without full consultation with your family."

"Thank you for saying that to us," continued the grandson, who appeared surprised not to have received a hostile response. "It makes me feel a lot better. I'm sorry if I sounded aggressive."

"That's fine," said Abraham, nodding his head reassuringly. "I understand." Satisfied with the progress they were making, he went on. "Did Mr. Alvarez express any views about how he'd have wanted to die? I mean, did he say to anyone anything about not wanting to go to intensive care or something like that?"

"My dad was a fighter," said the patient's daughter. "He was a well-known professor. He gave up his comfortable life to fight for freedom and justice in la revolución de Chile. He was jailed and tortured. He suffered because of his commitment to the people. When he had to leave Chile he decided to come to Australia, where he started again at age fifty. He came here and worked with his bare hands to save money and start a business. And he succeeded. He's given so much to us; he's fought for all of us—for you, as well as the people in his own country. The least we can do is fight for him now. We're really worried about killing people because they're old or weak or without defenses. That's what the Nazis did in Germany and the fascists in Chile. We can't let it happen here."

She was crying softly. Abraham continued to struggle to retain his own composure. "All I can say is that I do understand," he said. "I know from my own family . . ." After a pause he added, "Maybe this is a good place to stop. We'll need to meet again to continue the discussion but perhaps we've covered enough ground for today. Does anyone want to add anything before we finish?"

Everyone was silent, so he closed the proceedings.

20.

In the corridor outside, the team regrouped. Rebecca looked oppressed. "It's tough, isn't it?" she said. "I mean, they're really suffering. Mr. Alvarez is going to die regardless of anything we do. If things go on for too long it'll only make things harder for them."

"I know it's hard," Desmond broke in, "but dying's always hard and—I don't mean to be heartless—Mr. Alvarez isn't the first person to go through it.

And after all, he's had a full life—maybe not the easiest, but it's been long and eventful. I agree with Beck: I can't see any point in prolonging the suffering. As she said, he's going to die anyway. Keeping him alive will just add to the pain—and to the community's expense." He glanced quickly at Rebecca who gave him an appreciative expression.

Abraham winced at the nurse's familiarity with his registrar. "We'll have to wait and see what happens in the next day or so," he replied, "but I'm not planning to take steps here to prolong life artificially. At least none of the family tried to insist on him going into intensive care."

Rebecca looked at her watch. "We have another fifteen patients still to see. I need to get organized and I've got some questions to ask you. Maybe before we go on we could sit and go over them verbally, and then we could see the sickest ones."

As they walked to Abraham's office she asked plainly, "Prof, what do you really think about Mr. Alvarez?"

He was a little taken aback by her directness. "What is it you're thinking about?" he replied.

"I mean . . . I'm not sure . . . I was thinking . . ." She began haltingly, but then the words came in a torrent. "I was wondering how you decide what's best in a difficult case like this. It's clear that Mr. Alvarez is going to die, no matter what anyone does. The only question is when. Although it's sad, the family will have to confront it and go through the grieving process when they do. But it seems to me that we can slow down or speed up the process. I mean, if we wanted to, we could do all sorts of things to keep him alive. For example, we could—I'm not saying we would—take him to ICU, ventilate him artificially, dialyze him if he went into kidney failure, feed him through a nasogastric tube or intravenously, and so on. We could keep him alive for a while longer, which—given what his grandson was saying—would be seen by the family as a good thing.

"But to keep him alive would also carry a lot of negative consequences. It'd be very expensive, and we all know that we're struggling to be able to pay for the health system as it is rather than improve it. It'd mean that one ICU or hospital bed wasn't available for someone else who needed it—maybe for someone whose life could be saved altogether by coming to the hospital. It'd take up the time of the nurses, who could be spending more time with other patients. It'd take up our time, too. And, most important, it'd prolong the pain and suffering for Mr. Alvarez himself and for his family.

"Ultimately, it's the consequences that count, but the ultimate consequence for Mr. Alvarez—that he dies—is the same whatever we do. When these other consequences are taken into account it seems to me that the balance is strongly in favor of not keeping him alive, even if he and his family want that to happen." She stopped, evidently a bit surprised by her own intensity. After a pause she added meekly, "What do you think?"

They were at Abraham's office now. He opened the door and they entered the room. He motioned to Rebecca to take a seat in one of the armchairs, automatically went over to the cabinet to pour himself a drink, and then sat on the couch. He was trying to decide how best to respond to the registrar's question. He wanted to avoid sounding condescending and as usual decided that it was safest to start blandly. "These are big questions, Rebecca," he said. "Perhaps we can schedule some time in the next few days to sit down and go through the arguments. The view you've just expressed stands or falls on the idea that consequences are really the only things that are important. Some people believe—as it happens, I'm one of them—that consequences are only one source of ethical value among many that have to be considered when making a decision. Some of the others may in fact be much more powerful than the bare outcomes." He could see that this was not what she wanted to hear, so he added, "But we'll need time to talk this through. Before we do that we'd better discuss our patients. Let's come back to the big questions later."

He felt he needed to help Rebecca but didn't quite know how. This remained on his mind as the two of them went through the list of patients under their care. When they had finished, trying to find a way to return to the previous conversation, he asked about her preparations for the upcoming exams. He was surprised at her renewed eagerness to talk.

"Actually I'm in a bit of a quandary," she started off. "Medicine's all I've ever wanted to do and the fact that I'm doing it is really important to my family. We come from the country and I'm the first one ever to go to university. My mom brought us up and has had a big struggle to allow me to achieve my dream."

"She's been very successful," Abraham said.

"I love the work, but sometimes I feel that it's just too difficult," she continued. "I saw your response to the girl in ICU who'd tried to kill herself yesterday. In fact, to tell you the truth, when I heard the story I was distressed, too. I love medicine. I love the challenges. I love coming upon a problem and going about solving it, carefully and systematically. I can accept that it's not always possible to make a diagnosis and even that not all my patients will survive. I can accept the long hours of work and study and that I'll always face a battle to balance my personal and professional lives. What I'm not sure about is whether I can carry the emotional burden, whether the weight of suffering is too much to bear.

"You probably don't remember it but once when I was a third-year student you asked me to interview a dying patient. He was an elderly man who'd been in a Japanese prison camp during the Second World War. He told us how in the camp he'd been a kind of doctor—a first-aid officer really—which meant that he sometimes had to decide who could be saved and who couldn't. After the war he couldn't free himself from all the misery he'd lived through and the guilt he felt about the decisions he'd made, and he spent the rest of his life alone, unable to establish close personal relationships. When we saw him he was dying of a brain tumor. He was philosophical about it, saying that in response to pain and unhappiness there's only so much empathy you can store up. Beyond that point, you're kind of full—anything more no longer has meaning. He wasn't depressed; he was just tired. He accepted his death but said that not much would have changed if it had come a few decades earlier. I often think of that man and know that I don't want to end up like him. I'm only twenty-six—the same age as Flora in ICU. And I don't want to end up like her, either."

Abraham's phone rang. It was Jenny, his long-suffering secretary.

"Abraham, where are you?" she exclaimed. "You have a room full of patients waiting to see you at the clinic. What are you doing?"

21.

Jenny had organized Abraham's outpatient clinics for many years and well understood his foibles. She took great pride in her work and he always tried to do as she demanded. On this occasion, as he arrived in the clinic, she looked a little dark but merely said, "You'd better get going. I'll call you to keep you moving if you're too slow."

There were already three people waiting to see Abraham, who described himself as a "specialist in internal medicine." This meant that his work covered a wide range of medical conditions. He saw people with heart and lung problems, gastrointestinal disorders, diabetes, problems of the joints, skin or blood, even some cancers. He reveled in the complexity of illness and the thrill of solving a diagnostic problem and finding a precisely targeted treatment. However, it was the less formal, less precise aspects of medical practice that never failed to evoke his fascination, to really move him. He was acutely aware that every person he saw, no matter how trivial or serious the underlying medical condition, drew on a personal story that shaped how he or she made sense of new life events. Illness was not just a matter of disruptions in the nature and structures of tissues: it was a disturbance in the field of meaning that gave shape and direction to a person's life course. Even supposedly minor conditions could stimulate a profound reflection about meanings and values. They could evoke fears, hopes, apprehensions, uncertainties the person might even be unaware of harboring, or precipitate reevaluation of major life themes, including work, relationships, and religious beliefs.

Sometimes patients would be shocked to find how illnesses they themselves assumed to be straightforward would shake them to the core. Sometimes they would actively seize on the opportunity to challenge things about their lives they had long taken for granted. Not everyone, of course, sought to utilize a visit to the doctor as an occasion to engage in a deep philosophical meditation. But for many, the modalities and vulnerabilities of the flesh were inextricable from the layers of meaning they accumulated around themselves, like a kind of outer skin, to orient and protect themselves. What was often most remarkable was how a particular symptom—a specific pain, a weakness, an episode of dizziness—could change everything. There was no bodily experience that was too small, too obscure, to be symbolized or invested in this way. And there was no shortcut to working through the intricate web of significations, which could only occur in the dynamic exchange with another person—not a friend, a relative, or a lover, but someone who could act as a guide, as a figure who could be fashioned and refashioned according to the needs of that moment and that experience.

In his clinics Abraham fell into a comfortable routine: he would pass from a discussion of a newly discovered fear to a reawakened hope, from wistful remembrances of childhood to deep-seated, unfulfilled yearnings. He felt he had a knack for identifying the moment when the tinge of meaning was needed to make sense of a symptom, or when a physical symptom had to be located in a broader framework of interrupted bodily experience.

For some people the disruption in the fabric of the everyday provoked by illness was gradual and controlled. For others it was like an explosion going off. Occasionally, it was the everyday itself that was the minefield.

Abraham called in a young woman whom he had not seen before. Reading her name from the sheet he had been given, he called, "Marina Bell, please," and led her into the consulting room.

The room, like all the others in the hospital except Abraham's office, was stark and functional. Abraham sat down on a swivel chair at the plain, plastic-topped desk. He waited for her to talk.

"I need help!" she blurted. "My life has become unbearable. I can't go on!"

Expressions of distress were familiar territory for Abraham. "Would you like to tell me your story?"

"I have agonizing problems before my periods each month. I've always had pain, but that's only a minor part of it. The main problem is what happens to my mood. I get angry and depressed, so much so that I can almost no longer function."

"What does happen?" he asked.

He scrutinized her while she was talking. "For three weeks of the month I'm okay. Then within a day I can't stop crying. I can't talk to people. I just want to die. It goes on for a week until my period comes. Then I'm okay again for another three weeks. It's driving me insane, literally."

"What do you do when you're feeling bad?"

"If I can, I disconnect the phone and just go to bed. I don't eat or drink. I just lie there, sometimes for three or four days. I think of dying, of suicide. If I had the courage, I'd do it. That's if I'm lucky. If I'm working I can't stay home but just have to plough on."

"What kind of work do you do?"

She hesitated, then smiled sadly. She had dark, penetrating eyes. "This might surprise you, but I'm a comedian. I perform either on my own or with a group."

"And you have to perform, even though you're feeling how you just described to me?"

"Yes. It's unbearable. Every time I do it I'm not sure that I can go on. Sometimes they have to physically push me out on stage. So far, however, I've managed in the end every time and the show hasn't ever had to be canceled."

"Where are you in your cycle now?"

"I'm six days before what I call 'the catastrophe.' I open a new show next week. It's been widely advertised—with lots of these flyers distributed—so there's nothing I can do to get out of it. I'm terrified about what might happen. Can you help me?" She passed him a leaflet. Her eyes flashed.

He asked her some more questions, carried out a brief examination, and told her a little about the treatments that were available. "But before trying any treatments I need to do some tests. I'm confident we'll be able to control the problem, Marina. Here's my phone number. Please don't hesitate to call me if you feel you need to talk to someone urgently."

"Do you think you can help? I'm really desperate."

"I won't be able to do much for this show, I'm afraid, but there may well be things we can do for later ones. How do you feel about that?"

The woman did not reply. Instead, she just burst into tears.

Abraham silently took her hand and held it for a few seconds. When she had quietened down he led her to the door.

After she had left the room Abraham sat for a few moments looking at the paper Marina had given him. Something about her predicament had struck a deep chord in him. Her chosen work was to bring laughter to other people's lives but she was able to do so only at the cost of considerable pain to herself. Of course, all people have to perform in some way, to put on a show, to present themselves publicly as composed, organized, and stable. And many—maybe most—personal interactions are distorted by expectations about what is proper. Humor is an important device for cutting through hypocrisy and for exposing the pretense underlying much of everyday life; in fact, ruthless, uncompromising honesty is one of the things that makes comedians funny. But in Marina's case—performing through her pain—the exposure of hypocrisy was itself no more than pretense.

He slipped into thinking about his own predicament, his loneliness, his ambivalence about his father, his misgivings about the way the hospital and medicine were moving, his uncertainty about his own authenticity and purpose. In his dealings with his patients, all this was hidden. Did this make him a hypocrite or was he just doing what was expected of him? Who is the authentic person: the one who really is as he seems or the one who refuses to play the game?

22.

Abraham winced a little when he saw the name of his last patient for the day. He braced himself, went out into the waiting room, and called her name: "Mrs. Timoshenko, please."

A Russian woman in her late seventies, Ursula Timoshenko was very small, thin, and stooped, and walked—or rather hobbled—in small steps. Her face was heavily lined and her demeanor perpetually and unchangingly grave. She perched herself on the chair and without waiting for an invitation began talking. She spoke with a heavy accent, in a soft, low voice but with precise articulation, perfect grammar, and careful punctuation. Her words came at a constant speed—neither fast nor slow—in an even, controlled, unvarying sequence.

"Doctor, I am very sick! I need your help. I've been to Dr. Bauer and he says I need an MRI scan of my liver and lungs. My blood tests show my condition is deteriorating. The anemia is worsening and the blood cells are irregular. I have the report here. It says that the red cells show anisocytosis and poikilocytosis. This is commonly seen in inflammatory and autoimmune conditions. I have pain all over—terrible pain—and it only gets worse. I'm very worried that I have cancer somewhere. The blood tests show many irregularities, which often occur in cancer. My blood sugar is rising. I have to get up in the night to pass urine every hour. It is definitely polyuria. This has never happened before. It's a common feature of diabetes. I know that I have been developing diabetes . . ."

Abraham sat back in his chair and tried to relax. He was accustomed to the routine. Mrs. Timoshenko always talked like this, in her unmodulated monotone, with an unvarying rhythm that was unbroken even by the need to take a breath. What was more, she always started in the same way: "Doctor, I'm very sick. I need your help."

" . . . The liver function tests show deterioration in the transaminases. I've never had this before and believe it may be the start of autoimmune hepatitis. Dr. Bauer confirms that this might be the case. He agrees that we need to look for hidden and sequestered antibodies . . ."

She continued with her mechanical drone. Abraham knew that, for some time at least, it was futile to try to interrupt. He allowed the words to wash over him, to engulf him. His mind wandered. Over the years, he had come to learn about Ursula's personal history. At the age of eighteen she had had the whole world at her feet. She was slender and beautiful, with long, flowing blonde hair—she had shown him pictures of herself. She was a brilliant student and was admitted to the university in her native St. Petersburg, at that time called Leningrad. She excelled at languages, literature, and philosophy. The war had just ended. Despite the devastation across Europe, and especially the Soviet Union, this was a time of promise, of renewal, of hope.

Dictatorships seemed to be crumbling and a new age of mutual understanding beginning. Ursula decided at that early age to devote herself to healing the cultural wounds of war. She would do this by allowing people around the world to share and enjoy the great works of literature, and thereby the grandeur and nobility of the human soul. She was to become a translator, from Russian to French, from French to Russian, and from both into English. Her life was to be a gift to cross-cultural understanding.

" . . . My father died when I was ten, and I'm sure that he had immune disease. I think that I've inherited it from him. I already have systemic lupus erythematosus, which means I have circulating immune complexes. My mutinous body is at war with itself. Autoimmune hepatitis can lead to chronic active hepatitis and liver failure. It starts with elevated transaminases . . ."

At the university, she was able to learn from some of the greatest thinkers of the age. By twenty-five she was offered a position in one of the leading universities in the country. By thirty she was working on her books. Her translations of Proust into Russian and Dostoyevsky into French and English became famous. She married Yevgeny, a handsome, promising young violinist, a Jew like her, who was committed to using music to foster national and international understanding. The end of Stalinism added to the sense of hope. She recalled the excitement of the news of Khrushchev's speech to the Twentieth Congress of the Communist Party: words had become potent devices; after all the suffering the process of healing had become a work of art and culture. When she was thirty-five her son Ivan—named after the second of the Brothers Karamazov—was born.

" . . . Look at the results of these tests. The ALT, which should be 40, is increased to 68, and the AST, which should be 50, is 96. My immune system is very badly affected. We need to look for other causes of hepatitis, including viruses and granulomatous diseases . . ."

Even though the dream of universal understanding wasn't realized—the Cold War, resurgent authoritarianism, and anti-Semitism saw to that—she continued her work, and the family continued to live a comfortable, even privileged, life. Nonetheless, when the opportunity to leave the Soviet Union arose in the late 1980s she decided to take it and, with her husband and son, she emigrated to Australia. She and Yevgeny were in their fifties and brash and confident. They retained their sense of adventure and their readiness to confront new challenges. But the move turned out to be a tragic mistake.

" . . . The arthritis is out of control. I have rheumatoid arthritis. It was shown by the blood tests you did in 2007. Look, here are the results. The rheumatoid factor is 63, when it should be 39. I have the other features of rheumatoid arthritis. I have . . ."

Despite their eminence neither of them could find reliable work in the new country. Yevgeny gave occasional concerts and his recordings still sold—he was an acknowledged exponent of the music of Prokofiev and Scriabin—but Ursula was unable to obtain a university position. Their limited savings were soon exhausted. But worse—much worse—Ivan died within a year of their arrival.

" . . . The fatigue has seeped through to my bones. In addition to the tiredness, there is the anorexia, the synovitis, the generalized weakness, the polyarthritis, the inflammation, the lymphadenopathy. I have had all of these . . ."

Her son had been living in another city, trying to strike out on his own, and she had demanded—in her imperious way—that he come to visit her. After an angry conversation he had acceded to her request and died in a car accident on a country road on the way home. Both parents took the tragedy very hard. Ursula blamed herself for her son's death.

Abraham knew he had to do something to bring the consultation to a close, but he had been here before and knew how difficult this was. He shifted in his seat to indicate that the time was nearly up, but it was to no avail.

" . . . The dyspnea is getting worse. I can't walk more than twenty meters without having to stop. My breath is failing, like my unbreathed memories. I think I might have a pleural effusion. This is common with lung cancers and infections. Small cell cancers can develop slowly over many years. They can be associated with cough and hemoptysis . . ."

Their lives were in ruins. Yevgeny never played in concert again, only taking up the violin occasionally to revive sad memories. Ursula started to experience physical symptoms—first vague aches and pains, which gradually extended and became more severe. Words had been her business, so she bought a medical dictionary and started going through it. She was shocked to find that she suffered from a great many of the ailments named there. She had arthralgias, arthritis, chills, constipation, colic, dyspepsia, fatigue, fever, fibromyalgia . . . She became an expert in medical terms. Gradually, the self-diagnoses became more elaborate and sophisticated: she now had ischemic heart disease, congestive cardiac failure, autoimmune renal disease, rheumatoid arthritis, leukocytoclastic vasculitis, systemic lupus erythematosus, and so on. She would seek out medical specialists to confirm the diagnoses and discover new ones. Nothing they might say could shake her convictions about her multiple afflictions. Time after time, she would be escorted out of the consulting room, still talking, or else the doctor would simply get up and leave, while she continued her relentless discourse, unabated.

" . . . The rash is worse. It's terrible. Abraham, you must do something to help! The rash is caused by the vasculitis. Dr. West said many years ago that I have leukocytoclastic vasculitis. I had palpable purpura, macules, papules, vesicles, bullae, subcutaneous nodules, and urticaria. He performed a biopsy that showed possible inflammation in postcapillary venules. I have the report here. I will show you . . ."

Words were, and remained, her life. She savored their taste and their texture in her mouth. Abraham marveled at the ease with which she had moved from the lexicons of Proust and Dostoyevsky to that of medicine. Sometimes she would come up with a technical term that he did not know, which he would jot down to look up later. Sometimes he would tune out, allowing the drone to continue in the distance, enjoying its reassuring, mechanical rhythm, like the sound of distant traffic. If he did this, however, he would often be jolted back into the present by a demanding question, sometimes repeated forcefully: "What do you think?" "Will you order the blood test?" "Can I have the MRI?"

" . . . The lupus is causing problems. It was diagnosed by Professor Johannsen many years ago. It started with myalgias and arthralgias and mainly affected the metacarpophalyngeal joints. I have also had cutaneous manifestations and am worried about renal and hematological involvement. The blood weeps in my heart. I have many antibodies: antinuclear, anti-DNA, anti-Ro, anti-La . . ."

Her life had been steeped in culture and music. She had studied in the best universities. She had been celebrated and respected. With her husband she had traveled the world. She had grown up with the hopes and disappointments of the October Revolution. She had seen a war. She had fled persecution. She had lived at the cutting edge of the twentieth century, with all its nobility and its bloody horrors. She had given birth and then lost her child. She had struggled for the triumph of ideas and sensibility. Now, however, as her last years approached, she was a shriveled, lonely old woman, twenty thousand kilometers from her birthplace, reduced to rambling endlessly about ailments she didn't have, reciting not poetry but lengthy excerpts from *Harrison's Principles of Internal Medicine*. Her words were once the weapons that would heal the world; now, ironically, they were no more than a pathetic cry of anguish, a sad song of despair, of lost chances, of unfulfilled hopes and shattered dreams.

" . . . I am sure I'm developing diabetes. I have to get up every hour to pass urine. Every hour! I can't sleep, or if I do go off to sleep I wake up after only a few merciful moments to go to the toilet again. And I'm so thirsty! I have to drink whenever I get up. That's the commonest sign of diabetes. Polyuria and polydipsia. Dr. West said many years ago that I was at risk of developing diabetes. He looked at the blood tests then and he knew. I don't eat anything sweet but my glucose levels are . . ."

They had to finish. "Mrs. Timoshenko," Abraham interrupted brusquely, "where is the pain?"

"The pain? The pain is everywhere! It's terrible. I take morphine syrup prescribed by Dr. Goldstein but it doesn't take away the pain . . ."

"Does the morphine help at all?"

"Maybe it helps a little, but the pain is still there, lurking treacherously. I feel pain wherever I am and whatever I do. I've had the pain since my renal cancer was removed. This could mean that the cancer is still—"

"I'm afraid we'll have to finish soon. If I gave you some additional medication would you take it?"

" . . . What medication?"

"I'd like to try some stronger medications . . ."

"You gave me a new medicine last year and I couldn't take it. I have reactions to many drugs. When I took penicillin I developed red lesions over my entire body. Dr. Bauer said—"

"If you remember, the last time I gave you a new medicine you only took one tablet and experienced a number of severe problems that seemed very unlikely to be associated with the medication. I'd like to try again . . ."

"If you could find me a medication that would take away the pain that would be very good. The pain is there all the time. I can't close my eyes without experiencing pain. I can't sleep for the pain. The morphine is not enough to . . ."

"But Mrs. Timo—"

"And I have the rash. It's leukocytoclastic vasculitis. The vasculitis was diagnosed by Professor . . ."

Abraham was standing up. "Please, Ursula, just stop for a moment," he implored her. "I'm trying to help you but I do have to finish now. We can talk further next time. There are many things we can try to alleviate the pain. However, whenever I recommend a new medication you refuse to take it. If you don't take what I suggest it won't help you . . ." He started moving toward the door.

She didn't budge. "I don't need to change my medications. If I change I have too many side effects. People with autoimmune conditions are more likely to suffer bad effects of medicines. You must help . . ."

Abraham sighed in defeat. "Mrs. Timoshenko, please just tell me what you think needs to be done," he said weakly, from the doorway.

"Dr. Bauer agrees that I need a new MRI of my back and liver. Also, we need some more blood tests . . . Oh, I felt the bad pain just now. I can't walk up the street without having a severe pain all the time . . ."

"I'm afraid we do have to end now. I know that this is a difficult illness for you. However, if there's anything I can . . ."

Abraham opened the door and looked around. Mrs. Timoshenko was still talking.

23.

The lunch group was assembling in its usual place, a table in the corner of the cafeteria most distant from the serving counters that had been chosen in the hope that it would both be quieter and soften a little the sense of undifferentiated starkness that pervaded the factory-like atmosphere. In reality, the noise of voices and clanking dishes barely varied and the uniformity of the plastic-covered tables and chairs was undiminished across the large space.

Harry Krokowski bustled up to the table, looking flustered. "Hello, everyone. Sorry I'm late. It's been completely crazy in the ED today. It's as if there's been a natural disaster that's created an instant epidemic of coughs, colds, cuts, and scratches. It's been overwhelmingly busy, even if not deeply satisfying."

"That's interesting," said Jonathan Bitic, the director of surgery. "In the operating rooms lately we've been flat out, too. Every list is full, and there's not even time allowed for morning or afternoon tea."

"That's because everything in the hospital—including the operating suite—has been cut to the bone," said Nic, "although I'm not sure that's quite the right image."

Ian Moloney and Madeleine Silverstein had become engaged in a conversation about the CEO's statements about health care costs. "She's right about the rising cost of health care becoming a big problem for all developed countries," Ian was saying. "What she didn't point out is that it's a result of our own success. The aging of our population means that there are fewer people in work to support those who've retired. What's more, this has happened at exactly the same time that health care has become much more expensive because of the cost of new drugs and machines."

Madeleine agreed with him. "At the directorate meeting last week Damien from ICU said he'd done some calculations and found that the daily cost of keeping a patient in intensive care had doubled in the last twelve years, while the doubling time for GDP is twice that. He's calculated that if the trend continues we'll be spending nearly a quarter of all our earnings on health care by 2020. That'll mean that there'll be lots of other things we won't be able to support, including education, sport, and the arts."

Others joined in the conversation. "There's no doubt that we have a problem on our hands," said Allison Wong, "and I for one don't have any answers. But I get very unsettled when Margaret Wilson talks about cutting off care for elderly people or those with incurable disease in order to reduce costs. After all, isn't that what medicine's supposed to be about: caring for sick and vulnerable people, regardless of their circumstances?"

"We have to remember that debates about limiting health care to elderly people aren't new," responded Ian, pondering his tea. "After all, resources are always scarce, everywhere. In ancient Greece and Rome it was accepted that the sick and the elderly should be allowed to die or—better still—should actively bring on their own demise. It's always been recognized that the infirmity of age was part of the inexorable tragedy of life. But today anyone can be kept alive by our technological wizardry."

"That's right," added Harry. "Pneumonia was once known as the 'old man's friend.' Maybe one day—perhaps not too far away—we'll have to set a limit on the age when people can receive health care. After seventy years, for example, there'd be no entitlement. This'd preserve health care resources for those whose lives would be most enhanced by them."

"Do you know where the expression 'pneumonia is the old man's friend' came from?" interrupted Nic. "I looked it up once. It's actually a misquote from William Osler. What he really said was 'pneumonia may well be called the friend of the aged. Taken off by it in an acute, short, not often painful illness, the old man escapes those cold gradations of decay so distressing to himself and to his friends.' That's probably as true today as it was in the 1890s."

"I'm not sure that I'd set the limit at seventy, though," commented Jonathan. "That could mean that a few of us here are about to shuffle off our own mortal coils!" He chuckled and threw back the last of his coffee. "What about ninety-five?"

"There's a very serious point, though," Allison responded. "Setting an age limit to care is just a new form of discrimination. Elderly people are no less entitled than others to claims on society's resources just because they happen to be old. Besides, they're the ones who built up the resources through lifetimes of contributions, so maybe if anything, they should be preferred in decisions about resource allocation."

"I agree with Allison," said Madeleine. "It's quality of life, not age, that counts most. If someone's active and still productive they should be treated like anyone else. A problem arises when the quality of life's poor and a person still wants to go on living. What do we do then? Whose judgment should prevail? The patient's, the family's, the doctor's—"

" . . . the CEO's, the chief financial officer's?" broke in Nic, with his mouth full.

Everyone laughed, but Madeleine continued, warming to her subject. "It's offensive and cruel to people with disabilities to judge their lives on the basis of arbitrary standards, usually based on popular culture images of youth and beauty and sexiness. No one has a right to judge another's life, to say when it's useful or useless, to pronounce about when someone should live or die."

"Look, Madeleine," rejoined Harry, "no one can disagree with you. But even you have to admit that there's a problem here that we have to address, not in philosophical terms but practically, at the level of the hospital, where actual decisions have to be made about who gets what, when, and how. I like the CEO as little as everyone else—I disrespect her dress sense and, like you, think that a pharmacist might not be the best person to run a hospital—but, whether we like it or not, it's her job to balance the budget, to keep the whole thing afloat. She has to do this against a background of expanding demands and need and an obdurate workforce like us that continues to insist on our right to make decisions however we see fit. I don't have any answers but I can certainly see the problem."

"No one says that there's not a problem, Harry," said Allison, "but what disquiets me—what alarms me!—is the plan to introduce rules limiting treatment for old people coming into the hospital and offering bonuses for the staff members and departments that are most successful in cutting costs. In our ward we now have Freedom to Choose 'consultants' flouncing around approaching patients trying to get them to say that they don't want to be intubated or go to ICU, even when this has no relevance whatever to their current illness. If this process continues, old and sick people will no longer be able to have the confidence that they can receive care when they need it, and they'll constantly feel under pressure to suffer—and die—at home. I don't think that'd be a step forward."

"It's noticeable," said Ian, "that in all this discussion about fiscal plans there's no mention of caring, of respect, of maintaining trust, of relieving suffering, of all the things we entered medicine to achieve. What is it that we're coming to?"

"What we're coming to is the end of lunchtime," said Nic. "Abraham, old boy, you've been uncharacteristically quiet today. Usually you don't let the rest of us get a word in edgewise. Are you okay? Maybe you should have the last word."

Abraham shifted in his chair. He had been thinking about his conversation with Rebecca and about Mr. Alvarez, Mrs. Gurewitz, and Flora.

"I've only one point to add," he replied, "and that is we have to remember that the allocation of health resources has wide social consequences." Then he added, almost as an afterthought, "If we're to have a change in the fundamental precepts of medicine, if we're going to move from caring for our patients—and for each other—to crassly saving money by cutting down on cleaning costs, by eliminating patients' morning and afternoon teas, by extending the shifts of already overworked doctors and nurses, and then—most sickeningly of all—by refusing to care for the elderly people who've spent their lives working, paying taxes, and paying our wages, it should be as the outcome of a public debate around competing needs, priorities, and social values. It shouldn't occur through the arbitrary decree of a disreputable bureaucrat shamelessly trying to balance a budget and maximize her performance bonuses, or a pathetic communication consultant ticking a box."

The vehemence of his words surprised even Abraham himself. There was a pause, then Harry said, "Powerfully expressed, Abraham," adding, "like everyone else, I have to get back to the front line . . . Thanks everyone for the conversation. See you tomorrow."

"And I've got to go, too," added Jonathan. "Got to get back to cutting the operating room back to the bone, or whatever."

"Well," concluded Nic, "we've solved another great problem in the world. What's our topic for tomorrow? How about peace in the Middle East?"

24.

"Mrs. Da Silva . . ."

"Please call me Betty."

"Thanks for that. I'm Abraham Nevski. And thank you for agreeing to talk with us today. I'm going to get the students to ask you some questions and then we're going to discuss some things among ourselves. Will you be happy with that?"

The patient nodded assent. "George," Abraham continued, "could you please tell me what you know about Mrs. Da Silva?"

"Okay . . . Betty's a middle-aged woman sitting quietly in bed . . . She might be a bit short of breath . . . She came into the hospital . . . five days ago . . . Um . . . She's got an intravenous cannula in her arm and a drip set up next to her bed, but it's not connected . . ."

Abraham could see that George was trying to remember back to the previous session in which the patient's story had been largely deciphered from the clues they were able to observe. It had probably seemed straightforward at the time but now he was struggling. Abraham looked carefully at George. He was wearing a large badge that proclaimed brightly 'Hello, I'm George' with a smiley face underneath. Although at this moment he appeared awkward and uncertain, Abraham speculated that to his peers he presented himself as extroverted and confident.

"Thanks, George. That's a start. Tracey, please go on."

The young woman took up the narrative with striking enthusiasm. "Betty's hands are a bit . . . she's got arthritis . . . she has some bruising on her arms . . . and there is a four-wheeled walker next to her bed . . ."

Abraham now scrutinized Tracey closely, going over her features one by one. Height: medium. Hair: blonde. Jewelry: earrings and bracelet. No makeup. Eyes: grayish blue. Lips: full. Skin: unblemished. Clothing: short skirt and blouse. Putting all this together, the overall impression was of a warm sensuousness, which contrasted with the formality of the current setting. Abraham hoped that Tracey expressed the intensity she was displaying now in whatever she was doing. He wondered about her inner life, whether like Flora in the ICU she was driven by some deep, abiding secret passion, whether she was loved and loved someone, whether she was surrounded by people she could trust. He wondered if she'd ever made love . . .

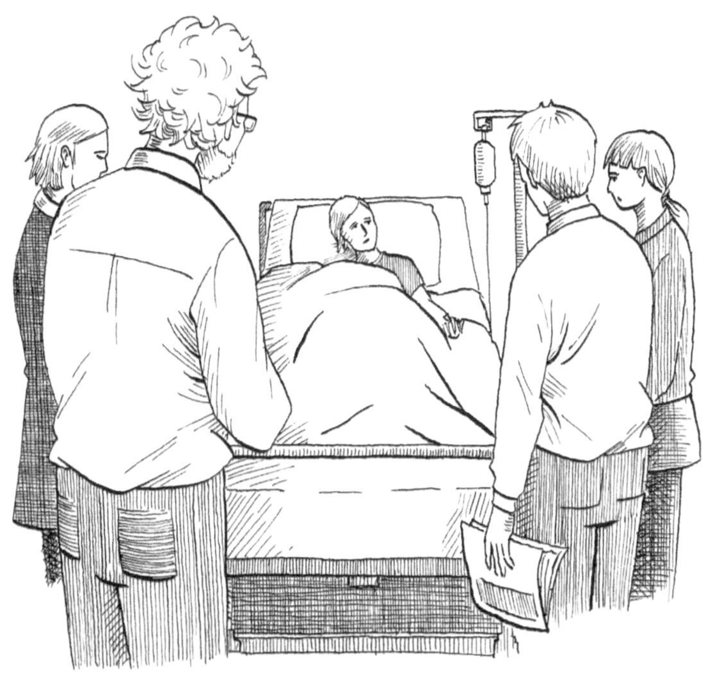

Looking at the pretty, bright young woman in front of him full of generous enthusiasm, radiating hope and promise, Abraham was reminded of the predicament of his own life, of his loneliness and yearning for intimacy. It was years now since he had felt cared for by anyone. Once Stephanie had fallen ill it was assumed that the entire burden would be his. He accepted the responsibility willingly, of course—first to care for Stephanie herself, then the children and his parents—but that didn't mean that he didn't need care himself. It was only now, looking at Tracey grappling to acquire skills that were second nature to him, that he realized his own inner desolation. He felt a vast invasion of loneliness. He had his work, of course, but the truth was that this was just a place for him to hide, and even here he felt increasingly under siege.

"Could she have rheumatoid arthritis?" the young woman was asking eagerly. Her face was shining with anticipated triumph.

Abraham extracted himself from his dark daydream. "Yes, that right. Very good!" He did his best to match her enthusiasm. "And what do you think's the purpose of the IV?"

The student examined the intravenous equipment. "She's received an infusion of . . . 'meripenem.' I think that's an antibiotic. Is that right?"

"Yes, it's a powerful, wide-spectrum antibiotic. Please look closely at her legs, which are clearly visible from the way she's sitting. What do you notice?"

" . . . They may be a little wasted?"

"And what about her face?"

There was a pause. This time another student answered. "It's round—maybe she's Cushingoid?"

"That's good, Carmen. Is there anything else you can see around the room?"

"She's got some asthma inhalers over here!" another student exclaimed, triumphantly.

"Okay. There are a few other things, but that's most of them. Who'd like to try to put everything together?"

There was silence. "Bruno, do you want to try?"

"Um . . . She's got rheumatoid arthritis and an infection . . ."

"That's a good try, but what about everything else? Carmen? Tracey?"

There was another pause. "Well, let me tell you what I think," said Abraham, "and then, as usual, we'll ask Mrs. De Silva to explain what's really going on . . ."

He was running on automatic pilot again. He was sure that the students hadn't noticed anything. "Mrs. Da Silva . . . Betty, is a middle-aged woman with chronic rheumatoid arthritis, a neuromuscular condition, asthma, and an additional underlying structural lung disease, the details of which are uncertain. Her lung condition's gradually deteriorated but she manages adequately at home with oxygen. She's on long-term treatment with steroids for her presumed autoimmune conditions. On this occasion she was admitted with a lung infection, which has responded well to antibiotics. This is not the first time she's experienced an episode like this: in fact, there've been many in the past. In spite of her difficult illness she copes reasonably well at home with the aid of a close and supportive family, which includes her daughter and grandson." As usual he was caught up with his own cleverness, and he paused for effect. "How did I do, Betty?" he asked.

"Wow, that's spot on!" exclaimed the patient, obviously impressed. "You got everything right. But tell us all how you knew."

Gloating shamelessly to himself, Abraham could see that the students were wondering the same thing. He loved playing Sherlock Holmes. He explained, addressing them. "We agreed that she has rheumatoid arthritis from the appearance of her hands. She also has wasting of her thigh muscles, which suggests a separate neuromuscular condition. We know from the inhalers that she has asthma. But she walks with a walker that contains oxygen cylinders. This must mean an underlying lung problem that's separate from the asthma, the arthritis, and the muscle weakness. It must have deteriorated gradually to allow her to establish a routine by which she can move around in this manner. She takes steroids as immunosuppressants. This is evident from her facial appearance, which Tracey noticed. Also, she's wearing a medical alert bracelet, which is no doubt on account of the steroids, which can be dangerous if stopped suddenly. The lung disease and the steroids make her vulnerable to lung infections. She's been receiving meripenem, so this is almost certainly the reason for her admission to the hospital. The fact that she needed such a powerful antibiotic suggests two possibilities: she was very unwell when she came in and there was no time to decide exactly which antibiotic would be most suitable, or that she's had many infections in the past and has multiple antibiotic resistance. The second possibility is the more likely one for two reasons: first, that she's so well now, five days later, and is not even needing oxygen; and second, the appearance of her bags neatly stacked in the corner makes it apparent that she's been to the hospital many times before, so much so that she has a system for coming in—it's even possible that she keeps a bag packed at all times."

"How did you know she was coping well at home and had a supportive family?"

"That was easy. She's wearing a wedding ring and on the walls are hand-drawn children's pictures from someone called 'Nicholas.' I'd guess that the pictures are done by a four- to six-year-old, which would make Nicholas clearly her grandson. There's also a card from 'Maria and Nicholas,' so I speculate that Maria is Nicholas's mother. There's no male person mentioned, so I imagine that Maria is separated . . . but . . ." he noticed that the patient looked upset, "maybe this is something we don't need to talk about now. There are other things we might have observed, but perhaps this is enough for the moment."

As always, Abraham was intoxicated with his success and had consciously to limit his own enthusiasm. He liked showing off in front of the students and allowed himself this indulgence. "That's about as much as we can say from the end of the bed—that is, it's what we're able to take in at first glance, before we've even asked Betty a question. It's quite a lot; you have to agree. No doubt there are also many other things we're not able to infer. Bruno, why don't you try to fill in the details by asking Betty some questions?"

"Okay . . . Um . . . Betty . . . What sort of work do you do?"

"I'm on a sickness pension now, but I used to be a nurse."

"Okay . . . Um . . . Can you tell me who you live with?"

"I live with my daughter and grandson."

"You live in your daughter's house?"

"No, she lives in mine. My daughter divorced when Nicholas was two and both of them moved in then. It works out pretty well."

"Nicholas is your grandson?"

"Yes," replied the patient. "He's autistic and needs a lot of care. Maria goes off to work and I look after Nicholas four days a week. He doesn't say much but we spend a lot of time together. I read to him and he loves music. He's my little sweetie. People say autistic children don't express themselves well but I know everything he's thinking."

Abraham noticed that the patient's voice had softened a little when she started talking about her grandson and how her eyes were now glowing. "I wonder if he also knows what you're thinking," he said, without really knowing why.

"It's true. We're connected. I'm a bit scared about what will happen to him when I'm gone. Maria's too harsh with him. She gets frustrated because he doesn't talk. But you just have to know how to listen to him. In fact, it's because of him that I came to the hospital."

"What do you mean?"

"I'm always short of breath and sometimes don't realize when I'm sick and need help. I often delay treatment and that can be dangerous. But Nicholas always knows when my condition's become worse. Yesterday I was playing with him—we were sitting on the couch together—and he suddenly became very still. At first, I thought that he'd heard something outside, but I listened and couldn't hear anything. Then he cuddled up to me, silently, and put his head on my chest. He just stayed there like that. I realized at once what he was saying—that I was really sick and needed to get to the hospital quickly. I called the ambulance at once. They told me that if I'd delayed even a few more minutes they would have lost me."

"It sounds like a beautiful relationship," Abraham said appreciatively.

"It's all I live for," she said, her voice cracking with emotion. Then she brightened. "As a matter of fact, I think I can hear a small voice now!"

The others turned round just in time to see a woman with a stroller come through the door. When he saw her, the child jumped up and ran to his grandmother. The old woman and the child embraced with laughter and tears, like old friends who hadn't seen each other for a long time.

The room, which a moment ago had been dark with illness and pain, had become lucent with joy and love. "I think we might leave," Abraham said quietly to the students, and the five of them stole out. The patient, engrossed in her grandson, didn't seem to notice their departure.

25.

Abraham had a couple of hours to work on his article. Before getting started he settled in one of the leather armchairs in his office, a glass of whisky in his hand, to relax and gather his thoughts.

Abraham's vision was to make the deep content of medicine come alive as a full-blooded practice that included the powerful experiences of pain, joy, despair, magnanimity, and wisdom that illness could evoke. He had been struck by what appeared to him as a paradox in the way doctors understood the meaning of "ethics." On the one hand, they thought that to be "ethical" meant acting in a conventional, predictable manner, as if they were simply following a guidebook on fixing common problems. On the other, it meant responding to unexpected challenges presented to them in the course of everyday practice, which often required them to reflect critically on their assumptions and to draw on whatever resources were available in order to improvise some kind of workable solution.

It was this that he wanted most to write about. A problem with medicine as it is often practiced, he thought, is that it fails to respond to the uniqueness of individual circumstances, thereby missing the chance to draw on the deep knowledge generated out of the experiences of all the people involved—including the practitioners. What's more, in Abraham's experience, most doctors didn't understand their own responses to medical challenges, nor did they reflect much on their own experiences. Abraham prided himself on his ability to do this. That's what had gotten him through the last couple of years.

Stephanie's death had been almost unbearably painful for him: certainly more difficult than any illness of his own would have been. What made matters worse was that it was only after she had left him that he had come to realize how much he needed and depended on her. As selfish as it sounded, he could not help feeling deserted and abandoned.

He was aware how irrational such feelings were and he half wished he didn't have them. But part of his injury was due to the fact that his children were angry at him for the disasters the family had encountered. The dark chasm that had opened up in their lives with Stephanie's death, the fracturing of the closeness and love that had held them all together, had afflicted all their lives. But he was supposed to be the one who was there to protect them. And when trouble—real trouble—struck he had been shown in their eyes to be impotent. He had tried to find a way of explaining to them that he was a wounded party too, but he couldn't. They professed their concern for him, of course, but he knew that a gulf had opened up between him and them that would never be closed.

The one person to whom he might have turned in a time of such dire need was his mother. In her time, she alone had provided him with unconditional love, no matter what the circumstances. Now, however, she was suffering from dementia, and it was he who had to support her. At least he could take satisfaction in the graciousness and simple gratitude she invariably displayed.

Gratitude and graciousness were not words that could be used to describe his father. Mordechai had good qualities, which Abraham greatly admired, such as the intense radicalism of his thought that seemed to come so naturally to him. Even now, in his declining years, whenever Abraham spoke with his father he came away with new ideas or a perspective that had not previously occurred to him. What's more, Mordechai could be warm and gentle. Abraham pictured with pleasure a moment long past, in his childhood, when his father was smiling softly at him, an expression of love in his eyes. He tried to hold the scene in his memory, to savor it, to extend the pleasure, but it slipped away as quickly as it had come.

But more often than not Mordechai was harsh and cruel. He regarded life not as a source of joy or pleasure, not as an opportunity to care and love, but as hand-to-hand combat. His bitterness was directed toward everyone but— at least, this is how Abraham experienced it—most intensely to his son. Ever since he was small Abraham had felt that his father regarded him with hostility. Mordechai would humiliate Abraham publicly, criticizing his clumsiness in front of friends or even strangers. When Abraham was recognized for his successes, when he was awarded prizes or degrees or honors, when he published books, was married or had children, or even celebrated an important birthday or anniversary, his father never so much as sent a message of support or recognition.

Mordechai could also be aggressive, even vicious. His mother tried to stand up to him, but often this only made matters worse. These were painful memories and Abraham tried not to dwell on them. He employed a technique he had developed at a time in his mid-teens when his father was at his most erratic and his parents' arguments were at their most intense. He consciously disavowed any personal effect of the high emotion that prevailed in the family. He told himself that he was self-sufficient, that he could manage on his own without the need to rely on others, including his own parents.

He finished the glass of whisky and turned to the computer.

26.

He started by rereading what he had already written:

> Medicine has two components: a technical and an ethical one. The technical part is concerned with facts and achieving certain outcomes. The ethical part is where the outcomes are identified, where we choose our goals and make decisions about what we ought to do.

It was a bit clumsy, but all beginnings are hard.

> This article seeks to expose a paradox that exists within the ethical domain. Ethics is called upon simultaneously to serve two very different tasks. On the one hand, it poses difficult questions about underlying assumptions, values and goals, reasons and justifications to help guide decisions and actions. This function of ethics is radical and subversive. It takes nothing for granted and respects no authority. On the other hand, ethics is at the same time called upon to serve an opposite function—to regulate conduct and to ensure that all social actors do what is expected of them, that they act in a prudent and predictable way. In this function, there is no

room for radical questioning or risky iconoclasm. If society is to function smoothly, there is a need for stable, predictable patterns of behavior, and this is what ethics seeks to deliver.

This is okay, he thought. What's needed now is to turn to the problem of ethics in medicine itself. He was pleased to see that that was exactly what he had, in fact, done:

> I would like in this article to focus on how ethical issues arise within medicine. These issues occur at many levels. They occur in relation to large-scale questions about values and society, about our relationships with each other and with nature, about the impact of new developments in science and medical treatments, and the extent to which we should embrace these innovations or take steps to contain them. They occur in relation to the nature of the social relationships, the relationships of trust and power, which can be the source both of confidence and caring, and of exploitation and betrayal. And they occur at the level of individual experience, the local or "microethical" level, where one person engages another face to face, where we encounter suffering and pain, bitterness and gratitude, love and resentment, caring and trust.
>
> In individual cases many issues may come together. To quote a personal example, I might be faced with the dilemma of whether or how I should care for my aging mother, to whom I was once very close but who has now been diagnosed as suffering from Alzheimer's disease. I may consider questions of a personal nature in relation to society generally and perhaps to wider philosophical and social considerations. I may reflect on my personal relationship with her, the debt that I owe her for the love and care she has provided to me, and on questions about the distribution of resources in a society that is itself aging. I may wonder about my personal responsibilities and the responsibilities of society in general to care for its older citizens. In practice, I may encounter all these issues within the flux of my everyday life, in the context of my other relationships and activities.

Why I should care for my aging father might be more difficult still, thought Abraham. He poured another glass of whisky and started writing:

> Although my primary concern is with medicine, many of the issues that arise are of wider relevance. Ethical considerations inhabit the very core of our sense of who we are. They reflect the primordial, irrefragable bond we have with others that is the condition of all meaning and value. They emerge out of the responsibility we unavoidably incur simply as a condition of being human. These experiences of ethics include purely philosophical reflections but are not limited by them. This is because we do not come to ethical decisions exclusively through a process of thinking or rational argument: rather, we draw on the whole range and variety of our embodied, sensuous lives, our memories of illness and pain, sexuality and love, and our hopes and fears about the future.

He was happy with how easily the words were flowing today. Sometimes it was like this, but at other times each word had to be extracted and each sentence fashioned and refashioned as if he were shaping a block of wood. The argument that followed had now to turn to the more personal dimension:

> To recognize that ethics plays a fundamental role in our lives does not, of course, tell us how to act. Decisions about what we should do may remain difficult regardless of the extent of our ethical sensitivity. This may be because the circumstances with which we are dealing are uncertain and complex or because we ourselves may feel ambivalence or conflicting emotions. Sometimes the facts have multiple interpretations or there are intractably opposed forces at play. It is a common discovery, for example, that physical suffering can become a fecund source of insight and wisdom, and may greatly deepen relationships and engender new purposes and hope. Or things can go the other way. While advancing technologies can bring major benefits, including pleasure, the relief of illness, or access to new possibilities, by displacing activities with ethical content in favor of purely technical ones they can also lead to an erosion of meaning, to a degradation of intimate human experiences and the undermining of traditional, community-based systems for generating meaning.

The last sentence was a bit of a mouthful but Abraham decided to leave it for the moment and return to it later.

> There is obviously a need to sort through this uncertainty and complexity. For all the attention that has been given to these weighty questions, however, the gains have been surprisingly modest. This is partly because of the paradox mentioned earlier: while ethical thought can facilitate and provoke fundamental questioning, at the same time it also tends to impose limits on what is possible, to ensure conformity to existing social norms or patterns of thought. In fact, the conservatism has usually predominated, even among approaches presented by their authors as radical and iconoclastic. The dominant discourses have not in general supported a questioning of the conditions and assumptions that generated the problems they are seeking to solve. This in turn reflects the fact that the inexorable forces driving modern society forward—including science and medicine, money and power—also sweep up our own theoretical reflections on them, which are therefore implicated within and co-opted by them.

" . . . the inexorable forces driving modern society forward . . . sweep up our own theoretical reflections on them." Abraham was pleased with the expression and repeated it to himself a couple of times. Then he looked at his watch. It was time to go. He was looking forward to a quiet night at home by himself. He would take up the next installment of the article when he could again catch some time, maybe tomorrow or the day after.

LATE NIGHT PHONE CALL

27.

braham was awakened by the telephone.

"Professor Nevski, this is John Blair, the Emergency Department registrar at Swamp Road Local Hospital. I don't know if you're aware that your father, Mordechai, has been brought here for assessment."

Abraham's heart missed a beat. "No, I wasn't aware," he said. And then, trying to control his voice, "What's the problem?"

"He was found by one of the carers visiting his home to be confused and she called an ambulance."

"I see. Have you had a chance to assess him yet?" He felt hot and his head was swimming.

"Yes. We've taken the history and examined him. I wanted to talk with you before we decided what to do."

"Thank you very much for that, John. I appreciate it," he said evenly. "I'd be grateful to hear what you've found. Also, if you have any questions about his medical history please feel free to ask."

"Thank you. Mr. Nevski . . . er . . . your father . . . as you know . . . lives alone, having separated from his wife, and receives lithium treatment for bipolar disorder. He's a former heavy smoker and drinker and has emphysema, with several serious chest infections over the last two or three years. He appears to have become somewhat of a recluse and has become increasingly lethargic and introverted over the last few months . . . He was found by a carer on the floor in his house . . . er . . . confused and disoriented and . . . ah . . . soaked in urine. Er . . . on examination, he was . . . um . . . slightly unkempt and confused, in that he didn't know where he was or the date and couldn't answer simple questions about current affairs. He was not . . . er . . . very cooperative with the examination . . . He had a temperature of 37.5 degrees and a blood pressure of 105 over 80. His chest was clear, he had two heart sounds and no added sounds, and his abdomen was non-tender . . ."

The young doctor on the other end of the phone paused to await a response. Abraham's anxiety had started to subside. He replied, as he knew he was expected to do, in a slightly didactic fashion. "What was your differential diagnosis, and did you undertake any tests?"

"I thought he could have an infection—perhaps a chest or a urinary tract infection. I can't rule out a head injury, maybe following a fall, although there are no signs of trauma. I'd want to rule out a metabolic or toxic cause, including lithium toxicity. I've done a chest X-ray and a brain CT scan and have sent off some pathology tests. When we see the results we can start treatment."

"You've done well. I'm confident he's in good hands. Please tell whoever you hand over to—and put in the notes—that I'd like to hear how he's doing and that I'm happy to be contacted at any time. If everything's okay I'll visit tomorrow afternoon, but I'll be happy to come in immediately if you need me."

"I'll pass on that message. I'm sure they'll call you if anything goes wrong . . . Um . . . I don't think that'll happen, though."

"I hope not. Thanks again, John. I hope the rest of the night goes well. Good night."

Abraham hung up the phone and sat for a few minutes trying to take in what had just happened. It sounded like a routine admission but even minor medical issues in an elderly person can turn serious. Still, the resident had been careful and thorough and maybe, he thought, if his father was sick enough he'd just lie quietly and cooperate with the doctors and nurses . . . Abraham knew only too well the difficulties associated with doctors mixing in with the treatment of their relatives and determined that in this case he would take particular care to maintain a respectful distance.

He looked at the clock. It was two a.m. He had a seven o'clock meeting and then a heavy day ahead of him.

PART 4

SUFFERING AND DESIRE

28.

It was the next day. The team of four—Abraham, Rebecca, Ashis, and Desmond—were preparing to conduct their daily review of the patients in the ward. Abraham noted with disdain the fact that Desmond was wearing a garish, fluorescent purple shirt and, with even greater annoyance, that the young doctors made it obvious that they appreciated it. As they were standing in the corridor, a young woman of athletic build, primly dressed in a cream shirt and beige tailored pants and walking at high speed, came up and introduced herself breezily.

"Hi!" she said in a high-pitched voice, with forced friendliness. "I'm Susanna, one of the new Freedom to Choose communication consultants. Just popping by to say hello. Got to get to know everyone. How are we today?"

She waited for a reaction but the doctors and the nurse, taken by surprise, just looked at her blankly. She was unfazed. "A plan for everyone. Big job. We're keen," she continued, in the same high-pitched voice.

There was still no response. "Well," she said after a few seconds more, still without any obvious concern, "better keep moving. Remember, we're here to help. Always ready and waiting."

And with that, she was gone. The stunned silence continued. "I'm not sure what that was about," commented Abraham sarcastically after a few more moments, "but I'm really looking forward to getting to know her."

The others smiled weakly and they returned to their work. "Rebecca, can you update us on Mrs. Gurewitz?"

"Sure, Prof. After our ward round the other day Ashis and I met with Mrs. Gurewitz's daughter, Anika. I explained to her that we'd investigated her mom very thoroughly and had treated her vigorously but we couldn't find any evidence of a reversible cause for her problem, which was obviously very serious. I pointed out that, taking into account the time in St. Mary's Hospital, she'd had nearly two weeks of full treatment but, apart from a few short periods of some awareness, she'd steadily deteriorated. I told her that we didn't think our treatments were doing anything now and we felt that it was the right time to respect her mom's wishes about quality of life and independence."

"Beck was awesome, Prof," interrupted Ashis. "It was a really difficult conversation but Mrs. G's daughter was calm and understanding."

Rebecca went on. "I . . . we . . . said that we felt that we should stop the treatment and keep her mom comfortable. She was happy . . . er . . . comfortable about that. So we stopped everything, except for the morph and the benzo, as we'd decided.

"Everything was pretty well stable for about twelve hours, then about midnight I got a call from the ward saying that Mrs. G had woken up. I was still in the hospital so I went round to see her. She was sitting up in bed, wide awake. I talked to her for about ten minutes. She knew she was in the hospital and that she'd been sick but couldn't remember anything more. She said again that she trusted Anika to decide for her and that when she was ready to die she'd be able to accept that. I didn't push the issue."

"Was that when you called me?" asked Abraham.

"Yes, it was probably about two o'clock by then. We thought that maybe the treatment was having some effect after all but that it had just been delayed, so we restarted all the treatments, including the antibiotics and the anticonvulsants. I left the ward about two thirty."

"I hope you managed to get some sleep," said Abraham, reflecting on his own disrupted night. He turned to Desmond. "Can you report what's happened since, from the nursing point of view?"

"When I came on this morning I spoke with the overnight nurse. She'd kept a close eye on Mrs. G the whole time. She said that almost at the moment Rebecca left, Mrs. Gurewitz lost consciousness again and completely returned to her previous state. I can confirm that in the time I've been on she's remained deeply unconscious, just like she's been for the last three or four days."

"Ashis and Rebecca, have you seen her during the day?"

"Yep, Prof, I've had to change her IV twice," said Ashis. "She hasn't responded at all to me, even when I put the needle in her arm. I agree with Des. I think she's exactly like she was yesterday."

"And I did a full neurological examination on her just before. It's true. She's back to where she was. It's really weird."

Abraham tried to sum up. "This is certainly an unusual case. Here's an old woman who suddenly loses consciousness. No cause can be found. She doesn't respond to weeks of treatment, then when treatment's withdrawn she wakes up. When we restart the treatment she loses consciousness again. She's had a huge number of tests, none of which have shown anything abnormal. She's had several different treatments, so we can't actually blame any one of them. Now, she's deeply unconsciousness again and not responding to anything we do."

There was a silence. Abraham took a deep breath. He was genuinely baffled. It was possible that any decision would turn out to be the wrong one. "Taking everything into account, it's hard to argue that we can do anything now but stop the treatment again. It's unsettling, but—"

"So you want to stop the treatment again, is that right?" interrupted Desmond.

"Yes, that's what I'm proposing," Abraham said. "I'm not pretending that I have the answer. I don't. But I think that's the most judicious course of action to take here."

"I agree the case is unusual," said Desmond, "but we need to know what direction we're heading in. My nurses are getting concerned about the lack of decisiveness in the medical management. I mean, we're chopping and changing, aren't we? One minute we're giving full treatment, then the next none at all, then full treatment again, then nothing. It's hard for us, and no doubt also hard on the old woman's daughter."

"There's no point in my apologizing to you, Desmond," replied Abraham curtly. "We can't control everything that happens in the world. Mrs. Gurewitz is choosing her own, very idiosyncratic, way to die." He secretly hoped for support from the registrar but didn't feel able to ask for it. This time Rebecca didn't let him down.

"I can't see any alternative. I have to say, though, that I'm finding this case pretty challenging, too."

"Okay, let's go back to yesterday's treatment plan, then," said Abraham. "Desmond, could you ask the nurses looking after Mrs. Gurewitz to pay particular attention to her conscious state and to call Rebecca, Ashis, or me if there's any change?"

"All right, Abraham, but let's just hope that this time we've got things right."

29.

"How's our other unconscious patient doing—that woman we think might've had an unusual drug reaction? What was her name—Mrs. Dreyfus, wasn't it?"

"Actually, I'm a bit concerned about her," replied Rebecca. "Her temperature's gone, the blood pressure's fine, and her bloods are okay but her mental state hasn't improved at all. She's still pretty well unresponsive, although Ashis says that she reacted to him when he was changing the IV early today."

"Yeah, it was crazy, Prof," the young man replied. "When I first went to see her she was lying there with her eyes closed. I called out to her but she didn't answer. As I was putting in the new drip she seemed to wake up. She opened her eyes and watched what I was doing without saying anything. She recoiled a bit when I poked her with the needle but she still stayed silent."

"Her daughters are with her," Rebecca added. "They both arrived yesterday. So far I've only had a chance to speak with them briefly."

The group entered the room and Abraham introduced himself to the two women. As he did so he took them in quickly. Although of similar age—he guessed mid-fifties—they were very different in appearance, the taller one dowdy with crudely dyed blonde hair and a weather-beaten face and the other—decidedly more elegant—carefully coiffed with freshly ironed clothes. They were sitting in armchairs in the far corner of the room, arranged so that they could see their mother, who was lying in much the same position as she had been when the team had left her the previous day.

"Hello. I'm Professor Nevski," he said, giving no indication of the scrutiny to which he had already subjected them, "one of the doctors looking after Mrs. Dreyfus, and this is Rebecca, our registrar; Ashis, our resident; and Desmond, one of the nurses. Are you Mrs. Dreyfus's daughters?"

"Yes, I'm Maggie," said the weather-beaten one, "and this is my sister Josephine. We met Rebecca a bit earlier."

"You've come down from the country. Is that right?"

"I have," said Maggie. "Jo comes from the city."

"Welcome," said Abraham meaninglessly. "How do you find your mother today?"

"She seems a bit better," said Josephine. "We got in yesterday and came straight here. Last night she was hardly moving and didn't seem to understand anything, but today she's opened her eyes a bit and seems to be moving a little more in the bed. I think she's a bit better."

Abraham continued to study the two women carefully. "She's a very independent woman," the elegant one continued, "but she can also be rather eccentric. She's always insisted on doing things her way. Maggie and I really haven't had much to do with her for a few years. Our father died about ten years ago, and then she took up with another man. He died about two years ago. Is that right, Mag?"

"Yes, it was two or three years ago," the other daughter replied. "After our dad died Mom changed a bit, and we lost touch with her, although Jo and I have stayed close to each other. Mom can get a bee in her bonnet about things, which can sometimes be hard for everyone else. We don't know much about her medical condition, especially about how she's been lately."

"We do know that she's always suffered from depression, though," said Josephine. "When we were little she'd sometimes sit for hours without moving, even when we needed her to make dinner for us. It was very hard on Dad."

"Thanks, that's useful. If you don't mind, we'll examine her now and then we can talk further. I expect that you have a number of questions you'd like to ask us."

"Yes, we do. Do you want us to wait outside?"

"That'd probably be most convenient. If you stay close by we'll come and find you when we've finished. It'll only be a few minutes."

The daughters left the room and Abraham and Rebecca examined the patient, with the intern keeping notes of the findings they dictated. As he had promised, Abraham then went out into the corridor to find the sisters. They were engaged in earnest conversation and seemed surprised to see him.

He apologized for startling them. "We've finished seeing your mother and Rebecca and I'll be happy to answer any questions you might have."

"Er . . . we trust you and the hospital," Maggie said, "but it seems clear that she's pretty sick. Can you tell us, Professor, if you think she'll pull through?"

"It's true that this is a serious condition," replied Abraham, "but if our diagnosis is correct, she should recover fairly quickly."

"Do you mean that she'll go back to where she was before this illness?" Josephine asked.

There was something about the daughter's intonation that made Abraham uncomfortable but he couldn't identify exactly what it was. He chose his words carefully. "There appears to be no reason why she shouldn't recover fully. But we can't at this stage absolutely exclude the possibility that there's an underlying process that's causing the problem. If that turns out to be the case then our prognosis may change."

Maggie's response reinforced his discomfort. "How long will it all take? I mean . . . when will you know if she'll recover?"

"We really can't say, but I'd be very hopeful that we'll have a clearer picture within the next forty-eight hours. Do you have any other questions?"

"No, thank you, Professor. We're grateful for your kindness."

The team moved on. Abraham turned to the others. "What did you make of that? I can't quite put my finger on it, but I've got a strange feeling that there's something odd going on here."

"I think I know what you mean, Prof," said Ashis. "They seemed impatient to get it all over and done with."

"And they weren't especially relieved when we said we thought that their mom would recover," added Rebecca.

"I guess we'll find out what if anything's going on soon enough," said Abraham. "Maybe it's just that they're stressed and anxious and are seeking an opportunity to bring about a reconciliation with their mother before she dies. Let's move on to the next patient."

30.

"How's Mr. Alvarez today?" It was now nearly a week since the elderly man had been admitted to the hospital and Abraham was not expecting the answer to be favorable, but the response from Desmond was more intense than he had anticipated.

"He's become the patient from hell!" he replied. "We knew he'd be difficult to nurse, but he's broken new records. He's not stopped yelling for the last twelve hours, mostly incoherently. He's been screaming foul abuse at the nurses. He's refused to eat, and when they've tried to feed him he's tipped the food on the floor. He's moved his bowels and then thrown the shit across the room. When the nurses have tried to clean him up he's lashed out at them violently. He's exposed himself repeatedly and refused to keep his clothes on. When his relatives have come to see him he's abused them, sometimes without even recognizing them."

Desmond's voice rose as he kept speaking. "First I put on one nurse to sit by him, expecting him to be irritable and aggressive, as expected with a head injury. Then I put on another, then a nurse and a security guard, and then I had to put him in the procedure room to give the other patients—and us—some peace and quiet. The only positive is that after shouting for twelve hours the poor bugger's usually so exhausted he sleeps for two.

"The worst thing, though, is to see the effect on the family. They're committed to him and pretty well bloody idolize him. But when they see him like this they're just speechless with despair. It's bad enough for us. My nurses are saying—and I agree with them—that they're entitled to work in an environment free of threats of violence and abuse. I can't even start to think how difficult it must be for the family.

"Here's a guy who's been a government minister, a successful businessman, a pillar of his community, and a model for everyone who's met him. I know that at the meeting the other day his relatives said they wanted to keep him alive no matter what. But they didn't know it was going to be like this. Jesus Christ! Isn't it his right to die with dignity? Wouldn't it have been better for him, for them, and for us if he'd just died quietly? For God's sake, we should let him go in peace! If necessary, we should even have the courage to help him on his way."

Desmond's face was flushed and his anger almost palpable. Abraham stole a glance at Rebecca and Ashis and noted to his dismay that both had been deeply affected. They were obviously siding with Desmond. Abraham hated the nurse's certainty and his ability to beguile others into sharing his views.

His own voice quivering with anger and frustration, he answered as best he could. "This is certainly an unfortunate case, Desmond. There's no doubt about that. But death's always been a complicated and unpredictable business. It has always been and it always will be. Like all of us, you yearn for a way to simplify the unsimplifiable, but it can't be done. You want easy answers to difficult questions, but they don't exist. You want to cleanse life of its untidiness, suffering of its pain. You want to turn the hardest thing we ever do—die—into a simple technical act. But you can't do it because it's not possible."

He stopped for a moment and wondered whether he should go on, whether this was the right moment. Abraham would not normally choose to conduct such a conversation in front of the junior doctors. But it was Desmond who had started it, and now he had no choice. Involuntarily, his voice rose. "As much as you'd like all these things, they're out of the grasp not just of you but of all of us. That's because suffering isn't a betrayal or negation of our humanity. It's rather an affirmation of it. As regrettable and painful as it may be it's not our job to sanitize death, or for that matter, to purify life of its uncomfortable or inconvenient excesses. Our job is quite different. To be sure, we have to manage the patient's symptoms and make sure that he doesn't suffer pain or physical discomfort. But it's much more than that. Our job is to enter into his world, to be a witness to the last great dramatic act of his life, to acknowledge and honor his and his family's predicaments, and to go a short distance with them along the way."

He paused again. His heart was still beating fast. He waited a few moments and then spoke in a softer tone: he meant it to be half an order, half a peace offer. "Let's see Mr. Alvarez and then talk with the family again."

He knew that in comparison with Desmond's vivid speech his own sounded abstract and insipid. He wished he had the nurse's charisma, his ability to charm the young doctors and nurses. Desmond, giving no sign that he had even heard Abraham's reply, led them to the procedure room, which was at the end of the ward next to the drug and utility rooms. They went in. The patient was lying on a low bed in the middle of the room. To their surprise he was sleeping quietly. His hands were bandaged, and the bandages were tied to the bed frame on each side in order to restrain his movements. The only other person in the room was a nurse sitting on a chair in the corner reading from a folder. She smiled faintly at them in response to their greeting.

With some apprehension they untied the bandages and woke the old man gently. He was obviously confused, but he remained calm and cooperated graciously with their attempts to examine him. He was unable to speak clearly but he did appear to understand some of what they were saying to him, making disconnected grunting noises. Abraham looked into the heavily lined face. The man's complexion was swarthy, he was unshaven, and his scant scalp hair was disarranged. His pale eyes were accentuated by bushy eyebrows. Together, these features gave his face an earnest and open, even youthful appearance. Abraham was jolted. Mr. Alvarez looked just like his own father! A once-proud man now reduced to incoherent grunts and obscene behavior.

They retired to the corridor outside the room and Abraham reopened the conversation. He knew he had to seize control and win back Rebecca and Ashis. "We've evidently been lucky to find Mr. Alvarez in a quiet moment. No doubt, however, his mental state will continue to fluctuate greatly. We need to review his meds and make sure that enough sedation's available to avoid the violent excesses Desmond's described. I think it's important to avoid physical restraint if at all possible, as this is invariably distressing for everyone involved."

He was trying to make his language sound more colloquial, like Desmond's, but could tell he wasn't succeeding. Rebecca responded, her voice shaking a little. "Would you be happy for me to start a combination of morphine and sedatives in doses that could be adjusted in accordance with Mr. Alvarez's needs?"

"Yes, that'd be very appropriate. If changes need to be made the nurses can call us at any time and we can increase the medications as much as needed. I realize how difficult a situation like this can be and that it's important for everyone to feel adequately supported. We should therefore make sure that we explain our approach and give them the opportunity to express any concerns they might have."

Abraham hoped that this would be enough to end the matter, at least for the moment, and that Desmond would for once restrain himself from replying. He was disappointed. "Abraham, I respect the approach you're taking," Desmond said insincerely, obviously still seething, "and I know we've been in this situation before, but aren't we being hypocritical here? We know Mr. Alvarez's going to die. He's had a horrific brain injury for which there's no treatment. We've made the decision that he's not a candidate for surgery or for intensive care. But what are we doing instead? We're just sedating him. But does this do anything more than prolong the suffering for him and his family?

"There's hypocrisy everywhere here. Physical restraints are obviously unattractive and upset everyone. But why are they worse than chemical restraints, which is what we're planning to use here? It's certainly not because they're more dangerous; in fact, we're prepared to increase the sedation up to the point where he may even die as a result. Also, we talk about 'respecting' our patients. Here's a man who's lived a full and productive life, who's loved and revered by everyone who knows him, who's now being kept in a state of humiliation while his life slowly ebbs away. The family should be allowed to remember the proud, dignified man who was still able to run the business at the age of ninety, not this crude, violent, confused shell of a man who throws excrement and screams obscenities. Surely, if we were acting with humanity we wouldn't be extending the humiliation but facilitating a quiet and dignified death. And this would be easy: all that would be necessary would be to give a single, sufficient dose of the exact medications we're prepared to give him in small doses over what could be many days.

"The hospital has a policy called Freedom to Choose. I know as well as you do that the reason behind this is not to increase freedom or dignity or patient autonomy but to save money for the hospital and the health system. I know that, despite what they say, the bastards who push this policy don't really care how people die, whether it's at home with their families around them or uncared for in some stinking old people's home. What they really care about is that it's not in this hospital, costing a lot of money, and eating into their personal bonuses—or, if it is in the hospital, that it happens as quickly as possible. What's more, I can't stand those 'communication consultants' who snoop around my ward pretending to be concerned and sincere. But even if the underlying motive's wrong that doesn't mean that the program can't be used to do some good. You said that it's not our job to purify life and death of their excesses and inconveniences. But surely reducing suffering—including the time spent suffering—is exactly what our job should be."

Without looking in their direction Abraham could feel that Rebecca and Ashis had now been fully won over by Desmond's powerful rhetoric. He had been ambushed and was furious at the nurse's insubordination and readiness to manipulate his junior doctors. Now all he had available to him was the naked authority attached to his position. He kept his voice low and articulated his words precisely. "Your argument is powerfully expressed, Desmond," he replied, "and I know it has a lot of support both in the hospital and in the community. But what I understand you to be proposing—that we should be able to make decisions about when a person's life is dignified or undignified, worthy or unworthy, and if the result's unfavorable, to go ahead and either allow them to die or actually kill them—I think deeply challenges the basic nature of our profession and our relationships with our patients. It goes against the ethical commitment we make to our patients that comes before everything else, that's at the basis of everything we do."

Why would someone take up the profession of nursing, he was thinking to himself, to be no more than a crude technician or a cheap rhetorician? It's our duty to listen and respond to our patients' cries for help. They give us access to the most private, most secret, most intimate parts of their lives. In return, they expect us to accompany them in their illnesses, to help them negotiate the obstacles along the way, to witness, record, and validate their suffering. This is where the ethical content of his work resided, not in crude calculations about outcomes and consequences. The final outcome had to come second to the relationships and decisions that produced it.

He needed to be firm in his directions to the team, at least for the sake of Ashis and Rebecca. "I know it doesn't help to say this, but Mr. Alvarez's case is obviously very hard," he said, using his most authoritative professorial tone. "There's a clear line between alleviating or palliating the suffering of someone in pain or distress and acting in accordance with our own views about what's an acceptable or 'dignified' way to die. There's no evidence that Mr. Alvarez himself is experiencing physical pain, and the views of the family are that they'd rather have him alive in any condition than not at all. But even if that weren't the case, our hands would be tied. The profession of executioner is perhaps a valid one; certainly, in some places it's socially sanctioned. But it's a different profession from that of a doctor or nurse. The difference doesn't depend on motives or consequences or on the personal qualities of the carer: it's imbedded in the relationship between the carer and the patient that's the bedrock on which we all stand."

There was a silence. Desmond glared but for once didn't say anything. Ashis looked uncomfortable and averted his eyes. Rebecca was close to tears.

Abraham tried to find a way to change the subject. He adopted a deliberately conciliatory tone. "We'll no doubt continue this discussion, in relation not only to Mr. Alvarez but also to many others long after he's gone." He turned to Rebecca and Ashis "Is there anything you'd like to say?"

Rebecca stammered a reply. Her voice was ragged. "I . . . I . . . find it so incredibly difficult," she said. "It's so hard . . . The pain . . . He's such a . . . The family . . ." Tears were streaming down her face and she was sobbing uncontrollably. She cleared her throat. "I'm sorry, but you'll have to excuse me," she said, and before the others had a chance to respond she turned and sped off down the corridor.

31.

Abraham felt completely drained. He needed a whisky and time to recover. He suspended the ward round until the afternoon and headed for his office.

He walked quickly along the corridor, trying to shut out the sights and sounds of the hospital. He tried to ignore the all-pervasive sense of pain, of fear, of the impending possibility of loss. He tried to close his mind to the sounds of anguish, of suffering, and of sorrow that echoed all around him. He tried to shield himself from the musty, rancid smells of decay and failure that were seeping into his pores. And he tried not to think of his own part in all this, of his complicity, his aloofness, his frustrating inability to escape his own fastidiousness.

He entered the room, put on a CD, poured a drink, sat down at his desk, and started up his computer. He opened the article on which he had been working, trying to decide how to take up the interrupted threads. Unable to concentrate, he just sat, glass in hand, staring into space.

32.

Abraham and Ashis, joined again by Rebecca, filed uneasily into the meeting room. This time there were only four relatives waiting for them. Abraham recognized Diego, the son, Sofia, the daughter, and two of the grandchildren. He noticed at once how tired they looked. They moved straight to business.

"The purpose of this meeting," Abraham said flatly, "is to make sure that you're fully informed about Mr. Alvarez's medical condition and to give you the opportunity to ask any questions and express any wishes you might have.

I know that this is very difficult for everyone. As usual, I'll ask Rebecca to start with a brief summary of the medical facts."

"Thanks, Professor Nevski," said Rebecca. The young woman was subdued, her hair a little disheveled, and she was frowning slightly. Abraham could tell that she was still affected by the morning's disagreement. Her voice was duller than usual. "When we spoke last time we expressed our view that Mr. Alvarez was so ill that it was really impossible for him to survive, and we still think that. The underlying problem is that he's had a very large bleed into his brain. We've repeated the scans and, if anything, the problem is worse now than it was. However, when we talked last time we also said that we couldn't predict how long things would take or exactly what the process would be. Unfortunately, our caution has been justified by the course of events. It often happens that people with brain injuries become confused and, as we say, 'irritable.' They can also sometimes express themselves in ways that are not consistent with their usual character. This is what's happened in this case. However, all we can really do here is wait and provide support as needed. Mr. Alvarez has a nurse caring for him full time and we're giving him medications to calm him down. When we saw him this morning he was quiet, and I've just checked up on him now and he's asleep."

"Thanks, Rebecca, that's really helpful," said Abraham. He was aware of how hollow his own voice sounded. "It's important for us to admit that the extent to which Mr. Alvarez's brain function recovered—if that's the right word—was more than we'd expected. When he came in he was deeply uncon-scious, and I personally thought that he'd remain that way. However, I was wrong. He did wake up. He was very confused by what was happening; in fact, I think it's unlikely that he knew anything about what was going on at all. There was a time when we had to decide how to manage his very active behavior. We think—we hope—that we have the right approach now, but we'll have to wait and see to be sure. We know how hard it's been on you—and indeed, it's been hard on us, too. I apologize for any distress any of you have felt about the way things have turned out."

"You are right, Doctor." It was Diego. "This has been the hardest day of our life. I never thought I would see my father like this. But we are very grateful that he is still alive."

There was a pause, then Sofia spoke. "We do want him alive," she said with quiet intensity, "but I don't want to see him like that again. It's been too hard for our mother."

"And the rest of the family." The grandson, too, was subdued and pale.

33.

"Do you have a minute, Rebecca?" Abraham asked. "Can we go over a few things before we finish?"

"Of course, Prof," replied Rebecca, who was hardly in a position to refuse. "Where should we talk?"

A few minutes later they were sitting together in the cafeteria going through the list of the patients in the ward. For each one, they reviewed the key issues to be resolved, the treatment plan, and the expected stay in the hospital. This patient was much improved but would require a few days in a rehabilitation facility before being strong enough to return home; that one was still unstable and would need to be observed closely for a while longer; yet another required review by a speech therapist to confirm that she'd improved sufficiently to resume eating and drinking. While they were talking Abraham watched Rebecca closely. He was impressed with her command of detail, her commitment to her work, and her readiness to admit when she was uncertain or lacked knowledge.

As they were finishing Abraham recalled their earlier conversation. "How are you feeling in general, Rebecca?" he asked directly. "When we spoke last time you raised concerns about a few issues. Do you want to talk more about them?"

"Thanks, Prof. I do need to talk." The words burst out of Rebecca's mouth. "I've been thinking a lot about Mr. Alvarez and Mrs. Gurewitz and I'm not really sure that we're doing the right thing for them. I mean, they're both dying. In both cases there's nothing that can be done to change the final result. In both cases we've had to decide about the levels of treatment and we've agreed that we won't do anything to prolong life. In both it's difficult for the relatives to see their mother or father or grandfather or whatever in a state they've never dreamed of before."

Her expression became grave. "I can accept all that. But what I can't understand—what I want to know, what I need to know—is why it wouldn't be more humane just to give a medicine to bring about a quick end. Wouldn't that be kinder, more dignified, and more respectful than extending the pain for everyone, as we are? Wouldn't that be better?"

Abraham was struck with the urgency with which Rebecca spoke. She did not hide how preoccupied she was with these issues, or her sense of inner turmoil.

He wondered blankly how best to reply. He knew she would encounter the question many times, but he also knew he didn't have the answer. The memory of Stephanie's last days floated into his mind. He saw her lying there, in pain, in need. But all he could do was watch. Why couldn't he answer Rebecca?

Dying was always loaded with meaning and pain, saturated with suffering and blood, and its stains inevitably lingered on in the lives of the survivors. His wife's death, his parents' looming deaths, his own death—he was struggling helplessly to understand these. Who was he to lecture this young woman about such momentous questions?

In any case, he had a sense that while Rebecca appeared to be stating an argument she was really asking a deeper question. What was that question? He watched how she pursed her lips when she sought to emphasize a point, how a faint frown passed quickly over her forehead when she was seeking a word or expression that was eluding her, how she slightly closed her eyes when she was encountering a painful idea. He wondered where the intensity had come from.

But she hadn't finished. "I know there's a problem with the amount of health care people need in the last months of life, and our society won't be able to sustain the existing system indefinitely. I know there's a big argument about this and that people are looking for ways to avoid unnecessary treatment for elderly people. But that's not the main thing for me. I'm trying to imagine myself—or my mother or grandmother or grandfather—in the position of Mrs. Gurewitz or Mr. Alvarez. I wouldn't want to be kept alive as a vegetable just because no one had the courage to do what was right and let me die—and I'm pretty sure *they* wouldn't either. Where there's only pain, no life may well be better than just bare life."

Her eyes were wide and she looked very sad. Abraham wanted to reach out and touch her, to show that he understood, to soothe her tender vulnerability. A lock of hair fell across her eyes, which she flicked away automatically with the back of her hand. He kept his own hands still.

"These are difficult questions, Rebecca," he started, realizing at once how empty this was as a response to such an impassioned plea. He needed to be more direct and honest, but he felt empty himself. "I can see how upset you are and I'm moved by your eloquence and depth of feeling." This sounded condescending. He tried again, watching her reaction carefully. "I appreciate the force of your reasoning. Personally, however, as I was starting to say yesterday, I don't think it's right that it's always just the outcomes that count. Consequences are important, of course, but they're not everything. In fact, I doubt that this conversation would be happening at all if ethical deliberation were no more than a matter of calculation of outcomes. I'd go even further than this and say that not only are consequences not everything but neither is reason the dominant or decisive component of ethical decision making. Ethics isn't—or, at least, isn't entirely—a matter of calculation at all: not of outcomes or motives or character traits, or any other particular criteria."

He knew he was failing in his response to her. She had asked him for help and all he could offer in reply was a stilted theoretical lecture. He wanted to find a way to explain that although we commonly assume that ethical decisions are made by starting with a set of principles and then measuring the proposed actions against them, in reality we move in the other direction. It's actually our primordial bond with others that comes first: it forms the basis for our concepts of ourselves, of our identities, of consciousness, of truth, and of reason. It's this, not reason, that makes us who we are.

"You've said that what ultimately counts is that in the long run both Mrs. Gurewitz and Mr. Alvarez will be dead and our job is to choose the course of action that produces the least pain and suffering. Speaking very personally, I can't see it like that. I don't believe it's our job to judge, to adjudicate, to decide what's the best or most moral action. Our job is just"—he said "just" but he knew how big it really was—"to listen and to hear, to be there for those who are suffering, to accompany them in their pain, to go with them on the deep adventure into the unknown on which they're embarking."

He stopped talking. He knew the implications of what he was saying. In any given setting the course that has to be taken might not be the one that minimizes pain and suffering. Instead, it might serve other purposes: to fulfill the promises and responsibilities of a lifetime, to preserve trust, to maintain loyalty—and to do these things and others in difficult and sometimes contradictory circumstances. Sometimes we have to put ourselves on the line. We have to be able to make decisions that conflict sharply with what we would want for ourselves. We have to be able to stay true to those who have placed their trust in us.

This was, at least, how he'd sought to live his own life. But how did he really measure up? He thought of his own recent experiences and the fog of loneliness and sadness that had engulfed him. He remembered the girl on the train. He thought about his patients. He hoped that his decisions would turn out to be the right ones, but what if they didn't? What if Rebecca and Desmond and the CEO were right? He was well aware that to the outside world he appeared confident and assured. Only he knew how beleaguered with uncertainty and self-doubt he really was.

He finished with forced simplicity. "In many cases it's not possible to conclude that the outcomes that we end up with are the best ones. All we can do is our best."

He realized to his surprise that his heart was racing and his chest was heaving. He averted his gaze from Rebecca. They were both silent for a long time.

34.

Rebecca's pager went off, giving both of them a start.

"What was that?" asked Abraham.

She gave a sigh. "It's just Emergency. They've got a patient they want me to assess but it might take me a little while to get down there."

"I'll do it," said Abraham. "I've got time and I have to go over there anyway."

They parted, and Abraham went straight to the Emergency Department. As usual, the place was buzzing with activity, cramped and chaotic. Patients were lying in beds in cubicles, open to view by whoever was passing, or in corridors on movable gurneys, or in wheelchairs. Some had bandages on their feet or arms or head; others were clutching small children; still others were simply sitting forlornly, staring into space, looking scared, worried, nauseated, or in pain, uncertain about what was to happen next. Lights blazed from the ceiling and the bare walls, and the floors reflected the sounds of a hundred people talking, groaning, shouting, protesting, pleading together. This is medicine at its most intense and dramatic, Abraham thought, but he always marveled at how, in the midst of the apparent madness, the young doctors and nurses would move around smoothly, going about their business coolly and methodically.

When they were not with patients, the clinical staff sat in a centrally located, raised area known locally as "the bridge." Abraham spotted Harry Krokowski sitting at one of the computers in this area. He greeted him and asked about the patient Rebecca had been requested to see.

"Hi, Abe," replied Harry, "it's good to see you. Yes, we have Dr. Vilgis.

Do you know him?" Harry Krokowski had worked in the Emergency Department at the Royal Prince John Hospital for as long as Abraham could remember.

"No, I can't say I recognize the name," replied Abraham.

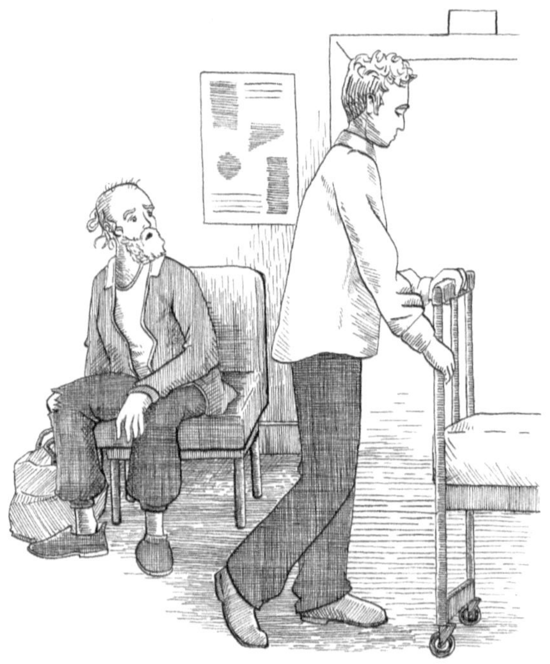

"That's surprising. He's one of our frequent flyers. I've seen him maybe five times in the last year. They drag him in and we usually send him straight home. Maybe that's why you people in the wards haven't had the pleasure of getting to know him so well."

Although he regarded Harry as a friend, Abraham disliked the offhand manner he sometimes adopted when talking about his patients. Different health care workers used different strategies for dealing with the stresses and traumas of their jobs. Harry's strategy was gruffness and bravado. He knew that his direct manner sometimes irritated Abraham and, perhaps in response to what he regarded as Abraham's excessive refinement, no doubt exaggerated it for his benefit. Despite the undertones the two men respected each other as caring and careful clinicians.

Abraham was familiar with the style of interaction with Harry and played his part. "I'm sorry to take you away from saving lives, but perhaps you could tell me a little about him."

"Sure. Dr. V.'s a retired GP in his seventies who's suffered from severe multiple sclerosis for many years. He's completely disabled—barely able to move—and we think he also has advanced dementia. He lives in a nursing home, where he seems to get pretty good care. He has a permanent indwelling urinary catheter and significantly impaired ability to swallow, making feeding him difficult and even dangerous. We understand that at home—at the nursing home—he mainly just lies there staring into space. That's what they say, and it's consistent with what we see here.

"Now, Dr. V. has a sister, Dora, who's completely devoted to him. She and the Doctor have always lived together. When he was working she looked after the household and the surgery. Since he's been sick—at least ten years now—she's come every day and sat with him from morning till night. She insists that she can communicate with him and that he understands every word she says."

"Is there any evidence for that?"

"None that we can see. We talk to him and he just lies there, staring into space. She talks to him and he does the same. But she firmly believes that he knows what's going on. What the heck, she might be right! But it doesn't seem to lead to any practical outcomes.

"The real problem is not that she talks to him but that she insists on feeding him. Because of his swallowing problem the speech therapists have said that he can only have thickened fluids, preferably given by a naso-gastric tube when he's sitting up. Dora knows this but insists on feeding him day and night: chicken soup, chicken, you name it. Because of this he develops a rattley chest, sometimes actual pneumonia. And that's why we see him. He's sent in here by the nursing home, always with Dora, asking for admission on account of a lung infection. We think that the whole thing's futile and a waste of time and that they should just let events take their course at home, so usually we just give him a shot or two of penicillin and send him back. They continue IV antibiotics in the nursing home for a few days and then he's back to where he started.

"Dora's never happy with this approach. She always tries to demand more treatment. She says he's being neglected at the nursing home, that we're neglecting him, that he needs tests and drugs, that she's going to lodge a complaint with the police, the government, the Queen, whatever. We try to placate her, then send him home by ambulance. It usually works fine."

"If you have such a well-developed and effective system," Abraham interceded sarcastically, "why have you called me?"

"Well, this is the second time he's come to the hospital in two days. We saw him yesterday and everything seemed to be going according to plan. However, he returned this morning with a note from the nursing home doctor—who's pretty good—stating that he's really no better. Much as it goes against our grain we feel we need some advice from you guys upstairs. He's in cubicle fifteen. Oh, and you'll be surprised to know, Dora's with him. Have fun!"

Abraham found cubicle fifteen and quickly looked over the patient's notes and the results from his recent tests on the computer screen. The history appeared to be exactly as described by the emergency doctor. The curtain was drawn around the cubicle. Abraham pulled it aside a little and peered inside. He saw a patient lying prone on the bed and a woman sitting on a chair beside him reading a book. "Can I come in?" he asked.

He entered and continued talking. "I'm Professor Nevski. Dr. Krokowski has explained some of the story to me. I presume you're Dora. Is that correct?"

"Yes, it is, and this is Dr. Vilgis. We're very grateful for your assistance."

"Would you mind explaining what's brought you here?"

Dora, a plump woman with gray hair, a heavily lined face, and thick, black-rimmed spectacles, was conservatively dressed in a brown cardigan and pleated skirt. She spoke in a slow, deliberate manner, with a careful precision in her choice of words. Her brother was a thin, elderly looking, unshaven man, lying stiffly under a sheet with his mouth slightly open. His face was impassive and he was looking straight up at the ceiling. He made no movement or other response as Abraham entered.

"Dr. Vilgis and I were here yesterday. He's suffering from a bout of pneumonia. This is not new, but it is more serious than usual. He is having trouble breathing and has very congested lungs. Because of his medical condition—he has multiple sclerosis, you know—he has difficulty moving or coughing, which means that any chest infection can become serious very quickly. Sometimes we can treat him with antibiotics at home, but not this time."

Abraham questioned Dora closely for some minutes about her brother's medical history and the present illness. Her answers were clear and concise and she seemed to have every fact at her immediate disposal. After a while he said, "You obviously have a very complete knowledge about your brother's condition. I'd now like to talk with him personally."

"Of course, you can do that, Professor," Dora replied, "but you won't be able to obtain much information from him directly. When he comes to the hospital he has great difficulty expressing himself. When he's at home he can talk a little. Sometimes even that is hard, but I can always understand him. Of course, he understands everything you say. He's still a very brilliant man."

Abraham directed himself to the patient. "Dr. Vilgis, do you mind if I ask you a few questions?" The patient made no response, continuing to lie stiffly on his back with his eyes open, apparently looking at a fixed point above him. "I know you find it difficult to talk at times, but it's important for me to try to find out what's troubling you." No response. "Can you tell me what the problem is that's brought you here?" No response. "I hear you've been having trouble with your breathing. Is that correct?" No response. "Perhaps you could tell me where you are at the present time." No response. "Can you squeeze my hand to show me that you can hear what I'm saying?" No response. "Or maybe you could blink your eyes." Nothing.

Abraham turned to Dora. "I don't seem to be able to detect any replies to my questions. Could you communicate with your brother in a manner that would allow me to ask him some questions?"

Dora replied, matter-of-factly. "Whenever he's anxious it's more difficult for him to communicate. At the moment he's very anxious both about being in the hospital and his illness. We may have to wait until he's a little better to be able to talk with him more fully."

"You talk with him at home?"

"Yes, all the time. He can't always answer very clearly, but I can usually understand what he says. He was always a great talker, so his speech difficulties are very frustrating for him."

"You see him every day?"

"Yes, I live nearby. I'm his main carer. He lives in a nursing home where there are, of course, nurses and doctors. But they never pay him enough attention. I usually arrive at about eight thirty in the morning and leave for home at seven o'clock in the night after he's eaten and is ready to go to sleep for the night."

Abraham was impressed. "What do you do during the ten-and-a-half hours you spend with him each day?"

"We read together. I read the newspaper aloud, then one of his favorite books. He's a great reader, you know. He always has been. Then I get him his lunch and we listen to some of his favorite music. That sort of thing. The days go surprisingly quickly."

"Have you always been so close?"

"Oh yes, since we were small children. He's two years older than me, but much cleverer. We've been a good team. He supported me when he was fit and able. Now I support him."

"Have you or he ever married? Do you have any children?"

"No. I guess we're very private people. We've always kept to ourselves. I'd have liked a family, I suppose—I love children—but the opportunity never arose. We're luckier than most, however, because we've always had each other."

Under the watchful eye of the sister, Abraham examined the patient to the extent that he could, the man retaining his rigid, inert position, providing no assistance and giving no indication at any time that he was aware of what was happening. Abraham knew instinctively that he had to exercise great care with everything he said. When he had finished he made a show of addressing the patient, speaking very formally.

"Dr. Vilgis, my assessment, and the results of the tests already performed, support the diagnosis of pneumonia. Because there's been no improvement over the last twenty-four hours, and indeed, there may have been a deterioration, I think that it's desirable for you to be admitted into the hospital for a few days. You'll be treated with intravenous antibiotics and it'll provide us with an opportunity to undertake whatever additional tests appear to be indicated. Would you be happy with this plan of action?"

There was no response from the figure on the bed, but Dora was very appreciative. "Thank you so much, Professor," she said effusively. "It's our privilege to be under your care. Dr. Vilgis is no doubt also very grateful for your attention. We both hope that his improvement will now be rapid."

Abraham left the cubicle and made his way back to the bridge to write up his notes. Harry Krokowski was still there. "I've seen Dr. Vilgis," he said impassively. "He's a true gentleman. I agree that he has pneumonia and would benefit from a few days in the hospital. We'll be happy to take him."

"Thanks, Abe," replied Harry, smiling broadly. "How did you find Dora?"

"She was very helpful and proper. She's also certainly very devoted to her brother."

"Completely. I've never seen them separated."

"Although Dora spoke at length about her conversations with her brother I found it difficult to elicit any responses from him. Have you been able to speak with him in the past?"

"Never. In fact no one has, either here or at the nursing home. Dora's always adamant that he can understand everything everyone says and that she can communicate with him freely but no one has witnessed him making any comprehensible verbal or motor response for years. There's a theory that it's all in her mind."

"Are you one of the adherents to that theory?"

"Abe, you know me. I'm a skeptic. As much as I'd like to believe it, I've never seen anything that convinces me that the doctor's doing anything but staring into space. Maybe you'll be able to solve the mystery up in the wards. Thanks for taking him off our hands."

Abraham left the Emergency Department, troubled and perplexed by what he had just witnessed. He called Rebecca to tell her about the new patient.

35.

It was lunchtime. Nic was speaking. "Did you hear what happened, old boy? You know Brucie Spalding, the anesthetist? Apparently, he had an affair with one of his students—that good-looking young girl Sophie, who did a term with us. She's now a registrar in his department. He was teaching the post-grads. It seems that the class went well and a few of the students went out with Brucie for a drink afterward. The story I heard is that everyone except Sophie went home and, well, one thing led to another. She's now accusing him of taking advantage of her when she was drunk. Marg Wilson's summarily dismissed Bruce. He's gotten fired, just like that, after ten years of service. And apparently he doesn't have a leg to stand on. If you screw a student you're in the wrong. That's all there is to it."

Madeleine was incensed. "Yeah, I know about it and it serves him right. There's a power relationship between a teacher and a student and this means that there can be no sexual relationship between them. Ever. Period. It's always rape."

Abraham joined in the discussion. "That's a very strong statement, Madeleine, but I agree with your main point. Sexual relations between teachers and students are always wrong and the same applies to doctors and patients. We have to accept that. Actually, what I can't understand is how sexual transgressions happen at all. In my own experience, relationships between doctors and patients or teachers and students are completely nonerotic. When I see a patient, when I examine a body—male or female—for me, it's stripped of all its sexual character. It's just like a machine. The clinical touch is inherently different from the sexual touch. I don't know what the difference is, but it's fundamental."

"That's a very interesting idea, Abe," responded Nic. "I've never thought about it like that but what you say rings true. When I approach someone as a doctor, the possibility of a sexual relationship with them just doesn't arise. I enter into a kind of de-eroticized process. Merely thinking about it now makes me feel a bit weird. I don't think I could convert what you're calling the 'clinical touch' into a sexual one if I tried."

"It's probably got a lot to do with how we're trained," said Madeleine. "But maybe there's a psychological aspect, too. I've always thought that Bruce Spalding was a bit weird, and he always struck me as being sleazy. I wouldn't be surprised if he's had some sinister psychopathology all along that's showing itself only now."

"I don't know anything about Bruce," said Abraham, "and I don't like the idea of condemning someone before he's even been tried. But I don't think that it's just education or psychology either. I think there really is something about these relationships that actively prevents sex. I wish I knew what it was." Abraham had, in fact, often wondered about this when seeing patients. From the outside at least, some of the actual physical actions one undertook during an intimate examination might look the same as those that occurred within an erotic interaction. But, he knew, to both parties involved, the meanings were almost completely the opposite. What it was that distinguished the two so clearly, however, was a mystery.

"It's probably not too difficult to distinguish between what happens in a clinical consultation and an erotic encounter," said Nic, as if reading Abraham's thoughts. "But what interests me is what goes wrong when it does. I mean, Brucie Spalding's just an ordinary bloke. He's always struck me as a decent ethical practitioner. It's true that he might've had an eye for the girls but I never thought of him as a pervert. Yet somehow he lost his way and crossed the line. He's paid the price, of course, but I wonder why he did it. Mind you," he went on, "not everyone pays the price. Look at Des Ray: it's well known that he screws all his nurses and no one seems to care. Is that a double standard or what?"

What I really wonder, Abraham was thinking, is why sex is so difficult for me. It's true, he thought, that no matter who it was, when he went to examine a patient all eroticism vanished. That was no doubt a good thing, but he sometimes wished that everything didn't have to be so complicated for him, that he didn't have to be so safe all the time. When he heard Nic talking about Desmond he couldn't suppress a pang of envy, half wishing that things were as certain for him as they were for the nurse. But maybe their personalities were just different.

He tuned back in to the conversation. Madeleine was still fulminating vehemently about Bruce Spalding. "Relationships between teachers and students and between doctors and patients are sacred," she was saying. "We have to set rules and enforce them. If there are gray areas they'll be exploited, and the boundary will become progressively less distinct. We have to be firm, even if the two people involved say they're in love."

"You're a tough woman, Madeleine Silverstein," said Nic. "You've convinced me never to have sex with a student or a patient, or at least never to tell you about it if I do. Maybe that's the moral: if you do it, don't get found out, because it could put at risk the reputation and standing of the whole medical profession, even if not the nursing one. Look, this is a great discussion. I love sitting round talking about fucking students but it's my clinics they pay me for and I'm already late for this afternoon's. I've got to go and unless I'm wrong, Abe, you've got a lecture to give. Thanks as usual for the great chat. Oh, and, old boy, don't get too cut up about Brucie. I bet you he's not agonizing about the philosophy of the clinical and the erotic touch; he's probably at this very moment making the most of his extra spare time out in the marketplace, finding another lay."

36.

Abraham hurried to his lecture. When he entered the room a hundred or so students were seated, waiting expectantly for him. "Hello, everyone," he said, trying to catch his breath. "I'm sorry I'm late. Let's get going right away."

He stood up straight. "I've been asked to talk with you about ethics. This is a crucially important subject but I'll bet that few of you actually have a clear idea of what the word means or its significance. My job is to show you that ethics is central to everything you'll ever do in your professional lives."

He stopped for a moment to take a breath. He looked around the lecture hall. No one looked particularly interested. A few students were doodling on the notepads in front of them. A couple of them were talking to each other. He glared at them and went on.

"When ethics is discussed in relation to medicine, it's often made to seem like something added on, an extra chore that has to be endured unless some way can be found to avoid it. Not only do we have to think of all the hard stuff—lists of possible diagnoses, investigations, and treatments, including the entire pharmacopoeia—but now there's this soft stuff, too! As well as lists of drugs and their effects we're supposed to go through lists of ethical principles and make sure they've been satisfied. Isn't it just twenty-first century political correctness?

"Not really. Ethics isn't just a fashionable add-on to clinical medicine: it's in fact what medicine's all about. It's not merely an additional checklist we have to go through to pass the exams: it's why we want to pass the exams in the first place. It's not just another set of rules that must be followed: it's the basis on which rules are written, and on which they may be criticized and thrown out.

"Some people talk about ethics as if there are just a few rock-solid principles—autonomy, 'do no harm,' justice, that sort of thing—but this is a serious misunderstanding of what ethics is all about. Ethical issues are everywhere. They pervade every aspect of our lives. In the clinic, we always need to ask: why has this person come to see me? What are they going through? What do they want of me? How will I know when we've gotten there? Why am I here in the first place, doing the job I am?"

He paused briefly. He noticed that a few students were taking notes while others were sitting looking at him expectantly. Another appeared to be sending a text message.

He went on. "We spend all our days grappling with ethical issues, usually without even realizing it. Consider the following. It's morning and you're the only one up. You've forgotten to buy milk and there's only enough for one bowl of corn flakes. Do you use it and leave the others in the house to fend for themselves? You're running late for the university and your mother calls to say that her back's hurting again and that you have to call your grandmother. Do you change your plans and go to see your mom, and do you immediately call your grandma? You're on the road and you see a driver swerving about, evidently drunk, on drugs, or sick. Do you try to catch him at the next light and convince him to pull over? While you're stopped at the light wondering what to do about the drunk, a collector bangs on your window asking for money for the Children's Hospital. Do you give her a few coins or do you tell her to get lost?"

Some members of the audience were starting to look interested. He went on. "You get to the hospital and run around frantically trying to see all your patients before the Professor's ward round. This person's frightened, that person's sad, another's exalted, another's uncertain. All have things to tell you. What do you say to them as you whizz by, with no time to talk?

"You're on the round and the Professor asks you to tell the group about a patient's history. She's told you about her secret extramarital affair that is making her very depressed. Do you tell the group? You know that the woman in bed ten with terminal cancer has just decided she wants to live two more months to see her daughter's wedding and that the man in bed sixteen with a drug overdose has felt lonely and depressed ever since his partner of fifty-five years died. What do you—or the Professor—have to offer these people?

"After the round another student tells a crude sexist joke. Do you laugh? You have a lecture on ethics before lunch. You know there's no question on ethics on the exam and you've got an anatomy assignment due in tomorrow, which you haven't even started. Do you go to the lecture?"

The students were obviously somewhat surprised by what he was saying. Most had stopped writing and were listening attentively. He continued, relentlessly.

"It's lunchtime and you bump into an old school friend who finished her BS last year and went straight into a highly paid job with a drug company. She offers you business-class airfare to Geneva to go to the World Medical Student Society Congress. Do you accept it? You rush out for a dentist appointment your mother made for you and you overhear the dentist talking on the phone about how BHP shares are about to go through the roof because of some big merger or something. Do you call up your broker and tell him to spend all your life savings?

"It's afternoon. You have a class in the operating room and the patient's under anesthesia. The consultant urges you to perform a vaginal examination on her to confirm the diagnosis of ovarian cancer before he makes the incision. Do you do the examination? In OR, the surgeon's being even ruder than usual to everyone—nurses, interns, students. Do you say anything?

"You get away from OR, snatch a cup of coffee, and race to the Emergency Department for the last class of the day. A patient's in severe pain with an acute abdomen. The others in your group are already lined up to examine him, even though it's obviously causing him additional pain. Do you take your turn? The ED is short staffed and the harassed resident suggests that you take over stitching up an elderly man who has a laceration on his scalp. You've never done it before and it'd be terrific experience. Do you stitch up the elderly man?

"Classes are over and some friends ask you to come down to the local bar with them to have a few drinks and shoot some pool. You've got work to do, but it'd be nice to relax for a bit. Do you go? Your boyfriend—or girlfriend—calls your cell and complains that you're not spending enough time with them. They'd like to spend some time with you tonight, maybe sleep over. Do you put them off? You drop into a café for a takeaway souvlaki. As you walk into the shop you see a sign scrawled on a wall across the road, 'Meat is murder.' Do you buy the souvlaki? You decide to buy a Slurpee instead and the shopkeeper accidentally gives you fifty cents too much change. He's got more money than you. Do you tell him about his mistake?

"It's late and you're driving along the freeway on your way home. As you're speeding along you see a young woman on the side of the road, obviously disturbed. Do you slam on the brakes and race back to help her? You get home and a couple of your roommates who've had a bit too much to drink are having a noisy argument that sounds like it could turn nasty. Do you intervene? You brush your teeth and flop into bed, dead tired, about to fall asleep. The phone rings. The answering machine in the hallway is on and you can hear from the message that it's your mom again. She sounds distressed. It's the last thing you feel like doing, but do you get up and grab the phone?"

He stopped, this time for effect. The room remained silent. He spoke more slowly and in a slightly softer voice. "Ethics is not about rules that everyone has to follow. It's mostly not about terrible dilemmas: do I let this person die? Do I perform this amazing, life-saving procedure that costs millions of dollars? It's mostly about clarifying one's own values and communicating with others about theirs. It's the part of medicine where two people come together and meet in the middle, on an equal footing.

"A computer can't be ethical because it can't tell, or respond to, a story, no matter how sad or how funny. Two people can't avoid ethics in their relationship, because ethics is exactly what makes them human in the first place. Ethics is the part of medicine that lies outside of technical calculations, of the computing of possibilities, of lists and protocols. It's the part where you wonder 'What's the purpose of this consultation?' 'What am I trying to achieve?' and where you have to decide 'What should I do for this person now?' It's the context for the technical discourses of anatomy, physiology, biochemistry, pharmacology, and all the rest of them. Without it, none of what we do would make any sense."

The torrent of words stopped. Abraham realized that he had been completely carried away by his own rhetoric. Returning to the mundane reality of the lecture hall, he looked around again. A few students were sitting upright, their eyes fixed on him. Others, however, appeared to be staring vacantly into space, a bit like Dr. Vilgis. The student who had been texting on his phone was still doing so. After a brief pause, Abraham sighed. "Thanks everyone for listening. If you have any questions about anything I've said, feel free to email me."

37.

There were two patients waiting to see Abraham. The first was Christine Fellegi, a middle-aged woman who suffered from a kidney problem and high blood pressure. From time to time she also suffered bouts of depression, in part brought on by her illnesses and in part by her difficult relationship with her husband.

He called her into the consulting room and—as usual—observed her closely as she entered the room. She had a slight, familiar limp from a congenital condition but Abraham thought that her gait was stiffer than usual and wondered if she was in pain. Her sad eyes were set deep into her rough-skinned, craggy face. She had straggly, graying hair. "Hello, Chris," he said. "It's nice to see you again."

He knew Christine's story well. She had come from a working-class family and had had little education. Before marrying she had worked as a sales assistant in a men's clothing shop and had been independent, if not confident. She had actually met her husband in the shop where she worked. An immigrant from Hungary, just off the boat, he was looking for some work clothes prior to starting his first job as a laborer on a construction site. Alone, looking for female companionship, and attracted by the shy, plain teenage girl, he asked her out. György was the first boyfriend she had ever had, and she fell in love without delay. When he proposed marriage a couple of months later she readily agreed and they set out on life's adventure together.

The adventure, however, turned out not to be uncomplicated. She had stopped working soon after the marriage in the expectation that she would become pregnant. That didn't happen and they never found out why. She was demoralized and shamed by what was assumed by both of them to be her failure. Her husband had many affairs, often taunting her with the fact that he was spending the night with someone younger and more attractive than she was. Occasionally, he would come home drunk and beat her, demanding sex at the end to deepen her humiliation.

The one bright spot was that he was financially successful. Industrious with the savings he was able to accumulate from the menial jobs with which he had started, György eventually opened his own business importing food and household items from the newly flourishing economy in his homeland. But even this didn't help Christine much because she was allotted no more than a pitiful amount of money to run the household. Almost every time she had come to see Abraham she had cried and talked of leaving her husband. She never had, turning instead to religion, seeking solace and peace in the ancient liturgies and rituals of the Anglican Church.

For a few minutes they talked about Christine's medical problems. Abraham examined the results of blood tests he had ordered at the last visit by consulting the computer on the desk. He conducted a brief physical examination. He noticed bruising on her arms and back but did not comment on it.

When they had resumed their seats he suggested some medication changes and arranged a follow-up blood test a few months later. Having completed the formal medical business of the consultation, he sat back carefully in his chair and, with a tone of voice that was deliberately softer than the one he had been using, said, "Is there anything else you'd like to discuss?"

The patient hesitated a moment, then replied in a manner that suggested to Abraham that she had planned the response. "György hit me again yesterday. I've got lots of bruises and I'm aching all over."

She paused for a moment, then continued. "It's been really hard over the years," she said, "but I know I've made my choices. I've been going a lot to church lately and in spite of how difficult things have been I feel I can find a way forward. I'd like to talk it through with you. If now's not convenient I can come back later."

"Chris, I'll be very happy to talk with you but we need to make sure that we have enough time. Let's go out and talk with Jenny and find a time either tomorrow or the next day at the latest. Also, please don't forget that if you need me you can call any time."

38.

"Hello, Abraham! It's wonderful to see you again. You're looking so well! Have you been out in the sun? I think you might have lost some weight . . ."

Abraham had known Jocelyn Chauchat for nearly ten years. She was a flamboyant woman in her early thirties with an ever-changing hair color. She consulted him about a variety of medical problems and often also took the opportunity to talk about personal issues. She had told him about an abortion she had undergone in her late teens, which—she said—she had not discussed with anyone else before. She had talked about the frustrations and guilt she experienced in her daily interactions with her elderly mother. She often delighted in relating to him details of liaisons she had with various lovers.

"I have so many things to tell you!" she exclaimed expansively. "I've had such an exciting time. I've been in and out of love since I last saw you. He was such a gorgeous guy. It was a real whirlwind! Really great sex, too! It's such a long time since I've had so many fantastic orgasms . . ."

As Jocelyn spoke, Abraham involuntarily took on an air of cool formality. He knew that sexuality was as important in the clinic as everywhere else and that medicine couldn't be quarantined from its influence and power even though, like his fellow professionals, he sometimes tried to act as if it were. He had often reflected that we can only interact with each other as embodied individuals, as people who know and experience the world and each other through physical contact. It was because of sexuality that both our own and other people's bodies had meaning for us. The sexual imperative drives everybody forward and its force is discharged through the experience of other bodies as different, as tantalizingly unattainable, as incompletely known and knowable.

"He really made me feel amazing!" she was continuing. "I mean, I really loved feeling wanted, feeling desired. The best thing was the sense that someone else was appreciating, enjoying, savoring my body."

Abraham reflected that he, too, yearned to be desired, and that since his wife had fallen ill neither he nor anyone else had "savored" his body.

"I don't suppose you can understand what I'm saying," she continued. "After all, you're a man, you're happily married, with children, with money— if you don't mind my saying so—and you don't know what it's like to have a disease you live with every day, with a body that's let you down, that's like a flashing light to other people saying, 'I'm dangerous, don't desire me!'"

That the medical encounter is itself a sexually charged field, Abraham was thinking, is an open secret. If sexuality is the fluid in which we all swim, illness is like a disturbance in this fluid, a perturbation that can create powerful surges and eddies. Coming to terms with an illness often includes relearning how to live with one's own body, how to ride it, how to trust it, how to open it—with all its flaws and imperfections—to others. Helping people make their way through this process of relearning and remapping was an important part of his job.

He had to work with both senses of sexuality, with the broader one—that is, the ability to connect with another person's deep experiences—as well as the more familiar, narrower one. The two were closely connected; after all, on the one hand, actual sexual contact only becomes possible because other bodies already make sense and pose problems for us; and on the other, the hypothetical meaning of another person's body is only evoked because of the thrill of the possibility of physical contact.

Jocelyn sat back in her chair. She rearranged her hair and tilted her head delicately back and to one side, with carefully controlled coyness. "I wonder if they know how much I really need them, how much I yearn to be loved," she said abstractly, adding, almost as an afterthought, "and if they realize how hard I'm trying."

Abraham looked at her closely. She was still young enough to carry the bloom of sex on her face. Her blouse and jeans were firmly fitting and she wore high boots, which together gracefully highlighted her sumptuous feminine curves. An array of jewelry—a necklace, earrings, rings on her fingers—and carefully applied lipstick and mascara further proclaimed her body as a potential site for sexually charged exchanges.

He regarded other people's bodies as his business. He loved looking at and imagining them and felt no shame or self-recrimination in doing so. He loved looking at their different shapes and contours, he was aware of the varying scents and aromas they generated, and he imagined their range of textures and tactile consistencies. He could appreciate the pride and power, and softness and sensuality, both men and women experienced in relation to their bodies, and knew the uncertainty and insecurity that could so easily be evoked. He enjoyed the thrill of looking at the body of a woman, despite the ambivalence he felt when he did so. Years of talking with patients had convinced him that everyone is capable of imagining the penetration of another's secret spaces. He would observe discreetly the soft curves of a breast, the contour of a nipple under clothing, the outlines of hips and buttocks, the gracefulness of a hand, the clarity of unblemished skin, the redness of lips, the liquidity of hair. Bodies had shapes, densities, tastes, and smells. The face was infinitely expressive and evocative, as could also be a graceful movement, a body shape highlighted by a fold or drape of clothing, an attitude, or a pause. The vagina—every woman's vagina—was a place of darkness, of lust and passion, of fecundity, of power, a forbidden place, always present, yet always marked as dangerous, tantalizing, and prohibited territory.

Abraham luxuriated in the bodies of those around him. He tried to imagine how they experienced themselves and the proximity of other people, the daily functions of moving and eating and defecating, and the more elevated sensations of pain and pleasure, and how they experienced love, and making love. He observed women and men, colleagues, patients, students, strangers. Yet he was constantly amazed by the fact that at the moment an actual relationship crystallized—a contact with a patient, an interaction with a colleague or student—all imaginative content would suddenly vanish into the routine disciplines of that relationship. Whenever a specific interpersonal territory was entered—clinical practice, everyday collegiate associations—the laws of that territory took over. He sometimes tried to resist: for example, as a thought experiment he would try to imagine making love to a patient or colleague, but he could never bring the image to mind. His own body resisted, implacably and obdurately. Then despite his noble scientific intentions he invariably felt revolted and even ashamed of himself at having embarked on the experiment at all.

He marveled at the power of the system. It was always on the point of explosion, of breakdown, of eruption into lust and desire but, remarkably, that never—or almost never—happened. When he tried to explain it, the boundary between the two—the boundary between the clinical touch, the palpation of an abdomen searching for evidence of pain, inflammation, or cancer, and the caress of sexual desire, the foraging for sweetness and mutual care—seemed diffuse and elusive. But at the level of his own inner impulses it was a boundary that in reality was as sharply defined and effectively guarded as any border crossing between hostile states.

Abraham methodically went through the clinical process with Jocelyn, discussing symptoms and medications. He conducted a cursory physical examination, recording the details of her blood pressure and other findings. As he was finishing Jocelyn asked, theatrically, "Abraham, darling, would you mind checking my breasts today? It's been some time and you know how I dislike doing it myself." Without waiting for an answer she removed her blouse and bra and sank back into the couch, presenting her naked chest to him.

Abraham was simultaneously embarrassed and titillated. However, he had been in this situation before and trusted himself to continue. Despite the thrill he felt in being exposed to Jocelyn's unmistakable desire he assumed a formal, slightly stern manner and took care not to return her gaze. He concentrated on the examination, proceeding in the prescribed, routine manner, observing with clinical precision the physical features of the breasts and palpating them to exclude the possibility of a malignancy or other abnormality. At the same time, however, he allowed himself to note their smooth, graceful contour and the sharp prominence of the nipples. He felt their firm but pliable, solid but still liquid, consistency, which recoiled softly and gently to his touch. It was easy to imagine her partner's pleasure when offering his sexual touch, his kisses and caresses. He could almost feel the soft pliant tissues under his own tongue, taste the nipples in his own mouth.

But Abraham's touch could not be a caress. It had to be a clinical exploration, strictly scientific and instrumental, unerotic. Overcoming his momentary mental lapse, he regained control of his fantasies. With an effort, he turned his reflections deliberately to what it was that distinguished the touch of the doctor and the lover. He tried to be scientific. From an anatomical point of view, the muscular movements were the same. But oddly, the meanings generated by the two actions were opposite. How could that be possible? He couldn't answer the question, but for now it really didn't matter. What counted was that he was back on safe territory. He was back in the land of medicine, physiology, and clinical reasoning. He breathed a faint sigh of relief. He was once again the compliant subject of the regime that deeply controlled his body.

"Your breasts are fine, Jocelyn," he pronounced, with well-practiced clinical precision, "although if you're concerned I'd be happy to arrange a mammogram for you. Also, your blood pressure's good and the remainder of the examination today is normal. You can get dressed now. I'd like to change some of your medications, I'll explain in what way . . ." And the consultation was brought to a close.

PART 5

SWAMP ROAD HOSPITAL

39.

It was Friday night and Abraham had at last finished work at the Royal Prince John. He was heading for the Swamp Road Local Hospital to visit his father. It had been years since he had visited the local hospital, even though it was within his own hospital district and, strictly speaking, was a branch of the RPJ. As a small district hospital, it was a place to which patients with less serious illnesses were sent. The medical staff rotated through the various hospitals in the district, so Abraham was sure that the care his father received there would be satisfactory.

The woman at the reception desk directed him to Ward 2C. He found his way there and introduced himself to the nurse at the nurse's station in the center of the ward. "Hello," he said breezily. "I'm Professor Nevski. I'm here to visit my father. Can you please tell me which bed he's in?"

The nurse was engaged with copying something from a computer screen to an exercise book. Without looking away from what she was doing she replied expressionlessly, "He's in bed three."

Abraham waited for her to say something more. When she didn't, he turned to look for the bed numbers. The rooms were arranged in a circle around the central station, and bed three turned out to be diametrically opposite to where he was standing. He walked around the nurses' station, looking in through the half-opened room doors on the patients in the other beds as he did so. He was not used to being a visitor rather than a doctor and was immediately struck by the different manner in which he was regarded. Even though he had introduced himself as "Professor," which he only did when he needed to emphasize his status, the nurse on duty seemed uninterested in his presence. No doubt she's busy, he thought, even though that's no excuse for a failure to acknowledge him as a close relative of one of her patients. He made a note to provide feedback in a tactful manner to the head nurse when feedback was requested.

The door to bed three was slightly ajar. He pushed it open and froze. Instead of a bed there was a mattress on the floor, and on the mattress was a naked, wizened, elderly man whom Abraham only just recognized as his father. "Dad!" he exclaimed. The patient appeared not to hear him, but before Abraham could say anything more he let out a piercing scream.

"Get away from me, you vermin!" the man cried. "Don't come near me!"

"Dad, it's me, Abraham," Abraham half shouted. He knelt on the bed, which he felt immediately was soaked in rancid-smelling urine. His father's face was twisted and full of hate.

"I'm being held against my will. You'll all pay for this. You're all scum, vermin." There followed a string of expletives.

"Dad, it's me, Abraham, your son," he repeated, coming close to the elderly man. "How are you feeling?"

"Get away! I don't need you or anyone! I don't like you. I don't respect you. I don't hold you in any esteem!"

This was the way his father used to talk, but Abraham was still overcome by amazement. Trying to control his emotions, he picked up the chart that was lying on a bench next to the window. The observation pages showed that his father had a high fever and low blood pressure. Under "general observations" someone had written "confused and aggressive." He flicked through to the medication sheet. His father's usual medications had been charted, together with a powerful tranquilizer, of which he had already received many doses during the day.

His heart pounding, Abraham turned and left the room. He walked directly to the nurses' station and behind the desk to one of the computers. Swamp Road Hospital was, technically speaking, a branch of the RPJ, which would give him access to their system. He quickly entered his password details and called up his father's pathology results. The results from the tests he had discussed with the resident the night before were displayed. He was dismayed but not surprised by what he saw. He picked up the phone next to the computer and dialed "9." After a few seconds the receptionist answered. "This is Professor Nevski," he said in a deliberately authoritative tone. "Can you please page urgently the registrar responsible for Ward 2C?" He could hear his voice shaking as he spoke but he did his best to maintain his professional voice and intonation.

"I'll do that for you immediately, Doctor," the receptionist replied. "Please hold the line." A minute or so later he heard a woman's voice.

"Hello. This is Dr. O'Hallaran."

"Hello, Doctor," he said. "This is Professor Nevski here. My father is a patient in Ward 2C. The patient—my father—is delirious, febrile, and dehydrated and has been hypotensive for the last four hours. The tests ordered last night show that he's in renal failure and has a serious infection, almost certainly of urinary tract origin. He doesn't have an IV and hasn't yet received any antibiotics. He's received nothing but tranquilizers all day, even though he clearly has a treatable medical condition. Would you be able to come up to the ward as soon as possible and start some treatment?"

"Certainly, Professor," Dr. O'Hallaran said in an uncomplicated and clear way. "I'm just in the next ward. I'll be there in two minutes."

"Thanks," said Abraham simply and hung up the phone. The test results were still displayed on the computer screen. The figures were similar to ones he had seen hundreds of times, although never before in connection with his own father. He had a sense of unreality, of horror, of which he was only dimly aware.

No more than a minute had passed. A young, somewhat familiar-looking woman was standing beside him. "Hello, Professor. I'm Carly O'Hallaran. I don't know if you remember me. I'm the registrar covering this ward tonight. I was in one of your third-year classes about five years ago. It sounds like your father's pretty sick. I haven't seen him before, and he wasn't handed over to me when I started a couple of hours ago. Would you be able to tell me what's been happening?"

In his distress Abraham was moved by the young doctor's gentle but efficient manner. He felt safe in her presence. "My father came into the hospital last night. The ED registrar called me. It sounded like a possible UTI and he arranged a panel of tests, which he said he'd check in a couple of hours. It looks like he didn't manage to do so. As I said over the phone, my father's dehydrated—actually severely dehydrated—febrile and confused. His blood pressure hasn't been above 80 systolic for hours. The path results show renal failure—maybe due to dehydration and the drugs he's been taking—and strong evidence for a UTI. He needs an IV drip, some saline, and antibiotics."

"Sure, I'll get that happening right away," the doctor said. She turned to the nurse who was still sitting at her computer copying out data. "Nurse," she said, "could you please set up an IV for Mr. Nevski in bed three? I'll put it in immediately. Also, we'll need an antibiotic. I'll give him ceftriaxone one gram stat. Thank you."

"Yes, Doctor," the nurse replied in a servile tone, glaring spitefully at the two of them.

Abraham followed the doctor into his father's room. His father hadn't moved. When he caught sight of the new arrivals he started shouting just like he had before. "Let me go! I'm a prisoner here! Keep away! You're all my enemies!"

Barely holding back tears, Abraham knelt once more on the urine-soaked sheet and took the old man's hand. "This is Dr. O'Hallaran. She's going to put in an intravenous drip and then we'll start some antibiotics. If everything goes well you'll be feeling a lot better in no time."

His father snatched his hand away from Abraham and glared at him with a crazed glint in his eye. "Keep away, you scum! I demand to leave here. I want to go home."

Abraham was about to respond to this when the nurse from the station spoke from just behind him. "There's a phone call for you," she said.

"A phone call?" said Abraham. "How could that be? No one knows I'm here."

The nurse just shrugged her shoulders and walked out of the room. Abraham followed her back to the station where the phone he had used a few minutes before was off the hook. He picked it up. "Hello, this is Professor Nevski."

"This is Denise Roland," the caller replied. "I'm the director of nursing here. Nurse Jones tells me that you have accessed a patient's data without authorization. I have to tell you that this is a breach of privacy. You're not entitled to access medical records without permission."

Abraham was incredulous. "I'm sorry, Denise, but you're evidently not aware of the situation here. My father was admitted to this hospital last night. He has septicemia and renal failure and hasn't yet received any treatment. I am a professor of medicine in this district and have legitimate access to the hospital system. In addition, I've been my father's physician for ten years. My father's life depends on starting treatment. It may already be too late."

"We value our ethical responsibilities in this hospital," was the head nurse's reply. "You do not have a right of access to the hospital records without a letter from the patient authorizing you to do so."

"I'm sorry, but I'm not going to talk about this now," said Abraham, almost speechless with exasperation. "I'm going back to the patient." He hung up the phone. Nurse Jones was still sitting at her computer, copying out figures. He did no more than glare in her direction before moving back to his father's room. The doctor was finishing bandaging up the IV site in his father's right arm. His father was lying quietly now, perhaps asleep, on the freshly changed bed.

"Is there anything else you want me to do?" asked the young doctor. "I hope he'll be all right now." Her smile was kind and reassuring.

"No, thank you," Abraham replied, smiling grimly in response. "I guess we just have to wait and see now. I'll stay for a little bit and let him rest."

PART 6

THE PAIN OF OTHERS

40.

braham was once more on the train to work. There were the usual people—the schoolboys, the office workers, the failed businessman—traveling in their usual manner. It should have been another ordinary morning, another instance in the inexorable routine of travel, work, and domestic life, with its regular, predictable rhythm and its repetitive if reassuring pulse.

But somehow things had changed. Abraham recalled the incident with the red-haired girl and looked around tentatively, half expecting to see another person in a similar state of distress, but luckily, there did not appear to be any impending disaster today. He had been very shaken by the incident with his father, whose life now hung in the balance. How do you prepare yourself for the death of your father, he wondered. All your life you know that it will happen one day, but when it draws close you find yourself completely defenseless. He had already experienced wifelessness, and his mother's Alzheimer's meant he was halfway to motherlessness. What would fatherlessness be like on top of all that? He would be alone, with no one to care for him, to know his fears, his hopes, his annoying and endearing idiosyncrasies. He still had his children, of course, but they had to live their own lives and they were still at ages when it was he who had to be there for them.

He was himself no longer a young man. He hadn't complained when his life for years seemed to be moving very slowly. He had been secure and comfortable, even in the midst of the torridness of the hospital world. Then, he'd had a happy marriage and was savoring the growth of his children. But now that equilibrium had been disrupted and the certainty of his world—his ideas, his attitudes, and his most cherished assumptions—suddenly seemed to be teetering on the brink of collapse.

He thought of the patients in the hospital—Mrs. Gurewitz, Mr. Alvarez, Mrs. Timoshenko, Mrs. Fellegi, and the others. They knew he cared for them, but perhaps—as with Jocelyn Chauchat—they didn't realize how much he needed them, how much he needed to be needed. Did he care only for this reason, because he depended on their love and respect, the love and respect that had always been insufficient or lacking from his own father? And if that were true would it make a difference? Would it somehow diminish or erode the authenticity of his commitment to his patients?

He reflected on how rapidly and unexpectedly things could change. This had been brought home to him forcefully once when he was a young medical graduate working in the Emergency Department of a big public hospital—not the Royal Prince John. It had been the day before Christmas and the patient was a middle-aged man with back pain. He was a schoolteacher who lived alone; he had told Abraham that his only relatives were his sister and his mother. The pain had come on over the previous few days and had become quite severe. He was not handling it well and so was seeking advice from the local hospital. At first this had seemed a simple, routine problem. However, when he had come to examine him Abraham had been struck by how anxious and scared the man was: in fact, he was literally shaking with fear. He must know something I don't know, Abraham had thought. He noted some weakness in the right leg. It could have been due to a slipped disc—a common problem—but despite his callowness Abraham had a feeling that it was more than this.

The Emergency Department that day had been noisy and hot. There were people passing close by, just outside the curtain of the cubicle in which the man had been placed. Abraham, himself perspiring, examined the man from top to bottom. Just as he was finishing he had found a single enlarged lymph gland above the left collarbone, which he could only just feel with the tips of his fingers. He had learnt—as all medical students do—that this could be a warning sign of something serious, so he had told the man that he needed to perform a biopsy, which he had done then and there. He had taken a needle, aspirated some tissue, and made a smear on a glass plate. It took about a minute. He sent it off to Pathology. "The result will be available in an hour or so," he had told the man. "You can go home if you wish. Otherwise, if you want to wait I'll come back when I hear from the lab."

The man had chosen to stay and Abraham had gone about his business.

A few hours later he had remembered him and hurriedly called the lab to see if the result was in. The women's voice was matter of fact. "Yes, we have the result. Do you want me to read out the full report or just the conclusion?" The conclusion was enough for the present. "It reads 'Cytology of lymph node shows signs of aggressive malignancy. Diagnosis: metastatic adenocarcinoma, etiology unknown.' Is that all?"

A silence. Then " . . . er, yes, that will be all." He had gone to the patient. The atmosphere was still stifling, choking. The man was still sweating with fear. Abraham had thought to himself, he knew all along. I wonder where the intelligence has come from. He's only forty-two and his life is almost over. He has only pain, suffering, misery, and despair ahead of him. Abraham had wondered what he had hoped for. When he was young he must have dreamed. His parents no doubt imagined him happy, healthy, perhaps married with children. Now they would have to watch him die, alone, disappointed, unfulfilled.

There was nothing he could say to him. "There's nothing I can say to make this any easier," he had said. The news he had to give was terrible. "I'm afraid the news is not good." There was no easy way of putting it. "It seems that there's a tumor of some kind. We don't know where it came from but it's likely that this is the cause of your pain. You'll need to see a specialist but there's no need to stay in the hospital. I'll make you an appointment for as soon as possible." He turned to go. He'd seen this man twice, once in the morning and once just now. He'd come with an apparently simple, common problem and now, the day before Christmas, he was leaving with a death sentence. Abraham had felt like an executioner.

The train was pulling into the station. Abraham alighted, with the sense that he was carrying a heavy burden.

41.

"What's the latest on Mrs. Gurewitz? Wait, let me guess: when we go into her room we'll find her sitting up eating breakfast and reading the newspaper!"

"I'm sorry, Prof, but actually she died in the night."

Abraham started. "What are you saying, Rebecca? She died? But when we saw her late yesterday afternoon she was quite stable."

"Yes, I know. She was discovered by one of the nurses at about two a.m. I only just found out myself five minutes ago."

Abraham made no attempt to hide his astonishment. "That's extraordinary! I was sure that the dying process was going to be stretched out for days—in fact, I was worried that it might turn out to be many days."

There was a tense silence. The three doctors and the nurse looked at each other. Rebecca was the first to speak.

"It was a difficult case, wasn't it?" she said weakly. "But at least her suffering is over."

She looked like she was about to cry. Abraham knew how vulnerable Rebecca felt at the present time and regretted having added to her distress. Also, despite his surprise he knew he had to be careful not to undermine the morale of the group, so he added, "Yes, and I suppose it was merciful that in the end things happened so quickly."

"It would be good to know just why she died, though, wouldn't it?" Ashis said. "Do you think we can get an autopsy?"

"No, unfortunately that won't be possible," replied Rebecca. "Apparently, the night registrar called the daughter. I understand that she's refused a post-mortem examination."

"Maybe we could convince her. If we said—"

"Why would we want a postmortem?" cut in Desmond sharply. "Just for our own self-gratification! The old bird's died and the family has said what they want. We have to accept that and move on."

Abraham was aware of the pressure the team was under. As much as it irked him to do so, he realized he had no alternative but to agree with Desmond. "It's true. Ours is an inexact science," he said sententiously. "It would be satisfying to know why Mrs. Gurewitz's death occurred in this way and at this time, but it sometimes happens in medicine that we can't know everything. And Desmond's right: her daughter's been through a hard time. We might just have to write this one off as a case we couldn't understand."

Desmond looked embarrassed at Abraham's unexpected support for him and shifted uneasily from one foot to another, uncharacteristically lost for words. Aware of the others looking at him, he added, "It's not as if we don't have plenty of other things to keep us busy. Mr. Alvarez is still giving trouble. Last night he was so nasty I was worried that the nurses would put in a demand for political asylum."

He was trying to lighten the mood but no one smiled. "Let's keep going," said Abraham.

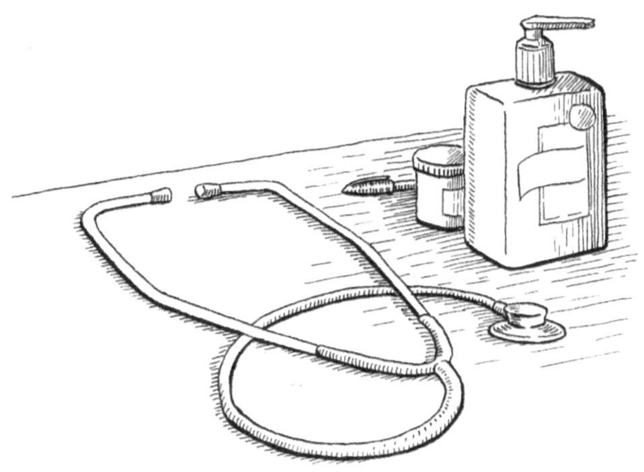

42.

The next patient had come to the hospital because of severe pain in his back. Everyone in the ward knew that his daughter was about to have a baby, his first grandchild.

"Hello, Mr. Tzorvas, how are you today?" Abraham asked.

"Pain! . . . I have pain in my side . . ." he answered. "I can't breathe . . . Aagh! . . . It's too much! . . . Help me!"

"Can you show me exactly where it hurts?"

"Here." He gestured weakly. "It's too strong!" He breathed heavily.

"Do you mind if I feel where the pain is? Is this the place?"

"Yes, it hurts there. Oooh!"

"What about here?"

"Yes, there too."

"What about . . ."

"Aaagh! Aaagh! It's too hard. Please make it stop!"

"I'm so sorry to hurt you, but in order to treat the pain effectively we have to understand what's causing it."

"I know you do, Doctor. I am sorry to be such trouble to you."

"You're no trouble. Of course, that's what we're here for. Is the pain there all the time?"

"There's some pain all the . . . time, but sometimes it's . . . aagh . . . worse." Mr. Tzorvas breathed heavily and closed his eyes. His forehead was covered in sweat. He writhed slightly, but as this evidently only made the pain worse he stopped abruptly and remained rigid instead. After a few moments he shifted in the bed and let out an involuntary scream. He showed his shame. "Oh, Doctor, I'm sorry." He had tears in his eyes. "I just can't help it. How long will this go on?"

The patient's wife, who had been standing a few steps behind the doctors, stepped forward tentatively. Tears were rolling down her face. "Doctor, he's in such pain. It hurts him so much. Is there anything I can do?"

Mr. Tzorvas let out another scream, this one higher pitched and louder than the others. He closed his eyes for a few seconds and then opened them again. He placed his right hand very gently over his left flank but he dared not undertake any movement more vigorous than this. He was still breathing very fast. "Aagh! Oh my God! Oh my God!"

Abraham turned to Mrs. Tzorvas. "I know this must be very hard for you. Your husband is obviously in great pain. We'll give him an injection to take away, or at least dull, the pain. But we do have to examine him to find out how best to treat him."

She took both of Abraham's hands in hers. "I know, Doctor," she said, imploringly. "We trust you. Thank you for all you're doing. It's very hard for us."

"Thanks for your understanding." He turned back to the patient. "Mr. Tzorvas, it seems like this pain's different from what you've been having over the last few weeks. Is that right?"

"Yes, it's much . . . Aaaaagh! . . . Oh my God! . . . It's . . . much . . . worse . . . Doctor, I really don't know how much more of this I can take. I haven't eaten or slept since last . . . Ahh! . . . I'm so tired."

"Doctor," Mrs. Tzorvas broke in, "he hasn't eaten anything. I'm so worried. He has to eat."

Abraham brought the examination to a close. He had established what he wanted. The pain in the patient's side was new. It was different in location, character, and severity from his usual loin pain. And on top of everything else, his side was extremely tender to touch. He had no doubt the implications were sinister.

He pondered briefly what he should say to the man suffering so grievously in front of him. He could see how agitated he was. But despite the obviousness of the suffering he, Abraham, felt strangely aloof. It was as if the man's pain was keeping the two of them apart, driving a wedge between them. The trouble was, Abraham could not imagine the pain himself. Try as he might, he could not conjure up in himself the travail that was completely engulfing the body before him. His own lack of sensation made him feel almost guilty. He knew he could be moved by a comment, a confession, a concern. He could empathize with joy, with sadness, with uncertainty. He could recognize despair and the distress associated with betrayal. He could even, he thought, experience pleasure vicariously. But he couldn't feel another's pain.

He made an effort to place within his own body the searing, scorching tide that he could see overwhelming Mr. Tzorvas, washing over him, submerging him, drowning him. He tried, but he couldn't do it. It wasn't possible to take on his physical anguish.

He turned to Mr. Tzorvas. He needed to tell him the truth. This was not the pain he'd come to accept, the pain of the scar tissues, the necessary burden he needed to pass through, like a purgatory, before emerging on the other side, no doubt to leave the terrible experience behind in the same fog in which it was already shrouded for everyone else.

Abraham looked deeply into the man's face. His eyes were bloodshot with the ordeal. They were also filled with tears, this time tears of fear. Before Abraham could speak, he said softly, "Doctor, I'm scared."

Taken by surprise, Abraham was disarmed. Suddenly, tears welled up in his own eyes and a lump formed in his throat. He did his best to control his emotions. He took the man's hand and replied, also softly, shaking his head slowly, "I know. I know. I'm sorry." Then, after a pause, he said simply, "I think you might be right." Then turning to the nurse, he instructed, "Please give Mr. Tzorvas ten milligrams of morphine intravenously right away. He can have as much as he needs after that in order to control the pain."

There was no more to be said. Abraham turned and walked out of the room. The rest of the team followed him. Outside, they discussed the technical details: the tests, the drugs, who else they needed to get involved. But Abraham was overwhelmed by the dire outcome of his clinical assessment for this man and his family. He, Abraham, would go back to his everyday life, to his own family—or what was left of it—and to his frivolous and not so frivolous pleasures. But for this family, everything had now changed. He thought again of the look in Mr. Tzorvas's eyes—the look of pathos and of pleading, resignation, and humility. Mr. Tzorvas was an ordinary man, poorly educated, a factory laborer. But he could accept his fate, and like everyone else, he could glimpse the poignancy of the moment, which just happened, this time, to be his own moment.

One day, as for everyone, it would be Abraham's moment.

43.

"How's Mrs. Dreyfus today?" asked Abraham.

"Yesterday was eventful," replied Rebecca. "Her conscious state's continued to fluctuate, so I've started to wonder if we had the diagnosis right. I organized an MRI scan of the brain and an EEG, just to see if there was something inherently wrong with her brain. The MRI was normal, but when she went down for the EEG she had a seizure."

"How interesting!" said Abraham. "Maybe there is some underlying brain pathology after all. What did the EEG show?"

"Funnily enough, not much," replied Rebecca. "They'd just completed the test and the neurologist said that he'd already looked at the traces and decided they were normal when the seizure came on. Apparently he examined her neurologically after it'd finished but couldn't find any specific pathology."

"And how is she now?"

"Last night she'd returned to her previous state of minimal responsiveness," answered the registrar. "I haven't seen her today."

They entered the patient's room. As on all the previous occasions she was lying on her back with her eyes closed. Abraham observed her closely for a few moments. She was breathing quietly and evenly and her general appearance was of peacefulness and rest. She was lying with her hands clasped on the sheets in front of her. Her right wrist was connected to an IV line and tubing from a urinary catheter emerged from the foot of the bed. At the far end of the room sat the two sisters close by each other. Jo was leaning her head on her sister's shoulder; there was a sense of pathos about them and both looked exhausted.

Abraham approached the bed and lightly touched the patient's left hand. To his surprise, she opened her eyes and looked him up and down dispassionately.

"Hello, Mrs. Dreyfus," Abraham responded. "How are you today?"

"I've got a bit of a headache," she replied. Then she added, "That's a nice tie you're wearing, Doctor."

"Thank you for saying so; it's one of my favorites," replied Abraham smoothly. "It's very nice to be able to talk with you. Do you mind if I ask you a few questions?" The patient merely looked at him blankly. "Can you tell me where you are at this moment?" Abraham asked, in time-honored fashion. Mrs. Dreyfus made no response. "What day is it today?" No response. "What year is it?" No reply. "A moment ago you called me 'doctor.' Can you say what makes you think that I am a doctor?" The patient remained silent but continued looking at him with blank eyes. "I can see you don't want to talk right now." Abraham tried to sound gentle. "Would you mind if one of our team came back to see you a little later? You might feel more comfortable talking then."

Again the patient made no response. Rebecca and Abraham set about listening to her chest and heart and completing the other formalities of the examination as they had done many times before. Then Abraham turned to the two daughters and said, "This is a very interesting situation. From our point of view the condition that brought your mother to the hospital has resolved. However, apart from the rather remarkable comment she made to me a few minutes ago, she remains mute and unresponsive. Has she spoken to either of you in any way?"

"No, Doctor. We've been here almost day and night for the last four days. We've sat by her bed and have tried talking with her but she's not made a sound. The poor darling, we can't bear to think what she's going through. Do you still think that she's going to recover?"

"I have to admit that I'm not certain what's going on. There may be more to this than we thought. I assure you that we'll continue looking and will keep you fully informed."

Abraham was struck by the devotion shown by the two women and immediately felt a pang of shame at the way in which, in their first meeting, it now seemed he had so grievously misjudged them. "I appreciate that this is a difficult time for you both," he said. "I can't say how long the process will take; it's possible that it'll be many days before the nature of the illness and the final outcome becomes clear. It's important that you look after yourselves. You'll not be of much use to your mother if you become ill from exhaustion."

"Thank you, Doctor," said the younger sister. "We do appreciate your advice, and I'll make sure we get some rest. But she's our mother and our place in a situation like this is by her side."

The doctors and the nurse moved on to the next patient. "They're very loyal, aren't they?" said Rebecca. "I wish we had a few more families like theirs."

44.

"The next patient's an interesting one," said Rebecca. "I admitted her myself late last night. Her name's Mrs. Simpson. She's a seventy-two-year-old woman with chronic, severely debilitating rheumatoid arthritis who was found unconscious in her bed by her husband. It seems that she's had a devastating stroke. Her husband has a medical power of attorney and he and the rest of the family demanded that no treatment be initiated. As a result, we admitted her to the ward for palliation only."

"This sounds like a straightforward case," said Abraham. "After all the complex and puzzling patients we've had recently I should think we're due for at least one we can understand!" He could see that not only Rebecca but also Desmond and Ashis agreed with him. "Can you tell me anything else you know about her?"

"Well, apparently she used to be very active and vigorous. In fact, in her youth she was a successful sportswoman. I think they said she was a runner. She developed rheumatoid arthritis about twenty years ago that, according to the family, has caused constant pain and significant disability. They're well off and she's seen all the best specialists in town, a few of whom I've spoken to. She's had a number of operations on her hands and neck and she's taken a long list of painkillers, including several different narcotic agents. She was largely confined to a wheelchair, although she could walk short distances with difficulty with a cane.

"Yesterday, things were just the same as ever—or at least that's what they thought. She didn't complain of anything unusual during the day and went to bed about eight, in the usual manner. When her husband came in a couple of hours later he felt that there was something strange about the way she was lying and tried to rouse her but couldn't. She was floppy and didn't respond when he shook her. He called the ambulance, which brought her to the hospital."

Abraham looked at Rebecca's face as she spoke. She was so young, so intense, so earnest! Desmond and Ashis remained silent. In the background, two nurses were moving another elderly patient in her bed. Abraham noticed that the blinds had been drawn against the bright sun outside.

"When she arrived, and when I examined her a little later, she was deeply unconscious. There were no localizing neurological signs to suggest an injury to a particular part of her brain. The blood tests and the CT scan of the head didn't show anything abnormal—although, of course, a stroke doesn't necessarily show in the early phase of injury. Regardless, the staff in the Emergency Department thought that a stroke was most likely and confirmed this with the neuro reg. They told the family they were going to recommend admission to ICU to make sure that she was kept safe while the picture was being clarified.

"But that's when things became complicated." Rebecca's eyes searched Abraham's face. "Mrs. Simpson has three daughters, who are very close, well educated, and articulate. Her husband has medical power of attorney but one of the daughters has taken on the role of family spokesperson. She spoke clearly and authoritatively—and, I have to say, a bit aggressively—declaring that the family didn't want life-preserving treatment and that their mom had made it clear that if she ever had a stroke she wouldn't want to live in a dependent state. As a result, the daughter refused ICU treatment and asked for her mother to be allowed to die. She herself contacted the Freedom to Choose consultant on duty, who came round immediately and helped her fill out their forms."

Sensing Abraham's response, Rebecca added self-consciously, "It turned out to be Susanna, the woman we saw the other day; she was actually quite helpful." She went on: "At the same time, I confirmed that this was the wish of the whole family. Accordingly, we agreed not to pursue treatment and transferred her to the general ward for palliation only."

Her summary finished, Rebecca waited breathlessly for Abraham's response. She evidently expected his praise for the thoroughness she had exercised in managing the admission. She seemed surprised to see that instead he was frowning and shaking his head. "But . . .what's . . . the matter?" she asked tentatively.

Abraham continued to frown. "There's something about this that just doesn't sound right," he said. "I'm not quite sure what it is. It's a bit too neat."

"What do you mean?" she asked. The disappointment showed on her face.

"Let's go through the story step by step," he replied. "She's a seventy-two-year-old woman whose only medical condition is rheumatoid arthritis, which has nonetheless caused severe disability and pain and for which she takes many medications. She was completely well when she went to bed, with no indication of any impending problem. Her husband finds her and recognizes that something's wrong. She undergoes tests which are consistent with a brainstem infarct but not conclusive and the family's adamant that she be allowed to die."

"Yes, that's right," said Rebecca tentatively.

"On the evidence we can't say definitively that she's had a stroke. It might turn out that she has, but all we can do at this stage is infer that this is a likely possibility. The absence of any known underlying condition or pre-existing symptoms or neurological findings apart from unconsciousness would be against this kind of stroke. You're correct that the CT scan wouldn't be expected to show anything yet, but this isn't positive evidence in support of the diagnosis. Accordingly, we'd have to say that there's a reasonable level of uncertainty at this stage.

"Under such conditions, a family's position would normally be to grasp at straws, hoping that the problem was a reversible one, rather than assuming the worst and demanding immediate withdrawal of treatment. Also, it'd be surprising if there was absolute unanimity in a family with respect to such a complex and controversial decision, even if they were close and talked together. It's too neat, too clean."

"But what do you mean? What do you think's happened?"

"I don't know yet. It may well turn out exactly as you've suggested, that she's simply had a devastating stroke from which she'll die. You may be right. But—and I'm only thinking aloud here—from the story you've told me we can't rule out a deliberate act, either by the patient herself or by someone in the family."

"You mean . . . you think . . . that it could be a suicide attempt or . . . attempted . . . attempted . . . ?" Abraham could sense that Rebecca was inwardly burning with shame at the implication that she might have missed something so important.

"Murder is a very strong word, and I certainly don't have any evidence for that. What's more, the fact that the husband called the ambulance so swiftly would be a strong argument against any complicity of his. Let's not speculate too much now. We should see her, look at the test results, and then talk to the family. Are any of them around to talk?"

Desmond, having listened to the whole conversation without comment, now spoke. "I think they're all here. The daughter came up to me just before and said that they wanted to talk with you when you arrived to make sure that the family's wishes were observed. She was with an older man, who I assume is Mrs. Simpson's husband, and two other women."

"Would you be able to take them into the interview room and we'll meet you there in about ten minutes?"

"If you wish," said Desmond. "It's important to talk with the family.

However, if she does turn out to have had a stroke—and it certainly looks like that to me—I think that there's a good enough story to justify withholding treatment, rather than keeping her alive for pure medical vanity."

Abraham felt himself bristle involuntarily. "Let's wait and see," he said. "I suspect that we'll know pretty quickly which way things are going."

Desmond left them and Abraham, Rebecca, and Ashis went to examine the patient and to scrutinize the results so far. They did this rapidly and, as Abraham had anticipated, merely confirmed the findings of the registrar. The patient was exactly as she had described—deeply unconscious but with no evidence of the cause. The neurological examination suggested a major injury to the brain but nothing to localize it to a particular region, as would often be the case in a stroke. The test results were also just as Rebecca had related.

Abraham sensed the skepticism of the other doctors and Rebecca's continuing dismay at his lack of trust in her judgment. He was by no means confident of his intuitions but was now committed at least to talking with the family. The three of them walked briskly to the interview room.

45.

The family was waiting: an old man—probably in his seventies, Abraham thought—and three women, one of whom, younger, sat apart from the rest. Mr. Simpson, bent over, exuded an almost palpable sense of suffering. Each of his hands was held by one of the two older daughters. Abraham asked the man to describe what he had witnessed the previous day.

Although obviously distressed, he spoke softly and clearly. He and his wife had been married for forty-five years and had had the closest and most trusting of relationships. He was a businessman and she had been a teacher. The last twenty years of their life together had been dominated by her illness, which had progressively limited her physical activity and was associated with great pain. The previous day she had seemed her normal self. She had spent the day reading and in the evening they had watched a little television together before she had gone to bed at her usual time. He had noticed nothing untoward during the day and when she had wished him good night it had not occurred to him that he would never talk to her again. His voice cracked as he described the events.

The daughters had little further to add. All lived separately and had not visited their parents for some time. The two older ones—Gillian and Christine—had their own families and their sister Helen, who had returned from overseas only a month or so earlier, lived on the other side of the city. Abraham asked about the patient's state of mind. Her husband stated that she was tired of her illness but otherwise was her usual self.

Abraham then turned to a close questioning of Mr. Simpson about the events of the previous night, asking him to repeat in detail everything he could remember, including words that had been spoken and expressions or gestures that might have seemed untoward. However, he had barely got under way when Gillian—the self-appointed family spokesperson—broke in.

"Professor, we don't need to go into this trivia now," she said testily. "As you will no doubt appreciate, we have all experienced a great shock and have other things to think about. I can't see any value in these discussions now."

Carefully changing the subject, Abraham asked her to explain how her mother had expressed her wishes about medical treatment to the rest of the family. Although Gillian couldn't recall a specific discussion she was adamant that her mother had indicated on a number of occasions that she would prefer to die rather than live in a severely disabled state. Christine added that she had had similar conversations with her mother over the years; Helen remained silent.

Abraham turned his attention one last time to Mr. Simpson. He apologized for adding to his distress but explained that there remained uncertainty about the circumstances of his wife's illness. He asked if he thought she might have been depressed. The husband replied that while she was not happy he did not think she was depressed. Abraham asked directly whether he thought there was any chance that she might have tried to commit suicide. The husband replied that his wife was always meticulous about taking her medications and he had watched her follow her usual routine during the day. Abraham questioned whether he had noticed any evidence around the bed or elsewhere of empty medicine containers and the husband replied that he had looked but had not seen any.

Gillian then broke in again to interrupt Abraham's questions. She spoke precisely, like a lawyer, with an inexplicable undertone of hostility. Her sentences were short and to the point. "My father has power of attorney. It is his view that treatment in the present circumstances would be burdensome and inappropriate. The whole family is in agreement that this is the correct approach to adopt. We love our mother but respect her right to choose how she might live. She has made it clear to all of us that she would not want to continue to live in a debilitated state. We have therefore made the decision to require you to withhold treatment in order to allow her to die peacefully."

Abraham turned once more to the husband. "Mr. Simpson, you're the one who holds power of attorney. Is it your wish to allow your wife to die?"

The old man cried softly. "I'd rather have her with me," he sobbed, "but I know that's a selfish thing to say. I agree with Gillian that the best course of action is to let her go, for her own sake."

Abraham closed the meeting, thanking the family members and apologizing for having subjected them to such close questioning at such a difficult time. He offered his continuing support, which included the possibility of their telephoning him if they wished to discuss anything with him.

"Professor," said Gillian, still talking like a lawyer. "What do you propose to do now? Will you comply with our mother's advance directive and the family's wishes?"

"We've just seen Mrs. Simpson," Abraham answered in a measured tone, "and her condition's stable at the present time. There's no treatment that I'd propose to give her now. However, it's only fair to repeat to you my uncertainty about the diagnosis of a stroke, as a result of which I feel that it would be appropriate to continue to provide hydration and other routine care at the moment. We'll keep a very close eye on her and will tell you immediately if her condition changes."

The staff members said goodbye to the family and left the room. As soon as they were out of earshot of the family members Abraham turned to the others. "What do you think?" he asked.

"I think we should respect the family's and the patient's wishes," the head nurse said.

"What does that mean?"

"I think we should provide comfort care only. If there's any evidence of distress we should treat that in our usual fashion."

Abraham thought aloud. "She doesn't have signs of a brainstem injury and the story of floppiness is inconsistent with a stroke. When I went into the room I wouldn't have been surprised to find that one or more of the family might have turned out to have been involved in whatever's happened, but I now think that's very unlikely. The husband's truly shocked by the turn of events and is only interested in doing what's best for his wife. He genuinely loves her. None of the daughters has been near the house for at least a week, so they haven't been involved in any foul play. There's something going on with Helen that I'm not sure about, and it's possible that she knows something more. I suspect, however, that we'll find out the answer soon enough if we just wait.

"For the moment, we won't withdraw care. We'll continue to provide whatever support the patient needs. We need to observe her closely, at least every half hour. I myself will come back and review her this afternoon."

"But aren't you going against the patient's and the family's wishes? After all, the husband has power of attorney, which gives him the legal right to refuse treatment."

"That's true, but we don't know what's going on here. Neither of us is in a position to decide to withdraw treatment until the facts are clear."

Desmond looked like he was going to explode. Rebecca, apparently still smarting from Abraham's rebuff to her, looked inconsolable. Abraham half closed his eyes and turned his head away to make it clear that he had made up his mind.

46.

"We have your favorite patient for you today again," said Jenny. "She's already here."

"Ah, Mrs. Timoshenko! How nice to see you! Please come in."

"Professor Nevski, I am so sick. Please help me!"

Abraham was once again on familiar territory. He relaxed into his chair, waiting for the inevitable monologue to be unleashed.

"I have terrible diarrhea. I have to go to the toilet twenty times a day. The stools are loose and pale. I am sure that I have malabsorption syndrome . . . I may also have an inflammatory bowel disease . . . I mentioned this to Professor Ricardo and he agreed that I should have a colonoscopy . . ."

The monotone continued as usual, unvarying, unceasing, inexorable. It was always the same: the lists of symptoms, the diagnoses, the tests, the scientific-sounding language. Abraham marveled at her command of the medical vocabulary. She knew more Latin terms than he did, archaic words which, no doubt on the authority of her anachronistic texts, she would employ as if anyone might use them in everyday language: abscessus, cochleare, alvus, decessus, marasmus, morbus, pabulum, tussis . . .

He recalled the discussions they had had over the years about literature and philosophy. She once told him that she knew *The Brothers Karamazov* almost by heart and to prove it recited a long tract from the section on the Grand Inquisitor. She was excited to hear of Abraham's interest in the philosopher Mikhail Bakhtin, who had lectured at her university and whom she had revered. He tried to imagine her as a young woman—vivacious, iconoclastic, sexually promiscuous, full of ideals and the determination to change the world.

"I think that my thyroid is overactive. I have many symptoms of thyrotoxicosis. I've lost weight. I have palpitations. My heart is heavy as my age is weak. It beats very fast for no reason. I timed it at a hundred and twenty in the night. It also beats very irregularly. I think that I might have atrial fibrillation. Can you order an ECG and a Holter monitor? I mentioned this to Dr. Bauer and he agreed that it should be done. Atrial fibrillation is very common in thyroid disease. I sweat all the time, for no reason, even when it's cold. That's not normal. Dr. Goldstein said that it could be due to thyrotoxicosis. Also, I cannot sleep. I lie awake for hours with my palpitations and my diarrhea and my polyuria . . ."

For years, Abraham had struggled to decipher the confused logic in Ursula's discourse. He had attempted to convert her ramblings into rigorous propositions—about her medical condition, about investigative strategies, about therapeutics, and to argue with her about the facts, to convince her that his recommendations were scientifically sound. Gradually he had come to understand that her use of the medical language was not to formulate rigorous propositions but simply as a mode of expression, as a vehicle to convey exactly the meanings that it sought systematically to suppress.

"I have a cough. I have never had a cough before. I can't stop coughing. Doctor, I sometimes think I'm going to choke. I cough up white sputum. It has small flecks of blood in it. When I was young we used to smoke and I was always exposed to other people smoking. Wherever we went there was smoke. Coughing up blood—hemoptysis—is a very dangerous sign. It commonly occurs with lung cancer or serious infections . . ."

She was not talking of disturbances in tissues, of molecular mechanisms gone awry, of interruptions to homeostatic processes. Her language, with its strange cadences and improbable connections, was not a scientific one. Her words were not signifiers of biological facts, carriers of empirical data. Rather, they welled up and burst forth from a deep source, as the eructation of some distant past, hidden in the mists of memory and fading time. Like the language of her beloved Dostoyevsky and Proust, they were a music of the soul—the sounds, at least, of her soul. An improbable music, to be sure, and one not understood by most of the people who met her.

" . . . I'm sure I had a fever the night before last. I was so hot when I was in bed. But it was not just hot. I was shivery, even though I was hot. This means that I must have had a fever. A fever could be caused by a lung infection. I'm worried about serious lung infections. Tuberculosis—it is *La Belle Dame Sans Merci*—is becoming common, and many people had it when I was growing up. It can cause a cough and fever and hemoptysis and weight loss. I need to have tests for that. We need to do microbiological studies and a CT of the chest. I have discussed this with Professor Ricardo and he agreed that it would be a good idea . . ."

Like the ancient languages of worship, her song—yes, she was singing—was an act of offering that carried its meaning in the medium of the utterance and not in the actual words themselves. It was like a sacred chant that called up the knowledge and experience of the ages. Like the prayers of the ancients it was inexorable, opaque. It employed the form and vocabulary of modern speech but spoke of times and places long gone.

"I'm worried about my kidney. Abraham, I only have one kidney. The other one was removed because of cancer. Cancer of the kidney is often not cured and can recur after many years. It can show itself in pain and weakness and hematuria and arthritis and shortness of breath and swelling of the ankles, and in the many other shocks that flesh is heir to. Swelling of the ankles!

Every night when I go to bed—I go to bed even though I don't sleep—my ankles are swollen. Sometimes I can hardly see them. I have pitting edema. This is a common sign of kidney disease and heart failure . . ."

Abraham could feel in his own body the deep residues of pain and sorrow of which Ursula sang. The tragic music conjured up the timeless suffering of generations of men and women, of ancient peoples displaced from their homes, of dispossession, of the murder of children, of atrocities too terrible to name. This was, however, not like the ancient incantations: it was not a song of praise to the grandeur of a God, or to a promise of eternal salvation. It was a song of despair, of the end of hope, of defeat and ultimate ruin.

"I'm very worried about my blood vessels. I'm sure I have atherosclerosis. My cholesterol is very high. Look, here's the result. The cholesterol is 5.8. Dr. Bauer says it should not be higher than 5.5. He says that this means that I have a high chance of having atherosclerosis. I think that my father had a heart problem too. He died when I was ten so I'm at high risk of heart disease myself. Yevgeny too has artery disease. Yesterday he was too weak to hold the violin. I also have shortness of breath and a cough. This is probably a sign of heart failure. The water in the lungs will be shown with the CT scan . . ."

In the scant interstices of her monologue Ursula pleaded for love and to be cared for. She yearned for the world she had briefly glimpsed but which had never been realized. In her song of melancholy desire she was calling out: "care for me, hold me, love me."

The phone rang. Abraham, jolted, picked it up. It was Jenny, his secretary. "Abraham, what are you doing? You have a room full of people waiting to see you. You have to keep moving!"

"Er . . . I'm sorry, Jenny. We must have lost track of the time. We're just about to finish now."

He turned back to the old woman, who had scarcely registered the interruption. "Mrs. Timoshenko, I have to finish right away. Is there anything you'd like me to do today?"

She took no notice of him. Instead, she went on, as if in a trance. "I have severe pain in the abdomen. Professor Ricardo thinks I should have another gastroscopy. The last one I had was in 2006 and he couldn't see the duodenum properly . . ."

Abraham stood up to emphasize that the time was up. He felt completely enervated. "I'm happy to refer you back to Professor Ricardo to discuss another gastroscopy. I wouldn't make that decis—"

"Dr. Goldstein also thinks I need a plasma electrophoresis. I—"

Abraham was at the door. "Mrs. Timoshenko, I don't want to sound rude but I do need to move on. I'm happy for you to call me whenev—"

"And the dizziness—"

"Look, you'll have to excuse me. I've just been advised that I have to go to see a serious case in the ward. I have to go. Please take your time. I'll be happy to see you in three months." And he walked out of the door himself, not knowing how he could otherwise resolve the impasse.

His last view of Mrs. Timoshenko was of her poring over her results sheets preparing for the next stage in her monologue.

47.

Abraham called in a middle-aged man he had not seen before—large and ruddy faced, with a slightly unkempt suit and tie. Abraham noticed that he walked in a hunched manner, avoiding eye contact with the other patients. The man entered the consulting room and settled down gratefully in the protected seclusion of the armchair.

"Hello, I'm Abraham Nevski. I'm pleased to meet you." He stopped and waited for the patient to talk. As it happened, he was bursting to do so and commenced with an energy and compulsiveness—and a loud voice—that caught Abraham by surprise.

"My lawyer suggested I come to see you," he said. "I've been charged before the Registration Board. I need to talk with someone about ethical behavior, someone who'll write a report about how I'm doing—"

"Perhaps you should start from the beginning and tell me the whole story," Abraham interrupted. "When you've finished we can discuss what I might be able to do to help."

"It's a long story," the man boomed. "I'm sixty-one. I was born in the United Kingdom. When I was eighteen I had a relationship with a girl. Just as the relationship was ending she became pregnant. We agreed that we couldn't afford to keep a baby and she decided to put it up for adoption. I didn't see her after we split up and I never saw the baby." The patient was talking very fast, with hardly a break between his sentences. Abraham felt the intensity of his speech almost as a physical force.

He continued with the same urgency, although a little more softly. A few years later, he explained, he had moved to Australia, where he went to the university and eventually began a medical course. He completed his training as a general practitioner and set up practice in a working-class suburb. He loved his work and believed that he was good at it, often working up to seventy-five hours a week. He had lots of girlfriends but never married. One day, in about 1994, he received a phone call. It was a woman's voice. She said that Quentin didn't know her but that she wanted to meet him. He wondered if it was some kind of hoax or prank but nonetheless agreed to meet her at a café in the city at a certain time.

"I didn't know who she was," he went on, "how old she was or what she looked like. I got there early and studied every woman who came in. None seemed to be of interest until one young woman walked in and my heart froze. She was the most wonderful, most beautiful woman I had ever seen. I was completely overwhelmed. I didn't know where I was or what I was doing. It wasn't sexual; it was spiritual. She was radiant, almost glowing with beauty. She walked straight up to me without looking at anyone else in the restaurant and said, 'You must be Quentin. Hello, I'm Doreen. Margaret told me about you. I hope you don't mind my seeking you out.' I still didn't understand and could hardly speak. I didn't know what was happening."

It turned out that she was the daughter he had never met. She had been adopted at birth and was brought up in a family in which she was comfortable but never really happy. She had studied nursing and worked in hospitals around London. Her adoptive parents were kind but uninspiring, and when she was eighteen they told her that she had been adopted. She wasn't surprised or upset about that; in fact, she thought it explained many things—her isolation, her sense of not fitting in with the family, of looking at the world from the outside. She decided that she wanted to look for her parents, but at that time adopted children were not permitted to contact their biological parents. She was unhappy about this but got on with her life. A few years later, when she was twenty-four, they changed the law so that people were entitled to find their parents. She put in an application and about six months later was contacted by the Department of Social Welfare. Apparently her birth mother had agreed to meet her. They had a good meeting, as a result of which she has established a continuing but not very close relationship. Doreen asked Margaret—the birth mother—who her father was. At first, all Margaret told her was Quentin's name and Doreen tried to find him in the phone book. She rang all the people with his name but got nowhere. She went back to Margaret, who then said that she thought he might have moved to Australia.

Doreen pressed Margaret for more details and Margaret eventually contacted someone in Quentin's family—an elderly aunt, who was still alive—who told her that he had gone to Sydney about twenty years previously. So Doreen got on a plane and came to Sydney to continue her search.

He paused for a breath. Abraham remained silent. Quentin went on in the same pressured manner. "It took me some time to recover my senses. I can't even remember how I replied. For many years I hadn't given a thought to the child I'd never met. I was dumbfounded. On that first occasion we talked and we talked and we talked. It was like a miracle, as if we'd known each other all our lives. Time seemed to evaporate. I remember looking at my watch at one point and being astounded that five hours had passed. Eventually, it was late and we said goodbye, agreeing to meet a few days later. The experience was so overwhelming I needed time to recover, to make sense of what had happened, and I'm sure she did, too. Over the next few days that first meeting began to seem like a dream; in fact, I started to wonder whether it had really happened. However, when we did meet again it was just the same: she was just as beautiful and our connection was just as strong."

Abraham, spellbound, scrutinized him carefully as he kept talking. He seemed to be in a kind of trance, completely engrossed in his memories. The words were tumbling out of his mouth, in quick succession as if no effort was needed to produce them. His look was far away.

Over the next two or three months they had seen each other regularly. They had a sense of danger and knew that they needed to take great care. They had no idea where things would lead. However, a force had been released that they couldn't resist. They met, they talked, they went out to restaurants, to movies, to concerts together.

"I introduced Doreen to my friends but, of course, we didn't tell them the background to our growing relationship. We were careful not to have any but the most formal, proper physical contact with each other. But at the same time a love was growing, an intense, powerful love like I've never known, before or since. We became very comfortable in each other's presence, which was natural because we were spending so much time together. I was working just as hard as ever, but during the day I felt uplifted, intoxicated, as if I was being carried on a cloud.

"One day, we were at my house sitting on the floor watching television. I don't know how it happened. We were sitting near each other, but apart. I can't remember what we were watching. One of us must have moved, perhaps just by accident, and our shoulders touched, ever so slightly. It was like an electric shock passing through my body, and I could tell that Doreen had the same feeling. We turned and looked into each other's eyes. The moment was irresistible. It was like in a movie. We could have been watching ourselves on television. We kissed, lightly at first, then more deeply, a kiss like I had never imagined possible. We held each other tightly, silently, for many minutes. We knew we were in danger but there was nothing we could do about it.

"We made love that night. It was the most beautiful experience I have ever had. But I knew—we both knew—that we were on the verge of an abyss. That's where I am now: on the edge of the unknown, about to plunge into territory we had never before visited."

The man's face was glowing. He was reliving events that no doubt he had already retraced many times. It occurred to Abraham, who felt the discomfort of having intruded into a deeply private experience, that Quentin had forgotten about his presence altogether. But as the man paused, he urged gently, "Go on."

"Doreen moved into my place and for three years we lived in perfect happiness. Well, maybe 'perfect' is an exaggeration, because we carried our dark secret with us wherever we went. We were always concerned that our friends would suspect the truth—even though that was unlikely, because there was in fact little physical resemblance between us. We felt an abiding guilt about what we were doing. We knew that society would disapprove of our relationship but at the backs of our minds we also hoped that the purity of our love could overcome everything.

"After three years she became pregnant. This greatly magnified both the joy and the terror we'd already experienced, to the point where these emotions became almost unbearable. We had no one to confide in, no one to talk to. At first, I thought that we—she—should seek a termination, but after talking with Doreen I realized that this would be very damaging. For me, this was a repetition of what had happened twenty-eight years previously. She could only say that she was glad that her mother's pregnancy had not been terminated. We decided to go ahead and have the baby. I'm convinced that this was the right decision. The baby was born into a space filled with the love of his father and mother, both for each other and for him. He was wanted in a way that my daughter had not been wanted, and maybe I myself had not been wanted."

Abraham was simultaneously mesmerized and appalled. He tried to imagine what it would be like to find oneself in a relationship of such intensity and perversity, but he was unable to do so. He shifted uneasily, searching for a way to intervene, but Quentin went on.

"We continued to live as a family, with unabated affection, care, and commitment, but now the doubts and fears accumulated ever more rapidly. We tried to find a way out, for example by convincing ourselves that maybe we were not really father and daughter, that there'd been some mistake, or even a malign conspiracy. When precise genetic testing became available we decided to submit to a test, knowing that our fates hung in the balance. I remember the sense of foreboding when I delivered the samples to the lab. I felt that all the joy we'd experienced, the easy, natural connection with Doreen, the deep love and commitment to our son Benjamin, the early mistakes that had caused her such suffering but which had been partly expiated by the miraculous time we'd spent together, the void of pain and neglect that had been filled by a plenitude of care—I felt that this was about to be dissipated, annulled, as if it had never happened, as if it had been no more than a wonderful dream.

"My dark forebodings were not misplaced. The test came back positive. I opened the letter myself. The result, typed in bold black capitals—POSITIVE—remains ingrained in my memory. Maybe it was positive for them; for us, it was as negative as anything could ever be. It was like a judge donning a black cap. My head spun, the earth seemed to swallow me up. I was falling into that abyss. I knew that there would be no way out."

His voice now changed. He had recounted the events as if they related to a fairy tale, which just happened to be his life. Now he was reaching the conclusion of his narrative, which Abraham knew would be grim. Like a child listening to a story where the worst was yet to come, he braced himself.

"After that, it was only a matter of time. Doreen went back to England, but we couldn't last and she returned to Australia; then she left again. Eventually, we settled on an arrangement whereby we'd live apart and try to build separate lives, but I'd see Benjamin at least two or three times a year and I'd continue to support both of them. I cannot tell you how black those next few years were. When one thinks of falling through space one imagines that it'll last only for a few seconds, maybe for a few minutes at most, even if it ends badly. Doreen and I were spinning, plunging through the abyss, for months, for years. There was nothing but blackness. The space that had been filled with hope and promise and love had been replaced by a vacuum."

The intensity was now blunted, as if it had expended itself in the fire and poignancy of the words just uttered. He now spoke more slowly, laboring his words, which hung heavily in the air. Abraham, still engrossed, became aware that he could hardly bear to hear what would happen next. He felt—he couldn't say why—that he was going through the experience himself, that it was his story that was being told. He tried deliberately to retrieve his clinical objectivity. He hoped that the patient had not noticed how involved he had become.

"Both of us found other relationships, and both of us married. Inevitably, both marriages were unhappy. We both told our spouses our secret. Doreen is still with her husband, although the relationship is a loveless one. My marriage ended in total disaster. My wife always knew that she could never replace Doreen and was wildly jealous of her, even though they'd never met. She couldn't bear the unbreakable bond she knew we had with each other. The hostility grew and when she left me and filed for divorce she cited my relationship with Doreen as the precipitating cause. I tried to be magnanimous, but she wanted retribution. She reported Doreen's and my relationship to the police and to the Medical Registration Board. At first, they took no action, but she pursued the matter relentlessly. She vowed that she'd destroy me and Doreen and what was left of our relationship. After years of her agitation the police took up the matter and I was charged with incest, with the further claim that my supposed moral turpitude inevitably puts my patients at risk.

"The case is to come up in a few weeks. Doreen has offered to come over to give evidence but I've insisted that she be spared this pain and indignity, so she's written a letter to the judge that we'll present in lieu of her appearance in person. Here's the letter in case you want to read it. At the least, it'll support the veracity of the facts I have reported to you. If I'm found guilty I'm fearful that I will therefore also be prevented from practicing as a doctor.

"That's why I'm here. My lawyer says that I need to find an expert witness to testify that I'm not a danger to my patients. You're famous for your work in ethics and we thought that maybe I could talk with you a few times and you could write a report saying what you think about my personal qualities and ethical standards. My life has come full circle. I'm deeply humiliated. I've lost everything. Are you prepared to help me?"

He stopped talking. Both of them remained silent. Abraham realized that he was expected to say something.

Like the speaker himself, he felt enervated and depleted by the animated confession. As a professional witness he knew the danger in this moment—the danger of succumbing to the temptation to provide comfort, to demonstrate empathy. As on countless previous occasions he struggled to resist the urge to affirm the patient's experience, to come directly to his aid.

A full two minutes passed. The two men sat looking at each other. Eventually, Abraham spoke. "Thanks for your story," he said. "I'll take it on." He paused for another moment, then added, "I'll read Doreen's letter. If you have any further material, as I'm sure you will, I'll be keen to read that, too. We'll need to meet a few times. I'll ask you questions and engage you in conversation about matters of ethics. At the end, I'll be prepared to give evidence in person or write a report.

"You need to be aware, of course, that I'll report the facts as I see them, and that I make no commitment in advance to a favorable assessment. It's important that you understand this. If you're comfortable with this arrangement I suggest that you talk with my secretary and arrange the appointments over the next couple of weeks. Are you happy to proceed in this way?"

The response was weak and undramatic, but at least Abraham had not given anything away. The patient was in any case by now too distracted to do anything else but accept. "Thank you," he murmured. "I'm sorry to have gone on so long. I'll send you all the materials and make the appointments. I'm sincerely appreciative of the fact that you at least take me seriously."

"I can assure you of that without hesitation," Abraham replied, relieved that he was now back on more secure ground. "I appreciate that it's been difficult for you to tell your story with such force and detail. I look forward to our next meeting." He rose, to indicate that the consultation had ended, and the patient—himself, no doubt, familiar with such signals—also rose. They shook hands and Quentin left the room. Abraham sat for a few moments, composing himself. He looked at his watch. He still had several people to see before taking the students. He let out an audible sigh and went to call the next patient.

48.

Out at the reception desk, Jenny was anxious to talk to Abraham. "I have a message for you from Rebecca," she said. "She wonders if you could telephone her before your session with the students."

He called the registrar. "Thanks for ringing, Prof," she said. "It's my afternoon off, and I was hoping to be able to get to a class and wanted to update you on our patients before I headed off. I hope you don't mind.

"Most of our patients are pretty much the same as they were this morning. Ashis has done all the jobs we gave him to do. Four people have gone home. Mrs. Simpson's still unconscious." Her voice cracked. "But something unexpected's happened. Mr. Tzorvas—the man with the pain in his side—died early this afternoon."

Abraham was shocked. "What? Mr. Tzorvas? How could that be possible?"

Rebecca registered his dismay. "I'm as amazed as you are. Apparently after we saw him the Freedom to Choose people came to see him—they must have been scanning the notes—and told him that the doctors had decided that his condition was terminal. They talked with him and his wife and they signed the forms to stop treatment except for the morphine. The next thing I heard he was dead."

Abraham had a strange feeling of disorientation, which resembled nausea, a bit like after his wife died. He had spent years struggling against the very idea of Freedom to Choose and now its agents were taking over the management of his own patients. They were even stalking the wards to inveigle them to sign away treatment plans on which he had already signed off.

But even worse than this was what this case showed him about himself. This morning he had marveled at his own power to pronounce a death sentence—as with the man in the Emergency Department that day before Christmas—but now it was his impotence that was overwhelming him. He had known Mr. Tzorvas was sick but he had had no idea that he was hours minutes—away from death. Was there something crucial he had missed? Maybe he hadn't examined him carefully enough. Maybe there was a test they could have done that would have shown why he was in such pain. Maybe there'd been an urgent, reversible problem that had escaped his attention. Abraham's entire power lay in his clinical skills, in his ability to assess a patient and in his capacity to reason. If he made critical mistakes like this he had nothing left. Above all, he hated being wrong.

He thought of the monthly audit meeting where the other doctors would subject his judgments to detailed criticism. He would have to justify, to make excuses for, his mistakes and omissions. His face burned in anticipation. "How could that be?" was all he could say. "This morning things looked bad, but there was no evidence of a problem that was imminently threatening his life."

People don't just die, even when they are sick. They hang on to life: the more dire their condition, the more tenaciously they cling. He could see Desmond's smugness and the Freedom to Choose consultant's satisfaction. It almost seemed to be the outcome they wanted. He had to appear to Rebecca to be coolly under control.

"I suppose this shows how complex clinical practice really is," he said insincerely. "Sometimes unexpected things happen. I suppose we have to look on the bright side. We'd correctly concluded that there was a terminal process. This way, he's been spared a lot of pain."

"I'm glad you say that," said Rebecca, the strain still obvious in her voice. "I was hoping it wasn't my fault, that I hadn't missed something I ought to have seen. The family is pretty desolated but Des and I have been trying to explain to them how he's been saved a great deal of suffering."

Abraham winced as he hung up the phone. Two deaths, Desmond, the Freedom to Choose consultants. It was not his best day.

49.

"Bruno, tell me what you know about Mr. Adams."

"Mr. Adams is a middle-aged man—I'd say about fifty. He's a thin man of slight build lying comfortably in bed, connected to a heart monitor and with an intravenous infusion, through which he's receiving . . . err . . . the anticoagulant heparin. I can see from the card above his bed that he was admitted to the hospital two days ago under the General Surgical Unit. I can also see that he's undergone a recent operation and has a horizontal row of staples closing a wound about ten centimeters long in the lower part of his neck . . ."

As Bruno was talking Abraham's mind was wandering. Two unexpected deaths in one day. How could that be possible? And what could it mean? Very little occurs in the clinic without warning. Being able to predict what will happen next—what the ancient Greeks referred to as "prognosis"—is one of the most ancient of the medical arts, much older than therapeutics, the science of treatment. Obviously, not everything can be cured, but it's rare for someone to die unexpectedly, or at least without the appearance of the well-documented clinical signs. Two patients! What was he doing wrong? Was he losing his clinical skills? Abraham thought again of the monthly audit meeting and shrank with embarrassment. He would have to try to excuse himself, like the countless lesser physicians whom he himself had persecuted in audit sessions over the years.

Bruno was still talking. "In addition, because he has his pajama shirt unbuttoned I'm able to observe that he's had previous chest surgery—from the scar, most likely a heart operation. In fact, as I listen closely I can hear a tapping sound, which may well indicate an artificial heart valve. Looking around the room I can see no signs of additional illnesses, such as diabetes or asthma, for example in the form of blood testing equipment or inhalers, and there are no walking aids or other paraphernalia that might provide clues about his functional capacity . . ."

Most patients who came to the hospital were cured, or at least recovered enough to go home. The daily business of clinical medicine was, like most jobs, routine and unremarkable. It was only when things went wrong that one became aware of what one was taking for granted. Abraham was usually confident of his judgments, but now, today, he was not so sure. He looked at the patient on the bed in front of him. Would he, too, be dead tomorrow?

" . . . On the bedside table is a book about animals in Africa and a pair of spectacles and the remains of his breakfast. And there's a photograph of a dog. However, I can't see any flowers or other evidence of his relationships with family or friends, so I can't comment on that."

Bruno stopped, flushed with his success. Abraham, stirred from his own reverie, tried to look pleased, too. The students were obviously learning their lessons well and had greatly improved their powers of observation. "That's excellent, Bruno," he said, with a weak smile. "I couldn't have done better myself. Congratulations. You've noticed even quite subtle things." This was familiar ground for Abraham. "Now, are you able to tell me what it all means?"

"Er . . . Mr. Adams . . . had a heart operation some time ago . . . and now has had an operation on his neck . . . Could that be his thyroid . . . ?" Bruno was deflated by the additional challenge.

Abraham was struggling to return to the present. "That's correct. Would anyone else like to add any further interpretations?" he asked the remainder of the group. There was silence.

The students were looking to him for help. Of course, they expected him to know the answers to his own questions. He needed to show them—and himself—that he was in control, that he had not lost his powers.

"Well," he went on as usual, "let me have a go, and then we can ask Mr. Adams some questions." The pressure was on him now, but the role of sleuth was one he knew well. He narrowed his eyes slightly and focused his mind completely on the task at hand, computing the clues mercilessly. The words came out almost mechanically.

"I believe Mr. Adams was born with a congenital heart abnormality, for which he underwent an operation to replace a defective valve some years ago. My reason for thinking this is that the chest scar is old, meaning the heart problem developed many years ago, probably when he was a young man. His slight build suggests that his growth may have been impaired by illness, supporting the congenital hypothesis and making other causes of heart disease—such as infective and autoimmune causes—less likely. He had an artificial valve installed; I can tell that from the sound it's making, as well as from the presence of the heparin infusion, which isn't needed with natural valves. I speculate that in spite of the valve replacement he's had ongoing problems with his heart—maybe arrhythmias or irregular rhythms, which became sufficiently serious to require administration of a drug called amiodarone. I further speculate that he developed a side effect of this drug, thyrotoxicosis, or hyperactivity of the thyroid. His thinness and slightly drawn facial appearance suggest recent weight loss, supporting this hypothesis. The thyrotoxicosis associated with amiodarone can be difficult to treat and may require surgery to remove most of the thyroid, which is undoubtedly the operation that's just been performed. The operation's been successful, in that Mr. Adams is able to eat and drink freely, as indicated by the breakfast dishes. However, I note from the heart monitor that the heart rate is still fast, indicating that his thyroid hormone levels are still high; this is expected because these take some time to fall—days or even weeks. All other things being equal, I'd expect him to be able to go home within the next day or so."

Abraham stopped, aware from the students' faces of the mixture of admiration and despair they were experiencing. Just when they thought that they had made real progress with their clinical skills they found that their knowledge was still at best only very rudimentary. They were wishing they already had his skill, his certainty.

Assuming his well-practiced air of modesty, he reassured them. "Of course, I realize that you'd not have known a lot of what I just said. That depends on specialized knowledge. In any case, I may be mistaken in my inferences. Let's ask Mr. Adams himself. Mr. Adams, did I get any of the facts right in my summary?" He was professorial again now.

"I couldn't understand the technical language, but I think you were exactly right."

"Thank you. Why don't we take a history? Tracey, I think it's your turn to ask some questions . . ."

"Thanks, Prof . . . Hello, Mr. Adams, my name's Tracey. Do you mind if I ask you a few questions?"

"Nah, go ahead. But call me Pete. That's me name."

"Okay, thanks. Can I ask you how old you are, Pete?"

"I'm forty-eight."

"What was it that brought you to the hospital on this occasion?"

Abraham looked at Tracey. She was young, luscious, and vivacious, glowing with health and vigor. Would she be dead tomorrow, like Mrs. Gurewitz and Mr. Tzorvas? He imagined her, like Ophelia, floating down a river, covered in flowers.

"I had an overactive thyroid and needed an operation to remove it."

"What were the symptoms you were experiencing?"

"I was hot 'n' sweaty 'n' losing weight and me heart was beating fast."

"Do you know why you became . . . why your thyroid became overactive?"

"It was jes like ya professor said: it was because of the heart drug I was takin'."

" . . . And what about your heart condition? I mean, did he . . . er . . . were we right about that?"

"About me having been born with a heart problem? Yeah, that was right too."

"Can you tell us about that? I mean, when it started and what happened after that."

"Me heart condition? Sure. I was always sick, even as a little kid. I was always tired 'n' thin. I could never walk or run like the other kids. But it wasn't until I was about six that me parents took me to the doctor. He looked me over and said he thought I had a heart problem. I then had to go for lots of tests and see lots of specialists. After that, I had to take lots of tablets and I wasn't ever allowed to do sports. They said that they'd have to operate eventually, but they didn't want to until I'd stopped growing. I was so sick I didn't actually grow all that much anyway, as you can see. But I had the operation in the end when I was twenty-one."

"And how've you been since then?"

"I was a bit better but not normal. I still can't walk far, and the heart goes a bit crazy from time to time. That's why I had to take that drug with the long name."

Abraham could see that the man was becoming a bit impatient with the student's questions, which he had no doubt answered many times in the past.

He felt that in any case the main details of the case had been fully explained. He was genuinely pleased with Bruno's initial attempts to decipher the clues available—it at least showed that he was on the right track. He was also relieved that he had been able in his distracted state to piece together the details of the whole complex story without the students noticing anything untoward. Attempting to bring the session to a conclusion he asked, or rather stated, with a tone of finality in his voice, "Okay, that's good. Does anyone have a last question to ask Mr. Adams?" Without concealing what he was doing he looked at his watch.

"I just have one more question." It was Tracey, who was back from the river. "Pete . . . I was thinking . . . you were sick as a child, you've been sick all your life . . . What's it been like . . . to have a heart problem like this?"

With barely a moment's hesitation the patient replied, simply, "It's wrecked me whole life."

He went on. "I'm nearly fifty and I've not been well for a single moment in all that time. You kids take being healthy for granted—or, at least, I imagine you do. You can do anything you want. You're studying to be doctors. I've spent me whole life—since pretty well as far back as I can remember—going to doctors, being tested, taking drugs, getting sick, and staying in bed trying to get well enough just to be able to breathe normally. I couldn't do sports. I couldn't go out with girls. I couldn't study. I was the black sheep in the family, the odd one out in the school. I was the poor sucker who was in and out of hospital; that was all I was to them, to me family, me friends, me teachers.

"All I wanted was to work with animals. My dream was to be a vet. I would have loved that. I like every type of animal. I can understand them and they seem to be able to understand me. But to be a vet you need to do well in school, or have lots of money."

He stopped briefly. There was a deep silence.

"Me parents were poor," Mr. Adams continued. "They had to spend a lot of money on medical costs—and even though I really tried I was never well enough to succeed. In me last year in school I was in hospital three times. I studied as much as I could and didn't do too badly, but it wasn't good enough to get into university. It wouldn't have worked anyway 'cause the next year I was even sicker, and the year after that I had the op. So I've never been able to work."

He paused for a moment. No one said anything. He went on. "Me dad died a few years ago and me mom's old now, so I had to move out of home. I live by meself—or rather, I live with me animals. I got lots of them—at last count thirty-one in all. I got a dog, Mavis—that's her in the picture there. She's half border collie and half kelpie. She's a good dog, clever and very loyal. I also got three cats, fifteen fish, and twelve birds. They're me family. They're all I got."

He went on. "I got a bit lost there. You asked about what it was like. I guess I've answered yer question. They can fix me thyroid, or whatever, give me new miracle drugs as they come out. But they can't fix me life. They can't give me the only thing I've ever wanted: just to live normally."

There was another silence. Abraham was reeling, horrified at his own lack of insight. He felt humiliated at the facile manner in which he had presented the man's problems, as if he were just a medical case, a purely technical device, ignoring the deep well of experience of which the physical phenomena were no more than the outward signs.

Mr. Adams was sitting motionless, staring impassively into space. Abraham breathed in deeply and, shaking his head slowly, spoke plainly. "Thank you, Pete," he said, with genuine feeling. "You've taught us—including me— an important lesson." Then he stood very erect in an attempt to convey a semblance of control and led the students from the room.

50.

It had been a terrible day and, despite his exhaustion, Abraham still had work to do before visiting his father in the hospital. He returned to his office and, to help collect his thoughts, he poured himself a whisky, put on some music, and sat down briefly in one of the armchairs. As he sat meditatively, his eyes caught sight of the letter given to him by Quentin Prince, which he had absentmindedly put down on the desk. He picked it up and started reading, perfunctorily at first.

To the Presiding Judge,

My name is Doreen. I was adopted at five weeks old. When I was 24, living in London, I made contact with my biological mother through an adoption agency. We had an intense reunion, complicated by our mutual mixed feelings and expectations. She said she was thrilled to find her long lost daughter but I was unsure as to how to be a

daughter to someone who was a stranger to me. A tumultuous year ensued as we struggled to process our feelings.
During this time I developed an overwhelming need also to
find my Father and to understand why he had not been
there when I had so much needed him.

My biological mother told me that Quentin had moved to
Australia and, after many months of agonizing, I decided
to go there to try to find him to fill the hole in my life. I knew
the city where he was living and his name but nothing else.
It wasn't easy. I telephoned everyone in the entire city with
his surname. I visited addresses that I had been given and
questioned people in the street just in case they might have
heard of him. I spent hours in my hotel room crying, in
panic and despair, wondering how it was all going to end.

Eventually, though, I did make contact and we met on
July 14th, 1994. It was a Thursday. The meeting was like
a miracle. I felt an instant mutual attraction to him. My
feelings were overwhelming. It was surreal. Quentin was
the most intelligent, humorous, charismatic man I had
ever met. Much more than that was the almost immediate sense of closeness, attachment, intimacy, and fascination that I felt, which was so different to the way one
would expect to feel on meeting one's Father. Amazingly,
he felt the same toward me. From the outset we agonized
about the strong feelings we were experiencing. How could
this be? Neither of us had felt such an easy and natural
bond with another before. But we were both confused and
scared. It was too much to bear and I decided to return to
continue nursing in London. Early the next year I went
to Australia again for three weeks. Our bond intensified
and we were in turmoil as to how to deal with the situation.
I returned to the UK and found out I had won a competition
in a national magazine. The prize was a beauty therapy
diploma course in London. By the time I had completed the
course in July 1995 I had made plans to go to Australia to
work as a Nurse.

Quentin and I lived together. Our relationship deepened

and we began to question the dates Margaret had given about the pregnancy. She had announced that she was pregnant just as Quentin was about to go to Australia to work with his uncle. Had she lied about who the Father was? There were no DNA tests in the '60s and false paternity claims were not uncommon. As Quentin was the son of a Doctor maybe she thought it would benefit her? We checked the dates the best we could and felt that there was indeed a basis for doubt. Still, as we quietly lived our life together, I was tortured by the clear possibility that it could still be true, despite our fervent hopes. I had the Father I had dreamed of as a little girl. He was there to look after me, care for me, love me. But he was also my husband and I loved him dearly with every particle in my body.

Eventually, the stress became too much to bear. We made the terrible decision to part. The day before I left for England, I found out that I was pregnant. I left anyway, full of trepidation and uncertainty as to what to do next. We had many long, agonizing phone calls. I got a job in a hospital in London. There was no way I would give up a child for adoption after what I had been through myself. Also, I was reluctant, having lost my Love, to have an abortion, and what's more, I'd often felt grateful I had not been terminated myself. I was bleeding a lot and I thought I was losing the baby. I had numerous scans and against the odds the fetus kept growing. As a woman with a life inside me I found myself willing it to survive.

I had no support in London and my parents were very cold towards me and it was winter. I decided, when I was 6 months pregnant, to return to Australia, knowing that Quentin would give me support and keep me safe. Our son Benjamin was born in Adelaide on July 22, 1997.

We continued to agonize about our situation. It was unspeakably painful. Despite our love we knew what we were doing was wrong. It became too much to bear and again we made the difficult decision to part. I returned to the UK when Ben was 5 months old. It was a bleak time—Quentin was devastated at losing me as well as his son but we were tortured. He never pressured me to stay. Being on the other side of the world though was too much and I didn't want Benjamin to miss out on having a Father as I had done, so I returned to Australia two months later when he was 7 months old. We tried to live a quiet family life but it just wasn't possible. When we finally had the DNA test that proved what I already knew—that Quentin really was my Father—the possibility of sharing a future together was finally destroyed. We made the painful decision to part and in July I returned to England with Benjamin for the last time.

Quentin supported me as I set up home in the UK and has always been a committed and loving Father to Benjamin. He has always been generous in the extreme, both financially and emotionally, in support of Benjamin and I. We have all suffered deep pain and regret over the years. When Benjamin was 9 I told him of his Heritage, concerned that he should know the truth and to this day he has a deep love for his dad who has always been open, loving, and committed as a Father. Over the years Quentin and I have struggled at times to maintain a good relationship, as my parents, and my subsequent partner, have been condemning of the situation, but we have all tried to accept what is and these days Quentin and I have a good relationship as we are united in our concern for Benjamin, who has matured into a fine, loving, insightful, and thoughtful young man who loves both his parents unreservedly. I would ask for some compassion and understanding in the final analysis of this very sad story. For Benjamin and the other children involved I would ask that it be considered that we have all suffered enough. We are very sorry for the pain we have caused and are just trying now to do the best for our child. Quentin is a good man and an exceptional doctor who truly cares about people. I thank you for your consideration.

Sincerely,
Doreen Patience

Reading the letter, Abraham thought of his own childhood and wished that he had been loved like Benjamin. He thought of the devotion shown to Mr. Alvarez by his family and to Mrs. Dreyfus by her two daughters. Mechanically, he collected his things and went off to see Mrs. Simpson, as he had promised to do, before visiting his father at Swamp Road Hospital.

51.

In Mrs. Simpson's room, Abraham spoke briefly to the nurse responsible for her care and then examined the patient. Although still unconscious, she was a little more responsive than she had been in the morning, which reinforced the feelings he had expressed about her illness.

He thanked the nurse for her assistance and turned to go. As he was leaving, he almost bumped into Helen, the third daughter, who was coming in to visit her mother. Flustered and obviously very agitated, she asked if she could talk with him as a matter of urgency. In spite of his hurry he felt he had no alternative. As soon as he closed the door of the interview room Helen burst into tears.

"Professor, I don't want my mother to die. I know my sisters think that it's best to allow her to go now, but I don't, and I believe that my father doesn't, either. I know it's been hard for Mom. She's really battled all these years. But there's no reason for her to give in now. Gill and Chris think that her life's not worth anything anymore and they want Dad to be able to move on while he's still young enough. I'm sure they mean well, but they're just trying to impose their will on everyone else. They've made it so hard for Mom. They've put pressure on her for years to go to a nursing home, but she's refused. That's why I went overseas. I couldn't stand the conflict anymore. I had to escape. It was better, healthier for me living away from home. But in the end I couldn't stay away: I had to come back. When I did, I was convinced that Mom had made up her mind to end it. She just couldn't resist any longer. She didn't say so directly but I could see it in her eyes and in her body. I don't know what she'd planned or what she actually did, but I'm sure she did something. She's a strong woman and she always knows exactly what she's doing. She only meant the best for Dad, but he just wanted to be with her, whatever her condition, and whatever it meant for them together. In the end, neither of them could continue to withstand the pressure. I tried to reason with her. I argued with her, but she rejected me. She shouted at me that I had left her. I was her favorite. She loved me best, but she accused me of betraying her. I left because it was the only way I could survive. That was the last conversation we had. I understand her. I knew she was planning something. She was doing it for love. There was nothing I could do about it."

"When was this?" asked Abraham.

"It was last week. Professor, I'm so confused. I love my mother and I want what's best for her, as well as for my dad. I know they love each other. He's happy just looking after her, but she thinks—she's been convinced—that she has to sacrifice herself for his happiness. I don't want her to die, but maybe that's the best thing for her. Who knows?"

She was crying softly. Abraham listened but for once could think of nothing to say. When she had finished he simply put his arms around her and held her for a few moments. He could feel the sadness in her body. He reassured her that he would try his hardest to make everything work out for the best. She smiled weakly through her tears, but he knew she was not reassured.

He looked at his watch. The train to Swamp Road Hospital was leaving in just over five minutes. He explained to Helen that he had to go and would talk to her tomorrow. He set off for the station in a rush. At that moment his cell phone rang. He answered it as he was walking. It was Gillian. "Professor," she said, "Helen might try to speak to you. Nothing she will say is true. She's unreliable and hasn't had contact with our mother for more than a year. She has no authority to speak on the family's behalf. Please don't talk with her."

Abraham was almost looking forward to his visit to Swamp Road Hospital.

PART 7

SWAMP ROAD HOSPITAL, AGAIN

52.

On the train to the Swamp Road Hospital Abraham was in turmoil. In spite of the original impression that his father was suffering from a routine illness, he knew that the reality was that his life now hung in the balance. Abraham had been shocked by the deficiencies in care, by the humiliating treatment both of them had received, and by the hypocrisy of the nurse who had called the director of nursing. Abraham could never forget an insult—a trait, he thought ruefully, he had no doubt inherited.

Over the years, he had spent many hours ruminating about his father. The oldest and the brightest son of refugees from war-torn Europe who had struggled to provide a better, more secure life for their children, Mordechai had been sent to an expensive private school and then to a university, where he had excelled. He had studied law and loved it. Although he had always wanted an academic career, to which, no doubt, he would have been well suited, it had not worked out that way and instead, given his erratic temperament and the demands of supporting a young family, he ended up working alone.

Abraham's father had a complicated personality. It was not just that its many facets included wild brilliance and creativity, intolerance, and cruelty. It was also that his moods could fluctuate from one extreme to the other, hour by hour. He could be active, energetic, and grandiose for weeks at a time, working and writing without a break, or he could sink into black despair and sit for days in his chair, saying nothing.

Now, during his father's illness, all this came flooding back to Abraham with renewed force. Events from his own childhood kept recurring to him, sometimes provoked by incidental experiences, reminding him of his father's moods. A few bars of music from a patient's radio evoked the occasions when they had been spectacularly elevated. Sometimes Mordechai would play music on the radio or record player at full volume and keep every light in the house burning all night and he himself would become loud and inflammable, uncharacteristically making crude sexual comments or jokes—for example, a lewd remark about a pretty girl in the street. The sound of the air ambulance arriving outside the hospital reminded him of the time Mordechai had almost bought a helicopter, to the family's bemusement and dismay. A picture in the newspaper reminded him of the time his father started a political party of his own—to Abraham's knowledge no one joined it—and left without notice to visit China at the height of the Cultural Revolution, declaring that he wanted to become "part of the struggle for change." When his father was raging, the whole family—including Abraham's mother and older sister—would live in fear for days or weeks, waiting for the episode to pass.

Mordechai made close friends and then—usually as a result of his erratic moods—he lost them. Every friendship he ever developed, without exception, ended in disaster. Typically, a client or business associate would become close to him, attracted by his warmth and sparkling wit, and then, when he became abusive and aggressive toward them, would break from him acrimoniously. Often the dissolution of these friendships generated financial and legal disputes. He was involved in endless battles, some of which went on for years. When he was on a high he would refuse all attempts to find a resolution; when his mood was lowered it was left to the family to end the impasse, usually by giving in to the demands of his antagonists.

His sole love was the law. In fact, the whole family lived, breathed, and suffered the law. He was known in legal circles as a brilliant and innovative thinker. Abraham could easily imagine that this might have been the case because of his father's extraordinary memory and his ability to make original and unexpected connections between ideas. With these characteristics and his searing logical ability, as a legal thinker he must have been very unconventional. The order and discipline of the law seemed strangely at odds with his father's mercurial and inconstant personality.

It was left to Abraham's mother to keep the family together. She no doubt suffered more than the rest of them. She had to withstand spiteful, angry personal attacks when Mordechai's mood was elevated and his abject, pathetic dependence when he was depressed. For Abraham's mother to have stayed there must have been a reason. This may have been that when he was in neither extreme he could be warm and attractive, funny, clever, dazzling, daring.

For the rest of the time, however, she defended her position in her own way, by fighting back, by absenting herself for days at a time—no doubt, Abraham realized in retrospect, to allow herself the opportunity to recover from the psychological assaults and uncertainty to which she was continually exposed. She did her best to protect her children from their father's excesses, but in this she was only partially successful.

Throughout his childhood, Abraham lived in fear of his father. He craved the certainty of knowing who his father was, or what he wanted of him. He aspired to live up to his father's standards and expectations, but these changed constantly and unpredictably. His father was for him both a lawyer and the law, but the code to which he, Abraham himself, was expected to conform remained recondite and opaque.

Walking along the dark street on his way to visit his father, more and more memories flooded back. The demands placed on him during his childhood had imposed a great burden and Abraham spent much of his time withdrawn and depressed. He had become superstitious, fearing disaster, unable to play with the other children. He recalled the time when he was about fifteen when his father had deliberately humiliated him and he had run out of the house crying. He was in a street just like this one. It was dark and he'd had nowhere to go.

For some reason, in a flash, it had become clear to him: he was entrapped, caught in the prison of his father's wildness, which was also a prison of his own imagination, from which he alone could make his escape. He had decided then and there to do so, to renounce his emotional dependence on his father and to set himself free. He had vowed to himself that he would never again be subjected by his father's oppressive and despotic demands. Now, he shivered as he relived that moment, experiencing again both the exhilaration and the nausea of liberation, feeling the heavy burden of oppression lift and the heavier responsibility of freedom descend.

This was no doubt an ancient and enduring story. The son had torn away from the father and struck out on his own. This was the moment when his father had the option of accepting his son as an adult, as an equal in the family and in life. But Mordechai was not capable of such magnanimity. He never accepted Abraham as an equal and never forgave him for his escape. The jealousy and resentment only intensified over the years.

Nonetheless, inexplicably even to himself, Abraham retained a deep sense of loyalty and love for Mordechai, who was, after all, still his father. He was responsible for who Abraham was, for better or for worse. What was more,

Abraham felt profound compassion for his father's weaknesses and mistakes. His father had not, after all, chosen his own erratic personality, of which he was as much a victim as everyone else.

Despite the torrid history, therefore, the two continued their relationship in an undeclared truce. Abraham visited him every week to engage in intellectual—if sometimes somewhat tense—conversation. For Abraham, this seemed a workable solution—and indeed, it had appeared to work for more than three decades. But now, Mordechai was sick, probably dying, and Abraham was engulfed by dread. It was as if he had been caught up by a great tsunami that was sweeping away the defenses so carefully constructed over all those years and exposing the primal disorientation and foreboding they were meant to obscure.

53.

Abraham arrived at last at the Swamp Road Local Hospital. After the phone conversation with the director of nursing he had tried to speak with the hospital's CEO to discuss the matter with him but his phone calls had not been returned. He had called the treating doctor in charge—a colleague of his—and had explained the lapse in treatment his father had suffered. The doctor apologized—weakly, Abraham thought—and had assured him that his father's treatment was now being properly supervised and that his condition was improving. Although Abraham was still seething he knew that he needed to be careful not to alienate the doctors and nurses looking after his father. After all, the quality of care a patient receives ultimately depends not on technical skill and know-how but on the personal commitment of the individual staff. Abraham was only too well aware from personal experience that insistent and combative relatives, even though they considered their role to be that of protecting their loved one from a heartless and uncaring system, often did their own cases more harm than good. The health professionals saw them as "troublemakers" who were calling their integrity into question, as a result of which their good intentions became less spontaneous.

This was not the result of a conspiracy but of complex, often unconscious, responses. The aspirations for care were often exemplary. Each ward had clear rules about how often a patient should be reviewed or turned or offered a bedpan or a hundred other things. However, even if all the technical functions were adequately discharged, the non-technical—what Abraham called "the ethical"—ones could still be seriously deficient. If a nurse or a doctor were unable in a particular case to establish a personal relationship based on respect and commitment to an individual patient, a crucial dimension of the therapeutic relationship was missing, and this could evoke a sense of discomfort and even hostility. Neither caring nor ethics could be reduced to purely instrumental acts or intentions: indeed, the inapplicability of instrumental values was a defining feature of both of them.

In any case, Mordechai had been in the hospital many times before and Abraham knew that he could be a very bad patient. Once, he had suffered a broken hip and when the surgeon had come to visit him the next day, after—as Abraham tried to point out—having saved his life through undoubted technical skill, his father had refused to talk to him on the basis that he had found his manner condescending. Later, he had established a hostile relationship with the nurses by calling them lazy and ugly. In these and other situations Abraham had done his best to calm the situation by placating the nurses and doctors, saying that his father was anxious and afraid and by trying to convince his father to act with greater circumspection. On both accounts he was at best only partially successful. On the present occasion he suspected darkly that the worst was still to come.

As it turned out, he was not wrong.

When he arrived at Ward 2C he made a point of approaching the nurses before visiting his father. He assumed a deliberate, proper—he thought slightly old-fashioned—manner. "Hello, I'm Professor Nevski, here to visit my father. How is he today?"

The nurse occupying the central nursing station—not the one from previously—looked him up and down and replied coldly, "He's all right," and went back to her work. A little taken aback, but seeing no prospect of further discussion, Abraham proceeded to his father's room, not knowing what to expect. He entered the room tentatively, half expecting another disaster. However, this time the room was clean and bright, with a bed at normal height in the middle of which his father was lying, apparently asleep. Abraham walked quietly up to the bed and stood for a few moments studying his father's careworn face. He was clean-shaven now and his few wisps of gray hair had been combed. His swarthy complexion and bushy eyebrows, which when he was inflamed added to his aspect of aggression and hostility, in this setting made him seem venerable and gentle. He was breathing quietly. An IV drip was mounted above the bed and its plastic tubing disappeared under the sheets.

During his whole life Abraham could not recall previously having seen his father asleep. He wondered if Mordechai had stood watching him, Abraham, sleeping as a small baby, as Abraham had done with his own children and as he was doing with his father now. Just as remarkable, he noted, was that he seemed—however briefly—to have accepted the role of the submissive recipient of care, so unfamiliar to him and so necessary for the nurses.

Abraham watched quietly. After a few minutes his father opened his eyes and gave a weak smile. Abraham touched his hand lightly and said softly, "Hello, Dad, it's me, Abraham. How are you today?"

His father replied, barely audibly. "I'm not so good. I don't like it here. Please help me leave. I'm not ready to die."

Abraham asked, "Can you tell me what's happened? Do you know where you are?"

"I'm in the hospital, but I don't know why. I can't remember coming here. The nurses . . ." Abraham strained to hear as his father's voice became almost inaudible. All he could catch was "cruel."

"You've been quite sick," Abraham explained. "But you seem a lot better today. You've had a serious infection. You're receiving antibiotics that seem to be working. Hopefully, you will be able to return home in a few days."

"That's good. I'm tired . . ."

Abraham's voice became urgent. "Dad, there are a few things I need to ask you. The hospital won't allow me to access information about you without your permission. Do you want me to be able to see your medical record?"

"Yes, of course, you have to. I trust you to take control."

It was a small gesture, but Abraham was deeply gratified by it. "Would you sign a consent form to indicate your willingness for me to act on your behalf?"

"Yes."

"I have some paper. Can we write it now? Perhaps I will start off with 'I hereby give my son . . .'"

His father's voice remained weak but nonetheless clear. "Take this down. 'I, Mordechai Nevski . . . add my address and the date . . . hereby give my son Abraham permission to obtain access to all medical information about me and to make whatever decisions he sees fit in relation to my medical care' . . . no, put 'in respect of my medical and other care.'"

Abraham copied down his father's words quickly and then presented the piece of paper to the old man, who took the pen weakly and, still in his recumbent position, signed his name in the handwriting that was so familiar to Abraham. Abraham folded the paper and put it in his pocket.

"Thank you for this, Dad. I need to ask you a couple of additional questions. Are you feeling strong enough to continue talking?"

"Yes, what do you want to know?"

"As I said before, you seem to be getting better, but if this doesn't happen and you get worse rather than better we'll need to decide what treatment's appropriate and what you'd prefer."

"What do you mean?"

"I mean, if, say, you became sicker than you are and we had to decide whether to seek treatment in intensive care, perhaps with a tube in your throat to help you breathe, for example, would you want that?"

"Are you asking if I want you to let me die?"

"Er . . . no . . . er . . . yes. I'm asking . . . Some people say they don't want to go to intensive care or be kept alive by machines . . ."

"Well, I rather like the idea of people tinkering with my body! I wouldn't mind being hooked up to a machine. I think it would be rather nice!"

Abraham's father was weak and his voice was faltering. Abraham couldn't tell if he was answering his question sincerely or whether this was just an example of his natural perverseness. He decided to change the subject.

"Okay. Maybe we'll talk more about this another time. Is there anything else you want to say to me just now?"

"No. I'm tired. I might just sleep a little."

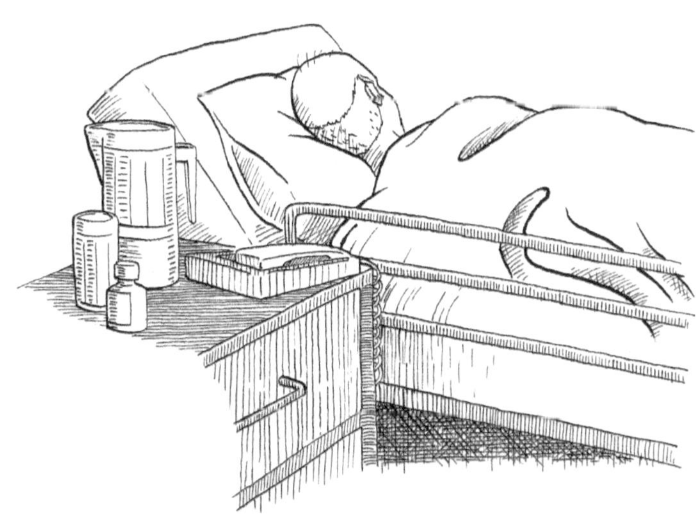

"Good night, Dad. I'll sit here for a while and then leave. Henny and Jack send their love."

"Say hello to them from me." Mordechai's voice was now barely audible again. He closed his eyes and drifted off to sleep. Abraham sat watching his chest move gently up and down for a few minutes, reflecting on the conversation they had just had. Even in these extreme conditions his father had refused to follow the conventional path. This was inconvenient, but for all the conflict and contretemps of the past, he knew that he had no alternative but to commit himself to remain loyal to him. He gently stroked the sleeping man's hand.

PART 8

MARINA ON STAGE

54.

Although it was a cold night and raining hard Abraham was determined to make it to Marina Bell's performance. In the time since he had seen her he had kept the flyer she had given him in his pocket. He wasn't exactly sure why, but her predicament profoundly unsettled him. He himself had spent long hours performing in front of his patients and others, concealing his personal emotions while making it appear that he shared theirs. He was intrigued to see how a clown, whose entire raison d'être was to make people laugh, could function under the conditions of almost catastrophic sadness Marina had described.

Waiting for a ticket, he realized that he was at least twice the age of the next oldest person in the line. He tried to look inconspicuous—he felt a little like a voyeur, visiting a single woman's comedy show alone. He reached the ticket office. "One ticket, for 'Faking It' please. I'd like to sit close to the front but not actually in the front row."

The young woman looked at him somewhat puzzled and replied, "Certainly, sir. Do you have any concessions?"

"What do you mean?"

"Do you have a pension card, for example?"

He wondered if she was making fun of him about his age, but she wasn't smiling. He could hardly tell her that his real mission was to undertake a medical assessment. "Er . . . no. Full price, please."

He took the ticket and made his way inside. Small and cramped, the theater had a simple bare stage at the front and a rather dingy bar at the rear. The other audience members seemed to be mainly men and women in their twenties. Trying to appear at ease, he bought a beer at the bar and then found his seat. After a few minutes the lights darkened and the show began.

Marina strode out, dressed in a white body suit.

"Hello, everyone. I'm Marina. Welcome to 'Faking It.' I'm a comedian, but I have to warn you right at the beginning that my show is actually a serious scientific exercise. I'm going to prove to you a simple proposition: that everyone is faking; everyone in this room is playing a part.

"Of course, this comes naturally to all the women here. Women are called on to act all the time—to be clever and beautiful and well behaved and sexy. No one is what they seem to be. Look at the friend or partner you came with, the person sitting next to you—assuming that you have a friend or partner at all—and think, 'What do I really know about him or her?' Well, I'm sorry to say, you know less than you think.

"You, sir, what's your name? Ah, Roger! Is this lovely lady sitting next to you your girlfriend? What's her name? Daphne! Daphne and Roger! How long have you been together? Six months! And you live together, do you? There, I knew it! Well, I bet that to all of you here Daphne and Roger appear to be an ideal couple; look at the touching way they are sitting together, holding hands—maybe bracing themselves for the humiliation that's to follow. Don't worry, I have a rule, I don't humiliate my audience—it would be very bad for business—but I do want to illustrate a point. Roger probably thinks Daphne idolizes him, is looking forward to the privilege of washing his socks and underpants, cooking, doing the housework, while always being ready to have sex with him any time. Daphne probably thinks that Roger only thinks about her and never dreams about getting it off with any woman he sees, including me, that he buys her flowers and chocolates because he loves her and not because he has a guilty conscience about what he thought about the girl in the short skirt he saw on the tram on his way home, that he's a simple man, who only wants to have a good time, and maybe in the future settle down and have children.

"Well, I've got news for all of you. None of this is true. At least not all of it: the part about men being simple was true, but that wasn't what I meant."

The audience was warming to Marina's narrative and there were murmurs of appreciation from around the room. "Roger spends half his day thinking about other women and Daphne dreams about—well, I'll leave it to you girls to say what you dream about. Daphne's sick and tired of housework and wishes Roger would do his share. Even though Roger supports feminism he's happy to leave the cooking and the cleaning to Daphne, despite the fact that both of them work full-time jobs. I've just told you a bit about what they think; I haven't even started to tell you what they actually do.

"Actually, I'm going to move at this point to safer ground—safer for me, because I'm really sick of those divorce cases where I'm named as the co-respondent. Look at me: young, beautiful, witty, well adjusted, rich—right? Wrong! You think you know me, but let me tell you how mistaken you are. If only you knew what an unstable cauldron of simmering toxic chemicals just waiting to explode I really am. Roger, you don't realize that if you'd said the wrong thing just a moment ago I would have burst into tears and stormed out of the theater.

"Everything we do is a show. That's natural for me, of course, because I'm a performer. That's what I'm supposed to do and what you came here to see. And to be sure, I'm exploiting that. But what you don't realize is that, like everyone, I'm a performer not just on the surface but deep down. This is how I really am. I'm just pretending to pretend. I'm even pretending to be a comedian, to be funny—I guess a few of you have already worked that out."

She had the audience laughing now. "What do you know about me? You think I'm a woman? Well, actually you got that one right, but that's about all. I spend my day—just like Daphne—trying to keep it all together. My period's due in three days. That might be a bit of information you didn't think you needed, but what it means to me is PMS."

Abraham was transfixed. He couldn't imagine what was to follow. He hoped that Marina had not recognized him in the crowd.

She went on: "PMS. Premenstrual syndrome. Every woman in this room has, has had, or will have PMS and knows what it's like to pretend that you're someone you're not for a week out of every month, trying to pretend you're not really a neurotic, babbling, crying, screaming axe murderer. You're just a decent, middle-class girl who likes getting up every day and going to work; who enjoys having swollen, painful breasts, stomach cramps, hot flashes, migraines, and a mind she can't control. Actually, come to think of it, what I like about PMS is that it's the only time in the month when I can really be myself. I'm not sure where the name PMS came from, but I realize that it was second best because mad cow disease was already taken.

"When I was preparing this show I wanted to know what other women who suffer from PMS experience and naturally—being a comedian—I Googled 'PMS jokes.' I was surprised to find that none of the jokes that came up were funny—that is, until it dawned on me that it was the week before my period and that during this time even the funniest jokes make me cry. But I did come across an answer to the question of how many women with PMS it takes to screw in a lightbulb.

"What's the answer? Does anyone have any suggestions? Two? Four? Eight? Well, I'll tell you. One. At least, in my house. Do you know why it only takes one? Because no one else in the fucking house knows how to change a lightbulb. They haven't even noticed that the fucking bulb has burned out. They'd sit in the house in the dark for a week before they worked it out. And once they worked it out they wouldn't be able to find the lightbulbs despite the fact that they've been in the same damn cupboard for the past eight years. But if they did, by some miracle, find the lightbulbs, two days later the chair that they'd dragged from the next room to stand on to change the fucking lightbulb would still be in the same spot! And underneath it would be the crumpled wrapper the bulb came in. Why? Because no one in the house ever carries out the garbage! It's a wonder we haven't all suffocated from the piles of garbage that are ten meters deep throughout the entire house. The house! The house! It would take an army to clean this . . .

" . . . Where was I? Ah yes, faking it. The other day I went to my doctor. He sat there looking serious and considerate, writing, occasionally looking up at me. But I had no idea what he was really thinking."

Abraham froze and held his breath. He wondered if the person sitting next to him had sensed his reaction.

Marina continued, "He could have been thinking, 'Oh no, not another woman with PMS—she's the third I've seen today. I have to pretend to be interested' or 'Only twenty-five minutes to lunch. I can hardly wait for that cheese sandwich. I wonder if I should order a cappuccino or a latte today' or 'That girl has nice breasts. I wonder what it'd be like to sleep with her.' Or maybe he was thinking about his own troubles, his prostate problem or his stomach ulcer or his impotence. I've no way of telling. All I know is that when he was trying to look interested and concerned about me, he was faking it."

Abraham suddenly felt numb.

"So here I am, a comedian, pretending to be funny. Is that funny? Only if the joke about the joke is funny. I know what you're all thinking—that you wish I'd just cut the psychoanalytical bullshit and start talking directly about sex. Well, I've got some advice for Daphne—who's six months into her whirlwind romance—and the other women here. I know that this shows a bias toward women and that it isn't fair to the men in the audience who also expect their money's worth. So when I'm finished I'm going to let Roger get up and give some advice to the men.

"Daphne, rule one: never do housework. Believe me, no man ever made love to a woman because she had a clean kitchen. Rule two: remember that a sense of humor doesn't mean you tell him jokes but that you laugh at his. Rule three: if he asks if he's your first, say, 'You could be. You look familiar.' Rule four: if he asks what sort of books interest you, tell him checkbooks. Rule five: if he asks if you're faking orgasm, tell him it's not that you're pretending, it's just part of your practice schedule . . . Hey, it's true that a lot of women fake orgasm, but look at it this way, that's only a small thing because the men they are doing it with are mostly faking whole relationships.

"It sounds like I'm criticizing men and I know I shouldn't. As a child I was always told that before you criticize a man, you should walk a mile in his shoes. It's a maxim I've always tried to follow. That way when you do start criticizing him, you're already a mile away and you have his shoes! And if you've chosen your man carefully, they're Gucci white leather high-top sneakers with crystal studs.

"Why are you here? Because you want to be made to laugh. But how are you made to laugh? By being told something you knew was true but were too uncomfortable to tell yourself you were thinking. Am I right, Daphne . . . ?"

The audience was laughing along with the performer but Abraham was trying to observe her as closely as he could. He wondered if he was the only person in the room who knew what she was really going through, how true her words were. Her jokes were funny, but they were funny only because they were jokes. He knew that she was really just telling the truth. What was to the others her humor was in reality a cry of distress. He looked at her face. He wondered if he could detect signs of the pain she was experiencing. He thought he detected lines of strain around her eyes and that her facial expressions—of humor, of uncertainty, of questioning—seemed forced. He listened to her voice. She was a good actor; her presentation was clear and the audience was convinced.

But like all sad clowns she struck a chord in her audience. She told them things they knew but couldn't admit to themselves; maybe that's why they were laughing. She concealed her own pain, only to expose that of the members of the audience. She was tricking them, coaxing them, challenging them, getting under their guard so that they could release the fears and anxieties with which they were struggling.

Abraham scrutinized Marina closely and suddenly realized that she was talking to him. He was a sad clown. The comments about going to the doctor hit home, but what they really meant was that she was doing exactly the same thing as him. When he had seen her the other day he had not realized that he was the one who was being observed. She was visiting him to obtain material for her show. He had spent an hour with her. He had thought that the purpose had been to find a treatment for her medical conditions but now it seemed that maybe it was really only to acquire a couple of jokes. Maybe she was just faking it!

His mind was reeling. He tuned back in just in time to hear her say that she wanted to die quietly in her sleep like her grandfather, "not yelling and screaming like the other people in the car he was driving." She had talked to him about suicide—so much so that he had given her his personal telephone number. Now she was joking about her own death. He had trusted her and, despite their brief encounter, he had thought that she trusted him. But now he was not so sure. Maybe no one really trusted him. Maybe everyone was faking it . . .

The show ended. As soon as the clapping had stopped and the performer had left the stage Abraham stood up and walked quickly out of the theater. He needed to get outside, to be alone, to walk in the night air.

PART 9

FIND YOUR PASSION

55.

braham had been so preoccupied with the events relating to his father and in the wards that he had been unable to make progress on his article. Accordingly, he had made a special effort to come in early to work on it before the ward round. He reread the few pages he had already finished and forced himself to turn to the task at hand:

> It is widely assumed in discussions about ethics that to proceed in a systematic fashion it is necessary to identify a "problem" or a "dilemma" that needs to be solved and then to find solutions to it. It is assumed that ethical problems are solvable and that the solutions can be discovered through the application of rational thought. While these may sound like inoffensive and natural assumptions, in reality they depend on deep preconceptions about the nature and role of reason and rational argumentation.

He was satisfied with these opening sentences. They showed how productive it was to start work early, when your mind was still fresh. He went on:

> The central values attributed to individual autonomy—the appeal to the universal abstract principles, the search for definitive "solutions" to ethical "dilemmas," the emphasis on outcomes rather than processes—also affirm and support prevailing cultural assumptions. Take medicine again. Dominant approaches to ethics regard autonomy, the individual subject, and freedom—understood in a historically limited sense of the individual in isolation—as key values. Arguments often presented as "radical"

support the legalization of euthanasia, the killing of disabled persons (including infants and elderly people), the application of genetic techniques to increase or improve physical capacity, unrestrained research into stem cells, etc. In many cases these arguments are no more than apologies for the prevailing technological regime. However, of greater importance than this is that they comprehensively set the agenda for all ethical debate. The conclusion that is reached in any particular case makes little difference because the damage has already been done: the task of ethical discourse has been reduced to rubber stamping—or refusing to rubber stamp—the conceptual status quo.

Abraham was pleased with the turn of phrase "rubber stamping the conceptual status quo," which he thought was very striking.

> The radicalism of these ethical theories is illusory because they disturb little in the status quo. They do not engage key issues that arise at the level of the lifeworld—that world of experience we share with others in our most intimate moments. They do not reflect on the fine texture of day-to-day decision making, the subtle adjustments we make in the continuous flux of communication, in response to our intuitions about others. They omit the diverse richness and complexity both within and between cultures that distinguish our personal and interpersonal lives.

He sat for a few moments admiring his fluent phrases. But then—he wasn't quite sure why—Marina came into his mind. What did he really mean by "richness and complexity," he wondered. Wasn't he himself just substituting sophisticated ideas for the messy facts of the real world? How could he find a way of avoiding the trap of merely replacing one empty discourse with another? He was disquieted by the questions but knew that in a paper of this kind he had no alternative but to proceed in a detached and authoritative manner:

> The roots of the concepts of ethics that prevail in contemporary Western societies derive largely from the changes in the understanding of the nature and role of reason that occurred during the intellectual movement around the mid-seventeenth century that became known as the European Enlightenment. The basic

conviction guiding this great process of ferment and change was the belief, inspired by science, that progress will occur inexorably toward greater knowledge and social and moral improvement as a result of the application of reason.

The traditional worldviews had provided unified, shared, stable ways of understanding moral and practical life. In the emerging view of the world, separate regions of discourse and action were distinguished, each of which had its own specific tasks. Science became the major intellectual practice devoted to the search for truth; ethics and jurisprudence assumed the role of carrying out the search for normative rules to guide action; and art became the site for the creation of and reflection on beauty. Each of these areas was the province of "experts," individuals with specific skills, knowledge, and authority whose activities were from now on by and large restricted to a single main field of activity.

Abraham stopped to think. He had come to the nub of the matter—the version of rationality that had proven so powerful. He decided to attack the issue directly:

> Perhaps the most crucial innovation of the Enlightenment, however, was the novelty of the concept of reason itself, according to which reason was now seen as a highly refined technical device. Rational thinking was identified with instrumental reason, the kind of thinking that seeks to realize clearly defined outcomes. The application of this reason became the key to all knowledge. From the point of view of the new science, the book of nature, which had now been deciphered, was literally written in mathematical characters. The possibilities and power of reason were considered unlimited. It was to be the tool that would render transparent the obscure complexities of nature and society. The new order was based on some very fundamental assumptions—for example, the "objectivistic" assumption that the scientist acted as an isolated, disembodied subject and that theory merely reflected nature and had freed itself from any contamination with culture. Its notion of reason was "closed," in the sense that it focused on certain truth, the elimination of ambiguity, the overcoming of uncertainty, and the extinction of difference. From now on, one particular kind of

reason became the standard for assessing and judging all theoretical claims and empirical phenomena.

Ethical theories were increasingly justified on the basis of single philosophical methods and general theories of human nature. Morality was given a very narrow focus; it was considered no more than a guide to action. All dilemmas were assumed to have a rational resolution. All discrepancies in moral views between individuals were to be overcome by the exercise of reason alone.

In the new regime, everyday dilemmas could only be interpreted within the limited framework available . . .

That didn't sound quite right; he had to say how the framework was limited. He deleted the sentence and began again:

In the new regime, everyday problems—such as my question about whether I should care for my elderly mother—had to be framed within a context that allowed limited options only. If, as a respectable thinker, I wanted to answer this question, I had to adopt one of the conventional possibilities. I had to formulate reasons that addressed such issues as whether she has useful cognitive capacity sufficient to allow her to be regarded as possessing personhood. The cold light of reason demanded that a calculation be undertaken to assess whether her continued life maximized the happiness of the whole society. Religious moralists would try to prove that to care, or not to care, was an obligation that derived from the existence of God. Others would try to identify universal principles that would illuminate or exemplify the specific case of this one woman.

Yet none of these options helps me answer my question. As elaborate as they are, the official discourses of ethics are incapable of representing the everyday experience of ethical life.

Abraham saved his work and turned away from the computer. He had made progress today but he remained strangely unsettled by the task that lay ahead. He would come back to the article and finish it later. Now he had to prepare himself for the day's activities. He had some things to read before the ward round—a couple of journal articles and some correspondence, and he also had to finish his report to the court on Quentin Prince. He left his desk, poured himself a whisky, moved over to his favorite armchair, and picked up the journal.

56.

He started reading the medical journal in a desultory fashion, but his mind wandered. His thoughts kept returning to the Swamp Road Hospital. He was still very disturbed about his father's illness, about the treatment that was being provided and, above all, about the intensity of his own reactions. He had imagined years ago that he had freed himself from his father and his insensitivity and cruelty and established himself on his own. Yet now, when in his heart he was convinced that Mordechai was dying, he was confused and disoriented. It was as if he was in free fall, plunging through space, with no control over the direction or the destination. He needed to understand what was happening. Who was his father? Who was he, Abraham? Marina, the comedian, had claimed that no one was truly authentic, was who he or she claimed to be, that everyone was "faking it." Could this really be true?

Unlike his relationship with his mother, Abraham reflected, he had never been able to understand the relationship with his father. He wondered if this was how it was for everyone, or even how it had to be. Maybe, he thought, the role of every father is open to question, including his commitment, even his identity. Certainly, as a figure of authority and order, and perhaps even as the classical psychological theory had it—as the competitor for his mother's love, Abraham had always regarded Mordechai with ambivalence. This was something he had always felt and always regretted. But now a curious idea occurred to him: perhaps the ambivalence itself might have somehow also been a productive force. What if it had been the ambiguity of his father, all those fears, doubts, and uncertainties, all that inflammatory unpredictability, which somehow had made it possible for him to develop his own sense of what was valuable. After all—this was the classical theory again—if the father is the device by which the existence of society infiltrates its way into an infant's developing psyche, and thereby becomes the symbol of the need to control our carnal desires, he is also the one who opens up the discrepancy between reality as we experience it and all the possibilities we can imagine. But this discrepancy is surely what drives us forward, what we spend our lives trying to make sense of.

These were heavy thoughts and Abraham gave some rapid shakes of his head to try to clear his mind. His reflection continued. Maybe, it is true that as the provider of authority and order, as the representative of the law, the father is supposed to provide the key to entry into society, the possibility of language, of personal identity, and of desire. But how could such complex tasks have ever been accomplished by someone as erratic and troubled as Mordechai? He wondered whether Mordechai himself had been aware of the paradox.

His father's greatest aspiration was to write a book. This was to be the Book of the Law, the book that exposed the falsehoods and misconceptions, the pretentions around legal thinking and practice. It would simultaneously have provided a definitive exposition of the foundations of legal reasoning and a devastating exposé of the institutions of legal power.

His father had worked on his book for the last three decades. It had become his singular objective, the goal toward which his whole life became aimed. He collected material from many sources and compiled notes, drafts, sketches, references to the complex history of different legal traditions. He employed typists to produce scripts of countless hours of dictated recordings. The accumulated material grew to encompass thirty-six volumes. His father's book had become part of the family's folklore. It was how he spent his leisure time, and as much of his work time as was available. It was to be his statement, his testament. It would demonstrate the nobility of the law, its purity, its relationship with the grand tradition of truth and justice; and it would also lay bare the corruption, the degradation of values, the subornment to the drive for power and money that had contaminated the purity of its ideal.

But it was never finished. When, after years and innumerable conversations, Abraham had eventually insisted on seeing the draft manuscript he was appalled to see that the text consisted of nothing but an elaborate compendium of aphorisms and quotations. "But Dad," he had said, "where are all your ideas and arguments? I thought you were going to put down your own theory of the law in the hope of reforming it. This isn't a book. It's just a collection of quotations."

As soon as he had uttered the words he had regretted saying them. His father's reaction showed how deeply wounded he was by his son's comment. He responded defensively, and then—characteristically—with full-bodied aggression, as if Abraham had scurrilously ambushed him in one of his street battles. "What would you know, you arrogant ignoramus?" he exclaimed angrily. "The great thinkers I've quoted say all I need to say. The ideas are all there. My message will be stronger if it comes from those with commanding authority. They are the models we have to return to."

Remembering all this, Abraham was touched and saddened. "The book" had been his father's lifetime goal, but it had been evident at that moment that it would never amount to more than a hollow chimera. Maybe, Abraham thought, that's why he's so resentful of me. He's spent his life battling for causes that would never be won. He's endured endless opprobrium from political enemies looking for opportunities to destroy him. For all his forbidding exterior, he was at his core soft and raw and vulnerable. Now, years later, Abraham flushed with shame for having exposed his father so cruelly.

When he was twelve his father and he had gone on a camping trip together. Abraham cherished the memory. It was the only time the two of them had really spent on their own, and it was one of the few periods in his childhood when he had felt truly happy. His father knew nothing about the outdoors—he would always prefer to remain inside reading a book—but the two of them together shared their new experiences, almost as if they were equals. He recalled his pride in sitting next to his father as they drove the long distances into the mountains in his old Humber. At one point they were caught in a snowstorm and nearly slid off the road. His father had made him promise he wouldn't tell his mother about the danger they'd faced. It was a secret bond they shared—maybe the only one.

A lump forming in his throat, Abraham recalled the camping trip, the helicopter, the embarrassing moments as his father raged in public. He recalled arguments with a waiter in a restaurant about the size of a fish, with a parking attendant who objected to being called at two o'clock in the morning to open the parking lot because his father needed to go to his office to do some work, and with a policemen who tried to direct him in heavy traffic. He recalled his own apprehensiveness as he had craved his father's love, knowing that he could never rely on it for more than a few minutes at a time.

He wondered how much insight his father had had into the pain he had imposed on his son, from which he, Abraham, had so determinedly tried to break free. Then, in a flash, it occurred to him: maybe he'd known all along; maybe it had all been orchestrated; perhaps it was he who—discreetly and without acknowledgment—had actually set him free! Maybe he had really known all along. Maybe, without asking for gratitude or recognition, he'd quietly done his job, to support and honor his son.

Here Abraham was, in his fifties, trying to understand who he was and the nature of his relationship with his father. He didn't know the answers, but he did realize that the flesh-and-blood father—the old man, not the cluster of arcane symbols—was more than a mere empty hulk. As pathetic as he may now be, he was the—still living—cynosure of histories and dreams, of possibilities and ideals, of struggles and defeats.

Abraham was still hurtling through space, revisiting aspects of the relationship with his father that he thought he'd left far behind. He wasn't sure of anything anymore. He was proud of his father's undoubted courage and respected the originality of his intellect. But he also hated him—bitterly, violently, with a vengeance.

57.

Abraham was getting ready to leave for his ward round when the phone rang.

"Doctor, I'm so sick! Please help me!"

"Ah, Mrs. Timoshenko! It's good to hear from you. I'd love to talk but I'm really busy at the moment. Could you call ba—"

"Abraham, I have such pain. Sometimes I think it's too much for me to bear. I have pain in my abdomen, pain in my chest, pain in my heart. I have spent most of my life dreaming about nobility and love and happiness. My whole world was once a hymn to beauty. But look at me now: an old woman crippled with the sordid refuse of time."

Despite his hurry Abraham was momentarily taken aback. "Please tell me more, Mrs. Timoshenko," he coaxed.

But the moment was lost. "The main pain is in the epigastrium. It is a dull, penetrating pain that comes and goes several times a day. Sometimes pancreatitis can cause such symptoms but Dr. Bauer says that the enzyme results don't support that diagnosis. He says that it must be a very rare syndrome and that I should ask you to conduct further tests. Do you think we need another MRI scan? Perhaps I should go back to Professor Ricardo . . ."

"Mrs. Timoshenko, I'm sorry I can't . . ."

" . . . Maybe I should have a biopsy. Then we would have a tissue diagnosis. The antibody levels are not a good explanation . . ."

As usual, Abraham was fascinated and compelled by the flow of empty language. He thought back to her opening metaphor. An old woman crippled with the sordid refuse of time. He did not want to let her down. Still, he was in a hurry and his anxiety was mounting. "Mrs. Timoshenko, I really have to go now. I'm so very sor—"

"And the leukocytoclastic vasculitis is playing up again. The rash on my arms has come back. The purpura was first identified by Dr. West ten years ago. Vasculitis can also affect the kidney. I need . . ."

"Mrs. Timoshenko, I don't wish to be rude but I have to hang up now. I will call you back when I have more time. I—"

" . . . and the fevers continue. Last night I experienced a series of flashes and spasms that suffused my entire body. This is prob—"

"Mrs. Timoshenko, I am going to hang up now. We'll talk later. Goodbye!"

Silence. Abraham collected his things and left for the ward round.

58.

"Prof, Rebecca asked me to say that she's on her way. She just has to check up on some results from a patient she saw during the night."

"Thanks, Ashis, that's fine. How are all our patients?"

"I think we're keeping up with the work. But there's some sad news. Mr. Alvarez died during the night."

Abraham recoiled in amazement. "What? Mr. Alvarez? But he was stable yesterday! Why would he have died so quickly? What happened?"

"I dunno, Prof. I only saw him a couple of times. Des started the morphine drip straight after the ward round and he calmed down a lot. That helped the family a fair bit, but they were all still pretty upset. I checked in on him before I left about five and he was awake but drowsy. I had a brief talk with the grandchildren and told them that we thought this could go on for days. When I came back this morning I heard that he was dead. Apparently a nurse found him about two o'clock. I guess it's for the best."

It really didn't make sense. Abraham shook his head with puzzlement. The unit audit once more loomed before his eyes. "Three deaths in one week, Professor Nevski!" his interlocutor was booming. "Are you aiming for the *Guinness Book of World Records?*" He felt sick. Three deaths! He really was losing control. The students thought he knew everything, but the reality was that he couldn't even tell when his own patients were on the point of dying.

And then there was Desmond, whose smug satisfaction was almost palpable. He could sense a derisory comment welling up and started to prepare his own defensive rebuke. But the nurse remained silent.

Abraham was not very good at dissembling, but for Ashis's sake he had to maintain his professorial demeanor. To hide his inner turmoil, in time-honored fashion, he resorted to a cliché. "It's very surprising, but that's the nature of clinical medicine. I always say to patients that I won't try to predict because every time you try to do so you're proved wrong."

He knew how unconvincing he sounded. Clinical medicine was the one thing he was good at; it was who he was and how he was seen by the rest of the world. The most basic thing about it was to be able to recognize how sick one's patients were. Yet on this matter he was failing repeatedly.

Or could there be another explanation? This had never happened before. What if the deaths were not completely an accident? The idea was too preposterous and he put it out of his mind.

"Hi, Prof. How are you today?"

"Hello, Rebecca. I've just heard the news about Mr. Alvarez . . . It was unexpected . . ."

"Yes, it did happen quickly." Her voice sounded tired. "I was on last night and looked in on him in the evening. The family was there and very sad. His son said that they didn't know if they could last much longer. So I guess it's a good thing that his suffering ended so swiftly."

"Have you spoken to them today?"

"I've been on the phone to Diego and Sofia. They sounded tired but relieved. They expressed their gratitude to you for your help."

Abraham looked at her closely, unable to determine whether she was being sarcastic. "That's nice," was all he could say. "I'll write them a letter expressing my sympathy. It was a difficult case."

59.

A fog of despondency hung over the ward round, but they had to continue. There were still Dr. Vilgis, Mrs. Dreyfus, and Mrs. Simpson to see. Abraham could see that Rebecca, tired and a bit disheveled, was struggling to concentrate.

He tried to sound businesslike, to maintain morale despite the blows they had suffered. "I meant to ask you, Rebecca. How did you find Dr. Vilgis, the old doctor with pneumonia?"

Rebecca was doing her best to maintain her composure. "He's still sick," she answered methodically, "but I think his chest's improving. We haven't been able to get any response from him personally. His sister's always by his side; in fact, sometimes she even stays overnight in the hospital. She tells us what he's thinking—or at least, what she thinks he's thinking. It's a weird situation."

"My experience has been pretty much the same, Prof," said Ashis, in answer to Abraham's look. "He never makes any responses to me. I had to change his drip yesterday and he didn't even flinch when I inserted the needle in his arm. I wish a few other patients would do that."

It was Desmond's turn. "None of the nurses have been able to elicit a purposeful response from him. His pupils react and from time to time he moves an arm or a leg a bit. But there's no evidence that he knows what we're saying to him."

Rebecca went on. "Prof, I asked the neuro and psych teams to review him. It seems they've both seen him in the past, going back years. The neurologists say he's got advanced multiple sclerosis causing severe paralysis and they think he's also developed advanced dementia. They say we can do a brain scan if we want but that it probably won't be any different from the one performed last year. The psychs agree that he's got dementia and have discounted other psychiatric disorders like depression or psychosis or catatonia."

"Does anyone think that Dora's claims to communicate with him are likely to be valid?" Abraham asked the question out of pure interest.

"I think the short answer to that, Prof, is no. And apparently that view's shared by the staff at his nursing home where he's lived for nearly seven years. They think that Dora's a bit dippy herself and that his bouts of pneumonia are caused by her feeding him when she shouldn't during the day."

There was a silence, which Desmond broke. "If he has such advanced dementia it raises the question of whether we should be treating him for his pneumonia, and certainly whether he should be receiving expensive antibiotics. Maybe this is another case in which our anxiety to keep people alive exceeds our capacity to judge what's the most ethical and humane course of action."

Abraham sighed to himself. This wasn't the discussion he wanted to have after all that had happened in the last few days, but he knew that there was nothing he could do to avoid it. He was worried that Rebecca and Ashis would be won over by Desmond's simplistic views. "What do you think, Rebecca?"

He was disappointed but not surprised by her reply. "I'm sorry, Prof, but if he's got advanced dementia I'm not sure what we're doing here, either. I mean, if Dora's right and he really does know what's going on and can understand the newspaper and the books and the music, that'd be one thing. But if he can't . . . I mean, what are we achieving?"

Her sense of desolation was palpable. Abraham could not deny that the point had validity and his heart was not really in his reply. "We do have Dora to think of. She's very vulnerable. Her life's completely wound up with his."

He could see that Desmond knew that he had the advantage now, as he moved in to strike another blow. "But Abraham, she's not our patient. He is. We surely can't regard everyone who passes by our hospital as our patient, just because they're related to a patient or once knew one. And we do have to think of the health budget. We all hear every day about how the hospital can't afford to keep its beds open. We're threatened with cutting down on the care we give to the community because we're keeping old people who can't even move alive. Surely that's the wrong approach."

Abraham both resented and envied Desmond's certainty. Complexity can never win against dogmatism. "But Dora might be right. Remember Billy? He's the one who keeps his entire family together. He provides meaning for his parents' and brothers' and sisters' lives. He helps keep alive the concepts of loyalty, care, and sacrifice. We can all be inspired and energized by his example."

"I don't think they're the same at all," responded Desmond, obviously enjoying the discomfort he was causing Abraham in front of the junior doctors. "In the first place, whereas Billy can be delightful, there's no evidence that Dora's right. No one, not us, not the people in Emergency, not the people in his nursing home, no one has witnessed Dr. V. making a meaningful response. But even if Dora were right it would still raise the question of whether we should be treating people like him—or like Billy for that matter—while we're having to turn away younger, otherwise fitter patients with curable diseases."

He hammered home his advantage. "I think we need to give careful consideration to whether we should be continuing to treat in this case or whether we should just let nature take its course. We've made mistakes in the past, which have no doubt resulted in unnecessary and avoidable pain and suffering. We have to learn from these mistakes. If we can't, one day we might find ourselves having to pay."

How he hated the nurse, especially when he was unable to refute his arguments! "I don't know what you mean when you talk about paying, but I resent the suggestion, Desmond, that we're causing pain and suffering. I wish the world was as simple as you present it, but unfortunately it isn't. What's more, I make the decisions here. For the moment at least, we're continuing to treat." He turned to Rebecca and Ashis. "In the meantime," he said, maintaining his peremptory tone, "could both of you start talking with Dora to try to find out what her needs are? If Dr. Vilgis were to die—and he will, one of these days—she'd be completely devastated. It's not just his life and happiness that's at stake but hers, too."

As Abraham finished he could see that Desmond was white with rage. Without saying another word the nurse turned away and stormed off.

60.

This was not the easiest of ward rounds. "How's Mrs. Dreyfus?" asked Abraham wearily, as they approached the room where they had seen the patient the day before.

At last Rebecca's voice lightened a little through her grimness. "Actually, there was an amazing event yesterday," she replied. "You remember how she commented on your tie? Well, a little later she just sat up and started talking to the nurses. She was completely coherent, talking about all the things that had happened. It seems that she was conscious the whole time."

"How interesting!" replied Abraham, trying to take advantage of this glimmer of hope in what was threatening to become a black morass of despair. "We did feel that there was something a little odd about the course of her illness, didn't we?"

"Yes, but that's not the most amazing part. When she woke up she talked to everyone except the daughters, whom she ignored completely. At first they tried to talk with her but when she refused even to show that she could hear what they said to her, they became very upset, booked their flights home, and left."

"Have we been able to find out anything more about Mrs. Dreyfus's story, in particular about her relationship with her daughters?"

"We know a little from an elderly man who came to visit just at the time that this was happening. He said—and we have no way of verifying this— that Mrs. D. had been estranged from the daughters for many years and thought that they were only interested in her money. But she's taken steps to make sure they don't get anything. It's apparently Mrs. Dreyfus's view—and the elderly relative's too—that the daughters didn't really care for their mom at all but were just trying to build a case for a share of her will."

"And where's Mrs. Dreyfus now?"

"After the daughters left she asked if she could be transferred to a private hospital, and so we arranged this for tomorrow. It's an unexpected ending, isn't it? I can't stop thinking about it. Why does one patient recover while another—like Mrs. Gurewitz—only gets worse?"

Clinical work—like life—can be confusing and unexpected. Abraham could see with complete clarity how hard it must be for Rebecca, a young woman trying to find her place in the world, trying to identify the goals and values that would guide her for the rest of her life. From the outside, medicine seems straightforward, but nothing could be further from the truth. Whether patients live or die, or even when they are cured, what seems most secure can often slip away without warning.

"Well, I guess we can't get everything right." He was almost embarrassed by his bland understatement. "We did try, and we did save her life, even if we missed some key facts along the way. Maybe we were deceived by the daughters' apparent devotion, but the patient wasn't . . ."

As Abraham was talking, Susanna, the Freedom to Choose consultant, appeared from behind them. "Hello, everyone!" she said cheerily as she breezed up. "Everyone happy? You'll be pleased to know we're making good progress with FTC. We're well on the way to making sure that everyone in the ward fills out an advanced directive form."

Her timing couldn't have been worse. Abraham, still feeling the guilt of his own insipid reply to Rebecca, let fly. "Susanna, we can do without your homilies," he said cruelly. "We've just been talking about a patient who could easily have died if we'd followed the Freedom to Choose protocols. In fact, I wouldn't be surprised if you'd already signed up her daughters. In medicine, however, the truth is more complex than you people can understand."

The poor woman looked confused at the unprovoked attack. "But limiting unwanted care means more for those who really need it," she stammered. "And I'm really just trying to do my job. Besides, who knows what truth is anyway?"

She was trying to hide how upset she was. Before Abraham had a chance to reply, like jesting Pilate, she turned and disappeared from sight.

61.

There was still Mrs. Simpson to see. Abraham told Rebecca and Ashis about his conversations with Helen and Gillian from the night before. As he did so, he noticed that Rebecca's demeanor relaxed further.

She smiled wanly. "We do have some good news today. I wanted to surprise you with it. Let's go straight in."

They entered the room. On the bed Mrs. Simpson was sitting up eating breakfast with a newspaper open in front of her. "Good morning, Mrs. Simpson. How are you today?" Abraham said, adding while trying not to sound ironical, "It's good to see that your appetite has returned."

"Good morning," the woman replied in a soft, cultivated voice. "You must be the professor. I've heard a lot about you."

"Yes, we've had a little bit to do with each other over the last day, although we were not previously on speaking terms."

She gave a weak smile. "It's true, I've been through a bit. But I'm still here and I guess that's a good thing."

Abraham could see that the woman was intelligent and reflective. He became serious. "Mrs. Simpson, I'd like to talk with you. Would you have some time now?"

"Of course, my first appointment is not for another hour."

"Do you mind if Rebecca and Ashis stay?"

"I'd rather we talked alone."

" . . . If that's what . . . Rebecca . . . ?"

"It's all right, Prof . . ."

The others left. Abraham pulled up a chair from the corner of the room and sat down in it. He waited for the patient to begin.

"I understand that you worked out what happened," she said.

"I think I have a reasonable idea," he replied. "but why don't you just tell me your story and then I can see how much I got right?"

"Can I have your assurance that anything I say to you will be in the strictest confidence?"

"I give you that assurance, with the qualification that if your safety or that of others is threatened I may be compelled to share the information."

"I'm willing to take that chance. Where would you like me to start?"

"Wherever you wish. From the beginning. There's no hurry. Take your time."

"You have such a gentle manner. I was once physically very active. I was actually a champion runner in my day." Her voice was quiet, melodious, and controlled.

"So I've heard. What was your distance?"

"Four hundred and eight hundred meters. I was very fit. When I was about fifty I developed rheumatoid arthritis. It's been an absolutely horrible process. It stopped me running, then walking, then doing almost anything. But the worst part of it has been that for the last twenty years I've not had a single day free from pain. Sometimes the pain is absolutely excruciating."

"Weren't you given medications for it?"

"I've seen almost every expert in the city—rheumatologists, pain specialists, surgeons, physiotherapists, acupuncturists, hypnotists, you name it. I've left no stone unturned. I've lived on a cocktail of medications that have allowed me to survive, although sometimes only just . . . Please don't get me wrong. I'm not complaining. This just happens to be my lot." Abraham studied her face carefully as she talked. It was thickly lined and he could tell that she was in pain even now.

She went on. "And I do have a great deal to be thankful for. There are many others worse off than me. What I have is a loving husband who's stood by me unconditionally and daughters who are committed to both him and me. Also, we're not short of money, and despite my disability we've been able to travel and lead a comfortable life."

She continued in her even, but nonetheless expressive, tone. "Although I feel quite well now, apart from being a little muddled, I have no doubt that I've been depressed for many months. My husband's been wonderful; he hasn't faltered for a moment in his commitment and his love for me. But if anything, that's made things worse. He's still relatively young and healthy. It's not too late for him to remarry, to travel, to enjoy life. A life with me is—and will ever be—no more than an unrelenting slough of hopelessness and despair.

"Of course, I couldn't talk about this with him—never in the past and never in the future. I did have conversations with Gillian and Christine, however, and they indicated to me—indirectly, but unmistakably—that they agreed with me that Robert's only chance of happiness was if I were to vacate the scene. I couldn't bring myself to live in a nursing home. I still have my wits about me—I hope you agree with that—and it would be more than I could bear, even worse than this!

"What about Helen?" Abraham asked, tentatively.

Mrs. Simpson's eyes darkened. "I don't want to talk about Helen," she said roughly. "She's lost to me. She was once my closest child, but . . . I don't want to talk about her . . ."

"I'm sorry I interrupted. Please continue with your story."

The soft, melodious voice returned. In precise and meticulous detail she related the events that had brought her to the hospital. She explained how she had, quite simply, conceived a plan to kill herself. She had searched the Internet and obtained instructions about the medications she needed to take and then purchased them by mail order from Mexico. She had done her homework well, choosing carefully so that she obtained drugs that would not show up in hospital drug screens, both in order to avoid the possibility that their effects would be reversed and to save her husband the ignominy and guilt associated with knowing that she had committed suicide. She had bought a large quantity of the drugs and stored them in a secret place, awaiting the moment when she would ingest them. She even took the step of carefully destroying all clues to what she had done, including the packaging and the correspondence with Mexico on her computer.

The subject of advance directives was in the news, so she had seized on this to inform her family at every opportunity that should she reach a point when she was disabled—she had deliberately used the example of having suffered a serious stroke—she would want to be allowed to die. She had expressed it even more strongly than this: she gave them the strict instruction that she not be taken to intensive care and supported by mechanical ventilation or other means. This was, she said, her genuine wish: were she in such a condition she would not want to be sustained in a vegetative state.

"The plan was ready to be executed," she continued. "The night before last—or maybe the night before that, I really have lost track of time—I took great care to keep up the appearance of normality. I went up to bed in the usual way. No special goodbyes, no notes, no meaningful glances—I was very careful. I took every one of the tablets I had accumulated and arranged myself in my bed. And the rest is silence, or at least, it was supposed to be."

She stopped. She was expressionless. They sat for a few minutes. "How do you feel now?" Abraham asked. "Do you still want to die?"

"I'm not sure that I ever really wanted to die," she answered, "and to tell you the truth, I don't know how I feel now. I guess I'm a little numbed. I really didn't expect to wake up and think about it. I'm surprised to be here. It wasn't part of my plan."

"What should we do now?" he asked. "Certainly, we can offer considerable expertise with respect to pain control."

"No, thank you for your offer, but I have access to the best specialists available, so that really won't be necessary. I guess I'll just return home as soon as I'm ready to do so and then reevaluate where I shall go next."

"Will you tell your husband what has happened?"

The woman instantly became very emphatic. "On no account must my husband learn anything about this. Under no circumstances, ever. It'd wound him grievously. He'd feel deceived, betrayed. I couldn't hurt him like that."

Abraham reflected momentarily on how he should respond. He did not normally like to give advice in matters like this, which were really none of his business. But this time, maybe because of his own heightened emotional state, he threw caution to the winds. "Your husband loves you," he said. "I have no doubt about that, both from what you've just told me and from what I saw yesterday. Where there's such a great love it's often better to share the deepest of secrets, even the most painful ones. I'm sure that he'll be able to understand, and what's more, you'll be able to bear the burden you both carry more effectively. It may even deepen your relationship and your commitment to each other."

He waited anxiously to see how she would respond. Her eyes widened for a moment. "Do you really think so?" she asked reflectively, then she said, "No, I couldn't tell him."

Abraham pressed on. "I can't guarantee anything, but from my experience it's very likely. I think you need to consider carefully what you do now, and that should definitely include confiding in your husband. Do you have any-one with whom you're able to talk?"

"I do talk with my family doctor but, of course, he knows nothing about my attempted suicide."

"I think he might be an appropriate place to start. With your permis-sion I could telephone him and discuss this conversation with him. I'll say that we've agreed that you wish to consider carefully how to raise with your husband the complex issues associated with your relationship, your love for each other, and above all, your commitment to his future happiness. Would you be happy for me to do that?"

She hesitated, and then replied wearily. "Yes, I suppose so. Thank you. I'm very tired now. I may sleep a little, if that's all right with you." A slight smile flickered on her face. "I've had a big day. When can I go home?"

Abraham assumed a more formal clinical manner. "From a medical point of view you'd be safe to go home this afternoon. In cases of attempted suicide, though, I'm obliged to seek a psychiatric clearance to make sure you're safe for discharge. It's my personal assessment that it's appropriate to allow you to go home, so this should be a mere formality. Can I have your agreement to call in the psychiatrist?"

"Is it really necessary?"

"I'm afraid it is. I apologize for any inconvenience."

"If you say so, Professor, I'll do it. Thank you for your kindness and care. It's made all the difference. Thank you also for your offer to assist in the future. I may well take you up on that."

"You're most welcome, Mrs. Simpson. Thank you for talking so openly and frankly to me. I'll come by this evening and say goodbye before you leave."

"Thank you again. Oh, and Professor, can I have your word again that you won't tell my husband or my daughters what I've told you?"

"You have my word, Mrs. Simpson. Goodbye."

62.

Abraham, heavily burdened by the events in the ward and in his own life, sought out Rebecca to go through the patient list again, just to make sure that this time they were not missing anything. He was starting to feel like an old man. His mind kept returning to the audit and the humiliation that awaited him. He was sure that the doctors and nurses he passed in the hospital corridor had already reached their decision; he could read the accusations and judgments in their faces. No sooner had they started, however, than Rebecca received a message on her pager that there was a new patient in Emergency to see, so they had to suspend their ward round yet again and head for the frenetic disarray of the Emergency Department.

They found the doctor who had sent for them. He was looking flustered. "Welcome to the madhouse," he said drily and, without pausing, went on. "We've got a patient I'd like you to see. Barry McLeod's a seventy-four-year-old horse trainer from the country who's been visiting his daughter in the city. While down here he's developed a pain in his side. He says he's used to pain, having fallen off lots of horses, and he didn't think much about it at first. But it persisted, so his daughter suggested that he drop by here for pain relief."

The doctor recounted the story in detail. Emergency was busy, as a result of which there had been a wait. By the time he had seen the patient, Mr. McLeod was in a very bad mood and anxious to go home. The doctor himself had felt under pressure and was somewhat annoyed; after all, it was not his fault the department was so understaffed. At first he assumed that the problem was just another trivial muscle strain, but when he examined Mr. McLeod he had a sense—he wasn't sure why—that it was more serious. He told the patient and his daughter that although it was probably nothing he thought they should do an X-ray just to make sure. The patient had started to leave but his daughter convinced him to stay.

"We did the X-ray," the doctor went on, "and the radiologist said he couldn't be sure but that maybe he did have a broken rib. He thought we should get a CT scan just in case. I explained that to Mr. McLeod and he was even less happy, as you can imagine. I can tell you, the last thing you need when the ED's full to overflowing and everyone's shouting at you to get things done yesterday is to have to convince someone to stay for another half an hour just to do you the honor of undergoing a test of some sort.

"He did stay, though, and we did the scan. I wanted to hurry them through, so I went down to get the results and I looked at the scans with the radiologist. Amazingly, it showed a pathological fracture in the rib and what looks like a renal carcinoma on the right side, which is no doubt the cause of the fracture. He wasn't very happy when I told him he had cancer, but at least this time he really did have something to be unhappy about. Look, he could go home, but I thought it was reasonable to get you guys to look at him to get him fixed up with some pain relief. Otherwise, he's just going to be coming and going here anyway."

Rebecca and Abraham found their way to the cubicle to which the patient and his daughter had been assigned. Normally, Abraham would have looked forward with relish to the challenge that was to follow but today he found himself wishing for just a few moments' respite to collect his own shattered feelings. With effort, he composed himself and entered the cubicle.

Inside was a thick set, elderly looking man, half sitting on the hard gurney, obviously uncomfortably, and a younger woman perched anxiously on a chair next to the bed. Mechanically, Abraham introduced himself and Rebecca. The patient scowled. "I'd certainly like someone to tell me what this is all about."

Adopting his time-honored practice, Abraham looked around for clues. He noted that the man's face was furrowed and weathered. He was dressed neatly but conservatively, wearing a slightly tattered white shirt and stained tie. His large hands were coarse, and his arms, like his face, were sun-scarred. On his right hand he wore a large, flamboyant gold ring. He was sitting awkwardly and Abraham could see that the mere act of turning toward him as he entered the cubicle had caused him to wince. Abraham then turned his attention to the woman, whom he estimated to be in her mid-forties. She, too, was conservatively dressed, although somewhat more elegantly than her father, and was wearing earrings and a simple necklace but no other jewelry. She, too, carried a grave expression of either hostility or fear.

The two were obviously in disarray. The doctors needed to know the whole story but to achieve this Abraham knew he had to convince them that he was on their side. He tried to put his own troubles out of his mind for a moment. "I'm a bit confused myself about what's happened this morning and I'd like to understand it better," he said strategically. "Can we just go over it in detail to make sure that we're starting from the same place? Then we can work out what needs to be done next."

The approach worked and the man responded readily to Abraham's invitation. "I've been down visiting Patricia—my daughter—for a few days and I had this bloody pain in my side." He winced as he said this, as if his own words had suddenly reminded him of the pain. "It was starting to get . . . the better of me and I asked Pat if she'd help me get some pain relief—if she'd buy some aspirin, for example. She thought it was better to see a GP so she called her own doctor . . . uhh . . . to see if she was available but she wasn't 'cause it's Saturday. So we ended up here instead. We got here about eight and talked to someone on the desk outside—I think she was a nurse—who said . . . that it sounded like a minor problem and that it'd be better if I went to a GP. We . . . uh . . . explained that we'd tried that and it wasn't possible and she said in that case we'd have to wait at least two hours. I wasn't too bloody happy about that but Pat insisted we stay . . ."

The information wasn't helpful but Abraham knew that he couldn't interrupt. As much as he wished to do so, as much as he was aching to get away, there was no way he could speed things up. "Eventually, a doctor came and said it was just a bruise but he wanted to do an X-ray to make absolutely sure there wasn't a break. He didn't seem . . . particularly interested, but that was all right, so long as he was doing his job. The X-ray took another hour— which means we'd been sitting here for four hours with nothing . . . to eat . . . or drink and nothing for the pain, which is why we'd come in the first place. I was a bit fed up by this time and me and Pat were about to leave when the guy comes up and says . . . uh . . . we need to do another X-ray. I'm pretty well at the end of my tether by now but Pat still won't let me go, so I agree and we wait for another hour. They do the scan—that was all right—and we wait some more. Still nothing to eat or drink and nothing for the pain . . . I say to the nurse can you give me something for the pain and she says no, we have to wait for the doctor to order it and they won't do so until they know what's going on. I tell you what, mate, this system needs changing. If I treated a horse like this I'd have the whole RSPCA on my back in no time."

The bitter flood of words continued. "So we're just getting ready to leave—this time I'm really going and Pat's gone off to get the car. The doctor comes in . . . and he just says, 'I've seen the scan and you've got cancer and it's spread to the bone.' Just like that: 'you've got cancer and guess what, you're going to die.' I say how do you know? Could it be wrong? And he just says there's no way it could be wrong and he needs to get a doctor from upstairs to come and see me. Then he turns and leaves. Pat gets back and asks what happened and I say he told me I'm gonna die. We were really floored. I mean, all I've got is a bit of pain. Doc, is it really true?"

Unlike the rest of the narrative the last sentence was uttered plaintively, imploringly. The man looked up at Abraham for the first time, and Abraham was now able to see the fear in his eyes. It was not just fear: it was also confusion and disorientation. Abraham knew how he was feeling. He could also see Mr. McLeod was convinced that what the doctor had said was true. Like the man with the back pain all those years ago, like Mr. Tzorvas, he had known all along . . .

Making an effort, Abraham put his own problems aside and concentrated on the man in front of him. "I understand now," he said, this time genuinely. "You've had a real shock. I'm sorry that you received the news so roughly. That's not how we usually do things here." He allowed himself to wonder what the doctor had actually said. On the one hand, it was possible that the patient, overwhelmed by what he was hearing, had only registered the words he had repeated, leaving out the context and the qualifiers. On the other hand, the doctor had certainly seemed annoyed and unsympathetic, and what happens behind closed doors—or curtains—is impossible to verify. However that may be, both the patient and his daughter needed the possibility of hope restored.

"It's true that the CT scan shows something abnormal, and we can't rule out a tumor," said Abraham. He used the word "tumor" deliberately, because he knew it was less confronting than "cancer." "We'll need to establish beyond doubt what's really going on. This'll require taking a sample of tissue and looking at it under the microscope. Even if it does turn out that there's a serious problem there are still lots of things we can do. There are all sorts of possible treatments. We'll talk to you about them when we have more information. And we can certainly give you effective pain relief; that's something we're really good at. And there's no reason why we shouldn't start right away."

Abraham had chosen his words carefully. He didn't want to make promises that he might not be able to keep. He had seen the scans himself and they certainly suggested the likelihood of a cancer. What's more, with kidney cancers of this appearance, once they had spread to bone they were usually unstoppable. This meant that what the Emergency doctor had said—the exact words he had used did not really matter—was likely to be true. But the father and the daughter needed to be able to imagine something positive: they needed to be able to imagine a future, however brief that may now turn out to be.

The daughter spoke for the first time. Her voice was thin and vacant, as if she, too, was still trying to orientate herself. "How long will Dad be in the hospital and what'll you do for him?"

Abraham and Rebecca provided the additional information, patiently explaining what was likely to happen over the next few days. They described the tests they would be performing and the kind of treatments they were expecting to use. By the time they had finished Patricia's manner had changed.

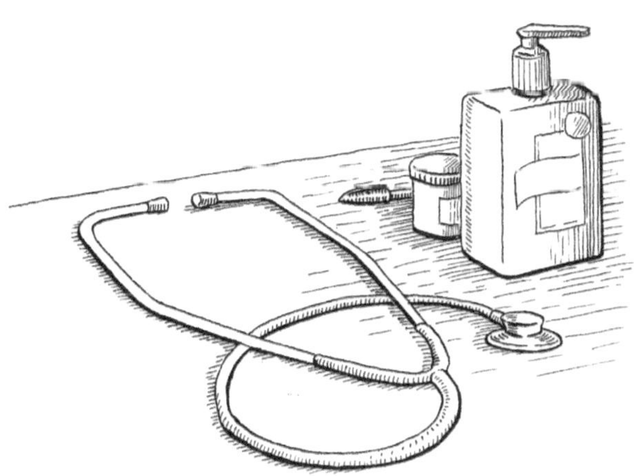

"Thank you for your kindness," she said, sad resignation now replacing hostility. "We had a shock. Dad hasn't been sick for a day in his life prior to this—apart from the inevitable injuries, falling off horses and so on. And he's only seventy. I guess we have to put our trust in your hands."

Abraham smiled weakly, unsure whether he was smiling for her or for himself. He loved complexity, but every once in a while things became too complicated even for him.

63.

Abraham was running late for his regular class with the students. On his way to meet them he saw Natalie Hermann, one of the palliative care physicians in the hospital. She was an attractive woman in her early forties with clear blue eyes and long blonde hair. "Hello, Natalie. I'm so pleased to see you! I'm just about to take the third-year students and I need a patient to show them. You wouldn't have someone who'd be suitable, would you?"

"Sure, Abraham. What do you need? A history or an examination?"

"Just someone they could talk to would be enough. It doesn't have to be anything fancy or exotic."

"In that case you could try Mrs. Newton in Ward 5A, bed ten. She has breast cancer and she likes talking."

"Thanks, Natalie. That sounds good. I'd better keep going because I'm already late."

The students were already waiting for Abraham in the ward. "Hello, everyone. I'm sorry I'm a bit late. We have a patient in Ward 5A. Let's go there."

Mrs. Newton was a middle-aged woman who probably looked older than her years. She had very sparse, fine gray hair, obviously reflecting the effects of recent chemotherapy. She was thin and her face was drawn and heavily lined, her angular features strikingly accentuated by the creases above her mouth. However, the overwhelming impression was not related to the appearance of her body but stemmed from a deep sense of sadness that seemed to seep out of her depleted frame. Abraham was struck by the somberness of the atmosphere the moment he entered the room. He puzzled over where it came from but could not identify its origin. "Hello, Mrs. Newton," he said. "My name's Professor Nevski. I'm teaching a group of medical students and am wondering if you'd be prepared to tell them your story?"

Abraham went out and waved the students into the room. As usual, they stated their names one by one and stood expectantly. Abraham started in the usual way. "Carmen, please tell me what you know about Mrs. Newton."

"Well . . . she's a middle-aged woman sitting comfortably in bed," the young woman began. "She's thin, although maybe not very thin. I can see from her arms that she's recently had a drip. She's lost much of her hair so

I speculate that she's been receiving chemotherapy, maybe for a malignancy of some sort. I can see from the magazines that she likes doing crosswords. I can tell from the card at the end of the bed that she only came in today. I suspect therefore that she's receiving regular chemo and has come in to receive a dose of medications. I can't tell what kind of cancer she has, but from her age and the fact that she's a woman I suppose one would have to think of breast cancer."

"Carmen, that's really impressive! Let's ask Mrs. Newton how accurate your speculations are. Bruno, could you ask her some questions?"

"Sure, Prof. Hello, Mrs. Newton. My name's Bruno . . . er . . . as Prof just said. As you know, I'm a third-year medical student. Would you mind if I asked you a few questions?"

"Go ahead."

"I wonder if you could start by telling us what brought you to the hospital."

"I've got breast cancer and, like your friend just said, I've come in for chemotherapy."

"How long have you known you have cancer?"

"Known? About six weeks. I had the lump for a couple of months more, though."

"Could you tell us what you first noticed?"

"I was in the shower and felt my breasts as I sometimes do and I noticed a lump. It was only small and I didn't think it could be important . . . Actually, I suppose I was worried and tried to put it out of mind. I really didn't think that breast cancer could happen to me. I didn't tell anyone about it and kept feeling for it every time I had a shower. After a while it started to hurt a bit and I got scared. Even then it took a couple of weeks before I was able to muster the courage to go to the doctor."

"Why do you think it was so difficult to go to the doctor?"

"That's a hard question. I know it really doesn't make sense. You think 'this can't be happening to me' and try to ignore it. Of course, pretending you don't have a problem doesn't make it go away. I hope you can learn from me—and maybe tell your patients that if they have a lump they have to have it checked out at once."

"What did the doctor say when you finally went?"

"He was very matter of fact. By that stage I'd already decided it was cancer and really didn't need him to tell me that's what it was. He looked very serious and said that we needed a biopsy right away. Nothing else. He got on the phone and the next day I was in the hospital having the operation. Once I made up my mind to go to the doctor things moved pretty quickly."

She had seen the surgeon, who had examined her breasts. He had said that they needed to do a biopsy but that if it was cancer the quickest and most efficient way to deal with it would be to go ahead and remove the whole lump as well as the lymph nodes under her arm. She had asked him whether he thought it was cancer and he had said that he was 99 percent sure it was.

"He kind of shrugged his shoulders as if to say, 'It's a bit tedious, but I've got to go through it.' I guess this is what he does all the time so it's understandable if he gets a bit bored. I wouldn't like to spend my life cutting up women's breasts, though it's good that someone's prepared to do so. All the same, it's easy for him to be bored, but it *is* my breast and my life."

The student was faltering, intimidated by the woman's direct manner. He flushed, uncertain how to proceed. Abraham came to his rescue. "We understand that the lump did in fact turn out to be malignant. Could you tell us how that was explained to you?"

"When I woke up after the operation the surgeon came up to me. His manner was the same. He didn't beat around the bush. He merely said, 'I was right. The lump was cancer. I've removed it and sampled the lymph nodes under your arm. It'll take a week or so to get the results on them, but if they're positive you'll have to have chemotherapy. Your doctor will refer you to a specialist who deals with these problems.' Then he said, 'You probably won't see me again. Good luck.' And he walked away."

Abraham himself faltered momentarily. He was remembering his own experience with Stephanie, his wife. He recalled how the news was broken to the two of them, in not too different circumstances. He remembered the feeling he had had at the time, of his whole world disintegrating, of floating through space, as if his own body was being torn apart, particle by particle. He could see Stephanie in front of him now. "How did you feel?" he asked, simply.

"It's hard to describe. In my heart of hearts I'd known it was cancer for weeks. But I was still devastated. I had lots of questions—the main ones being 'Am I going to die?' and 'What will happen to my family?'—but there was no chance to ask them. I was groggy from the anesthetic. I was lying on a hard gurney with a blinding fluorescent light blazing into my face. My chest and arm were throbbing. How would you feel?"

"It must have been a very difficult experience," said Abraham, aware of the understatement. "Did anyone offer you comfort? Were there other doctors or nurses around?"

"There was a nurse who kept coming up to me to take my blood pressure and check the drip. She seemed very efficient. But she didn't once look me in the face or address me by name. It seemed that once you've been found to have a cancer you're regarded as almost already dead. Maybe they can't bear to think about what's going to happen to you next, or they're too scared to talk about it, or they're trying not to imagine themselves having a breast lump. I think every woman lives with the fear of breast cancer. Every time you touch your breast for whatever reason you worry that one day there'll be a lump there and that'll be the beginning of the end."

The students remained silent. In his mind's eye Abraham could still see his wife, distraught and ravaged by the news of what was in store for her. He wished he could free himself of the image. "What happened next?" he heard himself say.

"The next little bit was okay. My GP arranged an appointment with an oncologist. She was straightforward, too, but at least she had some people skills. She explained that we needed to see what the lymph nodes showed and then decide on what kind of additional therapy I needed. In the meantime, she organized some additional tests to see if the tumor had already spread elsewhere. She explained that this was a small risk but it had to be done. I liked her and trusted her—I still do. It's not her fault, after all.

"We did the tests and then I went back to see her a week later. The minute I walked into the room I knew the news was bad. Her whole manner was different. Before, she'd been upbeat and calm. Now she looked like a judge about to pronounce a death sentence. Which I guess she was."

"Did you have anyone with you?"

"No. I do things alone. I've lived a tough life and rely on myself. In fact, everyone relies on me. I looked at her and said, 'Give it to me straight. Am I going to die?' And she looked me in the eye and just said 'I'm so sorry! I'm so sorry!' I'm not sure, but I think she was crying. It turned out that the tumor had already spread—to the lymph nodes, to my lungs, to my liver. It was only a little lump but it turned out to be a very aggressive tumor. She said that was very unusual. She hadn't seen a case so aggressive before. That doesn't make me feel any better, of course, but at least I can maintain my record of being unique! She offered me chemo but made it pretty clear that it would do no more than slow things down for a short time."

"So you're having chemo now?"

"Yes, I've already had two courses. This is my third. They're trying out some new experimental drug on me. Why not? I don't have anything to lose. I had the first dose this morning and suffered a bad reaction to it. In fact, they thought they'd lost me. I told you I'm unique. It was really weird. I could hear them talking—shouting—'Get this! Do that!' All the while I was calm, looking down on them from the outside. I was waiting to see what would happen. I kept asking 'Am I going to die?' and they just kept reassuring me. But I could see the fear on the young doctor's face and knew they weren't being honest with me. I was annoyed with them but couldn't do anything about it. I thought, 'This is interesting. I'm dying. I wonder what will happen next.' And I thought about my girls, alone and motherless, just like I was at their age. But the next thing I knew I was in my body again and waking up. A few minutes later everyone had gone and it was as if nothing had happened."

"This has been a terrible experience for you, and it's obviously not over yet. Can you tell us how you feel . . . about having cancer . . . ? Please, I recognize that this must be difficult for you to talk about. If you'd rather not we'll certainly accept that."

"No, no. It's really fine. In fact, it's good to talk. I haven't unloaded on anyone yet, so I hope you don't mind my doing so with you. You ask how I feel about having cancer. I can answer that question easily. I'm angry. I feel cheated and betrayed. I'm only fifty-six. I've never been sick in my life before. I've had to rely on myself since my mother died when I was twelve. I never knew my father. I left school early and supported myself by cleaning houses. I was determined not to spend my life being bossed about by others and went to the university. I worked during the day and studied at night. I finished a business management degree and then opened my own business. I buy and sell cosmetics. It's hard work; there are lots of competitors and they'll do anything to undercut or get rid of you. But I've succeeded against them. I might not look it, but I can be pretty tough, too.

"At age thirty-five I got married. I thought I was in love but he turned out to be a loser. I got pregnant twice before I ended up kicking him out. He couldn't handle my lifestyle, the long hours, the need to succeed. He just wanted to be at home. We didn't have a lot in common. I've never regretted telling him to leave. It made looking after the children hard, but then I always do things the hard way.

"My whole family depends on me. I've got two girls, who are eighteen and twenty, at school and university. My company employs fifteen people. I'm paying off a mortgage. What's going to happen to all these things? Why me? If I was religious I could blame God, but I'm not. You can't just stop someone's life in the middle like this.

"My children have taken it hard and I've tried to be firm with them. I've told my oldest daughter that she has to leave home. She could have stayed for a couple of years but she has to learn quickly how to live on her own. So I've made her find a place on her own. She'll have to find a job. She's moving out next week. It's more painful for me than it is for her, but it has to be done. I wish there was an alternative but we have no time to lose."

She was becoming very emotional and her voice was building in a crescendo. "I mean, if I'd been doing something wrong I'd understand it. I don't drink or smoke. I eat low-fat foods. I jog and I go to the gym three times a week. I'm not ready to die. I don't want to die . . . I don't want to die, but I'm not scared of dying. That doesn't mean I'm not scared. In truth, I'm terrified: I'm terrified of the pain, and I'm terrified of what will happen to my girls.

"I've worked so hard. I've worked to show everyone what I can do, that I could rise above my mother's poverty and humiliation so that I could see my children succeed, unlike her, who died when she was still cleaning floors. I've got goals that have not yet been achieved. But now I'm not going to be around to achieve them.

"I've had this dream. I always thought I'd live until ninety. I'd have my children around me, and their children. I'd have time for them, like I've never had. They'd come to see me, not because they had to but because they wanted to. I've had this image of myself as an old woman, with someone caring for me. Now it's not going to happen. Life's not fair."

She stopped talking. There was no sound but her soft sobbing, which she was trying hard to suppress. Abraham, trying desperately to suppress his own emotions, looked around the room. The students were white faced, obviously affected by the impassioned narrative. He thought he saw a tear on the cheek of one of them.

The pain was almost too much for him, too. He shook his head vigorously to try to drive out the image of his wife. Breathing heavily, he allowed a minute or two to pass, during which he gradually became aware of the sounds from elsewhere in the ward: the clattering of objects, beeps and bells, muffled voices. Eventually, feeling a bit calmer, he forced himself to speak.

"Would anyone like to ask Mrs. Newton any further questions?" They remained silent. After a few more seconds he turned to the patient. This was his usual closing speech. It usually came out mechanically but this time he had to force it past his own emotions. "Mrs. Newton, thank you for talking with us. It's really helpful for us to be able to hear what it's like to go through such a difficult time. You've shown us important things. Is there anything else you'd like to say to us before we finish?"

She addressed the students. "I just want to say to you: you're young, but you might not have as much time as you think. Decide early what you want to do and then go for it with all you've got. Don't delay. Don't make the mistakes I made messing around, wasting time. Find your passion early. Enjoy yourselves. I hope you all have wonderful lives!"

Abraham nodded to the students, who murmured their thanks and filed out of the room. He repeated his own thanks to her and then followed the others into the corridor. "Let's find a place to talk," he said and led the group to a small room reserved for family meetings. They sat down and remained silent. Responding to the somber mood, Abraham spoke softly. "How did you find that?"

There was another silence. Then Tracey said, "That was very sad. I feel so sorry for her daughters."

"We've spent months going to oncology clinic," George added, "and this is the first time we've seen the person behind the disease. We only ever talk about which course of chemo, or maybe the effects on tumor growth or size. We've never seen what's going on behind the scenes."

"I didn't know how to talk about death," broke in Bruno, "and I was anxious about raising such delicate questions. I can see now how it can be done, though I'm not sure I'll have the courage to do it next time, either."

"We don't have anything to offer her, do we?" reflected Carmen, in a half voice. "I mean, she's receiving chemo, which is just making her sick and even nearly killed her. Maybe it'll prolong her life by a few weeks but maybe it won't even do that. Perhaps it would be better just to let her die."

Abraham had been listening silently, respecting the deep effect the conversation had had on the young students. But, still feeling the pain evoked by his own memories, he had to respond to this last comment. "Assuming all that Mrs. Newton said about her cancer is true, it's likely that there's little that we can do to eliminate or even limit the effects of the disease. But that doesn't mean that we have nothing to offer her.

"A hundred years ago people got sick with breast and other kinds of cancer, just like they do today. There was no chemotherapy. True, there was surgery—sometimes performed under gruesome circumstances. But once the cancer had spread—as it has in this case—the treatment options were very limited. In spite of this, people still went to doctors and doctors still agreed to see patients. For the most part they did what we've done today. They sat with their patients. They offered them an opportunity to reflect, to make sense, to contemplate their successes and failures, their pride in their achievements and their unfinished projects. They became witnesses to suffering and accepted and honored the trust that was placed in them. As doctors we have a lot to offer beyond the drugs we prescribe and the operations we perform."

There was a long silence. Abraham concluded softly. "I think that might be enough for all of us for today. I'll see you next week." And he stood up and left the room.

64.

As usual, Abraham was late for his outpatients clinic. As usual, Jenny had been trying to track him down. Now he bustled in, carrying armfuls of papers and books.

"You have a patient waiting for you, Abraham," said Jenny. "What have you got there? You look like you're trying to set up a library in the clinic!"

"Oh, it's just something that's come up in the wards that I have to look up," Abraham replied. "I'm sorry I'm always so difficult for you to organize. But I do my best, really, and I don't know how I'd manage at all without you."

"It's okay! You're forgiven," she laughed. "But you'd better start seeing patients. If you keep them waiting it's me they get cross at, not you. Actually," she added, "it's not as bad as it seems because the first patient today—Marina Bell—didn't arrive."

"Marina? Did she call with an explanation?"

"No, she just didn't show up. Do you want me to rebook her?"

"Yes, if you would. Maybe just send her a letter with another appointment."

He called in the first patient. Mrs. Hörök was an elderly woman nearing the end of a long life that, like Mrs. Timoshenko's, had been full of tragedy. She saw Abraham with her husband, from whom she was inseparable. She had many medical problems, but Abraham's main tasks at this stage involved management of severe pain in her legs and attempts to assist the couple in finding ways of responding to their evident developing inability to cope by themselves at home. Abraham had talked with Mr. and Mrs. Hörök at great length over the years and knew their life stories by heart. He regarded himself as the chronicler of their history, as the person to whom they could recount their experiences and who could preserve them for others who came after them.

Their lives together had been a beautiful love story. They had been married for over sixty years. It was after the war that they met—both were refugees on the road after being liberated from different camps. He was twenty-seven and she was twenty-three. Mr. Hörök had been in Treblinka and Mrs. Hörök in Auschwitz. He'd been married before, but his wife didn't survive the war. She'd been a university student, studying literature and philosophy under the great philosopher Stanisław Ignacy Witkiewicz. Mr. Hörök's father had owned a factory that produced furniture. The family was wealthy and cultured and was taken by surprise by the brutality of the Nazis and the betrayal of the Poles. Mrs. Hörök's family consisted largely of professionals and intellectuals: her father was a lawyer and her mother had taught at the university. They were less surprised by the course of political events but unprepared for the abominations these events brought with them.

Both suffered terribly at the hands of the Nazis. She suffered sexual abuse and he—like other male inmates—was worked almost to the point of death. He developed tuberculosis in the camp, which was not to be treated until it recurred in Australia almost fifty years later.

They met in a makeshift camp in a small town near the Hungarian border in the days after the liberation. They both remembered the first time they saw each other. Improbably, it was love at first site. Both were emaciated and filthy. He had skin rashes and lice and her clothes were in rags. At the time of the liberation they had been provided with food and a few days shelter but both had decided independently that they would return to Warsaw to try to track down their families, so they took to the road along with the thousands of others. The first time they talked, on that fateful day at the refugee stop, they were unable to share their pain. It was too early. There had been too much suffering for any sense to be possible. What could ever be said they did not know. Rather, they just sat together, during a whole night. Not talking, not touching. By the morning both knew that their lives belonged together.

Together, they made their way back to Warsaw. Together, they scanned the lists of names of displaced persons seeking other displaced persons. They visited the ruins of their family houses. They walked through the rubble of the ghetto. They could find no one and nothing. Together, they decided that they needed to leave Poland, Europe, forever. They needed to make their lives elsewhere—where, they didn't know. All they had was their youth, their memories, and each other. The past was unspeakable—literally—but it held them together. It cemented their love.

Their odyssey took them across the ravaged cities and plains of Europe. They walked, they hitched rides on military vehicles and freight trains and buses. They made their way to Hungary, across Romania, to Odessa, where they found a ship that was leaving the next day. They approached the captain, offering their services as crew members. They had no money to give him and in reality they had few skills and little physical strength. But for once luck was on their side. No doubt out of kindness—and maybe moved by the obvious devotion they showed to each other—he took them on, saying that in return for doing odd jobs—cooking, cleaning, etc.—they could stay on his boat until they found a country that would take them.

Neither was able to say how long the journey lasted. Eventually, the ship berthed in Melbourne, where they were granted shore leave by the authorities. Walking through the streets for the first time—it was 1946 or 1947—they observed the starkness of the landscape, the foreignness of the streetscapes, the unfamiliarity of the habits. They couldn't read the signs; the buildings were from an age and a culture that was wholly unfamiliar to them. They felt like explorers encountering a foreign tribe for the first time. They were alone, in the farthest place in the world from the sites of their travail, of all the brutality and the cruelty and the misery. But they had each other. In the crowded street in that far-off place, dressed in the only clothes they had, with no other possessions or family, they embraced for the first time. They felt the warmth of each other's bodies and the solace and comfort of their love. Both of them had lost everything, but out of the loss a miracle had occurred: they had found each other.

At that very moment another miracle occurred. Perhaps—like the ship's captain—moved by their commitment and devotion or touched by the sad pathos they must have conveyed by their public embrace, a passerby approached them and spoke in their native Yiddish.

"Excuse me," he said gently. "You seem lost. Do you need help?" The speaker, as it turned out, had himself been a refugee from Poland, although he and his family had migrated to Australia some twenty years before. Like other

Jews settled in the country, he had retained his sense of that first moment of contact with the safe colorlessness of Australia.

"I'm sorry to intrude," he went on, "but where do you come from?" The couple lost no time in sharing their story and their predicament. They were already convinced that this was where they needed to stay. But they would require help with the immigration processes. They were assured by the stranger that this would not be a problem. The Jewish community had an established system for providing sponsorship and support for incoming migrants. He would take care of everything. They were obliged to return to the ship and talk with the captain. He would approach the authorities.

And that was how they ended up in Australia. Two days later they were legal immigrants in a country of which a few months earlier they had barely heard. They were part of a community that welcomed them and provided support: people who could speak their language and who understood—or at least acknowledged—what they had been through.

Of course, this was not the end of their struggles. They would never be able to expunge the bitterness and pain—of which Mrs. Hörök would be reminded by the tattoo on her left forearm every remaining day of her life. But it was a new beginning, and the purity of their love—which had saved them in Poland and had brought them to their new country—would continue to sustain them in the many decades to come.

It was now more than sixty years later. A lot had happened in the meantime, but in a sense, after those early tumultuous years, almost nothing. They worked hard but didn't become rich. He found work in a factory and she in an office. They saved enough money to start a small business selling furniture. It was enough for a comfortable but unspectacular life. They never traveled overseas. They never heard from any family members. They were unable to have children, a legacy of the sicknesses and physical damage they had suffered in the camps. But they were active in the community—contributing to its cultural life and participating with their new friends and adopted families in weddings, circumcisions, bar mitzvahs, funeral services. They attended the synagogue on special occasions but neither was able to pray to a God that had subjected them and their families to such privation and bestial cruelty.

Mr. and Mrs. Hörök had spent their lives together, ever since that first meeting in the small town. After the exceptional beginning it was perhaps an unexceptional life. But there was no moment at which their commitment for each other wavered. Now, at the end of their lives, they relied on Abraham to help them address the mounting obstacles they faced: Mrs. Hörök's pain and their mutual disability. The pain in her legs caused her unrelenting distress. Her husband would spend hours massaging her feet and legs, applying warm and cold compresses, tenderly seeking remedies that eased or at least blunted the pain. They depended absolutely on each other. Once, he had suffered a heart attack and was admitted to the hospital: this had been the first time in more than sixty years that they had spent a night apart. She spent the entire week sitting in a chair in their living room, crying. Abraham had raised the possibility of a nursing home, but they refused to consider any options unless they could maintain their inseparable partnership. They were open with him: they had lived their lives together and they were prepared to die together.

Today's consultation was no different from any other. Abraham sat with the two lovers, listened to the issues they raised, and made a few suggestions about Mrs. Hörök's extensive regime of medications. He hoped that his suggestions would help alleviate some of her physical pain, but he knew his real contribution was not related to pharmaceutical treatments. His role was more important and more enduring than this. In addition to the more mundane tasks he could safeguard their story, tell the next generation what they had been through, help preserve the memory of the depravity and cruelty of Nazism. As the witness to what their lives had been and what they had made of them he could confirm to the world how their love had ultimately triumphed, so that, just possibly, it might ultimately be shown that it had not all been in vain.

65.

"Hello, Mrs. Simpson. I can see you're ready to go home. I've just dropped in to say goodbye as I promised this morning. How did it go with the psychiatrist?"

The woman glowered at him. "I'm so angry and so upset," she said. "I just want to get out of here as quickly as I can."

Abraham was taken aback. "Has something happened?" he asked.

"I'm so upset!" she repeated, even more emphatically. "The psychiatrist came and he bullied me."

"What do you mean? Can you tell me what happened?"

"It started off smoothly enough. He was a young man and at first seemed very personable. He explained to me, as you did, that his task was merely to verify that I was safe for discharge. I understood that this was partly to protect the hospital against claims of negligence. He asked me to tell him why I had done what I had. I told him briefly—not in the detail that I conveyed to you this morning—but enough for him to understand, or so I thought. He asked if my husband knew and I told him that he didn't. He said that he thought that it was very important that my husband did know. He was really very insistent. I said that you and I had discussed this matter in the morning and that I'd agreed to consider it, maybe with the help of my local doctor. I emphasized, however, that at the moment I had absolutely no intention of telling any member of my family, that I thought it was unnecessary and would hurt them too much." She broke off.

"What happened then?" Abraham asked. "Did the psychiatrist accept your decision?"

"No, he became even more insistent. He said quite categorically that I had to tell my husband and that if I didn't do so he would tell him himself."

"I'm very surprised by that," said Abraham. "What did you do?"

"When the psychiatrist left I telephoned my husband and told him directly over the phone. I said, simply, 'I tried to kill myself. I lied to you. I deceived you. I betrayed you,' and I hung up. I haven't heard anything more from him. I'm now waiting for him to come to pick me up and take me home. This is not what I wanted at all." For the first time, her voice was racked with emotion. She was sobbing convulsively. "This is not what I wanted at all. It will hurt him so much! This is not a good ending. All I wanted was to end the pain. Now it has engulfed all of us. I would be grateful if you would leave me now."

Abraham was speechless. "I'm . . . I'm sorry for what happened . . ." he stammered. "I really didn't expect that . . . It is not how I . . . I'm so sorry . . . If you feel that I can help in the future please feel free to call me. My offer will always stand . . ."

She made no response. He said goodbye and left the room. He knew that he would not see her again.

PART 10

BACK TO SWAMP ROAD HOSPITAL

66.

The Swamp Road Hospital was becoming familiar to Abraham. Now, almost without thinking, as he entered through the large front doors, he set off on the route past the reception desk, to the elevators, up to the second floor, and then along the corridor to Ward 2C. He had tramped through the front door of the Royal Prince John every day for nearly twenty years. When he entered the Swamp Road Hospital, however, the experience was very different. He entered not as a doctor, whose knowledge and authority were valued, but as a patient or relative, who was powerless and vulnerable.

As he walked through the door he felt his heart beat faster and his chest tighten. Unlike the familiar predictability of the RPJ, which provided a sense of calmness and reassurance, the Swamp Road Hospital was a space of uncertainty and hostility, of crisis and impotence in the face of authority. Indeed, small events during the day—the smell of the particular floor detergent, for example, or the flickering of a fluorescent light—might set off the cascade of feelings. Abraham had listened as patients had recounted the experience of being transported unexpectedly into the emotional and psychological world of the hospital: for one, this had been triggered by the taste of tea in a polystyrene cup that she had experienced during her husband's long illness; for another, it had been the electronic beep in a supermarket that evoked the life support system in ICU that had briefly kept her son alive. Now he found himself in that liminal world of anguished uncertainty.

Abraham went straight to bed three. His father was lying there as on the previous occasions, but today his face was bruised, with an obvious black eye. When he saw him Abraham swallowed hard. "Dad, your face!" he exclaimed loudly. "What's happened to you?"

His father turned to look at him with glazed eyes. Whereas yesterday he had been drowsy but coherent it was clear that today he barely recognized his son. "What . . . ? Who . . . ?" he stammered, then turned his head dully away.

Abraham tried for a few minutes to engage him in conversation, without success. He needed further information and therefore left the room and approached the nurses' station. The nurse on duty was the same as the previous day. Abraham addressed her directly, "Hello. I'm Professor Nevski. My father appears drowsy and confused today. Can you tell me what's happened?"

"I've been instructed that if you want any information about your father you have to contact the director of medical services," replied the nurse unceremoniously.

"What are you talking about?" Abraham responded with incredulity. "He's a patient in this ward. I just want to know how he is." Despite his experience with the hospital system he felt a lump forming in his throat and tears of anger and frustration welling up in his eyes.

"That's all I can tell you," the nurse responded coldly and turned away.

Abraham picked up one of the phones on the desk and dialed the switchboard. "Hello, please give me the director of medical services," he said when the operator answered.

"I'm sorry, sir, but she's only available during office hours," the operator replied. "She should be back at nine o'clock tomorrow morning."

"In that case, can you please find me the consultant in charge of Ward 2C?"

"Of course, sir. Please hold the line and I'll contact him."

A few minutes later the consultant came on the line. "Hello, this is Dr. O'Brien."

"Hello, Dr. O'Brien. This is Professor Nevski, the son of Mordechai Nevski on Ward 2C. I would appreciate some information about my father."

"Ah, yes. Mr. Nevski has been a difficult patient. He was confused and aggressive today. He abused one of the nurses and struck out at another. We have had to administer a tranquilizer to control him."

"He has bruises on his face. How did they occur?"

"I understand that he fell out of bed."

"Why is he confused?"

"We don't know the answer to that. We assume that it's related to his underlying condition. He's difficult to treat because he's hostile to the nurses and has pulled out his IV line."

"Have you undertaken any further tests to consider other possible causes of the confusion? He has, after all, now received two days of antibiotics. He should be getting better at this stage, not worse. How have you examined, for example, a possible relationship with his head injury?"

Abraham was aware of the vulnerability of his position and knew that any suggestion of hostility or criticism of the treating doctor would not benefit his father. As much as it irked him to do so, he added meekly, "I'm not making any judgments, just seeking information."

"Mr. Nevski is a very difficult patient," the doctor repeated dismissively. "We're doing everything we can to assist him. Now, if you'll excuse me, I am being called to an emergency. Please don't hesitate to contact me again if you need further information," he added, with pointed insincerity. Then the line went dead.

Abraham was dumbfounded. He knew that his father could be sharp and rude. But this did not seem to be enough to justify the cruel treatment both of them were receiving. He returned to his father's room. Not much had changed. "Dad, can you tell me what has happened?" he pleaded.

"They want to kill me," his father replied. Then he continued, "I need to get dressed. Will you help me? I have to be before the judge in the morning. I have an important case to argue and there's an interlocutory injunction left to complete."

"Tell me about the case," Abraham said, half in resignation and half in despair.

"I've told them many times that the Act doesn't allow it. It's inconsistent with the new bylaws. Under Section 54, special permission is needed to transfer power to the trustee. If they don't accept this I'll appeal to the High Court."

"Dad, do you know who I am?" Abraham broke in.

"You're my son," his father replied. "What do you want of me? What do they all want of me?"

"Do you know where you are?"

"I'm home in bed, of course. Will you drive me to court? I'll argue from the doctrine of local powers. If they don't listen to me I'll sue them for malicious intent." He rambled on. Abraham felt a deep sense of helplessness within him. He was this man's son, a doctor, a professor of medicine. His father was a weak and vulnerable old man, however disagreeable he might be.

"Dad, I promise you I'll stand by you to the end. You can trust me,"

Abraham thought that he could detect a flash of recognition on his father's face. But it was only transient.

"It's nearly Shabbat," his father went on. "Is everyone here? Father doesn't like being kept waiting. We have to light the candles before starting the prayers." His father continued to talk in disjointed thoughts until his voice trailed off again and he lapsed once again into his drugged sleep.

"Dad, I have to leave. I'll see you tomorrow," Abraham said to the sleeping form. He had to pass the nurses' station on his way out. He stopped briefly, in a calculated gesture to show that neither he nor his father had accepted defeat. "Nurse, can you make sure an incident report has been filed in relation to my father's injury. Also, because he's confused he will need at least four hours of close observation. Please call me if there are any developments in his medical condition."

The nurse looked at him expressionlessly without replying. He left the ward feeling impotent and humiliated.

PART 11

INNER TUMULT

67.

"Prof, there's some really terrible, tragic news! Mrs. Dreyfus died!"

"What? But she'd recovered from her illness!"

"I know. We'd made arrangements for her to be transferred to the private hospital first thing this morning. But when the nurse went into her room to wake her up to start getting her ready she was dead."

"It's impossible! I can't believe it! She'd come through a really bad illness and she was better! She was sitting up talking. There was no reason for her to die!"

"It's true. We're all devastated. For days we think she's going to die any minute and then when she's almost completely better, when she's ready for discharge, she actually does die. It doesn't make any sense."

"I wonder if there could have been some medical mishap. What medications was she taking?"

"That couldn't have been it: we'd stopped everything. She didn't even have an IV anymore. It's truly a mystery."

"It just doesn't make sense! How have her daughters received the news?"

"We haven't been able to contact them yet. We think they're still in transit after leaving yesterday."

"We'll have to arrange a postmortem examination to seek a cause of death."

"Er . . . if you think so. I'll . . . arrange that . . . Prof, I feel completely devastated."

The last words were uttered with such pathos that Abraham felt a deep, cold sadness stab at his heart. He abruptly checked his own reactions. "Don't take it personally, Rebecca," he said gently. "You did an excellent job looking after her. We shouldn't forget that she came to the hospital with a life-threatening illness, and we treated it as well as we could, even if the final outcome was a bad one. I haven't said this before, but I really appreciate your caring approach and attention to detail, as well as your kindness and sensitivity. You're a good doctor and have much to be proud of. Sometimes unexpected and inexplicable things happen in medicine and this is one of them. I'm upset too, as you can see, but no one's to blame."

"Thanks, Prof," she replied, but he could tell that his words did little to comfort her. "Your support means a lot to me."

Their eyes met and they looked at each other for a long moment. Abraham felt a deep connection with the young woman who was so full of passion and tenderness.

68.

Despite the terrible weight of oppression they were all feeling, the ward round went on. As usual, there were some patients who were getting better, some who were much the same, and a few whose conditions had deteriorated. For each, the doctors went through the same routine of reviewing the facts, assessing the present condition, scrutinizing new test results, and going over and where necessary adjusting the treatment plan. Abraham was very familiar with the process—he had been through it countless times—and could normally carry it out almost by second nature. Today, however, he was struggling, overwhelmed by his inner tumult, his mind constantly returning to the death of Mrs. Dreyfus and its inevitable repercussions.

He felt disoriented, bewildered. In the mists of his perplexity he had to regain control, to decipher what had happened, to reassert the power of reason. Mostly, people come to the hospital with straightforward problems, are treated, recover, and go home. Some cases are more difficult and require careful thought and analysis, but here too the process is straightforward and systematic. The facts are collected and arranged, an array of possible diagnoses is identified, and a plan of investigation and management is developed and put into action. This aspect of clinical medicine is highly rational; everything that happens can be predicted and explained. Of course, one doesn't get everything right all the time, but even when mistakes are made it always becomes clear in retrospect what has happened, what known facts should have been given closer scrutiny, and what additional possibilities should have been considered.

Mrs. Dreyfus's death did not fit the pattern. Try as he might, Abraham could simply not think of an explanation for what had happened. People just do not recover from an illness and then die without reason; that possibility offended every fiber of his physicianly body. This was not just a matter of intellectual conceit: his entire personal raison d'être depended on the possibility of understanding the workings of the body and the disruptive effects on it of illness. He regarded every clinical case as a little mystery and had spent years honing his ability to observe and to analyze; to make connections; to recognize patterns, gaps, and incongruities; and to deploy the searing force of logic to expose the underlying processes. His reputation, his stature within the hospital, his self-esteem were built around these skills.

As irresistible as the force of his logic had been in the past, it did not seem to be so powerful now. Again and again, recently, his judgments had turned out to be wrong. As a direct result of this he now felt besieged from all sides. How quickly things can change! As long as he had been able to hold sway intellectually he was, within the hospital culture, unassailable, but he realized now how unstable that equilibrium had been. While he was successful he could live by his wits, without forbearing from speaking his mind—to colleagues, to the CEO, to anyone—but once his powers were seen to be failing he immediately became exposed and vulnerable. And nothing makes a clinician more vulnerable than the unexpected death of a patient. Over the last few days Abraham had had not one such death but four. It was almost inconceivable that such events could occur by pure chance alone. But the alternative was too painful to contemplate.

Once more, in his mind's eye he envisaged the unit audit. He would have to sit there, enduring the sneers of lesser colleagues savoring the opportunity to repay slights from past years. He would squirm in his seat—like he had made them do many times—trying to explain away his mistakes, his lapses, his inadequacies. A wave of nausea passed over him.

What made things worse was that this was only the latest in a series of events that had progressively swept away the certainties in his life. First there was his wife's illness and death and the desolation that followed, then the changes in the hospital culture, with the move to Freedom to Choose and its barefaced subordination of the values of medicine to crude economic considerations, then the deaths in the ward he had been unable to see coming. Pervading everything, however, was the now seemingly inevitable death of his father, looming as an opaque pall of melancholy. The key landmarks according to which he had oriented his world were either under threat or gone. The ground underfoot seemed insubstantial, shifting, treacherous.

In spite of his carefully cultivated appearance of humility Abraham relished the adulation the students heaped on him, and he loved to see the admiration in their eyes. He hated not knowing something or being shown up to be wrong. As long as he was in control he could affect modesty and pretend to be demure and gracious. Would his colleagues and the students now be able to see through this finely crafted exterior? Would they publicly declare him to be an imposter? Was he an imposter? Were all his supposed accomplishments and virtues no more than an elaborate artifice?

As Abraham's mind wandered he became aware that Rebecca was talking to him. She was asking him a question. It was something about Dr. Vilgis and his past treatments. With an immense effort he sought to curb the massive chaos that was going on inside him. Composing himself, he assumed a manner of studied coolness, as if nothing could surprise him.

69.

"How *is* Dr. Vilgis today?" asked Abraham, expertly projecting his air of normality.

"His chest's continuing to improve," Rebecca replied, also doing her best to sustain the appearance of business as usual. "In other respects, things are much the same as ever."

Abraham asked Ashis and Desmond for their observations, as much to gauge their states of mind as to obtain new information. He and the nurse would be working together for a long time to come and they needed to find a way to make this possible.

"Nothing much to report from me, Prof," Ashis replied in his usual phlegmatic way. "When I see him he's just lying there. Dora's with him from early in the morning 'til late at night. When she comes in they say prayers together—or rather, she says prayers. Then she reads the newspaper to him, and then she reads a book. She often plays music, too. She talks quite a lot, but he never answers."

"What music does she play?"

Ashis shook his head. "I really don't know, Prof. It's something classical."

"The nursing experience's pretty much the same," added Desmond, more subdued than usual but adopting a careful, businesslike manner. "We never see any response. We turn him every hour or two and he doesn't give any assistance. We feed him soft fluids, which he seems to tolerate satisfactorily and, though he coughs occasionally, there's nothing striking. The physiotherapist's been visiting him and she reports that she's happy with how things are progressing, too."

Grateful for the nurse's restraint, Abraham looked to Rebecca, who made it plain by her expression that she wanted to keep the ward round moving. To show that he was still in control he quickly reaffirmed the plan to complete the course of antibiotics with a view to returning the patient to his nursing home at the earliest possible date, and the group moved on.

70.

"Our next patient is Mr. Timmens," said Rebecca, "the man with the collapse they mentioned in handover. He's in bed twelve."

The room contained four beds, one in each corner. In these shared wards little that occurred regarding any one patient could be hidden from the others, although when required, a semblance of privacy was achieved by drawing curtains around a bed. What in other settings would be regarded as intimate personal details—such as private conversations with doctors and nurses, or the evident nature of major issues of treatment such as delivery of oxygen or intravenous fluids, or the presence of pain or shortness of breath—became known to all. Sometimes this openness undoubtedly caused inconvenience or embarrassment: the coughing or snoring of one person, for example, could be disruptive to all the others, and the nauseating smell of feces or vomit would at times pervade the general atmosphere for minutes after an event. Nonetheless, for the most part, the arrangement worked reasonably well, perhaps because the patients and their visitors recognized that discretion would be mutually beneficial, or maybe simply because of a resigned acceptance of a situation no one could change.

Each patient, in fact, kept a careful eye on the others. This generated a cautious and qualified sense of solidarity and mutual caring, with the qualification that each also kept his or her distance, watching—sometimes with a critical and not necessarily magnanimous eye—the passing parade. In fact, the transience of any particular bed allocation made closer relationships both inadvisable and difficult to achieve. Patients were often moved from one location to another without warning or explanation. Occasionally, the move would be for a reason—such as the need to be close to a particular piece of equipment—but mostly the word simply came from the top—no one seemed to know exactly where—to move the occupant in bed fourteen to bed twenty-six, and it was simply accepted and acted upon without comment or objection.

Abraham and Rebecca approached bed twelve. As usual, Abraham rapidly took in the situation. The patient was a middle-aged man sitting up eating his lunch—in fact, eating with obvious enjoyment, a rare occurrence in this setting. Close by him within the space of his cubicle—even though the curtains were open—were a woman and man of roughly similar age. The woman was plainly dressed, with short brown hair and thick-rimmed, inelegant spectacles, and the man, perched on a stool obviously too small for someone of his bulk, was dressed in heavily worn jeans and a stained T-shirt. The patient himself was unshaven, wearing a loose hospital gown, and receiving oxygen through a clear plastic tube in his nose.

But he was eating his dinner with relish. "Are you Mr. Timmens?" Abraham asked.

"Yep, that's me," the patient responded, barely glancing in his direction.

Abraham drew the curtain so that the group of them—the patient, the woman, the man, and the medical team—were suddenly together in the fabricated private space in the corner of the ward. "I'm Professor Nevski, and this is Dr. Sanderson. We're the doctors looking after you. Can you give us a brief summary of what it was that brought you to the hospital yesterday?"

"It was the collapse, Doc, I just sort of . . . collapsed . . . fell to the ground."

"Where were you and what were you doing?"

"I was just standing with Kevin and the boys in the bar and the next thing I knew I was in the ambulance. It was weird."

"Is this the first time this has happened?"

"No. I've had a few collapses since my car accident in 2000. I'm, like, just standing there and suddenly I fall to the ground. Sometimes I can't move my arm or leg. It used to be pretty scary. The doctors say it's because of the head injury. After the accident I spent three months in the hospital and when I got out I had to walk with a stick for a few more."

"That was some years ago. How have you been in the meantime?"

"I have to take tablets for my blood pressure and diabetes, but I've been okay really. The attacks have come on more often in the last year or two."

"Do you mind if I ask if you drink a lot of alcohol?"

"Nah, I don't drink much. I like going to the pub, but . . ."

"Do you go every day?"

"Most days."

"So yesterday you were standing in the bar and you collapsed. Did you have any warning?"

"Nah."

"Did you have any chest pain?"

"Nah."

"Did you have any palpitations—a sense that your heart was beating fast or irregularly?"

"Nope."

"Did you have any odd feelings in your head or arms or legs or change in your vision?"

"Nah."

The other man broke in. "I was standing right next to 'im, Doc. We was just talkin' and he, like, goes limp. He falls backwards and luckily I just puts me arms out and grabs 'im. I grabs 'im and puts 'im in the chair, but he's right out to it. He's groanin' something awful."

"How long was he unconscious?"

"About ten minutes, I reckon. We put 'im in the chair and called the ambulance. They come pretty quick. By that time he was awake but pretty confused."

"Were there any jerky movements of the arms or legs?"

"Nah, I don't think so."

"What color was he?"

"He was normal, I s'pose. Maybe a bit blue. That's what the ambulance guys said. It was pretty scary. I thought we'd lost 'im."

Abraham went on in this vein for a short time, with additional questions from Rebecca. They asked the patient about his other symptoms, his previous medical conditions, drugs he was taking, and so on. The man answered in short sentences, frequently embellished by contributions from the other two.

"Charlie," Rebecca asked, "can you tell us who you live with and what work you do?"

"I live with Wendy here. I was married once, but the marriage broke up after the accident. I'm unemployed. I used to be a welder. But I had to give it up 'cause I injured my back at work. That's a common thing for welders. There's a lot of heavy lifting. Not so much today, mind you. Today they have all sorts of hoists and lifts. In my day you had to lift all the equipment on and off the car yourself."

"So how do you spend most of your time these days?"

"Oh, I find lots of things to keep me busy. I read. I walk a bit. I meet up with friends."

"What do you like reading?"

"I like John Grisham books."

"Doc, can I say a few things?" the patient's partner broke in. "Charlie and me live together. We been an item ever since his marriage broke up and me husband left. We used to have a good relationship. He got a bit of money from the accident and we could afford a nice flat. But in the last few years he's really changed. I reckon it's the drink. We've argued about it a lot. He spends most of his time during the day at the pub." She paused briefly, then continued with intensity. "I don't like to have to say this in front of him, but he knows I think it and I have to do it. I think he's an alcoholic, but he won't admit it. He doesn't do nothing but go to the pub and drink. He spends all his pension on booze and we have to live off mine, and that's not enough even to buy food and smokes."

Charlie remained motionless, his head bowed, as if he knew and accepted what was to follow. She became more animated and raised her voice. "His whole personality's changed. He used to be such a reliable person, a good worker, easy to get along with. Now he's messy. He doesn't look after 'imself. Sometimes he just looks like an old derelict. He often comes 'ome drunk. If I say anything he gets annoyed. He can get pretty angry. He throws things. He hits me. He makes me do things I don't want to do—sexually, you know. If he can find someone else to fuck he'll do that—excuse the language, Doc. Once he even brought 'ome a slut and fucked her in front of me and then threw her out. Just to show me that he could. When he gets drunk he can be really violent. I've got the bruises to show it even now. I can show them to you if you want. Sometimes he just goes crazy and I fear for me life. I'm sorry to have to say all this, but you have to know. I'm at me wit's end. I need help. We need help. You have to help us."

Wendy was crying convulsively. Charlie sat there, staring at the remains of his lunch. Although there was no doubt that everyone in the room could have heard the searing accusations against him there was no sense of embarrassment. Kevin coughed uneasily, shifted uncomfortably on his stool, and looked into space.

After a long silence, Charlie said, "I may drink a bit too much but Wendy's exaggerating, as she always does. I can stop whenever I want to. Sometimes I don't drink nothing at all. If I do drink, it's just a few beers—no more than anyone else. Maybe I get a bit wound up from time to time, but who doesn't? We can be pretty rough with each other sometimes, it's true, but that's just how we are. Maybe I lose control occasionally, but I don't mean nothing bad. Wendy and me love each other. She's all I got. Things have been pretty tough. It's hard not having a job. No one wants to employ a guy in his late forties. I haven't been able to work since I injured my back, and the younger guys know more and can work faster anyway. What can I do? Sometimes I just want to die."

He was sobbing now, too. There was another long silence. Abraham, recognizing Wendy's desperation and Charlie's vulnerability, thought of his own predicament and his own desperation and vulnerability. Oddly, he felt for Charlie, violent as he might be, but still pathetic, naked—figuratively and literally—exposed by the semi-public accusation against which he had limited ability to defend himself. He sought to lower the intensity of the discussion a little. "There are obviously lots of things for us to talk about," he said with his practiced blandness. "I think we need to talk them through over the next day or so. Maybe something good will come out of this business. Rebecca, is there anything you want to say?"

He looked at the registrar and was shocked to see that she was deathly pale. She remained silent, so he continued with a few more questions to Charlie. After a bit more talk Abraham said, "We need to examine you, Charlie, but I think we might come back a little later and do that. Then we'll try to work out a plan. It's likely that we'll have to do a few tests. We may get some additional specialists to come and see you, if you don't mind. And we'll work out how to keep talking about the things we've just been discussing. Does that sound okay to you?"

"Yeah. I'll be here, Doc. Just let me know when you're ready for me."

Rebecca and Abraham pulled back the curtain and took their leave. Abraham deliberately avoided looking around to observe how many of the others in the room might have heard what had been said. The two of them went out into the corridor. Abraham could see that Rebecca, too, was struggling. Like the rest of them, she also was fighting vulnerability and desperation.

"This is a tough one. What do you think?"

Her eyes were deep with sadness. "I . . . I really feel . . . for that woman, Prof," she stammered. "She's so helpless, so desperate, so violated. But so is he."

"It is difficult," Abraham replied. "We can make sure he doesn't have a brain tumor and withdraw him from alcohol, and we can link both of them into counseling or even psychiatric care if need be. But we can't solve the problems in their personal lives, can we?"

"I've seen some violence against women," Rebecca said, still talking with strong feeling. "I know how dependent women can get. He's not a monster—just a pathetic guy with a drinking problem and a bruised male ego. But he's being cruel to her and she's trapped. She has nowhere to go."

Abraham sensed that Rebecca's words were coming from a deep source. Deliberately preventing himself from imagining what that might be, he softened his manner. "What do you think we should do?"

"I think she's stuck. Maybe nothing will help her. Maybe it'll continue until one of them dies." She met his gaze briefly, then quickly turned her eyes away.

71.

"We need to see Mr. McLeod, the horse trainer with metastatic kidney cancer we saw in Emergency." There was tiredness in Rebecca's voice, but they still had one more patient to review. "We've made a bit of progress. Ashis, can you summarize for the prof and Des?"

"Sure, Beck. We referred Mr. McLeod to the oncology team. They reviewed the scans and agreed that it looked like a renal cell carcinoma. They said they needed a tissue diagnosis and took a biopsy of the right seventh rib under local anesthetic in the ward. We don't have the full histology yet but there's already a preliminary report on the system that confirms that it's malignant.

"We also ordered a bone scan and some blood tests. The scan was done this morning and shows multiple lesions—probably malignant—throughout the skeleton. The blood tests have come back showing some liver function abnormalities, so we've also ordered an ultrasound of the liver. Things aren't looking good."

"It does appear bad. What about the pain?"

"We're doing the best we can for that," replied Rebecca. "I called the Palliative Care registrar to ask for advice. It seems that the main pain's coming from the rib, although he also has pain that's probably related to some of the other bone lesions. Since admission, the pain appears to have got much worse. The Pall Care reg suggested non-steroidals and high-dose morph in the first instance. Once the biopsy results are back, she said, we can also consider cancer-specific therapies, radiotherapy, and other treatments. She said she'll bring her consultant around to give more formal recommendations."

"What Beck says about the pain's right," confirmed the nurse. "When Barry first came up here he seemed reasonably comfortable, but then the pain immediately became worse. He was up most of the night screaming. For a tough guy like him that must be very unusual; the pain must be really bad. The morphine gives some relief, but any movement really stirs things up."

"Thank you for all of that. Perhaps we should see him."

"Before we do that, Prof, can we talk about his resuscitation status?" Rebecca asked. "Should we make a decision to limit or scale down his treatment if he suddenly becomes sicker? The Freedom to Choose communication consultant called me to say that she'd seen him and he ticked the box on the form that said he didn't want to go to the ICU. She suggested that we make it clear in the care plan that there shouldn't be any escalation in treatment."

"Regardless of what boxes he's checked, Rebecca—and what the Freedom to Choose consultant says—it's premature to make a decision to limit his care at this stage. It's increasingly likely that he has widespread malignancy, and if that really is the case his prognosis will be poor. However, we're still waiting for the definitive test results, and before we have them we won't be in a position to make a firm statement about the nature of the tumor and the extent to which it can be treated. What's more, when we do have the information we'll still have to talk with Mr. McLeod himself before making any decisions. For the moment, therefore, we'll regard him as being a candidate for full resuscitation."

Abraham breathed in deeply and braced himself for Desmond's reply, which he felt he could predict almost word for word. The nurse's face was hard with anger and contempt. But histrionically shrugging his shoulders, he merely said with a sneer, "Okay. You make the decisions here," and turned away. A few moments passed, then Abraham, still bristling, said peremptorily, "Let's go and see him."

72.

Mr. McLeod was sprawled across the bed, much as he had been when they had seen him in the Emergency Department. The bedclothes were in disarray and on the floor were various articles of clothing and a newspaper. Standing next to her father, holding his hand, was Patricia, whom Abraham could see at a glance was less composed and more anxious than on the previous occasion he had met her.

In answer to his question about how he felt, the man's response was immediate. "Oh, Professor, I'm bad, very bad!" He caught his breath as he was talking. "The slightest movement causes the sharpest pain . . . uhh . . . I've had plenty of pain in my life but never anything like this. When I . . . uuhh . . . move even a bit . . . it's like a shock through my whole body . . . The shots help a bit, and I really don't . . . like . . . uh . . . being a nuisance . . . but the worst thing is that I just can't sleep. Last night and the night before I didn't get a wink of sleep, not a single wink . . . I'm pretty tired, Doc. Can you give me . . . something to knock me out?"

Responding with concern, Abraham assured him that an immediate effort would be made to improve the treatment for the pain and that when the results of the tests that had been performed were available, a decision could be taken about the most effective, long-term overall approach to treatment.

Despite his discomfort the man replied graciously. "Thanks, Doc," he said. "I'm sorry I was so rude yesterday. I know you're all . . . doing your best. And I want to say that you . . . should be proud of these young doctors here. They've been wonderful to me. Both the beautiful young lady . . . and . . . the handsome young man! In fact," he managed a weak smile, "it turns out that I know the young lady's mom's family! They're neighbors of mine. Known them for years, actually. I've promised Beck that when she's next up she can come to our place and I'll give her some wonderful horses to ride."

Abraham glanced briefly at Rebecca, who was blushing demurely. Touched by the man's kindness, he thanked him for his sentiments and tactfully returned to the underlying reason for the tests. Mr. McLeod's reply was again straightforward.

"I don't understand the details, Doc, but I know it's looking bad. It seems like what the feller downstairs said to me yesterday might turn out to be right—that I've got cancer and I'm dying. Is that correct?"

This was a familiar exchange, and Abraham replied, as he had done many times in the past, with a careful statement that while a malignancy seemed likely it had not yet been proven, and that if this in fact turned out to be the case there would still be many possibilities for treatment. He explained also that some cancers grow slowly and others respond well to particular drugs, so even if the treatments couldn't cure the cancer they might well be able to control the symptoms for a while.

Before he was able to finish, Patricia broke in, speaking loudly, taking Abraham by surprise with her vehemence. "This is crap!" she said. "It's all just hot air! We've been here, at this hospital, for a day and a half and all we've done is sit around waiting. We've had a few scans, but all we're told is 'wait until the test results come in.'" She screwed up her face and raised the pitch of her voice. "In the meantime, my dad's lying here in pain. We ask for pain relief and nothing happens. I ring the bell and if I'm lucky someone comes fifteen minutes later. You heard him: he hasn't slept a wink. If someone doesn't sleep how could they ever fight a disease, especially one as serious as this? We need some action."

"I'm sorry, Patricia. I know it's hard. But we're—"

"Don't condescend to me. If this is your best, it's not good enough. You've got to do more . . ."

"Pat, please don't," said the patient. "Uh . . . it's not their fault . . . I'm the one with the disease . . . They're trying . . ."

"That's not what you said to me yesterday," said Patricia, by now almost shouting. "You were furious at that rotten doctor in Emergency who was so cruel. I don't know why you're . . ." She broke off in tears.

Everyone else remained silent. Rebecca moved over to Patricia and put her arm around her. She was sobbing loudly. Desmond spoke. "Pat," he said soothingly, "I know you've been here nonstop and you haven't slept either. Perhaps you should take some time off. We've got good nurses here. We'll take good care of your father."

Abraham, shocked by Patricia's outburst, was transported back to his own predicament at Swamp Road Hospital. Thrown off balance, he fumbled out some supportive words, but the rest of the consultation was clumsy and uncomfortable. The doctors conducted a brief examination of the patient and the party retired once again to the corridor.

Patricia followed them out. She was still angry and directed herself at Abraham with unremitting vehemence. "Professor," she said, articulating her words precisely, "I do not apologize for my strong language. My father is dying." Her expression was hard and vengeful. "You wouldn't know what it's like to have a father dying."

He smiled grimly. "I might know better than you think," he said.

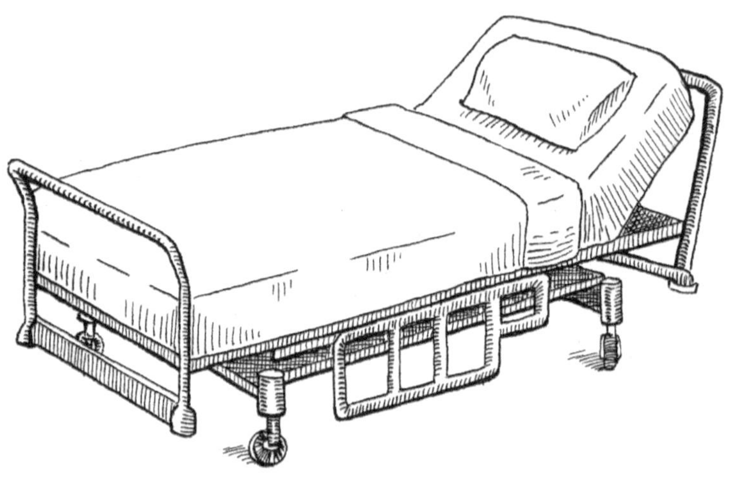

73.

The members of the lunch group were sitting around the table in their usual corner of the crowded cafeteria. Abraham, distracted, was pondering his sandwich, trying to make sense of all that was happening—his father's illness, the deaths of his patients, the new, oppressive atmosphere in the hospital, and the attack he had just experienced from Mr. McLeod's daughter. He felt depleted, desolated. It seemed that nothing made sense anymore. Everything was slipping away from him.

The others were chatting desultorily. " . . . There's some juicy gossip about Margaret," Nic was saying.

"I don't want to hear it," replied Harry Krokowski. "What's she up to now . . . ?"

" . . . How's that man in 4B with the lung cancer?" asked Madeleine.

"He's heading for surgery," replied Ian Moloney. "We're interested to see what they find. I'll let you know what happens."

"What happened with the old woman with jaundice you took from Emergency?" asked Harry.

"It's not looking good," replied Nic. "Ten to one it'll turn out to be a malignancy. I hate to say it, but I reckon her next port of call might be a Freedom to Choose communication consultant."

Observing Abraham's evident preoccupation, Madeleine sought to bring him into the conversation. "Abraham, how's it going with your dad?" she asked gently. "Are you okay?"

Abraham wasn't in the mood to talk but appreciated Madeleine's concern. "It's pretty hard," he replied flatly, still staring at his sandwich, "and he hasn't exactly received the best care. This isn't the first time I've been on the receiving end of medicine but it's by far the worst."

Madeleine was genuinely concerned. "I'm so sorry to hear that. How are your mom and kids handling it?"

Abraham really didn't want to get drawn into details but he had to answer. "I don't think my mother fully understands what's going on, though we do take her to see him from time to time. The kids were terribly wounded by Stephanie's illness, and the legacy of that's continuing, but I think they're doing their best." He looked up fleetingly at Madeleine, forcing a weak smile.

The conversation drifted to other topics. Someone raised the matter of Freedom to Choose and the signing of advance directives. Sensing that all eyes were on him, Abraham recounted his experience with his father. "I asked him if he wanted to give any directives and he interpreted my question as a sign that we wanted to get rid of him. I felt ashamed and humiliated."

Abraham's comment struck a chord with Natalie Hermann. "That's really interesting," she said. "We don't often ask relatives how they experience advance directives. We assume that they'll automatically be reassured that the wishes of their father or mother or whoever it is are being respected, but I suppose it's not obvious that that's always the case."

The raising of the subject of Freedom to Choose and advanced directives provoked immediate interest from the group. It was obviously on everybody's mind. Ian recounted his experience that filling in forms with long lists of treatments and preferences makes it harder, not easier, to talk about dying. "The problem is that it's all in the abstract," he said. "It doesn't refer to the actual problems the patient faces. In real life what inevitably happens is just the outcome you didn't expect, the exact thing you didn't talk about, so when you go back to the list it provides no help whatsoever. Incidentally," he added spitefully, "the so-called 'communication consultants' hovering self-righteously about the ward don't help, either."

Natalie agreed. "We see it all the time in Palliative Care," she said. "Statements or directives often can't be used because the circumstances have changed or hadn't been anticipated. I don't know how many times I've seen someone who's said for years that she'd never want to go on living if she had a stroke and then completely changed her approach when the unthinkable actually happened."

There were many nods of assent. The unpredictability of illness was something with which they'd all had experience. Madeleine was reminded of a particular case. "Sometimes the illness can even cause some good things to happen. When I was on the ward a few weeks ago we had a man with cancer of the esophagus—extensive disease that'll certainly kill him quickly. He was a poor old guy who'd been living for years pretty much as a hermit, estranged from his family. I don't know the exact details, but apparently he hadn't seen his children for nearly ten years. But when they heard he was dying they all rallied round. They visited him in the hospital and—as far as I could tell—reconciled their disputes with him. It meant that after years of suffering alone, bitter and resentful, he's now able to die in a setting of love and forgiveness. We were doing a routine ward round and he burst into tears telling us about it."

A few people nodded in agreement and there was a brief appreciative silence. The conversation then moved to concerns about whether the involvement of "experts" not connected with a patient's care might discourage doctors, nurses, and others from having conversations about death. One of the doctors commented that talking about death was not "a matter of ticking boxes," but was really an opportunity for "a conversation about life," about a person's hopes, disappointments, and achievements. It was the conversation that counted; often, the actual mode of death was of much less importance.

Once again, Natalie, who was intensely engaged by the conversation, spoke up. "That's a really important point!" she exclaimed. "I can't tell you how much effort we put in trying to teach it to the students and residents. The whole thrust of the advance directive approach is wrong because the focus on outcomes and decisions that it's based on obstructs the grieving process. It prevents people from reaching the point of calmness, the state of acceptance, which used to be called 'quietus.' It stands in the way of the ability to make sense of one's own death, let alone that of one's loved ones—"

"It's not just a focus on outcomes and decisions but also an emphasis on a particular kind of evidence and practice," Nic broke in, speaking with uncharacteristic sobriety. "The only evidence that's usually regarded as authentic is that based on measurable, empirical facts and outcomes. But the things Harry just spoke about—hope and despair, precariousness and vulnerability, disappointments and successes, and so on—are often not measurable: they refer to ideas that are too complex to measure and control in that way."

Acknowledging Nic's point, Natalie went on, arguing that while the advance directive approach is only interested in kinds of treatments and the mode of dying, when one talks with patients about end-of-life issues, it becomes clear that there is no tidy solution and that many different approaches are possible: one person might have a clear point of view himself; another might place his trust in a relative or friend; yet another might refuse to make a decision at all; and someone else might reject the question completely. "These different approaches aren't alternatives that people have to choose from. They're resources they can call on in different ways at different times. People don't even see the need to appear rational or to avoid contradiction. What's more, there's no reason why they can't change their minds as often as they like."

In his detached and fragmented state, Abraham's mind was drifting in and out of the conversation. On the one hand, he felt relief that many of the concerns that were perturbing him so gravely were shared by people whose opinions he respected. On the other, the more their words rang true the more disquieted he became. He felt the lack of certainty, the sense of ragged precariousness, in his deep heart's core. He knew he was supposed to fight but just now he felt so weak he could barely move. How he wished that there was someone who could share his burden, someone in whom he had the courage to confide! How he wished for his own state of calmness.

"It really does show how much complexity we have to deal with," Madeleine was saying. "I'm sure that over the centuries every skilled physician would have understood the points Nic and Natalie have just been making. In all probability they'd have taken them for granted and worked with them in their daily practice. But now, under the guise of efficiency and providing patients with 'freedom,' a large part of this process is eliminated in favor of a series of answers to yes and no questions. Instead of deep dialogues based on trust, we're constantly searching for simplistic, unambiguous instructions, even when the patient herself is crying out for something more. Doctors seem to have lost sight of the need to come to terms with the fear and the pain. That's what really matters in the experiences of their patients."

Abraham added to himself, "and in their personal experience, too!" Amid the nods of assent a sense of despondency hung over them. The members of the group straggled off back to work.

74.

The students were still perturbed by their experience with Mrs. Newton, the woman battling with breast cancer. Tracey recalled her exhortation to them to "find their passion."

"She really made us think, Prof. We've been talking about it all week. We've been trying to decide what our passions are. Some of us want to travel, some want to succeed in our careers, others just don't know. We thought we'd ask you what you wanted when you were at our stage."

The four of them waited expectantly for Abraham to reply. He took in their young, fresh faces and thought of his own uncertainties, even now, thirty years later. They assumed that he had found a path of wisdom and comfort that resolved all the doubts of his youth. If only they knew how wrong they were.

But they need not know and he did not have to tell them. What he could tell them about was his own passion, which—in spite of the battering it had taken along the way—remained yet unextinguished. He could appeal to them, like Zarathustra, never to relinquish their quests, so that they might give birth to dancing stars. "I hope my answer doesn't disappoint you," he began, "but I think I understand what you're trying to grapple with. I don't have many solutions, but I can tell you about a few of the conclusions I've come to along the way.

"When I was your age I just wanted excitement and adventure. For a time I thought about entering the police force because I liked solving mysteries and the glamour of being a famous detective appealed to me. But somehow I ended up doing medicine instead. I'm not exactly sure why, although it was probably just because I had good marks, it seemed interesting, and it didn't involve anything to do with figures. After the course finished I tried out lots of things and it took me a while to make any sense of where I wanted to go. I wanted to go to the edge, to find the limits of what could be thought and experienced. I traveled, worked in factories, went bungee jumping and white water rafting. I even tried working in the slums of Calcutta to help sick children.

"It was fun but it didn't provide what I was searching for, and in the end I came back home to complete my training and to think things through. It was only much later that I came to realize that what I was looking for was not on the top of some mountain or in some exotic place. It was here under my nose all the time. I learned it from a patient a bit like Mrs. Newton, a woman who was dying from a rare cancer. She taught me that the place to look for the extremes of human experience was right in front of me, in ordinary, everyday life.

"What Mrs. Terasso taught me was that the lives of ordinary people are full of adventure, passion, and despair. We think of everyday life as mundane, routine, tame. We sneer at the sameness of suburbia and the conformity of office work—certainly, I used to. But in doing so we ignore the real substance of the worlds in which most people live."

Abraham paused to try to judge the students' reactions. He half expected that they would be repelled by his stilted prose, dismissing it as the weird ideas of an eccentric old professor. But he saw that they were engrossed, their eyes fixed on him and their bodies motionless with expectation. He breathed deeply and went on, not really knowing what he was about to say.

"You don't need to climb Mt. Everest or swim the Amazon or ride a crocodile or wrestle a grizzly bear to go to the limits of what can be experienced. All the elements of the most extreme experiences and the most powerful qualities of human beings, good and bad—including love and hatred, pain and joy, loyalty and betrayal, courage and cowardice, faithfulness and dishonesty, generosity and meanness—are here, right in front of us, in ordinary daily life. They show themselves vividly and with special intensity during illness, and nowhere more than here in the hospital.

"People might live in houses and streets that look alike. They might own cars, plasma televisions, and CD players or spend hours playing computer games, watching *The Simpsons*, listening to pop songs on their iPods, or worrying about what brand of cornflakes they should buy. But they also fall in love, make love, betray and are betrayed, fall ill, suffer desperately, and grieve for their loved ones, who may themselves experience great suffering. They come to the hospital and they die, or their parents or wives or husbands or children die. And they suffer, just as deeply, just as authentically, as anyone has suffered in art or literature or history."

He could barely tell now if he was talking aloud or just thinking to himself. His own words had awoken in him—however fleetingly—his old fire. He knew that when he had finished, the same problems—the uncertainty, the doubt, the fear, the errors and limitations, the pride and vanity—would still be there. But for however long it lasted it was exhilarating to focus on what was still pure and clear.

"Medicine provides a window on the extreme experience of everyday life.

Those of us lucky enough to be a part of it have been taken places no one else has been. And we can go there, not just for the sake of abstract experience, not just to flaunt what we ourselves have achieved, but to help shape our own and other people's achievements, to participate in them, and to share in both the exaltation of success and the black despair of loss."

He had certainly had his share recently of black despair. It had been scary; in fact, he was still scared. Even now he was not sure if it was all too much to bear. He finished with an admonition.

"I don't want to scare you. People come to medicine for many different reasons. Some want to serve humanity. Some want to earn lots of money. Some have responded to pressure from their families. But once you've entered, there's no escape. This is a wager you cannot renounce. You'll be exposed to forces that are powerful and rewarding but can also be tragic. Your obligation—your inescapable obligation—is to remain true to your values and to be accountable for whatever decisions you make. You have to decide what these values are, what is important to you, what you want to achieve, how you want to be remembered; these values might turn out to be right or wrong, but they have to be yours. And when you do decide, when you take action, it has to be your decision and your action, for which you alone accept responsibility."

PART 12

SHATTERED LIVES

75.

"Hello, I'm Abraham Nevski. Please take a seat . . . Would you like to tell me your story?"

"My name's Dorothy Camello. I'm a psychologist and I want you to know from the beginning that I've lost all faith in doctors. I'm here because I need help, but I'd rather not be here at all."

She was a diminutive woman with delicate features, an open face, and a sad smile, elegantly dressed, with golden hair swept up into a bun. Despite the forcefulness of her manner, she exuded a sense of kindness and gentleness. From the tone of her voice it was obvious that she had been very wounded.

"I'm forty-one years old. Last year I started having pains in my tummy. At first they were mild, but gradually they became more severe. I work in a private clinic, and sometimes the pain was so bad that I had to interrupt a consultation with a patient. That was very embarrassing, especially as I see women who suffer from menstrual disorders.

"Then my periods became irregular. That was new—my periods have always been like clockwork, except when I was pregnant. I became worried and went to my local doctor. She organized a scan, which showed I had some kind of tumor on my ovary. The doctor was worried and sent me to Professor McDonald at the Women's Hospital. He looked at the scans and said he was concerned that it could be cancer and that I needed an immediate operation.

"I've never liked the idea of surgery but obviously I don't want to die. I told Professor McDonald that I was reluctant to have any operation down there and he scoffed at my concern, saying that I wouldn't notice the difference but that if I didn't go ahead the outlook was grim. I discussed it with my family—my husband Bill and two children—and we agreed to go ahead.

I saw Professor McDonald a couple of days later and asked him for more details. He said that he was 95 percent certain the tumor was malignant and that it would spread quickly if he didn't remove it. He even said that it might already be too late. This was a nasty disease—he was talking as if the conclusion had already been reached—and it killed lots of people my age.

"I told him again and again that I'd go ahead on the condition that he'd do the minimum necessary. I didn't want to be dismembered. My sexual relationship with my husband is one of the most precious parts of my life. We have a great relationship. I love having sex. I love the feeling of him inside me. Being a woman is who I am. It's my life and my work and my family and my world.

"I told Professor McDonald that I'd only go ahead if he'd take out the minimum amount possible. I didn't want to have a hysterectomy. My womb is very important to me.

"I was scared when I went to surgery. Bill was there and said goodbye. I really thought I'd never see him again. Professor McDonald came in, very cheery. I don't think he was taking it all that seriously.

"I woke up I don't know how much later. The first thing I asked was, 'What did they take?' The nurse wouldn't tell me anything—saying that it was up to Professor McDonald to talk to me and that he was the best. After an hour or so he came in—I was still in recovery. He said that it was a nasty, aggressive-looking tumor on the ovary and that he had to take everything. My heart sank and I asked, 'What's everything?' He said that he'd cleared out my ovaries, my tubes, and my womb. 'What about my vagina?' I asked.

"'That's still there,' he said. 'You won't notice any difference. In fact, you've finished having children so you don't need your uterus anyway. It'll probably be better without having to worry about periods.'

"He was flippant, as if it was nothing! I liked my uterus. I liked having periods. I liked the feeling that I could get pregnant if I wanted to—even though I didn't. When Bill came in I cried and cried. He tried to console me, saying that he loved me, not my ovaries, and that it was necessary to do whatever had to be done to save my life. Obviously, I knew this was right, but I was still hurting.

"Then the pathology came back. The tumor was benign. There was no cancer at all! The whole operation was unnecessary. Professor McDonald was amazed, saying he'd never seen anything like it. The tumor looked malignant and he was sure that this was what the pathology would show. He admitted that the extensive surgery was unnecessary, saying that he did it because it was better to be safe than sorry.

"Bill was stunned like I was but tried to look on the bright side. There was a bright side, of course. I wasn't going to die after all. Naturally I was pleased about that. But I couldn't get over the fact that I'd lost all my female organs—or most of them, anyway—for no reason at all.

"I'm a psychologist and I know that you have to work things through. I went to a counselor and talked and talked. But whatever I say or however I think about it, I can't get away from the fact that I'm no longer whole. I'm no longer who I was or want to be.

"Sex is not the same. I can't feel anything anymore. I've seen people who say that he must have cut some nerves. Professor McDonald says that my feeling will return but it's six months now and things are worse, not better.

"I don't get aroused. I just feel empty inside. When Bill comes near me for sex I just feel dead, or worse. Our sex life together used to be a major part of our relationship. We'd make love two or three times a week. Now I'm letting him down and we can't share our bodies like we used to. He tries everything, but it makes no difference.

"I know this can't last. I'm afraid for our relationship. I'm not the person I used to be. And I can't get over it. It was all for nothing. I told him not to take out anything that didn't need to be taken out. It was the last thing I said before going under the anesthetic. He was just flippant about it. I knew he didn't understand. 'You really don't need your womb anymore,' he said. 'Most women would be pleased not to have to worry about periods from now on.' As if he'd know! He's a man who thinks that he knows everything about women. He wants to control women. He thinks he's some kind of God.

"I feel empty. I feel dismembered. I feel violated. It's like I've been raped. I've had my most precious possession, my sense of being a woman, taken from me. I don't know who I am anymore. It's like I'm just floating some-where in the air. When I touch my body it's not *my* body—it's someone else's, not a woman's body; it's neuter, sexless.

"I went back to Professor McDonald for the post-surgery checkup. I told him I was upset and angry. I wanted an explanation and an apology. He admitted he'd made a mistake but said he had to err on the side of safety. He didn't apologize. He said that he was sure that my feeling would recover and suggested a physiotherapist who specializes in restoring vaginal sensation. I've tried it for months now. You put things in your vagina and try to imagine having sex. You try to get used to how your body is now.

"If I was dealing with a patient I'd probably do all the things the physio does with me. But it doesn't work. My life, my body, has been ravaged, denuded. And all for nothing."

She broke off and sat for a few moments, silently shaking her head. Abraham was very affected. "It's a sad story," he said slowly. " . . . How can I help?"

"I need help to regain control of my ordinary bodily functions. My hormones have gone wild since the operation. I can't eat or sleep, I can hardly walk, I have daily headaches, and that's only half of it. But I'm sure no one can really help," she said with a tone of sad resignation, still shaking her head. "Nobody can. I'm taking legal action against Professor McDonald. The lawyer said that I had to be careful. He'd argue that he was trying to save my life, and he is, after all, the most experienced person in the country in dealing with ovarian cancer. I said that I had to go ahead. It was something I had to do. Otherwise it would be like a woman who'd been raped just letting her attacker get away with the crime.

"It's already cost me thousands of dollars. We'll have to mortgage the house to pay the legal fees. Professor McDonald doesn't care, of course. His medical insurance company is fighting it. He doesn't have to pay a cent."

The physical injury can be healed, she was saying, but the deeper wound, the wound to the personality, her relationships, her life, will remain. Abraham reflected how limited, how barely significant, his role and his power really were. "I can certainly help with the hormones," he replied, "but I'm interested to know just one more thing. What do you want to achieve with the court case? I mean, what would be the best outcome? How will it help?"

"All I really want is for him to say he's sorry, to admit that he messed up everything—the operation, my ovaries, my life. I don't want money. I just want my life back, my body back, but I know that'll never be possible. If we get to court I'll be able to tell my story. The judge will be able to say that I was wronged. I'm not sure, though, if that will make any serious difference. What good will it really do?"

76.

"Your next patient is Mrs. Fellegi. Marina Bell hasn't come again. Do you want me to send her another appointment?"

Abraham was still haunted by the young comedian. He had felt traduced and used by her. He needed to see her to find out what had been in her mind, to prove to her that he—perhaps he alone—was sincere. But there was nothing he could do to compel her to keep an appointment. He felt like a jilted lover. "Let's try one more time," he said. "I'll write a personal note saying how concerned I am about her and suggesting that she make a time to see me. If she doesn't come this time there's nothing more we can do."

He ushered in Christine Fellegi, the woman who had requested a meeting to discuss her relationship with her husband. Turning his mind from Marina, Abraham recalled that Christine had indicated that she had found a way of coping with her problem through religion, which she had indicated she wanted to talk about with him. He called her into the room and, after the usual pleasantries, invited her to talk.

As previously, she needed little prompting. "My life with György is very hard. He can be extremely cruel. I think I might have talked a bit about our relationship in the past. It wasn't always as bad as it is now. When we first knew each other he was good to me. He'd just arrived from Hungary and was good looking and fun loving. And he loved me. He was my first boyfriend and I was a bit overwhelmed. I had a bad leg—it was something I was born with—and couldn't walk properly. When I was in primary school the kids used to make fun of me and call me names. I couldn't play sports, and when I was older I couldn't go to dances and was too scared to go to parties where I might meet people. I thought that I'd never get married. When György came along he didn't care about my disability. In fact, he seemed to like it; it was a part of me he appreciated and cared for. After I got over being shy with him we had great sex, too. We'd go all night. He loved my body and I loved being loved. I worked in a shop and he got work on building sites and in factories.

"The change happened when we decided to have a family. We tried for a couple of years and then went to a doctor to find out why I wasn't getting pregnant. It turned out that I'm infertile. They think it might be related to the problem with my leg, but it seems I couldn't produce the right eggs. They offered us IVF but we couldn't afford it, and anyway I thought maybe it was God's wish that I was like this. But György never forgave me. He started spending time with his friends and often came home drunk. He got violent, especially when I complained. One time when I yelled at him for forgetting my birthday and coming home stinking drunk at three o'clock in the morning he smashed me in the face and I had to have ten stitches. He had affairs. He'd even tell me about them. He'd say he was tired of me and was going out to see his girlfriend.

"Money got hard. I stopped working full time when I was trying to get pregnant and instead took part-time work cleaning. I still do that. He had some trouble keeping work—the building trade's hard, especially when you're a bit older—but he eventually found a stable job in an office. He controlled all the money in our house. He'd only ever give me an allowance, while he went out most nights with his friends drinking and smoking. The only place I go is church.

"The worst thing's the sex. Sometimes he'd come home drunk and get into bed with me. I'd pretend I was asleep so as not to encourage him, but often that wouldn't stop him. He'd come at me like an animal and there was no stopping him. In the end, I'd just let him do it. I never feel anything anymore. He just gets on top of me and goes until he's finished then rolls off and sleeps it off. Sometimes I wonder if he even knows I'm there. One day he came home as usual, reeking of tobacco and beer, and climbed on top of me. I just lay there as he did his thing. He burped straight in my face and just kept going.

"I was so upset I had to tell someone. We're Anglican, as you know, and I'm close to my church; it's what's kept me going over the years. There was a new priest in my parish, not young—about my age, but with a beautiful voice. I hadn't ever mentioned the problems with my husband to anyone before. I thought maybe this was God's way of punishing me for something I'd done. But I confided in our priest and he was very concerned. He said that it was wrong and that I didn't need to put up with rough treatment. It was the first time I'd ever thought that it didn't have to continue.

"The priest was good to me. I started going to church every day, just to get a glimpse of him. He's a respected member of the community, of course, and he has a wife and family, but he gave me a lot of help. He was so thoughtful and sensitive. He reminded me of the first days with György, though that's a long time ago now. One day I went into the church—it was a Thursday— just to pray a bit, and it turned out that there was nobody else in the church except him. He came up to me and asked how I was doing. I said that I was okay, thanks to him. We talked for a bit and there was this attraction. I've never felt anything like it. It was like a magnet. He was kind of glowing. Then I took his hand and said something like, 'I just want to thank you for being so good to me.' Well, that was it. We kissed, hot and passionate. I could feel he was aroused under his cassock. I was afraid someone would come into the church and find us but he said it was all right, no one came in at this time of the morning. We made love, then and there, on the pew. It was the most wonderful thing I've ever experienced. He was so loving and tender. No one had been tender to me for twenty years. It was like I was human again, young and pretty, without my bad leg. He stroked my body. He touched me in secret places, not for him, but for me.

"Since then, we've been meeting regularly. It's always in the church and always in the morning. We always make love on the pews and it's always wonderful. I'm always worried that someone will find us, but so far that's not happened. I know we can't continue. If we were found, he'd be ruined. His marriage, his job. I've prayed to God for guidance about what we should do.

"The newest thing is that György's fallen ill. He's got some kind of cancer of the blood and has to have chemo. He's taken it pretty bad and as usual takes that out on me. That's why I've got the bruises. But at least it's stopped him demanding sex. I hope it'll stay like that after the treatment.

"Doctor, do you think I'm doing the wrong thing? Are you shocked by what I've done? Do you think I'm a bad person for having an affair with a married man, with a priest? Please tell me what to do."

77.

Abraham's cell phone went off. It was Mrs. Timoshenko.

"Abraham, I'm sick."

"Mrs. Timoshenko, it's always good to hear from you, but today I have only a couple of minutes. I—"

"Abraham, I'm sure the cancer has come back. I can't eat. I have no appetite . . . I mean, anorexia . . . I have dysphagia. I'm losing weight. You have to help me."

He was struck by the urgency in her voice. "How much weight have you lost?"

"I don't know. I'm not scared. To suffer is my fate. It is the fate of the times. My hour of sound and fury is nearly finished. The epigastric pain is worse. The polydipsia and polyuria . . . the leukocytoclastic vasculitis . . ."

Her voice was barely audible. "Mrs. Timoshenko, if you really are sick you should come to the Emergency Department immediately. Otherwise, I'll see you as soon as Jenny can arrange it. I'll let her know and she'll contact you."

For once, she was silent. Abraham feared the worst.

78.

Abraham was in his office going through his mail. He saw an envelope with a British stamp on it and the address written in an unsteady hand, which looked almost like a child's. He opened it with interest, not knowing what to expect. When he read the first few sentences his heart froze:

Dear Professor Nevski,

You don't know me but I've heard a lot about you. I'm the daughter of Dr. Quentin Prince. I live in England. I am writing to thank you for all the effort you put into helping Quentin and to advise you of the sad news of his death.

Quentin told me a lot about how he was seeing you prior to his upcoming court appearance. I think you know the background. Quentin and I have had a very loving but impossible relationship. Our lives were greatly damaged by our Great Love. After we separated Quentin married a cruel, vindictive woman who pursued him, as it happened, to the grave. She hated me, even though we never met. I think she resented the fact that Quentin could never love anyone else but me. After the divorce she reported him to the police and harassed them until they took action.

It was alleged that Quentin was a danger to the community and to his patients. I know that he visited you to discuss his attitudes to his patients, including ethical issues. You wrote a very good report, which our lawyer was just about to send to the Court. We both cried at what you had written. You said that you had concluded that Quentin was a devoted doctor who was committed to his patients, that our relationship was a genuine love affair, and that Quentin posed no risk to his patients. We were so very grateful to you for writing such a positive, and true, statement.

Our Lawyer said that when they saw your letter the most the judges could do would be to reprimand Quentin. They said that we could relax because the case was as good as over. When we heard that, we were overjoyed. The Court Case has been a nightmare we have lived with for five years. We thought it was over now forever. We knew that we could never be together again but that at least this would end one part of the tragedy that was darkening our lives.

But just as we had one triumph the next disaster struck. The tabloid newspapers found out about the case and published graphic articles about it, even though they were supposed not to. They said in their headlines that it was shocking that a doctor who had committed horrible sex crimes was still practicing and that his patients should have been told all about it. They pursued Quentin and sat outside his house, taking photos whenever he looked out the window. He called me many times and we talked over the phone. He was so disappointed. He had thought for a few moments that at least the nightmare of the court case was over now and that he could go back to doing what he loved—looking after his patients. And they loved him too. But the Press wouldn't let him. They refused to leave him alone. They accused him of being a sex criminal even though as you pointed out that was not the case. He never did anything to hurt his patients or anyone else and they were never at any risk as a result of the love between Quentin and I.

In the last phone call I had from Quentin he was very depressed. He was crying over the phone, frantic. He said that he had gone past the point of all endurance. He had thought that the nightmare was about to end but in reality it was just the start of a new one. He told me that he did not know what he could do now. I tried to calm him. I pleaded with him over the phone. I could hear from his voice that I was about to lose him, to lose the only person I had ever loved, and who had loved me. We were both crying when we said goodbye. His last words to me were 'I will always love you.'

I heard from the Solicitor a couple of days later that Quentin had died. They think it was due to an Overdose but the autopsy report isn't back yet. When I heard the

news I was completely dumbstruck. It is as if a light has
gone out in my world that will never be lit again.

   I want to thank you for what you did. You are one of
the few people who supported us during the long night of
blackness we endured. It has now ended in the worst possible way but that is not your fault. I would end my own
life now too but I have to be here for Benjamin, our son. He
is all I have left in the world. We have both lost a Father but
I have also lost the only hope I ever had of love. My sadness
is infinite and I can only wait for the time when I will
eventually join Quentin and we can be together, safely, in
our love, until eternity.

   With Gratitude,
   Doreen

79.

Abraham now understood. A father is not just a flesh-and-blood person with
whom we happen to have a relationship, which may be good or bad. He has
many facets and many layers of meaning. He is the device by which we enter
and engage with the world. Not only is he the first stranger we encounter, as
the classical theory explains it, the one who fractures our secure relationship
with our mother: he is also the one who teaches us about desire, about the
striving for goals and the costs of fulfilling them. He is the one who shows us
what a tough place the world is, how harsh and cruel it can be, but how with
courage and pertinacity we can succeed against the odds.

   Abraham thought about some fathers who were known to him: Quentin
Prince, Mr. Alvarez, Barry McLeod. All had provided basic coordinate systems of values, according to which their children had oriented themselves
and mapped out their identities. In each case—and, he hated to admit it to
himself, in his own case, too—the father was a scaffolding around which lives
had been organized. This scaffolding—like the father himself—was multilay-
ered and multidimensional, encompassing as it did relationships, meanings,
and identities. Abraham felt a twinge; a role like this is a big responsibility for
one person to carry, especially someone as weak and flawed as his own father.

   This all seemed so clear now! Why had he not seen it before? That which is commonly referred to as "paternity" is not a single thing: it is in reality a collection of functions that happen to come together loosely around the figure of a particular person. But those functions, and that person, are not fixed, either in time or space. In fact, if the father becomes everything that falls into so many different categories, there may not be just one father. It is the child's job—Abraham was now thinking of himself—to try to define and control the idea of the father, but in reality this may be impossible to achieve because what is ultimately at stake is the whole space of his or her moral and imaginary life. Whether they had liked it or not, the conflict between his father and himself had been inevitable and inexorable; if there was ever to be a reconciliation, it could only be posthumous, and it had to involve a recognition of the wild and contradictory nature of the forces at play.

Like all powerful forces, those unleashed by the relationship with the father run the risk of going dangerously wrong. Abraham tried to recall some of the stories his patients had told him about their fathers. They showed that things could go awry in many different ways. Children caught in traumatic circumstances—a car accident, an assault, bullying at school—may feel a sense of betrayal by their fathers, who should have been there to protect them, and they might never reestablish a sense of security and trust. Where the father is absent he is often transformed into a myth—of an invincible protector, a powerful athlete, a freedom fighter—and the hopeless search for a replica sometimes becomes a lifelong quest. Where the father is for some reason seen as powerless and ineffectual, as emasculated, extraordinary feats may be demanded of him before the scourge can be overcome and the son can develop a sense of his own power. A cold or abusive father may evoke a lifelong questioning of identity or purpose. In all cases, the father comes to symbolize all the gaps the child has never been able to fill. There are always plenty of these, of course, but it is the father's fate to bring them together, to represent them, and to take on the responsibility of redressing them.

Returning to Mordechai, Abraham realized that he, like all fathers, was polysemic, encompassing many layers of meaning in his own life, which themselves had changed over time. His flesh-and-blood father was a sad and damaged human being. He was erratic, mercurial, unpredictable. He could be funny and clever or vicious and ruthless. He could be relentlessly logical or hopelessly confused. He could be powerful and courageous, or he could sink into a slough of pessimistic torpor. The course of his present illness, including the anguish and the passion associated with it, seemed a perfect epitomization of his life, which had been beset with ironies: the psychological unpredictability that belied the cool linearity of legal reasoning, the attachment to fixed principles that turned out to be no more than a commitment to change. But for all the contradictions and that contrariness, for all the bitterness and hatred, without even knowing what was happening, the two of them had maintained a persistent, uneasy residue of loyalty and respect—and maybe, just possibly, even of love. In spite of his belief that as a teenager he had been able successfully to free himself from his father he could see now that in reality he had never been without him for a moment.

If the uncertainty of fatherhood was the essence of the father then Mordechai had performed his role to perfection! A real father can never—maybe must never—fulfill the expectations that are placed on him. Abraham was not quite ready to forgive his father, but maybe it was in any case too late for him to do so.

80.

Abraham was determined to finish his article. He had to make sense of what was happening—not just with himself personally, but also with the events in the ward and the hospital. It was in times of pressure that the risk of losing one's nerve was greatest. It was important to stay calm and remain true to the full complexities of the clinical experiences.

He went over what he had written so far. He had discussed the key role of ethics in medicine, and he had criticized the dominance of what he regarded as a very narrow and limited kind of thinking in addressing its key underlying ethical concerns. He was pleased with what he read. What was needed now was a way of capturing the depth and fullness of the experiences of the clinic. He had to return to the problem of why he had a responsibility to care for his mother and father. The trouble was that he didn't know if he could answer this question. He tried to think through the issues by writing:

> The official discourses of ethics do not reflect accurately the everyday experience of ethical practice. In daily life, we make decisions about issues concerning values all the time. Whenever I engage another person, however large or small the interaction, I adjust my conduct in recognition of him or her. Whether I am interacting

with a student, a bus driver, a shopkeeper, or a lover; whether I am engaging in a dinnertime conversation, walking in a crowd, or driving on the road; whether I am making decisions about the care of a patient, a child, or my elderly mother, I remain acutely attuned to the proximity of others, to the effects on them of my words, my actions, my mere presence. In the continuous flow of these interactions, some mundane and inconsequential, some of great moment and consequence, I carefully adjust my words, my physical actions, my facial expressions, my bodily postures, in recognition of their needs, vulnerabilities, and reciprocal responses or lack of response. My daily life is replete with small decisions about my responsibilities for, and effects on, other people.

He stopped for a moment and thought of his relationships with his colleagues and his patients. He thought of Nic and Madeleine, and Rebecca, Ashis, and Desmond. He had a different relationship with each of them and fashioned each of his interactions with them differently. And then there was Mr. Alvarez and Mrs. Dreyfus and Mrs. Timoshenko and Mrs. Fellegi and Quentin Prince and the Höröks and Marina Bell and . . . and all the others. There were so many ethical issues, but so few of them were decided through a process of rational analysis and calculation. He had to get this point down:

Some of the decisions I make are explicitly considered and rationally based, and occasionally I may ponder issues of great moment and deep consequence. However, mostly, the ethical content of my life is intuitive and inconspicuous. Ethical discourse in the everyday does not follow rigorous philosophical theories. We do not start from universal, abstract principles or normative rules of conduct and then try to make reality conform to them. We resist and reject strict formulas and dogmatic principles. Instead, we engage in dynamic, open, and flexible dialogues with others as we negotiate our way delicately through densely populated fields of often-conflicting values. In doing so, we utilize whatever tools are available to us. We appeal to arguments; we engage in discussions; we call up memories, traditions, and past conversations; we apply fragments of theory. There are discussions about discussions and reflections on these discussions. Our conversations may be carried to completion or they may be partial, interrupted, and inconclusive. We abide this complex process of bricolage, this strange and mysterious polysemy and ambiguity, without demur or a sense of exception.

This seemed right. Abraham settled back in his chair a little and continued writing:

> In these practical dialogues that drive our daily lives forward we do not start from the premise that we are autonomous individuals setting out to establish and then control contact with others. We start from the assumption that we are inexorably and irrevocably enmeshed with others. Our relationships with other people are placed at the very beginning—indeed, even before they become differentiated as relationships. We start from the premise that our very uniqueness lies in our responsibility for others, a responsibility that cannot be passed off to another person, just as I could never have anyone else take my place in death. The uniqueness of my commitment to the other person with whom I am engaged in dialogue establishes my capacity to do only what no one else can do in my

place. This uniqueness and specificity of the "first person singular" guarantees my freedom. On the other hand, the continuity of my relationships and responsibilities, embedded as they are in thriving, rich, and intense dialogues and diverse cultures and ideas, insures against an arbitrary process of relativism or subjectivism.

Neither the starting point nor the process is closed or rigid. The outcomes of the ethical dialogues are often marked by a similar openness and polysemy. In ethics, there are no correct solutions. There is no single point of view or conclusion that distinguishes right conduct from moral error, or good from evil. There are no inviolable laws of moral action that command universal obedience; there are only processes with greater or less integrity, with more or less commitment to the openness and creativity inherent in the interpersonal space.

Our daily lives are textured by small, microethical moments, soaked with ethical resonances: the meeting of eyes in a train, someone giving way in a doorway, a gesture—or lack of a gesture—of kindness in the tea room, mundane interactions with family and friends. The larger-scale experiences of embodiment, puberty, sexuality, childbirth, illness, menopause, and old age all have deep ethical content. These experiences may provoke reflections on our personal goals and aspirations, the sources of satisfaction and frustration. From time to time we encounter—and may be perplexed by—dilemmas in respect of which we are called upon to make conscious decisions.

He liked the expression "our lives are soaked with ethical resonances" and wondered where it had come from. He tried it out in his mouth. It was an odd mixed metaphor, but it was the point he had been trying to find a way to express—that we don't live our lives by starting with abstract principles and then trying to beat reality into shape. Rather, from start to finish we are immersed in a remorseless hand-to-hand combat with reality. He began to write again:

When we engage another person in any interchange, we enter into a field of values that is unbounded and indeterminate. We find ourselves not seeking unambiguous solutions to questions concerning the ethical validity of propositions but, instead, negotiating trajectories of values within shared lifeworlds of experience. We proceed incrementally, in infinitesimal steps, as—by trial and error—we explore the contours of this lifeworld. In ethics there is no single, universally valid category of the good; there is not one method. There is an infinity of goods, and many frameworks within which ethical analysis and debate occur. This means that the domain of ethics is much larger and more fecund than is generally accepted within the paradigms of conventional ethical theory. It also means that this expanded domain—the microethical domain—is in general not the terrain of spectacular cases involving heroic decisions. Rather, it is the field of day-to-day communication and structured, complex interactions, of subtle gestures and fine nuances of language. In the medical setting it includes the space of the reverberating physician-patient interaction, within which the medical relationship itself acquires a specific form, and deep-seated, often fundamental issues of value are engaged and, at times, thrown into question.

I do not care for my elderly mother who has Alzheimer's disease just because she has useful sentient life or residual personhood, or because she is still capable of happiness, or because killing her does not maximize the happiness or pleasure of the rest of us. I do not care for her because she is of the human species, or because she has a soul, or because we are God's creatures, or because there is a rule or principle or moral law that says that I have to, or because I am or want to be a good person. I care, despite my own failings and hers, because of—or in spite of—my love and resentments, my misgivings and uncertainties, about her and about myself, because of opportunities seized and missed. I care because I must; because it is the right thing to do; because she is my mother; because caring is a condition of possibility of being human; because I feel compassion and sadness and loss; because I myself am bereft; because I see in the elderly woman the shadows of my own childhood and the poignancy of her past splendor dulled by the ravages of age, and the poignant contemplation of my own future. I care because it is ennobling to care, even in the meanest, most defiled and debased settings, not because victims are inherently noble but because the distinction between carers and the cared for is itself mistaken. I care because there is never a simple dilemma, a single question with an unequivocal answer. I care because I loved this person once and she loved me, because she was the rock on whom I could depend, who provided the starting point from which my own life was launched, because she cared not just for me but also for many others, including my own children. I care because she contains within her the assemblage of meanings and symbols for my life, the trail of a path traced over a long life; because her current predicament cannot be explicated in terms of "rationality" or "sentience" or "quality of life." I care for her because of her vulnerability and fragility, which is like the vulnerability and fragility she discerned and protected in my children and me. I care for her not because I can string together arguments to make a case. In short, I care with my reason, my emotions, my humanness.

Abraham's hands shook as he wrote these words. He now felt exhausted. He realized that although he could speak about his mother he was not yet able to talk about his father. That would take much longer—in fact, he was not sure that he would ever be able to do so in this way.

He had now said all that he wanted to say, but he had to bring the article to a close.

Ethics is a process of dialogue that involves communication across the boundaries of philosophy, personal values, cultural assumptions, and political and religious beliefs. Within it, individuals come together to generate and share new meanings, or indeed to define what it is that makes them individuals. Because of these characteristics it is inherently and irrevocably open, fluid, and anti-totalitarian.

We are all experts in ethics. We live in spaces shaped by ethical considerations. Our face-to-face relationships with others, our deepest and most private emotions, our mundane interactions during the conduct of our daily lives, all involve a multitude of ethical decisions, negotiations, and adjustments. In these relationships and private experiences we engage with each other and with the world as embodied subjects, as physical, carnal beings, finite and vulnerable, grappling with our fears and hopes, weaknesses and desires.

One does not have to go to exotic places, seek out extreme circumstances or look for fundamental innovations in science, technology, or culture to encounter ethical issues and the challenge of making ethical decisions. In the gray, commonplace continuum of the everyday there is heroism, joy, tragedy, suffering, honor, trust, loyalty, betrayal, altruistic caring, and ruthless egoism. There is even evil and good, cynicism and selfless virtue.

Even in the face of its social function to control behavior or stabilize social relationships, ethics is, and must be retained as, a domain of radical questioning, of reflection on and scrutiny of deep assumptions and strongly held values. It can be messy, untidy, inconvenient, and inconclusive. It should, however, never be allowed to give up its crucial meaning-creating mission.

He stopped typing and sat staring blankly at the computer screen.

PART 13

HEALING AND HOLINESS

81.

I n his office, sitting back in his armchair, whisky in hand, Abraham was reflecting. Medicine is an intense and challenging business. Although its primary task is apparently simple—to promote healing—what is involved in achieving this is in reality profoundly complex. This is because healing extends across all the areas of medicine; it encompasses the biological processes, as defined by the disciplines of physiology, anatomy, pharmacology, biochemistry, psychology, and so on; but it also has to consider goals, values, and meanings, and the impact of illness on personal life and social relationships. All the modalities of bodily experience may be drawn in, including birth and death, sexuality and love, happiness and grief, and pain, fear, and hope. In this way, healing brings together the disparate elements of medicine. It is what joins the great domains of science and ethics together; indeed, it is the suture of the wound that has rent them apart. Healing is the site where the knowledge of science is applied in the service of ethics, and where ethics as practical action encounters the conditions of science.

As the practical art of healing, Abraham reflected, medicine draws upon theory and knowledge, but ultimately what it aims at is action. Even in cases that seem on the surface to be straightforward, however, negotiating this transition can be very uncertain. As recent events in the ward had illustrated, illness can evoke intense fears and uncertainties, disrupt apparently stable family relationships, or threaten the basis of a person's livelihood. It can also evoke critical questioning of values and belief systems and provide a reminder for all who become involved of the tragic fragility of life and the obdurate inexorability of death. In all cases, the doctor himself is supposed to be a disinterested agent who not only offers knowledge and wisdom but also assumes multiple roles: of scientist, counselor, confidante, witness, mother or father figure, and moral and spiritual guide. The possibility that the doctor might have his own inner life, his own fears, anxieties, and hopes, never enters into consideration.

The impact of his father's illness and his wife's death had left Abraham empty, drained, and disoriented, and the other things happening in the ward, in the hospital, and in his family had further undermined the certainty of his world and his confidence in himself. His life, which had seemed straightforward—even if not without challenges—had suddenly become very complicated: indeed, it had become too complicated.

He enjoyed being a physician and knew he was good at it. Usually his judgment was reliable, even if, like everyone, he had occasionally gotten some things wrong. The rapidity of the deaths of Mrs. Gurewitz, Mr. Tzorvas, and Mr. Alvarez, however, had taken him by surprise, and he was completely preoccupied by the death of Mrs. Dreyfus. Again and again, brooding over this last case, he had looked for an explanation. He had gone through the medical notes in detail looking for clues and had scrutinized the results of the postmortem examination. However, he just could not make sense of it. In spite of his skills as a scientist and a detective this was one case he did not seem able to crack. He had followed all his usual methods, going carefully through the facts, consulting the literature, analyzing in full detail all the logical possibilities. While he knew as well as anyone that in medicine many things were never fully explained, that the world was always untidier and more uncertain than the theory would allow, nonetheless, here he could not escape the sense that there was something more, something that was escaping him. For someone who made a living out of working things out in his mind this was frustrating and disturbing almost to the point of physical pain. Abraham's head felt like it was bursting. He poured himself another glass of whisky.

Maybe, he thought, what was troubling him was not just his incapacity to understand what had happened but his inability to have prevented it. Maybe his disquiet was linked to his deep abiding sense of impotence in the face of the world. This was the secret that he managed so artfully to keep from almost everyone who knew him. Even those closest—friends like Nic and Madeleine and students like Rebecca and Ashis—imagined him to be in full control, at peace with himself. They couldn't know how wrong they were. He hadn't been able to stop Stephanie from dying or his family breaking up. Now, he couldn't even protect the patients in his charge. Despite his fine words he had done nothing to halt Freedom to Choose, which was inexorably gathering strength under his very nose. For all his fierce promises and elegant rhetoric what had he actually achieved?

Abraham was overwhelmed by a vast sense of emptiness. He believed he really had tried hard to do his job well, to be a good person. He replayed in his mind the peroration of his recent sermon to the students in which he had self-righteously exhorted them to take responsibility for their own actions. How sincere was that? He, Abraham, always talked about action, but the truth was that he was always only ever looking in from the outside. He was always merely watching other people act. He was never more than an observer, a witness. How he longed to be able to act himself.

82.

In spite of his state of disquietude Abraham forced himself to go to the regular lunchtime meeting. He didn't feel like being in company but he had to keep up appearances.

When he entered the cafeteria it was buzzing with activity. There was already a group of doctors sitting at the usual table. Abraham pulled up a chair, sat down, and pretended to look bright. There was the usual small talk around a mixture of personal and work issues. He hoped that no one would ask him how he was.

He scrutinized the company. There was Natalie Hermann, the palliative care physician; Harry Krokowski, the director of Emergency; Frederick Tauber, head of Neurology; and Allison Wong, Jon Bitic, and a few others. These were people with whom he had long felt comfortable, whom he had regarded as his friends. There was no one here he would not have trusted. But today he found himself wondering how loyal to him they would be in a crisis. What if he were really in need—for example, if he were in pain or dying? And how would they act at a unit audit? Would they accept that after years of service he was entitled to a few lapses, to make one or two mistakes? Or would they look at him with cold disdain, accusing him silently—or even not so silently—of neglecting his duty? And if the CEO seized upon this as an opportunity to attack him—and he knew she was actively on the lookout for such an opportunity—would they support him, or would they stand back watching while his bones were picked over in public?

Suddenly, Nic arrived, brandishing a piece of paper. "Hi, everyone," he said breezily. "Lovely day, isn't it?" He was standing next to Abraham and talking in a loud voice. "I've just received the latest newsletter from Margaret Wilson. I don't suppose that any of you have seen it because you were all sitting here having lunch when it arrived. So I've printed it out for your delectation. I quote, verbatim." He read from the sheet of paper: "'Thank you everyone for the great job you have been doing with the implementation of the Freedom to Choose program. Although I realize that there were reservations among some staff I think that these have now been overcome and we can all see how beneficial the program is. There is already evidence of a decline in bed stay days for patients at the end of life. Our chief financial officer has estimated that if the figures for the last month are maintained for the whole year the hospital will save well over a million dollars. In recognition of our success and as a sign of gratitude for the work you have all put in I am announcing that all senior staff members will receive a bonus with their next paychecks.' So congratulations, everyone, we're rich!"

The table erupted in angry comments. "Bloody hell!" exploded Harry. "That's disgraceful. I'm not completely opposed to Freedom to Choose, but I'm damned if I do what I do just to earn some filthy bonus."

"Exactly!" responded Jon. "I don't know what we're coming to. It just shows how much the world's changed. We used to be concerned with looking after the sick; now we're supposed to be just the representatives of the bean counters. What'll be next? A secret commission paid to doctors for bumping off patients who are taking too long to die?"

"That'd be pretty gross, but maybe it's not as incredible as it sounds. I'm already getting some not-so-subtle messages about the length of time people with terminal illnesses are staying in the hospital," replied Harry.

"I can't believe that any doctor would take action to kill a patient just to save someone money!" Allison said, with a grimace.

"That's the whole problem," said Jon. "We're not just doctors anymore. We're also gatekeepers," Jon said. "And the gatekeeper's job is to look after the owner of the gate, not those passing through it."

Abraham felt sick. It seemed that the whole world was being swallowed up by the emptiness inside him. Payments for killing patients? It was incredible that this could even be a serious topic of conversation! Could it possibly be true? He ached with his own impotence and ineffectualness. He clenched his fists under the table. Why did everything have to be so hard?

"Things really have changed." Natalie was agreeing with Allison. "Medicine used to be thought of as a calling or vocation. That goes back to whenever. If I remember correctly, the Hippocratic oath started with a pledge to the gods, showing that medicine was a sacred practice. Now it's just a job. It's assumed—by the CEO and the community—that the only reason we work is for the money."

"You're right about the oath," added Fred Tauber. "When I graduated we had to learn it by heart. It starts, 'I swear by Apollo, Physician, and Asclepius, the God of Healing.'"

"Maybe it's a result of having a pharmacist as a CEO," said Nic, who had now sat down. "Actually, I'm being serious here. If the people in charge are not clinicians they can't appreciate the nature of the deep commitment that clinical practice involves."

"I'd like to know more about the difference between a vocation and a job," said Harry. "Abraham, you're the intellectual among us mere worker bees. Can you tell us the difference?"

Startled, Abraham, who had only been half listening to the conversation, tried to conceal his distractedness. "I . . . don't know about being an intellectual," he stammered, trying desperately to organize a reply in his mind. "It's probably Fred with his German background who's a font of classical knowledge . . ." He recovered quickly. "The difference between a vocation and a job? Err . . . vocation was originally a religious idea, referring to a sense of being called by God to a sacred task . . . There's . . . an ancient history of regarding the healing professions as . . . holy or sacred. Medicine men and women were often priests or shamans, and because they dealt with dangerous matters like life and death, they were respected and feared . . . and sometimes regarded as dangerous themselves—especially when they were women; then they were called witches and sometimes burned alive." He was relieved that he had been able to make a response and hoped no one had noticed how much he was, in fact, struggling.

"I'm not sure that I'd want to restore every aspect of the tradition," Natalie commented, "especially the bit about the witches. But we've certainly lost a sense of the holiness associated with healing and the healing professions. Maybe not entirely, or at an individual level. For example, I often feel a special sense of inner pleasure that's hard to describe when something really special happens in the clinic. I'm not sure if you'd call that a religious feeling."

Abraham tried to remember the last time he had experienced a "special sense of inner pleasure."

"I thought for a moment when you were talking about holiness you were referring to our beloved CEO," joked Nic. "No, that's royalty, isn't it. Seriously, though, I sympathize with what Allison and Natalie have said—and," turning to Abraham and winking, "yes, and even with you, old boy. But I reckon medicine's always been a business. Doctors have always had to earn money, and their social status has always been important to them."

"That might vary a bit with different cultures," said Madeleine. "I'm reminded of the joke about the Catholic, the Protestant, and the Jew who were arguing about when life begins. For the Catholic a child's life began at conception, for the Protestant at the birth of the baby, and for the Jew when he graduated from medical school."

Everyone laughed. Madeleine went on. "Abraham's told us what a vocation is, but not what a job is. I'd like to have a go at a definition of that. I believe a job's an activity that focuses on the advantage of a particular person or group, rather than on the public interest."

"I think that captures the key idea," said Jon, thoughtfully. "Taken together, the two definitions—of vocation and job—show how dramatically things have changed. Medicine used to be a calling but nowadays is increasingly just a job. Can I ask everyone here, how many of you regard medicine as a vocation and how many as a job?"

"I think you have to ask one question at a time," said Harry.

"Okay," responded Jon. "Will those who regard medicine as a vocation or calling please put up their hands? There you are, everyone!"

"You also have to ask about who regards it as a job," interjected Harry.

"All right. Please put up your hands if you regard medicine as a job. Seven! I have a feeling some people might have voted twice!"

"That's because it can be both," said Harry. "It's not an either-or situation. I can respect the fact that doctors need to earn money to support their families or whatever without sacrificing—maybe that's not the right word—without giving up the possibility of a commitment to the work itself."

"I'm sure that's true, Harry," responded Jon, "but something's changed. Take this email from the CEO. That would have been unthinkable a few years ago. It's a sign of changes in the society. The whole culture's become degraded. Everything we do is judged in terms of dollars spent or dollars saved."

This time Fred spoke. "As the resident font of classical knowledge, I'd like to add that while it might be true that the culture continues to become increasingly materialistic, it's important to remember that the roots of this process go back a long time, as does this discussion about the loss of deeper religious or ethical values. There've always been debates about the loss of traditions, the decline of the West, and so on. But we shouldn't forget that the rise of the West and modern society also brought about a few small benefits, like, for example, democracy, the end of slavery, universal education, the ability of women to participate equally with men in social life, and a general increase in wealth. These changes are good, and they've all affected medicine, even if maybe they've sometimes come with a price attached."

"Great speech, Fred," said Nic. "And you've even made some good points. I'm sure you're right that there've been both gains and losses. But acknowledging that doesn't mean that nothing's changed. It doesn't counter the argument that in the modern world the concept of a calling is disappearing and being replaced, maybe not just by the need to do a job, to earn a living, but also to fit into some organization. After all, 'best practice' today is supposed to involve merely following rules, not making moral decisions."

"Also," added Allison, "it shouldn't stop us from trying to make an effort to stem the tide, even a little bit. For example, as older doctors we're able to influence younger ones coming up to think of their work as a lifelong commitment to service rather than just a meal ticket."

In spite of his dark mood, Abraham had to speak. "That's right, Allison," he said. "Even though society's changed, even though the role of traditional values and religion has declined, it's still possible for medicine to be taken on as a vocation and not just as a job. But we also have to accept that things are more complex; for example, that, as Fred said, the growth of the economy is not in itself a bad thing but has brought with it major benefits. Also, the increased access of women has changed the nature of medical work for the better. The vocations of today are different from the vocations of the past. Whereas once it was a single thing, with the voice that was calling being simple and clear and unambiguous, now there are many voices shouting at us at the same time." Lost in his speech, Abraham was now talking from direct personal experience. "Whereas previously, it may have been possible to devote oneself to a single set of tasks or values, today there are many possibilities, and many enticements and rewards. It's harder to commit to a unitary set of values, or even a single cultural or philosophical perspective. Today, whether we like it or not, we all have to be multicultural and pluralistic. That's not necessarily a bad thing. It doesn't mean that we can't make commitments. It doesn't mean that we're not revolted when a CEO shamelessly and scurrilously grants bonuses when patients die or are pushed out of the hospital more quickly. But it does mean that we have to keep reminding ourselves of our own reasons for doing what we do. And it means that each of us has to think carefully about every one of our decisions, about how we act, and what we personally are prepared to do to oppose what in spite of everything we still think is just wrong."

"That's a great speech, too, Abe," said Nic. "That makes two great speeches, which is pretty good for one lunchtime. I'm afraid, though, that as usual, just as we reach the really important bit, lunchtime's up, at least for me. I've got to get back to the front line. Thanks for the conversation, guys."

With that the group broke up.

PART 14

AN UNAVOIDABLE CONCLUSION

83.

braham had received a phone call from Yevgeny, Ursula Timoshenko's husband. He was almost incoherent with distress. While waiting for her appointment to see him Ursula had suddenly become very ill and had vomited blood. Abraham arranged for her immediate admission through the Emergency Department and for urgent tests. These showed that this time she really did have a serious illness—namely, cancer of the esophagus that could not be treated and would undoubtedly be fatal. An attempt to insert a rigid tube into the esophagus to allow her to take food was unsuccessful. The diagnosis and the dire prognosis were explained both to Ursula herself and to her husband, who were upset but understood what was told to them.

The next day Abraham came to visit her, at her request, alone. He entered the room and found her sitting up in bed surrounded by a large pile of books. He noticed at once that she was exceedingly thin and wasted. Her general physique had always been slight, but now it was no more than skeletal. She was wearing a pale blue nightgown with a lace collar that had fallen open at the front, obviously without her awareness. Her face wore the same sad grimace as ever. He could see at a glance that the books were in Russian, French, and English. A couple of them were open on the bed, suggesting that she had either been looking for a specific passage or had started reading and then lost interest. Without hesitating even for a greeting, Ursula started talking. She was speaking very softly, almost inaudibly, but with the same mechanical, monotonous rhythm as usual. She was obviously very distressed.

"Abraham," she was saying, "please don't leave me here. I will die if I stay in the hospital. I cannot be alone in the room. They're threatening me. I cannot sleep. I am in constant pain. They come in in the middle of the night to keep me awake. I ask for painkillers but they refuse. I ask for water and food and they say I'm not allowed to have them. They shine lights in my face to make sure I'm awake. I call because I need to go to the toilet and they refuse to come. I call and call. They come in and say that they are too busy and I will have to wait. I say it's an emergency and they say that's too bad. I tell them that I'm in great pain and they say there's nothing they can do about it but it may all be over sooner than I think. I ask them what they mean and they say just that—there may not be long to go, that I'm next on the list. I say that I want to talk to you and they say that even my precious professor can't save me. I say that I want to go home and they say that if I want to leave I'm free to do so. I ask them to bring me a telephone but they refuse to do so. Abraham, I'm scared. I don't want to stay here one more night. They've decided to kill me . . ."

"Mrs. Timoshenko . . ."

" . . . The other patient in the room. He came up to me and said I should shut up. He threatened me. I was scared. I didn't know what to do . . ."

Abraham was struck by something different in her tone. "Mrs. Timoshenko. Please stop for a moment. What you're saying is very serious. Who do you think is trying to kill you?

"It's not something I think. It's something I know. They told me so directly. They said, 'You're going to die. You don't have much time left. You're a troublemaker and we'll put a stop to that—'"

"Mrs. Timoshenko, Ursula! Stop again! You haven't answered who said this to you. Who's threatening you?"

"Yes I did. It's the nurses. The nurse who was here in the night. He said that I was going to die. I was a troublemaker and he would pay me back for that. I asked for the phone but he refused to bring it to me. I asked for water but he said he was busy and I would have to wait. Abraham, help me, I'm in pain. I need something. I need medicine. Abraham, only you can help me . . ."

"Mrs. Timoshenko . . ."

" . . . My blood test shows anikopoikolcytosis and leukocytosis. My liver function tests show raised alkaline phosphatase and alanine transferase. I have polyuria and polydipsia—"

"Mrs. Timoshenko, stop talking for a moment! You have to tell me who it was who threatened you. Do you know his or her name?"

"I didn't ask his name and he didn't tell me. He shone the torch in my eyes to keep me awake. I'm so exhausted. I can't sleep. I have to go home. Abraham, you have to arrange for me to go home . . ."

"Mrs. Timoshenko. What did he look like? This is important!"

"I don't know. He's a nurse on the ward. I asked to speak to his superior and he laughed and said that he was the one in charge. I said I wanted to call you and he said that my professor couldn't save me. It would make no difference . . ."

Abraham started. There was a pause. "You said you were in pain . . ." His voice showed no evidence of a reaction.

"I have pain all over. My legs, my arms, my back . . ."

"We can certainly treat the pain. You know what works for you better than I do. What would you like me to do?"

"Pain . . . Pain all over. I can't eat anymore. I need to pass urine every hour . . ."

"We can give you some morphine for your pain. You've had that in the past. It will certainly help with the pain now. Would you be happy for me to order that?"

"Whatever you say . . . I'm scared. I can't sleep. I know they want to kill me . . ."

"Mrs. Timoshenko. I have to go now. There's no way you can go home right now; you're too sick. However, we'll do our best to get you home in the next day or so. I'll talk to the nurses and order the morphine. I'll ask them to give you the phone whenever you need it, and I'll tell them that I'll be available all the time if needed."

"Abraham, don't leave me. I'm scared. I won't survive another night." She was pleading with him, with tears in her eyes. "Please don't leave me . . ."

"I'm really sorry, Mrs. Timoshenko, but I have to go now. I'll call during the evening to make sure you're all right. Please don't worry. We'll do everything we can to help you. You'll be safe. I'll make sure of that. Goodbye!"

As Abraham left the room he was aware of the elderly woman continuing her interminable monotone. He marveled at her stamina but felt a deep sense of pathos. This was her final predicament, and it was so ignominious. He couldn't decide what to make of her story about the events in the night.

Outside the room, Rebecca, Desmond, and Ashis were waiting. "How did it go, Prof?" asked Ashis cheerily.

Abraham shook his head slowly. "She's obviously aware that she's dying, but for all her linguistic skills, she's unable to put this into words, except in the most indirect and pathetic way." Turning to Desmond, he added, "It's my impression that she's finding being in the hospital difficult. I expect she's a difficult patient. How are you finding her?"

He scrutinized the nurse's face closely as he answered. "It's true that she's difficult," he replied, with complete naturalness, "but that's our job. I was on duty last night and spent a lot of time with her trying to calm her, but I'm afraid that I only succeeded in making her more anxious. She kept asking for things and I kept bringing them but eventually it became obvious that she just wanted someone near her. I probably spent a third of my entire shift just sitting with her. Toward the end there were a couple of emergencies and I just had to leave. We'll continue to give her whatever special treatment we can, but like it or not, from time to time we'll have to balance her needs against those of the other patients."

The nurse's response sounded plausible. "She thinks the nurses want to kill her."

"Yes, I was a bit concerned about the possibility of a paranoid delusion. Maybe it's an effect of her illness, perhaps the extreme malnutrition. It won't stop us giving her the best possible care, of course."

84.

"I've been meaning to ask you, Rebecca. What's happened to what's-his-name—you know, that old doctor with multiple sclerosis and probable pneumonia?"

"You mean Dr. Vilgis? I'm afraid he died."

"He died? When?"

"Just last night. We gave him three days of high-dose triple antibiotic therapy and he just didn't respond. He was found by a nurse early this morning."

"But when we last saw him he was improving."

"Yes . . . actually, yesterday he was pretty much the same as the day before. I assume it was the pneumonia that killed him."

He turned to Desmond. "How did you think he was yesterday from a nursing point of view?"

"To be honest, I didn't notice any change one way or the other from the moment he came in. He just lay there, eyes open, not communicating, in spite of what his sister claimed. I didn't have the impression that yesterday he was any different from any other time."

"This is not possible," said Abraham. "He has a condition that ought to be treatable. He's receiving the appropriate therapy. There's evidence that he's improving. Yet he dies without warning. There must have been some other event."

"Perhaps he aspirated again," said Rebecca. "His sister kept feeding him against our advice. Maybe that's what happened."

"I suppose that could've been possible. What's Dora's state? Has anyone contacted her since Dr. Vilgis's death?"

"Yes, I have, Prof," replied Rebecca. "I spoke with her for some time. She was naturally very upset. I offered to talk with her any time and suggested that she come in to meet with us to talk about her brother. She said that she'd get back in touch if she intended to do that."

Abraham was almost too astounded to talk. He tried to think of possible explanations. He also had to remain in control. He glanced at Desmond. "Ashis," he said authoritatively, taking a deep breath, "can you contact micro-biology to ask if they've isolated any unusual organism that was resistant to the treatment we were giving him? It's important that we know that because if it's the case other patients might be at risk."

"Will do, Prof, and I'll go through all the other results just to make sure there was nothing we missed."

85.

"What about Mr. McLeod?" Abraham held his breath as he waited for the answer.

"Oh, I thought the resident called you!" Rebecca said. "He died in the night!"

"Dead!" It was the familiar answer he so fearfully expected.

"I'm so sorry you didn't know, Prof. His pain continued to worsen. We progressively increased the morphine until he was comfortable, as you instructed. When I saw him at about six o'clock he was dozing peacefully. Patricia was much calmer, too. I talked to her briefly and she gave me a hug. We both cried a bit. It was very emotional. When I arrived this morning I heard that he'd passed away."

Abraham remained motionless. Mr. McLeod may have suffered from ter-minal cancer, but there was no reason for him to have died last night. He was in severe pain, and that was very regrettable, but it was not sufficient to claim his life. Abraham tried to conceal his dismay. "That's very unfortunate," he said drily. "It's unlikely that we could have done much for him, but now we'll never know."

Abraham scrutinized Desmond's face. He was expressionless.

86.

Abraham's system of observation and deduction had never let him down. Now, back in his office, with troubled but determined resoluteness he disciplined himself to apply the method with precision and rigor. When immersed in the role of sleuth he often felt intoxicated with his own power. Today, despite the wild, underlying turmoil, his mind felt like a steel knife.

Putting aside his unruly emotions, his familiar glass of whisky in hand, he took himself through the facts one by one in a cool, machine-like way. There had been six deaths in the ward in the last four weeks. This was in itself not completely unprecedented. Deaths certainly occurred: that was a somber feature of this kind of work. The patients in the ward were usually very elderly and, after all, had been admitted to the hospital because they were so unwell that they could not be managed elsewhere. In addition, it was always impossible to predict precisely the exact course of an illness. In fact, when asked by relatives—or occasionally, patients—how long someone would live, he always refused to give an exact answer, explaining that predictions invariably turned out to be wrong.

Of the six patients who had died four were clearly terminally ill, and a decision had already been made to limit their care. In two of these cases—those of Mrs. Gurewitz and Mr. Alvarez—an explicit judgment had been made that death was imminent, even if the expected time frame was longer than that which eventuated. It was acknowledged that the process of "keeping someone comfortable"—which often involved administration of opiates or other medications—could on occasion shorten the process, even if that was not the primary intention. Mr. McLeod also had an incurable cancer that would inevitably have killed him. However, his life expectancy was possibly longer; indeed, with careful treatment he might have lived on for weeks, or maybe months. In all these cases, though, the rapidity of the process was inexplicable. The patients simply did not seem sick enough to die when they did. They had not displayed the usual signs of approaching death, such as changed patterns of breathing and deepening levels of unconsciousness, and there were no other conditions of which Abraham was aware that might have explained a sudden deterioration.

He sat back in the armchair, concentrating hard, and took a sip from the glass. In the other two cases—those of Mrs. Dreyfus and Dr. Vilgis—the death itself was surprising. Dr. Vilgis's condition, while serious, was not significantly different from how it had been on several occasions previously. Pneumonia is serious and can cause death, but in this case it was being treated appropriately and, once again, the patient just did not seem sick enough to die. Mrs. Dreyfus's case was the most perplexing of all. She had had a life-threatening condition, but had seemed to have recovered from it. Unlike all the others, she was not regarded as seriously ill at all; what's more, the review of the facts and the post-mortem had not revealed anything. In her case, there was really no explanation.

If only one or two deaths had occurred, he reflected, he probably would not have worried. But six deaths in four weeks! It seemed incredible. What could be going on? Maybe some obscure infection was sweeping through the hospital. If that were the case it would, of course, be a serious emergency. But no, there was really no evidence for this; apart from Dr. Vilgis, none of the patients had shown any features of infection, and they had had no contact with each other. Although it was theoretically possible that a staff member was an unwitting carrier of a rare disease, Abraham had to dismiss this explanation as very unlikely.

Again and again, he went through the cases, one by one, in an attempt to explain what was happening. Doggedly, he laid out the common features: first, all the deaths were unexpected; second, in all cases, the patients were very unwell, even if not at the actual point of death; third, all were receiving a variety of medications, in all but one case intravenously and in some cases orally too; fourth, all were accommodated in single rooms; fifth, all were apparently alone at the time of death or for some period prior to death; sixth, all had died in their sleep at night, or at least were discovered by a nurse in the early hours of the morning; seventh, there had been no references to anything untoward or unusual, either with respect to the patients' medical condition or to treatment programs; eighth, in all cases there had been discussion among the team members about whether to sustain treatment, and in a few the question had been raised explicitly about whether it would be more humane to let them die rather than prolong their suffering through continuing treatment; ninth, in all cases there were complicated relationships involving family members that raised questions about the patient's continuing quality of life; and tenth—Abraham could not avoid adding it—all occurred in the pervasive current context of the discussions in the hospital about the need to limit care for elderly people being conducted under the name of Freedom to Choose.

However he looked at it, this was an extraordinary accumulation of circumstances and he realized that he could no longer avoid the conclusion he had been so doggedly resisting. Even if any single one of the factors could be explained, the chance of them all occurring together in six cases had to be regarded as vanishingly small. Further, even though Mrs. Gurewitz, Mr. Tzorvas, Mr. Alvarez, Dr. Vilgis, and Mr. McLeod were all going to die from their illnesses, that was not the case for Mrs. Dreyfus. He kept coming back to this case. There was no reason why she should have died. His own logic compelled him to accept what his heart had so frantically been denying. There was something rotten in the Royal Prince John Hospital. At least some of the deaths must have been the result of deliberate actions!

But who could be involved, and what means had they used? The latter question was not difficult to answer. Powerful and dangerous drugs were readily available in the hospital and the patients had intravenous drug lines. It would have been straightforward for someone with knowledge and access to drugs to enter a patient's room when he or she was alone and add a large dose of morphine or other medication to the drip. In all cases, the act itself would have been simple, quick, effective, and largely untraceable.

As to who was the most likely suspect, Abraham went through the possibilities. There were really only three. It was very unlikely that the culprit was Ashis. He had no motive and most of the deaths had occurred when he was off duty or elsewhere engaged in the hospital. Similarly, such acts would be inconsistent with Rebecca's character, and her evident distress on learning of the deaths showed that she had been as much taken by surprise by them as he was; he particularly remembered how shocked Rebecca had been after Mrs. Dreyfus had died.

That left only one remaining suspect. Abraham's mind had never felt so sharp or powerful. He could no longer resist the inexorable force of his own logic. The head nurse, Desmond Ray, had often—indeed, as far as he could remember, in all of these cases—taken a strong position against prolongation of treatment. He had an abrasive personality. He openly resented the subservient position of nurses in relation to doctors and craved the right to make his own decisions about medical management. He had full access to drugs. As head nurse he could come and go as he wished and no questions were asked if he stayed late or spent time on the ward outside his shift in order to complete outstanding paperwork. Abraham also recalled Mrs. Timoshenko's statements about Desmond, although in this case he had to accept that the nurse's version was more likely to be true than the patient's. And he recalled Desmond's words when discussing Mr. Alvarez, which had chilled him at the time: "If necessary," he had said, "we should even have the courage to help him on his way."

Abraham broke off his cogitation. His head was spinning and he felt nauseated with the horror of what he was convinced he had uncovered.

PART 15

MURMUR OF THE AGES

87.

"Oh, and old Mrs. Timoshenko died."

Abraham recoiled. "What do you mean?"

"Mrs. Timoshenko, the woman with cancer of the esophagus we saw yesterday. The scan had shown that the tumor was very extensive. She had lost a lot of weight—"

"She died?"

"Yes . . . er . . . She was found dead in the morning by one of the nurses. It was a peaceful—"

"Mrs. Timoshenko? Dead?"

"Well . . . yes . . . Prof . . . She did have terminal cancer . . . We knew that . . . She knew . . . She said . . ."

Abraham tried to contain his emotion. "How did she die?"

"I don't know. She was just found dead by a nurse in the morning."

"Did you ask for a postmortem examination?"

"I did. Her husband was so distressed he could hardly speak. But I understand that the family is Jewish and the burial has to take place quickly . . . I'm really sorry, Prof. Maybe I should have called you . . ."

"No, Rebecca, it's obviously not your fault. Thank you for your concern. I guess the death was expected. It's just that . . ."

"What?"

"It's just that she feared that she was going to die last night and I assured her that that was very unlikely . . . Well, she's gone now. She was a very sad soul. Do you know anything about the funeral?"

"No, I didn't ask."

"I've known her for so many years I think it would be proper for me to go.

I'll ask Jenny to find out for me . . . Maybe we should move on and see some of our surviving patients."

88.

Rebecca called. They had been asked to see a very difficult patient in ICU who could take a while to sort out. She wanted to know if Abraham would be able to visit her some time during the day. They made an arrangement for Rebecca to come to his office at eleven o'clock to acquaint him with the facts before going to the ICU together.

Two hours later Abraham was sitting at his desk working on his computer. There was a knock on the door. "Come in, Rebecca."

The young woman entered and sat down. Her expression was intense. "The case is, I think, a tragic and difficult one. The ICU registrar's contacted me to ask if we could help them think through what to do about it. The patient's a twenty-nine-year-old woman with cystic fibrosis. She has a ten-year-old daughter and a close and devoted family consisting of her mother and two sisters, as well as various friends who've provided support and care during her illness.

"Apparently, CF was diagnosed when she was in her teens but she was only mildly affected, with only a few hospital admissions until relatively recently. In fact, she's had a remarkably productive life already. She married at eighteen, completed a university degree in city planning, and works for a government department, or at least she did until she became ill.

"Last year everything started to fall apart. She had several episodes of pneumonia and her lungs deteriorated rapidly. The doctors were so worried that they put her in the hospital to look for reversible causes, but they couldn't find anything and ended up discharging her on her usual swag of medications months ago, just before Christmas.

"Two weeks ago she was admitted with a further sudden deterioration in her breathing. When she arrived at Emergency they thought she'd die then and there. She was transferred to the ICU but continued to deteriorate to the point where the mechanical ventilation was losing its effectiveness." Rebecca's face showed the strain she was under. "Because of the suddenness of the downturn and the absence of an obvious underlying cause it was thought by the doctors looking after her—the respiratory physicians who have known her all her life and the ICU staff—that there could still be an underlying cause that might be reversed, if only they could work out what it was. So they decided to put her on extra-corporeal membrane oxygenation to buy some time while they worked out the next step."

Abraham was listening intently to Rebecca's summary, taking notes while she talked. In his mind's eye he saw a picture of the patient: a thin young woman surrounded by family and friends lying in a bed in ICU connected to various machines and devices that were barely keeping her alive. One of the machines was the membrane oxygenation system, known affectionately to staff as "ECMO," the most advanced life-support technique available in the hospital. The size and shape of a washing machine, its principle was very simple: when someone's lungs stopped working and could no longer add enough oxygen to the blood to keep her alive, the machine could do this mechanically through a system of tubes running in and out of her body. Although the principle was simple the process was risky: to prevent the blood clotting in the machine the patient had to be given an anticoagulant, which increased the risk of bleeding elsewhere; and tubes and machines always carried the risk of infection. But the main problem with the technique was that it didn't always work. If the underlying problem couldn't be solved the patient would be trapped on the machine forever.

"I take it the ECMO was successful in keeping her alive," said Abraham.

"Yes, it was successful, but she's remained completely dependent on it. There's been no improvement in her lungs and her liver problem's worsened. ICU's now saying that they can't continue like this and a decision has to be made about when to stop treatment."

If the machine were disconnected the patient would die immediately. Furthermore, there seemed to be no other possible treatment. Lung transplantation had been considered but dismissed on the basis that it could not be done in the presence of the other medical conditions; in any case she was probably already too ill for such an operation.

If it were the case that there was no treatment left and a transplant was not available, this would mean that there was nowhere to go. "Has the problem been discussed with the patient or her family?" Abraham asked.

"I think that might be why we've been asked to get involved. Everyone else—the doctors who've known her for a long time, the ICU staff, the transplant people—are all personally involved and at loggerheads with each other about what to do now. I think we're walking into a hornet's nest."

"One that's already been stirred up, by the sound of it. I guess we'll just have to go and find out. What's the patient's name?"

"Her name's Briony Best."

The two took the familiar route from Abraham's office to the ICU. They negotiated the attendant and entered the ward. As always, Abraham was a little dazzled by the bright fluorescent lights that blazed there unceasingly. Rebecca knew where the patient's bed was and guided him there across the vast space. The door was slightly open. They peered cautiously around it and saw a patient sitting in a chair, obviously connected to various machines, surrounded by a group of people. "It looks like she might be busy now," Abraham said. "Let's start by going over the clinical documentation and talking to whoever we can."

They located the patient's notes and read through them together. The facts were almost exactly as Rebecca had recounted them. While it had been known for many years that Briony suffered from cystic fibrosis it was thought that she was one of the lucky ones and that it would cause her no more than a minor inconvenience throughout her life. When she had visited the hospital for her routine checkups, her condition was invariably reported by the clinician who saw her as "stable." But over the last year or so things had started to change. At first, she developed what seemed like no more than minor, annoying infections. By the middle of the year it was clear that her condition was deteriorating, as tests arranged during one of her hospital stays showed. She developed impairment of her liver function and a chronic, antibiotic-resistant infection in her lungs, and her weight fell to forty kilos. The present phase of her illness had begun two weeks earlier, in dire circumstances. The handwriting of the resident who admitted her communicated the sense of desperation and urgency everyone must have been feeling at the time:

> *29 yr old with longstanding CF. Now in respiratory failure. On 100% oxygen and mechanical ventilation but little effect? Moribund. Situation discussed with relatives. Will try ECMO . . .*

The unsystematic and incomplete documentation in the history was hard to follow, but it was clear that the response to the new technique of oxygenation was at first surprisingly good. A few hours later the same resident had written:

> *ECMO in place and functioning well. Oxygenation normal! Patient awake. Family present. Now just wait and see . . .*

The remaining notes comprised mainly technical details about machine settings; oxygen and carbon dioxide levels; and information about blood pressure, urine output, and so on. Abraham thought to himself, a little sarcastically, that this was probably as close as a medical record gets to a personal reflection on the great problems of life and death.

There were some brief comments from the various consultants who had been involved in her care. All were perplexed by the sudden and unexpected deterioration in her condition. The respiratory physician had written that he hoped that whatever had occurred would reverse itself spontaneously. The transplant consultant had been less sanguine, commenting that a transplant would not be considered "unless her general medical condition improved and the liver abnormalities resolved." The notes contained no indication that the patient herself or her family had been consulted about her condition, or even asked to express an opinion.

"Are you here to see Briony?" a voice behind them asked.

"Yes, I'm Rebecca and this is Professor Nevski. We're from the medical team," said Rebecca.

"Hi, I'm Emily, the nurse looking after her. Welcome. We'll be grateful for your input. Just ask if there is anything you'd like to know."

"We'll appreciate your help," said Abraham. "We've just gone through the history. How're things going now?"

"She's actually pretty stable now. The ECMO's still working effectively. Her oxygenation's almost normal and blood pressure, urine output, electrolytes, and full blood count are normal. She's been in sinus rhythm the whole time. She's able to sit up for a few hours a day and can eat and drink a little. But her liver function tests are still off—we don't know why—and the lung function tests from today don't show any improvement at all."

Abraham asked the nurse what Briony herself thought about it all.

"Oh, she's wonderful!" answered the nurse, effusively. "She's courageous and optimistic, and determined to get better. She's got plenty of support, too, as you can probably see from here. There's quite a group in there at the moment, playing cards together!"

He pressed the point a little further. How well did she understand how precarious things were, he was wondering. After all, her life was still hanging in the balance. She'd been on ECMO for more than two weeks, which was longer than anyone had been treated with it in the past. It was a new technique and there was no guarantee that it would remain effective indefinitely.

"I really don't think that either Briony or her family are able to think about the possibility of her dying. They know she was really sick when she came in, but she's got a husband and a ten-year-old daughter, Bree. I think she's really focused on being there for her child."

Abraham was struck by the obvious closeness the nurse felt to the patient. They had clearly spent a lot of time together. As if reading his thoughts, Emily went on. "She's actually the same age as me and I have a five-year-old child, so we have quite a lot in common. When her family's gone we talk a lot together. I guess I see her a bit as a friend as well as a patient."

As Abraham and Rebecca prepared to see the patient themselves, the nurse gave them some last-minute advice. "If you don't mind my saying, it's better to keep the visits short. She gets tired easily and the family doesn't like to be kept outside for too long. Come this way. I'll introduce you."

Briony was sitting in a chair with a deck of cards in front of her on a small table. A cluster of people were seated nearby: an older woman Abraham guessed to be her mother; two younger women bearing a distinct facial resemblance to the patient whom he assumed to be her sisters; and three other young women, no doubt personal friends. Briony, dressed in a regulation hospital white smock, looked pale and feeble. A large tube containing red blood emerged from underneath the smock and a similar one disappeared into the side of her neck. Both were connected to the large machine that stood to one side, making a quiet purring sound.

Abraham introduced himself and began in a friendly manner. "I'm one of the physicians at this hospital and I've been asked to see you. Would you mind talking with me for a few moments?"

"What's your role?" the older woman asked brusquely. "Why are you here?"

The directness of the question took Abraham by surprise. " . . . Er . . . I . . . um . . . I've been asked by the other doctors looking after Briony to see her . . . to review her treatment plan—"

"Well, Briony's seen lots of doctors today and she's very tired. Can you come back later?"

Abraham, still surprised, persisted. "I'm sorry to disturb your game, but I do need to see Briony. I don't know who you are, but I'd be grateful if you'd give us a few minutes alone."

The patient herself spoke, in a thin, breathless voice. "Mama, it's all right. I'll see him. I'll be able to manage." And then to Abraham: "Hello, Doctor, thank you for coming. I'd rather my family and friends stayed."

Abraham was struck by the obvious sense that he had intruded into a private meeting. He was taken aback, offended by the hostility toward him. Against his better judgment he couldn't resist asserting his authority. "It may be necessary for me to talk with you alone later," he replied, deliberately adding a stern tone to his voice, "but I'm happy to start with everyone else here . . ." He cleared his throat and started again. "As I said, I'm Professor Nevski. This is Dr. Rebecca Sanderson, the registrar in our department."

"What is your department?" asked the mother.

"I'm a general physician," said Abraham, maintaining his authoritative tone. "Because Briony's problem has so many facets to it I've been asked to try to form an overview of the . . . case"—he felt his own heart beating hard in response to the tense atmosphere but made an effort to appear calm and authoritative—". . . and to make some recommendations about future treatment."

Was this enough to take adequate control of the situation? He now knew that the family—or at least the mother—understood the precariousness of Briony's predicament, although he was uncertain about how consciously this feeling was held or whether it was shared by the patient herself. He turned to the older woman, "I assume you're Briony's mother. Is that correct?"

"Yes, I'm Briony's mother."

Abraham turned to the others. "Do you mind if I ask who you are?"

One of the younger women answered. "We're Briony's sisters, and these are her friends."

"Thank you," Abraham replied, with studied stiffness. He turned to the patient, not knowing what to expect. "Briony, I've heard a bit about you from the other people involved with your care and I've read your medical history. I realize that you were very unwell when you came to the hospital. That's why you're in the ICU. Can you tell me how you feel now?" He chose his words carefully, in an attempt to gauge Briony's and her family's level of understanding.

"I'm feeling better every day," Briony replied simply, in her weak voice.

"That's good. And how do you feel right now? Do you have any particular problems—pain, breathlessness, for example?"

"I'm a bit breathless, but it's really not too bad," the young woman replied, "and I do feel weak. Otherwise, I'm fine."

He was unlikely to make much headway with this line of questioning. He changed the subject. "I understand that you work in city planning?"

"Yes, that's right, although I've been sick for a while."

"Can you tell me how you see the future?" Abraham was really asking, Do you know that you're going to die? He could feel the others stiffen when he asked the question but maintained his gaze on Briony.

She didn't hesitate. "When I get better I'll go back to work. I'd like to do some more study."

Abraham persisted. "What do you think brought you to the hospital on this occasion?"

"I had a lung infection. I've got cystic fibrosis and that happens from time to time."

Abraham couldn't tell if the patient was being sarcastic or simply naïve. "Sure. But this was a serious infection. What do you know about your lung condition at this moment?" This time he was really asking, Are you aware that your lungs haven't improved and that you're only alive because you're hooked up to this machine?

"I'm just feeling better every day," the patient repeated.

Abraham realized that he wasn't going to get any further. The readings on the various screens displaying Briony's physical condition showed that her blood pressure and oxygen levels were satisfactory. He needed a way to end the discussion. At this point he would normally ask the family to leave so that he could examine the patient, and for a moment he was inclined toward this. But he wouldn't find out much more by doing so—the main purpose of such a move would be merely to tighten his control. He pulled back deliberately. "Thanks for talking with me. I won't disturb you any further, but if you don't mind I might visit you again a little later, perhaps tomorrow. Okay?"

"That'd be fine," the patient replied, showing little interest.

"Goodbye, everyone." Abraham directed his parting comment only in the general direction of the group.

He and Rebecca walked silently to the nurses' station where Emily was still seated. Abraham turned to Rebecca. "What did you make of that? I can't say that it was one of our most successful consultations."

"I think they know," Rebecca said simply.

89.

Rebecca and Abraham were sitting in Abraham's office. The young doctor was trying to explain why she felt so troubled.

"Prof, I sometimes find the practice of medicine so hard. I found seeing

Briony just now incredibly upsetting. I know that she and her family are suffering terribly, but . . ."

Her voice faltered and she broke off. She produced a handkerchief from under her sleeve and blew her nose. Suppressing his own feelings of emptiness and disorientation, Abraham spoke gently. "Take your time, Rebecca. These are big issues and we have to think them through carefully."

She sniffed a couple of times more and went on. "Look at Briony. She's got nowhere to go. She's stuck in ICU for the rest of her life. And it's our fault . . . I mean, I know that our intentions were good, but . . . all we're doing is keeping her alive. Good intentions don't count for anything. Look at all the effort we put into Wilma Dreyfus: we spent hours negotiating, counseling, caring. But what was it all for? For her to reject her daughters, who were maybe only there to secure their inheritance, and then to die unexpectedly? And what about Briony? She can't breathe anymore and only stays alive with the help of the machine. She can't move without the fear of disconnecting herself. We could say that there's a benefit in keeping her alive because she and her family get a little bit of extra happiness from being able to spend a few extra days together. But in fact, they're not happy at all. They know the outcome as well as we do, and the reality is that the extra days are just prolonging both Briony's suffering and theirs."

Rebecca was still talking through her tears. "I know that the CEO speaks a lot about the cost of beds and how the whole system's at risk from the aging population. That might be right, but even if it is, it's not my business. That's for her and the government or whoever to work out. But when my actions condemn someone to a meaningless life, that's relevant to me."

Abraham immediately thought of Desmond, whose views on this question he now knew well. He needed to give Rebecca guidance to ensure that she would avoid falling into the same trap. "Aren't you being judgmental there?" he asked. "How can you say someone's life is meaningless? How would we know? How would you know?"

Avoiding his gaze, she continued. "I know it can be difficult. Sometimes you can ask people in the hope that they'll tell you themselves not to start treatment. That's what they want to happen with Freedom to Choose. But I know it doesn't work. People just try to stay alive. If there's a small chance that they'll get better they'll take it, even if they're a hundred and it costs a million dollars. A small chance is better than no chance, especially where your life's involved. But with someone like Briony, it's obvious: she'll never be able to do the things a twenty-nine-year-old should be able to do. Simple things, like walk in the park, smell the breeze, or feel the sunshine on her skin. No one will ever be able to hold her, to hug her. She's stuck in that prison for the rest of her life."

"You're looking at Briony as if she's you," said Abraham, "and as if her life has to conform to some standard. And you're assuming that it's our job to impose the standard. But none of that's true. We're not moral police. We can't and wouldn't have the right to try to make the world conform to our own personal ideals. There's no ideal standard for what's good or bad, right or wrong."

Did he really mean this, he wondered as he was talking, or was he just trying to convince himself? Desmond thought his standard was clear-cut and incontestable.

"There's no algorithm that we can follow to decide on the best decision about a person's life. All we can do is muddle through, trying to do our best in complicated and sometimes contradictory circumstances."

As Abraham spoke, he experienced the familiar sense that his responses to the grand questions the young woman was asking were paltry and insufficient. It was not grand answers either of them needed.

"Prof, in cases like Briony's I often feel trapped. Everyone's tried hard, they've meant well, but we've created a situation in which we're stuck. We can't move forward and we can't move back. I'm not talking about whether to continue or withdraw a treatment or a technology. I'm talking about our own personal responsibility . . ."

They were talking about themselves. "It's true that we're trapped," replied Abraham, now as much out of weariness as conviction. "But it's a trap we have to be glad to fall into. The trap is the ethical basis of all human life. We start with the responsibility to others. That's the absolute beginning, the bedrock, not just of medicine but of all our values, our knowledge, even our faith. The focus on consequences—so dear to many doctors—is an illusion, an alibi, an escape. When the other calls we have to answer. Sometimes we get it wrong. I did with the girl in the train. Sometimes we're ineffectual, as we were with Wilma Dreyfus and Mr. Alvarez and Mrs. Gurewitz and countless others. But we had no choice then and we still have no choice. We're not slaves to a collection of abstract principles or norms of action set out in some code of conduct. Our actions can't be determined by our personal motives, however noble they might be. We don't start out to realize some set of fixed values or goals. We have to be true to our relationships, to the people who place their trust in us, who define us by their own experiences, their pain, their suffering, their travail, who are us. There is no other way."

Rebecca was again on the verge of tears. "Prof, this is a tough gig and I'm not sure I can do it. I'm just an ordinary person trying to live an ordinary life. Your standards are too demanding, too onerous for me. Like others, I need rules, simple rules, that are enough to make me confident that I'm acting decently. I'm not and don't want to be a saint. I just want the satisfaction that my actions are good enough."

"Rebecca, I understand what you say, but there *is* no escape. It's our fate. We're condemned to be ethical. Our lives are bound up with each other's. Once we've entered this path there's no other one we can take . . ."

He was tired, and he could see that she was too. She just shook her head. "It's easy for you," she said weakly. "You're so strong. You understand yourself and other people. Whatever happens never seems to ruffle or upset you. You never do or think or say anything improper. But I'm not like that. I don't know why I'm doing what I'm doing. I don't know why I'm here. I don't even know who I am."

Abraham, silently pleased by the intensity of the young woman's admiration for him, could find no reply. He wondered who he was but couldn't think of an answer.

90.

Abraham had been to many funeral services over the years and knew what to expect. This was a Jewish one. There would be the usual prayers in Hebrew and a brief eulogy expressed in euphemistic terms, delivered by a rabbi who in all probability had never met the deceased. As an atheist himself, in spite of his own Jewish background, Abraham generally found such events tiresome and insincere, although he recognized the importance of showing his personal respect and sympathy for the surviving family.

The service for Mrs. Timoshenko was in an old, rather nondescript building at the rear of a primary school he had not even known was there. As he entered, he noticed that it was an orthodox synagogue, a little surprising in view of Ursula's history of iconoclasm and liberalism. He assumed that the venue had been chosen hurriedly by Yevgeny, whom Abraham surmised must be bewildered and incapacitated with despair. He knew that in Jewish law a service for the dead was often held at the home of the deceased and required the presence of ten men. If this could not be assured—as, no doubt, in this case—the service was held in a synagogue. Abraham wondered fleetingly whether he would be able to find ten men to play this role when his father died.

In the center of the large, plain, rectangular room was a raised central area, square in shape, constructed in wood and marble. Here stood the rabbi and the cantor, in front of a reading platform on which the scroll of the holy law, the Torah, was placed, unrolled at the verse to be recited today. At the far end could be seen an elaborate alcove, marked by two wooden pillars on either side and decorated with floral patterns and stars of David, which Abraham recognized as the Ark, the storage place for the rolls of the Torah. The congregation—fifty or so in number—sat on hard wooden benches or stood untidily beside them, with the women to one side and the men to the other.

He entered and took a seat at the rear of the male section. The congregation—he assumed that only a few of them were mourners—were praying on their own. Each was whispering in a low voice, reciting words that Abraham couldn't catch and wouldn't in any case have understood. The plainness of the room produced a series of echoes, which came and went in soft cadences.

The effect was of a murmur with no obvious source that rose up and filled the voluminous space. It was like a muttering from the earth, as if the walls and benches themselves were talking. Abraham took in the atmosphere for some minutes. Then the rabbi began to sing. He sang the high, mournful chant of the desert, of the villages, of the townships, which itself echoed down the ages.

Then the congregation returned to its uncanny whispering, the incessant murmur, the disembodied voice that engulfed the whole. Abraham was struck with amazement. He had heard this sound before! It was Mrs. Timoshenko speaking, Ursula herself! The ancient voice, the evocation of suffering he had witnessed only last week, was reproduced here in this room, only hours after her death!

The rabbi rose once more. Now Yevgeny was standing next to him. This time the prayer was for Ursula herself. They were reciting the mourner's kaddish, the prayer for the dead, the ancient Aramaic hymn that the recently bereaved have intoned for thousands of years: "*Yishgadael vayishgadesh shema rebeh* . . . Blessed, glorified, honored and extolled, adored and acclaimed be the name of the Holy One."

This was Mrs. Timoshenko herself talking. The ostensible meaning was irrelevant: indeed, its banality only undermined and depleted the boundless beauty of the timeless chant. Ursula was being reclaimed by the ancestors with whom she had identified all her life. As the ancient prayer said, she had passed into eternity.

Abraham watched Yevgeny. He had aged. Ursula had always said that when one of them died the other would not survive long afterward. This was truly the end of an era—her era, his era, the era of their life together. Tears streamed down his face. His body looked eaten away with despair.

The ancient prayer was murmured by the multitude of strangers, who had never known Ursula or Yevgeny or their son Ivan. Like the nurses, the people here had not known about their achievements, the heights of the spirit to which they and countless readers of her books and listeners to his music had soared. This was the murmur of the ages, the murmur of sadness, of loss, of the fall. This was where words failed and then returned to succeed.

The rabbi and Yevgeny together intoned in mechanical cadences. "*Yit-gadal v'yit-kadash sh'may raba b'alma dee-v'ra che-ru-tay, ve'yam-lich mal-chutay b'chai-yay-chon uv'yo-may-chon uv-cha-yay d'chol beit Yisrael, ba-agala u'vitze-man ka-riv, ve'imru . . .*" Their tones were like a cosmic force that the other voices picked up and sent forth outward again, only to draw them inward once more, until finally they were no longer voiced by anyone but instead reverberated within, bringing harmony to the turbulent voices of all the bodies there, and everywhere.

Ursula's and Yevgeny's bodies were the texts of the age, texts disrupted, cacophonous, violated. Her world had been densely packed with words and music. The words were not merely the symbols through which her unconscious expressed itself. They were who and what she was. She had been the mélange of her almost randomly accumulated discourse.

Everyone needs a witness; hers had been Abraham. He had listened, he had received her passionate entreaties, even without fully understanding them. Now only the witness remained. Her cry, her lonely cry, was transformed, absorbed, into the cry of all and for all. What had once been Ursula now perdured as a living allegory, an untidy collection of fractured meanings and senseless babble, of sad complaints against the modern world she had abhorred and tried to renounce.

He understood now. She had called out to him. The actual words she had used had not mattered. What counted was her insistence, her doggedness, the purity of her imprecations. She had called out to him. He did not know if he had done his duty.

PART 16

MAKING SAND CASTLES TOGETHER

91.

braham, almost frantic, needed a strategy. He was aware that there was not yet sufficient evidence to prove who had perpetrated the crimes he was now certain had been committed. The criminal—and Abraham was sure he knew who that was—had to be coaxed into the open. So far, he'd been careful and clever. However, Abraham was confident that, given enough time, he would make a mistake. One mistake was all that was needed. Abraham would then have the evidence to prove his case. He had to bide his time until that moment.

There was no doubt about it: he was scared. But he also knew that now he had no choice. It was not merely that there was a criminal at large who needed to be brought to justice. Nor was it that other lives were at risk. It was that this, finally, was Abraham's chance to act. This was his chance to bring his life together, to show that he, too—like all those people he had been observing over the years—was capable of seizing control. This was his chance to prove to everyone—to Desmond, to the students, to Rebecca, to Nic and Madeleine, to his children, to his dead wife and his dying father, to himself—that he was more than an old academic windbag. This was his chance to show that he was a man of action.

Battling desperately to try to keep together a semblance of equanimity, he carefully calculated all the options and, after much indecision, eventually decided on a plan. He would make it known throughout the hospital that he was bitterly opposed to Freedom to Choose and was working to bring it down. Whenever the chance arose he would hint carefully that he was concerned that the program might be used as a cover for illegal acts. He would leave his suggestions vague and unspecified. He knew that the murderer would understand what was meant, while the other members of the hospital community would think that Abraham's insinuations were no more than rhetorical flair.

In order to give his quarry a false sense of security he would be careful not to suggest that he knew who he was. In fact, he would take elaborate steps to create the impression that he did not and would even plant the idea that he suspected someone else. Whom should he use as a decoy? He chose none other than the CEO herself. It was a private joke: in reality, as much as he disliked her, he—no more than anyone else in the hospital—could barely picture the revealingly dressed administrator furtively entering a patient's room late at night to execute a plan with the cool stealth and efficiency the murderer had repeatedly demonstrated. It was obvious that the actual murderer was an experienced clinician, and this excluded the CEO.

Sherlock Holmes himself could not have been craftier. As much as he longed to share the drama playing out in his mind—and his cleverness in responding to it—Abraham decided that the entire plan had to be kept to himself. This was partly because he did not want to expose his friends to potential danger, but the main reason was that he needed to give the murderer an incentive to act while he, Abraham, was still a solitary agent. Abraham calculated that his adversary would realize that, once shared, the facts could not be kept secret long and so he had to act before this happened. By deliberately exposing himself and increasing his personal vulnerability in this way Abraham was, therefore, offering a wager. He was keen to see whether it would be taken up.

He had to work completely in isolation. It would not always be easy to maintain this position. In fact already, more than once, Madeleine and Nic had questioned him about his obvious preoccupation, tacitly inviting him to share his burden with them. On these occasions, however, he had changed the topic with forced flippancy, signaling that this was not a subject he was ready to discuss.

Abraham knew that his strongest weapon was his skill at reasoning, his ability to solve a problem by the sheer, unrelenting force of logic. He would set aside a period every day to review and refine his campaign. His friends would think he was working assiduously on his articles. In reality, he would be seated silently in his armchair, whisky in hand, deep in contemplation, planning his next move.

92.

"Hello, Nic! It's nice to see you. What brings you to Ward 3B?" Abraham exclaimed.

"It's okay, old boy. I'm not checking up on you. Just taking a shortcut to gastro outpatients."

Abraham could see the head nurse standing with some of his underlings at the reception counter not far away. He spoke in a loud voice. "You'd better be careful," he said theatrically. "This is a declared Free Choice Zone. That means decisions about you might be taken freely without your knowledge. Sometimes they can be lethal. We're planning to put up warning signs at each end of the corridor."

"If you tried anything I'd claim political asylum immediately," replied Nic, who despite his obvious puzzlement could not resist the chance to join in on the repartee.

"That wouldn't work," responded Abraham, keeping a stealthy watch out of the corner of his eye. "We're under direct rule from the top. In fact, our elegant leader's in the habit of visiting us almost every night, of course usually incognito."

Exactly as Nic had left, Susanna, the Freedom to Choose consultant, swept into view. When she saw Abraham she slowed down and a look of uncertain expectation crossed her face. "Hello," she said with anxious cheerfulness. "It's so nice to see you again."

She faltered. Abraham, intoxicated with his new role, showed no mercy. "I'm glad it gives you pleasure to come here," he snarled, "but I have to ask you to leave my ward. Please do not feel that this is directed toward you personally. As you may inform your colleagues, from today onward Ward 3B is off-limits to Freedom to Choose staff."

He knew that the junior nurses would have no idea what he was doing but that the significance of the gesture would be very clear to Desmond. He tried surreptitiously to gauge the nurse's reaction but he had turned his face away.

93.

The various doctors involved in Briony's care had assembled in a small room at the rear of the ICU, not far from Abraham's office, to discuss how to proceed. Despite the mounting tension in the wards, Abraham had been asked to chair the meeting and had invited representatives from the many hospital departments with an interest in her condition. All the members of the group were known to him, although some more than others: among the less familiar ones was Kerri Yavuz, the recently appointed director of the hospital transplantation service. Abraham knew that, despite her outgoing personality and her interest in staff affairs, Dr. Yavuz had already acquired notoriety for her uncompromising nature and her insistence on controlling all aspects of decision making in her department, and he was keen to find out whether her reputation among the older physicians as one of the new breed of ambitious young doctors who made no attempt to conceal their determination to advance their careers was justified.

Abraham began, speaking formally. "Hello, everyone. Thank you for coming. As you know, we're here to discuss the matter of the care of Briony Best, a young woman who's been a patient in the ICU for the last seventeen days. I suggest that we proceed as follows: first, although we, of course, know each other I think we should start by stating in what capacity we are each attending this meeting; I'll then ask Rebecca to give a brief overview of the case, and then ask Ian, Damien, and Kerri to state their views about the current state of affairs. After this, we'll have a general discussion about where to go next. Is everyone agreed with this process?"

There were nods and general comments of agreement. "Okay, I'll start. I'm Abraham Nevski, a general physician, who's here to help provide an overview to Briony's care."

"And I'm Rebecca Sanderson, Professor Nevski's registrar. I'm here to assist and to record our discussion in the case history."

"I'm Ian Moloney, a respiratory physician, who's known Briony since she was sixteen."

"Kerri Yavuz, director of transplantation."

"And I'm Damien Trentino, director of intensive care."

"Thanks, everyone. Rebecca, over to you."

"Thanks, Prof. Actually, I'm new to the case, so you all probably know more about Briony than I do. In brief, she's a twenty-nine-year-old woman with cystic fibrosis, who's married and has a ten-year-old daughter and a close family. CF was first diagnosed at age sixteen and remained of mild severity until relatively recently . . ." Rebecca continued, recounting in detail the patient's history, recapitulating the key events that had come to characterize the young woman's oft-repeated life narrative—the hospital admissions, the courses of antibiotics, the recent decline, and the last two weeks in intensive care. She finished the story in the present: "Currently, Briony's in ICU on ECMO, still oxygenating well. However, there's been no recovery of lung function and the question has been raised about what we should do now."

She stopped, and Abraham resumed his role. "This is obviously a very sad and difficult situation. Before I pass over to Ian, I think it would be helpful to list the possibilities open to us, without any judgments about which course we should take. It seems to me that there are four: the first is that her lungs recover, she's weaned from the ECMO, and continues her recovery outside ICU; the second is that her lungs don't recover but that she receives a lung transplant; the third is that they don't recover and she stays on ECMO for a time until the treatment is withdrawn and she dies; and the fourth is that she dies before any of these possibilities have the chance to occur." Looking around, Abraham noted perversely to himself that the starkness of the choices matched the barrenness of the room. "Does everyone agree that these are the options? Is there any other possibility?"

Again, there was general assent. He then invited Ian Moloney to speak.

"I've known Briony for thirteen years, since the diagnosis was first made. I've watched her grow up, get married, have a child, go to university, and become ill and nearly die. I've gotten to know her family, including her mother and sisters and her husband and daughter. As you know, CF can show a wide spectrum of severity. Until recently, Briony's been at the very mild end and has been one of our best functioning patients. In fact, for a long time she's been looked on with envy by many of the other patients her age, whose lives were much more affected than hers. For this reason the decline over the last year has been all the more unexpected and distressing for all concerned. Over this time she experienced a number of infections. At first, this just seemed part of the normal routine but it's now become apparent that there's been a steady process of decline. To give you an idea of how unexpected this all is, only three months ago I had a discussion with Briony about what she was going to do this year. She had high hopes of going back to school and study-ing for a post-graduate qualification. None of us was prepared for what's hap-pened over the last two-and-a-half weeks. She came in literally on the point of death. We were all amazed and scratching our heads about what could be going on, and in that context I suggested that we put her on ECMO to buy some time to allow us to work out what was driving the process and what we could do about it. At that time I thought there was a good chance that her lungs would recover, either spontaneously or with treatment. The fact that that hasn't happened yet doesn't mean that it won't. We still don't know what the underlying process is, whether it's treatable or whether it'll turn out to be self-limiting. For that reason, I'm strongly in favor of pressing on with treatment. What's more, given her underlying high level of functioning, those of us in the respiratory unit would be very keen to have her put on the transplant list to receive a new lung as soon as one becomes available."

The physician was speaking very quietly but his voice was quivering with intensity. The next speaker was the director of ICU.

"When Briony came in everyone thought she was going to die. Usually we don't accept patients into the ICU who are about to die. In this case, however, it was put to us that the patient had very recently been functioning highly, that the underlying process was not understood, and that there was a reasonable chance that whatever it was would turn out to be reversible. For this reason we agreed to use ECMO as a stopgap measure, as Dr. Moloney said, to buy some time. This is still how we see the use of this technology.

"Before going on it might be helpful to say a few words about ECMO. This is a relatively new technique for mechanically oxygenating blood. It's used almost exclusively in emergency settings as a short-term means to support very sick patients while some other treatment process is taking effect. It's most commonly used in newborn babies or small children with respiratory distress, but it's increasingly also being applied in adults with a variety of conditions. We have only ever used it for short periods; in fact, Briony's already been on the machine for ten days longer than any previous patient at our hospital. The process is expensive. In addition to the cost of the intensive care bed, the equipment and nursing requirements are also considerable, and it can only be used in the intensive care setting. Last and most important, it carries major risks of infection, blood clots, and hemorrhage. The risk of infection is obvious, and we do our best to minimize it by maintaining perfect sterile technique. To prevent the blood clotting in the tubes the patient has to be kept anticoagulated with warfarin or heparin. This increases the chance of a hemorrhage and essentially, there's nothing we can do about that.

"In Briony's case, we've only ever seen the use of ECMO as a short-term, temporary measure. It's true that it's worked well—it is, after all, a good and effective technology. However, in other respects her condition has either stayed the same or actually deteriorated. Her lung function hasn't improved;

in fact, the most recent CT scan shows that her lungs are basically now just a solid mass. And her liver function's deteriorated, for reasons we can't explain. ICU is only ever a bridge. It's our role to keep someone alive until an underlying reversible problem can be reversed. We're not a final destination where people can stay indefinitely. Of course, I don't need to tell everyone that we have lots of people being considered for admission to our unit at any time and that we're constantly turning people away, people whose lives could potentially be saved by coming under our care. Accordingly, we're not prepared to support treatment that doesn't work and isn't leading anywhere. For that reason we've proposed that the treatment cease if there's been no change in the next forty-eight hours and there's no alternative escape route, such as a realistic plan for lung transplantation."

The ICU director's logic was inexorable. However, his even monotone was not entirely free from emotion. Despite the cool peremptoriness of his conclusion he was unable by his grave facial expression to conceal his awareness of its tragic implications.

"Thanks, Damien. That's really clear. We'll have to consider whether any chance of recovery remains. However, before we do that, we need to hear from Kerri."

Kerri spoke slowly and deliberately. "My message is brief. As sad as Briony's case is, she's not a candidate for transplantation. I wish this wasn't the case, but it is. We have very clear criteria and she doesn't fit them. She's too sick, she has serious liver impairment, and she carries a number of infections that would disqualify her in any case."

She stopped there, looking coldly at Abraham. Her categorical and uncompromising tone surprised everyone. After a moment's silence, Ian Moloney responded, trying hard to control his anger.

"With respect, Kerri, that's a completely illogical position to take. For a start, we often transplant very sick cystic fibrosis patients. Indeed, the fact that they're very sick is exactly why we do transplant them. In the last five years we've transplanted nearly fifty patients with the condition. I know you've only been here for a few months, but we have very extensive experience of transplantation in this area and a success rate as good as anywhere else in the world. Second, we don't know the reason for the liver impairment, and it's very likely that it's a consequence of the ECMO itself. There are a few reports to suggest this, as I'm sure you're well aware. If that's the case, the problem is likely to be quickly reversed with transplantation. Finally, a few positive tests for infection don't mean anything; patients with this condition have all sorts of organisms all the time. If we want to, we can eliminate any organism, at least for a period, which we could do if there was a need prior to transplantation."

The transplant director gave no indication of having noticed the barely disguised barbs in the doctor's reply. She remained implacable. "It would be unfair to the many other patients waiting for a lung transplant throughout the country and irresponsible to both the community and the hospital to transplant this patient. The criteria I mentioned have been developed on the basis of extensive consultation and modeling of outcomes. As sentimental as we may be, it is important to recognize that there are costs incurred in caring for Briony in the manner she has experienced. In a purely monetary sense these are considerable. I estimate that she's already cost the community more than five million dollars. Against this, there are limited benefits either for her or for other patients. I believe the unambiguous conclusion from the best available evidence is that the cost of transplanting a patient in Briony Best's condition significantly exceeds its potential benefits. We have our rules. I do not apologize for them."

Ian was outraged. "We're not talking about economic equations here, we're talking about human lives." He was almost shouting. "Briony's not just an instance of a statistical model. She's a young woman who's already given significantly to the community, who herself has demonstrated admirable personal courage and public spirit, and who has a ten-year-old daughter for whom every day that she can spend with her mother is a precious gift. You talk about models and evidence but you ignore the human reality underlying them."

"Briony will not be transplanted."

Abraham could see that Ian Moloney was trying desperately to control his rage and hastened to change the subject. "Maybe we can come back to this question. Can we discuss whether there's any chance of recovery of the patient's own lung function?"

Ian was grateful for the opportunity to talk nonetheless. "Obviously, Briony's lung function is grievously impaired at present. But simply because we don't know why it's so impaired, we can't say that it won't improve. I acknowledge that things aren't looking good for Briony at the moment and I'd be the first to say that her chances of survival appear very limited. However, the stakes are high. She may have a small chance of survival if we continue with the ECMO, but if we withdraw it, that chance will be zero."

"We do need some endpoints," interjected Abraham, who had an idea that he thought might allow them to make some progress. "What if we agree on a set of criteria and then continue for another few days and then reassess? Then, at least we'd be able to agree on whether we're going forward or backward."

"I'm all in favor of measurable endpoints," said Damien. "We're determined not to continue on an open-ended basis. However, we're not insensitive and dogmatic." Abraham could not tell whether this was a jibe at the transplant physician. "I'd be happy to reassess in forty-eight hours on the basis that if there's no evidence of improvement we'll most likely proceed to withdraw the treatment."

Ian Moloney, no doubt sensing that a modest concession such as this was the best outcome he was likely to secure, indicated his acceptance of this approach. "I'm happy to work with Damien to define a few criteria that we can measure, and I'll be happy to reconvene in a few days. However, forty-eight hours would take us to Sunday, so I suggest that we make it seventy-two."

Abraham admired the doctor's tenacity and loyalty to his patient, but also recognized that time was running out for her. "Well, that sounds like a way forward, even if it is only short term. I know the question of transplantation is a contentious one but it's not something on which we need a definitive answer right now. I suggest that we defer further consideration of that for the moment. Before closing, however, I'd like to discuss briefly what the actual process would be for withdrawal of treatment. Would someone just turn off the machine? If that were to happen would the patient die then and there?

What would her death be like? Who would do it? Would it be one of us or would you expect a nurse to do it? And what would we tell the patient and her family? Would we let them choose the time? What would we do if they opposed the decision and tried to resist?"

Abraham was conscious of the heightened tension in the room in response to these questions. Rebecca, who was sitting next to him quietly taking notes, briefly stiffened. Ian shook his head in sad resignation, almost imperceptibly. The ICU director answered, with a measured sense of gravity in his voice. "We've started to think about that. It might not be straightforward. No one could just switch off the machine and stand there while someone asphyxiated. We've decided that the responsibility for carrying out the decision should be that of the senior doctor in charge, not a nurse or other employee. We're not sure how we would do it. Some have suggested giving an injection of morphine or a brief general anesthetic to reduce the patient's own level of awareness. Others have suggested a gradual reduction in the settings on the machine until unconsciousness ensues, after which full withdrawal may be undertaken. As to your question about what we would do if Briony or her family tried to resist . . . I really don't know."

"Maybe you could give the job to Kerri!" Ian muttered under his breath, just loudly enough for all to hear. Abraham looked over at him and could tell that he was fighting to suppress his tears. The transplant physician recoiled slightly but remained silent.

"These are difficult and painful questions," Abraham said, trying to find a less contentious note on which to finish the discussion. "I'm sure everyone here's deeply mindful of the point to which Ian so movingly made reference when he spoke of the importance of remaining aware of the human tragedy involved here, not just for the young woman herself but for her whole family, including her daughter and her large group of close and devoted friends. We've agreed today that the current treatment can't be continued indefinitely but that we'd base our decisions about how to proceed on firm, well-founded data. As part of my role I'll talk with Briony and try to ensure that she and her family are aware of the seriousness of the situation so that, at the least, they're not taken completely by surprise if the almost unthinkable has to happen." He sighed slightly and hesitated for a moment. "We plan to reconvene in seventy-two hours to consider the next step. Does anyone have anything to add before we conclude?"

Everyone remained silent. "In that case I declare the meeting closed. Thank you for coming."

94.

Abraham and Rebecca remained seated after the others had left the room. They sat for a moment in silence. Abraham could tell that Rebecca, like himself, was very perturbed. Their eyes met. "It doesn't get much harder than this," he said. Then, after another moment's silence, he added, "Are you up to seeing Briony now?"

Rebecca nodded. "We have to talk to her," she said.

As they left the room Abraham looked around, wondering how many lives had been decided within its plain austerity. Without talking, they made their way back to the ICU ward and proceeded straight to Briony's room.

She was sitting in the same place as previously. Everything else was unchanged. The machine was still purring away in the corner. The blood containing tubes still entered and left the woman's small body. The computer screens, flashing lights, and other paraphernalia were as before. The only difference was that this time the six visitors were absent. Instead, sitting at the table was a small girl deep in concentration drawing with crayons on a sheet of white paper.

"Hello, Briony," Abraham said brightly. "Do you remember us?"

"Yes, of course," the patient replied, "you're the doctors from the medical team." Her voice was weak but her greeting was less frosty than on the previous occasion. "I'm sorry my mother was rude to you last time. But she can get very anxious. This is Bree, my daughter."

"Hello, Bree!" Rebecca exclaimed in a sugary voice. The child looked up briefly without interest and immediately returned to her drawing.

The young doctor smiled kindly. "How are you today, Briony?" asked Abraham.

"I feel much better," the woman replied. "I really think I'm getting better. I feel stronger every day. I'm looking forward to getting out of here and back home." She smiled. "No offence, of course. I'm really grateful for all you've done for me, but I'm just about ready to get on with my life."

"What are you planning to do when you leave here?" He watched her face carefully for a sign that she understood how unlikely this was. He found nothing.

"I've got heaps to do! This year I'm going back to university to start my master's degree in city planning. It's something I've wanted to do for a long time. But most important, I'll be spending a lot of time with Bree. Just look at her. Isn't she beautiful! She's my pride and joy. I love the rest of my family, of course.

But there's no love like the love one feels for one's child. Whenever she's here it's almost as if I'm well again, running with her, playing, sharing her life. Bree, sweetheart," she said gently, "show the doctors what you're drawing."

The girl briefly looked up from her work again. "This is me and Mommy at the beach," she said, continuing to draw. "Here's the water. Here's the sand. Here's the sky. We're making a sand castle together. Mommy's holding the bucket and I've got the spade. Here's a big wave about to crash into us."

The girl chattered on. Abraham looked across at the young mother. Her face was glowing and her eyes were shining with happiness. "Was there something you wanted to talk about?"

"I think we'll come back later," he said. "It's nice to see you anyway." And he bent over toward the girl. "It's a lovely drawing, sweetie. Thank you for showing it to us. We might see you tomorrow." The two of them left the room.

95.

After Abraham's plan to smoke out the murderous criminal had been put into action it was not long before signs that it was having an effect started to emerge. The first response was an obscure, apocryphal text message on his cell phone from an anonymous source. It read: "fools step in where angels fear 2 tread—u r in dangerous territory—beware."

When he saw this, Abraham felt a glimmer of resigned satisfaction. The murderer had taken up the challenge. His strategy was working. The endgame was approaching. It was now only a matter of time. He kept the pressure on around the hospital and spoke increasingly provocatively, in the cafeteria, in meetings, and on ward rounds.

Not long after, the text message was followed by an email, again from an obviously false address. It contained a photo of a corpse found in the desert, accompanied by a story about a businessman who had disappeared without trace.

He was thrilled and excited, but for the first time in his life he also felt genuinely terrified. He was not just talking about action now, as he had so often done in the past; he was actually immersed in it. He was not just looking in from the outside, advising people from a comfortable, safe vantage point about their most "ethical" courses of action. He was an actor, putting himself at risk, committing himself to a decision, and then anxiously standing back and waiting for the consequences.

He could barely believe what was happening. Here he was, his father dying in the hospital, almost beside himself with uncertainty, self-doubt, and grief, stalking a murderer in the Royal Prince John Hospital, a murderer who was also stalking him. Here was he, Abraham, a peaceable professor of medicine, at the heart of a real-life crime drama.

As scared as he was, however, he resolved to keep his nerve. His messages were getting through. His plan was working. Now there could be no turning back. In any case, he now had nothing to lose.

Through his general demeanor and his carefully chosen comments in the ward and at hospital meetings, Abraham skillfully cultivated the impression that he was closing in on his prey. Speaking in double entendres, he dropped dark hints that suggested certainty and confidence. He could see from the faces of trusted innocent colleagues that to them his remarks seemed like eccentric riddles, but he was convinced that the murderer would know that he was speaking directly to him. Abraham wanted his adversary to conclude that the only way he could hope to prevent exposure was by more threats and intimidation, through increasingly explicit messages. In doing so, however, eventually, inevitably, he would be drawn into making a mistake. When he did so, Abraham would be waiting; all he needed was the slightest lapse and he would have his proof.

He marveled at the cleverness of his plan. It was risky, but if he maintained his resolve, his clinical rigor, he would prevail. He'd spent his life interpreting obscure signs in attempts to decipher complex puzzles. He was now approaching the defining moment that epitomized all that he had pronounced, to his students and others, over the years: this was his puzzle of puzzles.

Further messages followed, and Abraham sensed that his anonymous opponent was gradually becoming more desperate, losing his composure. But nothing had yet been given away. He had to be patient, to wait for the single loose comment, the fatal moment of carelessness. This was Holmes versus Moriarty. Eventually, no matter how much skill and professionalism his quarry might display, the mistake had to occur.

In the ward, he kept a watchful eye. Ashis and Rebecca registered their confusion. Desmond was taciturn, subdued. When Abraham made a provocative remark about Freedom to Choose he took special note of the nurse's strange, silent glare.

It was as if he was living in a dream. Gurewitz, Alvarez, McLeod, Vilgis, Dreyfus, and Timoshenko were all dead. His own father had perhaps no more than hours to live. His vision was clear but clouds of black fog hovered all around.

PART 17

LAST VISIT TO SWAMP ROAD HOSPITAL

96.

Six weeks after his admission to the hospital Abraham's father's condition was no better, despite several courses of antibiotics and the initial improvement. Abraham and his sister had maintained a loyal vigil, but they realized that the end was drawing near. A family meeting was called. The doctor looked at the floor. "We have come to discuss what to do with his treatment," he started. "We've treated him for six weeks but are not getting anywhere." The doctor went on, but not once did he mention Abraham's father's actual name.

They agreed to withdraw treatment—none was being given now anyway.

That afternoon Abraham was with his father when Mordechai opened his eyes. "It's nice to see you," he said.

"Do you know where you are?" Abraham asked.

"Yes, I'm in the hospital."

"Do you know why you are here?"

"Yes, I'm preparing to die."

"That may be true." Abraham's voice was flat.

"What am I dying of?"

"We're not sure. We think it was an infection but we don't seem to be able to treat it."

"How long will it take?"

"We're not sure of that, either."

There was a pause. "Dad, did you enjoy your life?" Abraham himself was on the very edge.

"I'm not sure if I would say that I enjoyed life, but I can say that I exhausted it."

Another long, precious moment. " . . . Is there anything you want to say?"

" . . . I want to say goodbye to your mother Esther, to you, to Henny, to Jack . . . I want you to know that I tried to be a good father and a good lawyer. I hope I haven't disappointed you."

With that he closed his eyes and lapsed again into unconsciousness.

He died later that night. Visiting the Swamp Road Hospital for the last time, Abraham threw his arms around his sister. At least we've done our duty, he said.

PART 18

RIDING A CROCODILE

97.

braham returned to his office to find the place in catastrophic disarray. Books, CDs, and papers were on the floor along with many of his artifacts, two of which were obviously damaged. The rug was crumpled, one of the chairs and the small table had been overturned, and the pictures were awry.

On the desk was a typed, anonymous letter. His hands shaking, Abraham read it. "Don't venture into territory you don't understand," it warned. "Forces are in play that are more powerful than you." The last three sentences were especially menacing: "Do not ignore this warning. Accidents happen. Don't play with fire."

As he looked around the room the feeling of grim satisfaction that had come over him when he had seen the letter gave way to an overwhelming sense of desolation. His haven, his place of safety, his carefully guarded space of quietness and reflection, had been cruelly desecrated. It was as if his own body had been violated by the violent trespass.

For the first time he was not sure that he could go on. How could he have ended up like this? He was just an ordinary physician and here he was, the day after his own father had died, risking his life to solve six murders that no else yet realized had even occurred. How could it be that, in the midst of his grief, he found himself stalking and being stalked by an enemy of such formidable cleverness and ruthlessness?

He felt like he was in a trance. His life, his whole world, seemed to be in ruins. He struggled to maintain his resolve. A premonition that something terrible was about to happen welled up inside him, just as it had that day in the train when he had encountered Flora, the girl with the red hair. What would happen? Who would give way first?

The phone rang. It was Rebecca. She was very agitated and spoke fast. "Prof, I'm glad I've been able to catch you. Can you come quickly to ICU? Briony's taken a turn for the worse. She's had a brain hemorrhage and is deeply unconscious. They don't know how long she'll last."

"I'll come right away," said Abraham.

98.

When Abraham reached Briony's room Rebecca was waiting outside. "It looks bad. Briony was talking to Emily the nurse and suddenly lost consciousness. Emily tried to rouse her but couldn't. She called the doctors and they performed tests, including a CT scan of the brain. She's had a huge bleed in the left occipito-parietal region. The family members have been called and are on their way."

Emily was standing there, looking ashen. "I was just talking to her," she said. "She was sitting in her chair. We were comparing notes about our children. She was happy as she always is when talking about Bree. She laughed and said, 'I'll always be there for Bree.' Then she slumped in the chair. I called to her and shook her but she didn't answer. I could see at once that it was bad." The nurse gazed into space.

Inside the room Briony was lying on the bed. The inevitable tubes still entered and exited her body and the machine was still purring away defiantly in the corner. The patient lay motionless, her eyes closed. There was no movement of her chest. The only indication that she was alive was the trace of her heartbeat on the computer screen above.

Rebecca's eyes were wide with sadness. Among the group of people standing and sitting, Abraham recognized Briony's two sisters. When he looked at them they looked away. Everything appeared unusually vivid. He could hear the sound of sobbing and crying.

The door opened and Bree entered, accompanied by Briony's mother. The little girl ran up to her mother and threw herself on her. She was kissing and hugging her. The mother remained motionless, unresponsive. The girl was crying. She pulled at her mother frantically, at her hands, at her clothes, at her face. Briony's mother was with her trying to calm her.

The little girl shook her off. "Mommy," she screamed. "Mommy, don't die! Please don't die! Please, please, don't die!"

99.

Abraham and Rebecca were in shock as they left the ICU and walked across to his office. Neither said a word. Abraham was barely aware of traversing the long-familiar corridor and opening the door to his office. As they entered the room he noticed for the first time how distressed Rebecca was. Her body was hunched over, her face pale and blank, and her mouth clenched. The light frown lines on her forehead, which he had found so becoming, had become furrows of despair.

They were inside the office now. She looked around in amazement at the unfamiliar disorder. Her sadness cut deep into his soul. His own heart was bursting, for both Briony and Rebecca. He needed to provide solace, to give comfort for the pain. He thought of his father, of the murderer, of his life in ruins, of his fear. He tried to talk, but words would not come. He turned and locked the door.

They stood in silence, looking at each other, not knowing what to do next. She was swaying ever so slightly. He could take her hands, put his arm around her, reassure her. He tried to read her look. It was inquisitive, haunted, entranced. He was not sure what to make of it.

An abyss opened up in front of him. It was an abyss of danger, of danger greater than any he had ever faced before. He saw the risk of absolute destruction, of abjection, and annihilation. It was a risk greater than that of climbing Mt. Everest, of swimming the Amazon, of wrestling a bear.

This was the irreversible moment, the crossing, the point from which no return was possible. He leaped into the forbidden territory. With a sense of dread, his heart beating fast, he took the chance. He took her in his arms and kissed her on the lips.

He could feel the lace-like pounding of her heart. His own breath stopped. He waited for disaster. But it did not come. Miraculously, marvelously, as he moved toward her she surrendered herself to him. He could taste the sweetness of her mouth. He was intoxicated by her scent. It was an instant, a second, a minute, an hour, he could not tell. He held her tight. He wanted to care for her, to share her pain, her love, her comfort, her body, his body.

Leaping into the abyss, he plunged into the raging waters, surrendered himself to the danger, threw off the nameless years of denial, of inhibition, of relentless, uncompromising curtailment and propriety. For an instant all this lifted and he tasted the moment of freedom, of abandon, of the wildest possibility.

They kissed with their lips and their blood. His whole body was swept up with her liquid grace, her quivering vulnerability.

They looked into each other's eyes. He was shivering with love and desire, and she returned his gaze, with longing, with deep, quiet sadness, and with the unmistakable force of lust. He felt he could drown in the terrifying bliss of her fatal enchantment.

They moved to the couch. With her assistance he removed her clothes. First her top, then her skirt, then her underclothing.

He took in her youthful beauty. Then he caressed her, gently, reverently. Tentatively, respectfully, he explored her skin, her back, her thighs, her breasts. He savored the cool resilience of her soft flesh. He marveled at how in the course of his work he had examined arms and legs, palpated abdomens and breasts, and that though his actions now seemed identical, for him their meaning was somehow very different. He had often wondered about the difference between the medical touch—which could be gentle and, in its own way, loving—and the erotic caress. In the midst of his own pulsating ecstasy he now instantly understood that difference. The medical touch was unanswered. It dug down into flesh to understand what lay beneath it. The touch of sex was not an interrogation; it was a dialogue between two bodies. It was a call, an appeal, a hymn of praise, which was answered, with fineness and precision, by imperceptible movements, by the flooding of the senses, by touches, sights, sounds, smells, and tastes.

Abraham called Rebecca with his hands, with his lips, with his whole body. And her answer came at once, pulsating, vibrating, not as an echo but as another voice, in synchrony with his, mellow but clear.

She was answering his call. She removed his clothing, decisively and methodically. She unbuttoned his shirt and passed her hands over his chest. She held them there for a few moments, her eyes closed in silent concentration. He shivered at her gentleness, at her firm, unquestioning acceptance of his pledge to her.

She unbuttoned his trousers and gestured to him to remove them. He did so, and she drew close to him. She held him just as he was holding her.

He wanted to care for her as he had cared for no one else. He savored her body, first with his fingers, gently, silently, delicately, then with his cheeks and his lips and his tongue. He caressed the soft skin on her back, from her neck right down to her hips. Then her chest, her breasts, her abdomen.

He blew softly and inhaled the sweet smell of her pale skin; he tasted her nipples. He kissed her lips, her eyelids, her ears. He caressed her thighs with his eyelashes.

He moved to the innermost part of her. She showed him that she was thirsty for him. He tasted her juices. He drank from her bowl. In the steaming, pungent darkness he felt her moving under his lips, gently, silently, delicately. She signaled her pleasure and her desire for him, which was now unstoppable. She moaned, quietly, almost imperceptibly, sweetly.

He was intoxicated by the force of her desire, by her need. Come to me, she said silently. I want you. I need you. I love you, too.

As she guided him into her he plunged once more into the unknown, into that space, that forbidden place, of darkness and light, of lust, passion, and fruitful abundance. He knew of the danger but he had already abandoned himself to it.

They were sharing their flesh. He was hers and she was his, if only for these moments, these dangerous moments, of hope, joy, and nameless dread.

They were enfolded into each other's bodies. They pulsated together. For the moment, he experienced the deepest reverence, the deepest gratitude. He felt deep inside her. She was precious, delicate, exuberant. He opened himself up to her as she did to him.

He held her young voluptuous body tight, tighter, tighter still. He wished they could come forever closer. For a moment the dark cloud that had engulfed him lifted. His tender love opened up to become a world that was glowing, numinous. For a moment, he could face all challenges, surmount all obstacles, no matter how remorseless and intractable. For a moment, the great recent sadnesses of his life, the death of his wife and his father, the betrayals, the cruelty, the ruthlessness, the avarice, the deviousness, the pain, the suffering, for a moment, he could triumph over all of them.

The whirlpools of sensation swirled around them and seeped deeper and deeper into their tissues, overcoming them, drenching their consciousness. They joined in a perfect fluid of feeling. He melted into her sweet flesh, and she into his. He held her tight and he cried. He cried for his wife, for his children, for his parents, for his patients, for all those suffering people he knew and didn't know. He cried for the past and the present and the future. He cried out of sadness, out of happiness, and out of love.

They lay there, quietly. He gently touched her cheeks with his lips, then her eyelids, her ear lobes, her neck. As lightly as he could, he stroked her luminous body, limp and satiated with the joy they had shared.

He hugged her softly. "My darling," he said through his tears.

100.

They lay there together—for minutes, hours. Abraham was lost in a world of mists and light. He had feared that the world was about to collapse. Now, it seemed more beautiful, more luminous, more alive than he had ever known it before.

He lay next to Rebecca, still holding her tightly, still caressing the soft skin on her shoulders and back, still inhaling her intoxicating perfume. Out of the mist, improbably, unexpectedly, new images were taking shape, new shapes coming into view. For the first time since his wife had died he allowed himself to think of a future . . . "Rebecca," he started to say, "I . . ."

He hesitated, trying to utter the words that had so long been denied to him. He wasn't sure if he had actually spoken or was merely thinking. It was as if he was drunk: drunk with the pleasure, with the scents, with the warm softness, with the great bloom of caring and joy. As he was struggling with his words, Rebecca opened her eyes. She looked at him plaintively. "Prof," she said, "it was me."

He was still struggling to find the courage to utter the words he wanted to say and it took a few seconds for him to register that she had spoken. He adored her soft tenderness, the delicate vulnerability in her voice.

"Prof, it was me."

"What do you mean?"

"I was the one who gave them the morphine. The patients . . ."

It took him a few seconds to understand what she was saying. His look turned to horror.

"The morphine? The patients? You?"

"Yes. It was me. I gave the fatal doses to Mrs. Gurewitz, Mr. Alvarez, Mr. McLeod, and Dr. Vilgis. I gave the fatal doses. I did it. It was me."

He stared at her blankly. He was incredulous. "You?" was all he could say.

"I couldn't bear to see them suffer. I didn't want to kill them. I just wanted to help them find peace."

They looked at each other. His mind was numb.

"Prof, there's so much pain. It's too much for me . . . I'm so sad." Tears were streaming down her cheeks.

He thought his heart was bursting. He wanted to comfort her, but he had no more to offer.

"Mr. McLeod?"

"I came in late. He was screaming with the pain. He pleaded with me to help. He knew my mother and loved horses. He was a strong man but he begged me, like a baby. He implored me to end his suffering."

"What about Dr. Vilgis?"

"I sat with him for hours after Dora left. He was being exploited by her. He couldn't respond, but he was suffering, too. I'm sure of that. I looked at him. I stood over him. His eyes fixed on mine. He couldn't say anything but I could hear what he was saying. He was pleading for me to help him. I gave him the morphine and kissed him on the forehead. He smiled, ever so slightly. Do you remember Billy? His brother George said that the little smile didn't sound like much but to them it was everything. That's how it was. I know what George meant."

"What about Mrs. Dreyfus?"

"I had nothing to do with her death. It was a complete shock to me."

"But she was the one who convinced me that there was a plot, that the deaths were orchestrated."

"The last time I saw her was when I was with you. I'm sure she died of natural causes."

Abraham could not believe what he was hearing. His whole world was crumbling. "And Mrs. Timoshenko. What about her? She accused Desmond . . . and then she died."

"I sat with her, too. I looked in on her before I went home and she was already unconscious. Her husband, Yevgeny, was there. We talked. He told me about their life together, about the music, the literature, their son. He was bereft. He said he didn't know if he could survive without her. I held his hand and told him that the time was very short. Desmond was there too. He was gentle and caring. When I left, Mr. Timoshenko was holding Ursula's hand up to his face, washing it with his tears. I tiptoed out of the room. I don't know what happened after that."

For all the horror he now felt, Abraham realized that he loved Rebecca no less. He was overcome by the pathos of what he was hearing. He looked at her, lying next to him—her perfect, naked body, all sensuousness and sorrow. Is it possible to kill out of such sweetness and tenderness?

"What about Margaret Wilson?"

She was beyond crying now. "After Freedom to Choose was launched she called me every day. She asked me to come and see her. At first, she said she wanted to help me, one woman helping another to succeed. But that changed quickly. She told me it was my responsibility to control the numbers in the ward. Then she said if I didn't do what she wanted she'd make sure I never got a job anywhere in the country again. She asked me to spy on you. I was to report on what you said about her and Freedom to Choose. She asked me about your habits and I even had to describe your office in detail. She was very interested to hear that you had a bottle of whisky in the cabinet. I thought everyone in the hospital knew that.

"I tried to avoid her but I couldn't. When there were patients who were taking too long to die or get better she would contact me and demand action. She even called me about Briony. Prof, I'm afraid of her. I'm ashamed. I'm scared."

As Rebecca was talking Abraham suddenly saw how everything fitted into place. He understood now how the CEO had taken advantage of the pure-hearted, naïve young woman. He saw how Rebecca herself had become a victim of the scheme that under the guise of freedom and dignity had sought so ruthlessly to limit the care of their patients. And he could see how the young doctor had been used to execute the CEO's plans in the ward while Margaret herself was applying increasing pressure on him, through the text messages, the letter containing the hollow, empty threats, and the trashing of his office. All the clues had been there; why hadn't he been able to make sense of them? He was overwhelmed with shame and humiliation at how blind he had been. As much as he had disliked the CEO, he had never been able to imagine that she could sink to such levels of baseness. If he had been just a little more clever, how much tribulation, how much heartache could have been avoided!

And what price would now have to be paid for his failure? What would become of Rebecca? How could they abide the consequences of her terrible actions?

"You're so strong," Rebecca was continuing. "You can bear everyone's suffering and pain. You can carry it on your shoulders. You can take on other people's burdens so that their loads are lighter. But I'm not strong or brave. I'm just an ordinary person with my own weaknesses and failings. All I wanted to do was to help people. It's too much for me to bear. Prof, I'm so sad."

Rebecca's words echoed in Abraham's head. He was shaking with fear and sorrow.

101.

He was shaking violently. Rebecca was still talking. He rose from the couch and went to the cabinet to pour himself a drink.

"What will happen to me now?" she asked. Abraham was wondering about the same question.

The bottle was almost empty. Perhaps I am drinking too much, he thought, incongruously.

He returned to the couch and, sitting very close to Rebecca, held the glass in one hand and threaded his other arm around her. Her heart was still beating fast. Her skin was still smooth and fine, but now it was sticky, almost gelatinous, with sweat. He felt the gentle rhythm of her breathing. He could still taste her sweetness in his mouth.

There was a banging somewhere in the distance, or perhaps it was in his head. Rebecca was still talking, explaining, confessing. She was there naked, beautiful.

The knocking continued. His head was spinning. His hands were shaking.

The door burst open. It was Desmond. Abraham could feel the nurse's amazement as he took in the scene. "What on earth!"

Abraham and Rebecca remained where they were, transfixed. He pulled her more tightly to him. There was nothing else he could do. Then Desmond gave a scream.

"Abraham!" he shouted. Abraham was aware that he was running toward him.

"Abraham! Don't drink the whisky!"

Abraham felt a blow as their bodies collided. Desmond tore the glass out of Abraham's hand and hurled it across the room. There was a crash as the glass hit the wall, then a tinkling as the fragments landed.

The sound echoed in Abraham's head. He was dazed, amazed. He stared at the nurse. What was Desmond doing in his office? Why had he attacked him in this way? What had he done with the drink he had been holding? The sound of shattering glass was still resounding in his ears.

Rebecca was now shouting too. He wondered if he was dreaming.

"What's . . . what's going on?" he stammered, trying desperately to recover his senses.

Slowly the mist began to clear. Desmond was standing, quivering. Rebecca was still beside him. "I . . . I think . . . I think . . . we . . . need to talk," he said haltingly.

102.

The three of them were sitting in the office. Abraham and Rebecca had quickly thrown on their clothes. Rebecca's hair was in disarray. Abraham was sitting on the couch and Desmond and Rebecca in the armchairs. Desmond was holding the almost empty whisky bottle.

"I tried calling your cell and your office phone," said Desmond with intensity, "but you didn't answer."

"I had the cell off," said Abraham, "and . . . I . . . er . . . we . . . were distracted . . . What is this all about?"

"Something terrible has been going on in the ward over the last few weeks," Desmond continued in the same tone. "You know as well as I do. First Mrs. Gurewitz, and then Mr. Alvarez, Mrs. Dreyfus, and Dr. Vilgis. I was sure that they received assistance with dying. I don't know who was doing it but I was convinced it was something to do with Freedom to Choose.

"As you're well aware, I've felt strongly that we shouldn't treat dying patients too vigorously just to keep them alive for the sake of doing so. You and I, Abraham, have had some pretty torrid arguments over the years. Freedom to Choose at first seemed like an opportunity to ensure that patients aren't overtreated, although as I was saying the other day I fully realize that the reason for introducing it has nothing to do with freedom and autonomy.

"But that's beside the point. I oppose unnecessarily prolonging treatment or keeping patients alive simply for the sake of doing so, but I'm not in favor of active euthanasia, and I'd never do anything to kill a patient myself. I've thought about it a lot and I just couldn't do it.

"Someone was killing our patients. I don't know who it was, but I know how they did it. They came in during the night and gave them a large bolus of morphine. The patients were all receiving morphine through their IVs and would therefore all have morphine in their bloodstreams, so this meant that it was untraceable. At least, this was the case with Gurewitz, Alvarez, and Vilgis. Dreyfus wasn't receiving morphine; in fact she didn't even have an IV anymore. I don't know what happened to her; it's still a puzzle. But with the other four, I do know. I don't know who did it, but it was only the patients who were about to die. I reasoned that the person concerned either wanted to shorten their suffering or was trying to reduce their time in the hospital to save money. When the CEO sent round her memo congratulating us on our success in cutting down the average length of hospital stay I concluded that it must have had something to do with her. At the very least, she seemed to have a close interest in what was happening in our ward.

"I knew that you were anxious about what was happening and were talking loudly in the hospital about Freedom to Choose. There was a lot of discussion among the nurses about how you were trying to provoke a fight with the CEO. I didn't want to get involved—it's none of my business, and you and I, admittedly, haven't been close. I thought the best way for me to behave was to keep my distance. I wanted to find out what was happening in the ward and I came in on a number of nights just to observe.

"I also kept an eye on the drug inventory. That's my job anyway, but I was especially careful because of what was happening in the ward. The morphine usage was high, but it was within the limits of what had been ordered. I concluded from this that the cause of death in the patients who died was a rapid administration of the entire dose they'd been prescribed.

"Last night I came in late and took a look around. I walked around the ward and up near the procedure room, to my surprise, I met the CEO herself, dressed in her usual flouncy clothes. She was surprised to see me, too, and got very flustered. She said that she'd been working late and had to check a package for a vendor number or something before heading off home. She'd never done that before and it was obvious that she was lying. She tried to make small talk about how things were going, praising me for the smooth running of the ward and the reduced bed stays. Then she asked about you, Abraham."

"What did she say?"

"She started by saying that you were one of the most respected physicians in the hospital. Then she said that she knew that you and I had not always had a smooth relationship. I don't know where she got that from but I suppose it hasn't really been a secret. However, I didn't say anything to disabuse her because I wanted to know what was coming next. She then asked me 'in confidence' if I'd noticed anything about you lately. I said no. She asked if I thought that you drank too much alcohol. I said no. She asked if I was aware of whether you'd ever used other drugs, and I said no. Then she left. I was very puzzled. I knew that you and she hated each other and the rumor was going around the hospital that you were out to get each other, but—especially in view of all this—it seemed very odd for her to be snooping around late at night, particularly when she was so taken aback at bumping into me.

"I lay awake all night trying to work out what might be going on. I'm sure she wasn't the person who gave the doses to the other patients; she wouldn't have the skill to do so, and in any case it would have been too dangerous for her to keep visiting the ward. I decided that there had to be a bigger, one-time reason why she was in our ward. Then I had an idea: she's a pharmacist and if she knows anything she knows drugs. She has all the keys to the hospital and I wondered if she might have entered the drug room by herself late at night. The room is at the far end of the ward and at that time there's usually no one else around. It was only her bad luck that I was there snooping and I saw her.

"When I came in this morning I went straight to the drug room and spent nearly an hour going through what was there, checking it against the inventory. All the morphine and the barbiturates were accounted for, as were the major tranquilizers and insulin—all the drugs I could think of that could be used for dangerous purposes. I was about to give up when I remembered that we'd had a supply of sodium oxybate that we'd gotten in a few months ago when we had that girl in with narcolepsy. I only knew of it because it was in the news at the time and the nurses had had a bit of a discussion about it. It's sometimes used as a party drug called GHB, and exactly at the time the girl was in, there was report about a party in the western suburbs where three people overdosed on it and had to be taken to the hospital, and we ended up with one of them in our ward. We'd looked up the drug and found it was a stimulant that became dangerous if mixed with even small amounts of alcohol. We were a bit amused that we had one patient for whom the drug was a lifesaver and someone else who was in because it'd been slipped into her drink.

"I looked for the sodium oxybate in the drug room but couldn't find it. I checked the inventory and no one had taken it away. I couldn't remember when I'd last seen it but I was sure we wouldn't have had another patient who'd needed it. During the morning I kept thinking about it. I decided that the CEO must have taken it. That's what she was trying to hide. But what was she going to do with it? Then just as the shift was ending, it struck me. She's the CEO, a pharmacist, with access to the full hospital drug inventory, with access to every room in the place, prowling round the ward late at night on some business that she wants to hide. She's taken the sodium oxybate and she's asked about your alcohol intake. It sounded mad—like some crazy crime thriller—but maybe, just maybe, she intended to spike your drink.

"I didn't know how to raise it—you and I haven't been friends—but I decided that I had to let you know. I called your cell and then your office phone number but there was no answer. I knew you were in the hospital and that you usually answer your phone, because everyone has to remind you about appointments you've forgotten. When my shift ended I decided to come around to your office myself. I came over here and banged on the door. I could tell you were here because I could see the light under the door. I thought maybe I was too late. So I broke in. And you can see from this bottle that I was right. There's not much left, but you can see the residue in the bottom of the bottle. I'm surprised you didn't notice it."

"I had my mind on other things," said Abraham. "But I did notice that the bottle was emptier than I recalled. She must have emptied out some of the whisky to ensure the concentration was right. That's pretty dastardly, emptying out such good whisky."

The others ignored Abraham's weak joke. "What would have happened if he'd drunk it?" asked Rebecca, with wide eyes.

"It acts within about five minutes," said Desmond. "It causes confusion, coma, and then cardiac arrest."

There was a silence. For once, Abraham was completely lost for words. Eventually, he said quietly, "I guess I owe my life to you, Desmond. But saying thank you isn't enough. I owe you an apology."

"It's true, you've been bloody rude to me over the years," said Desmond, "but I've taken that as just part of the rough and tumble of ward life."

"No, it was worse than that," said Abraham. "I didn't trust . . . I . . . I thought . . . I imagined that you were the murd . . . um , , . that you'd administered the morphine to those patients. I was trying to trap you."

"What do you mean? How amazing! Why would you think I would do such a thing?"

"I put two and two together . . . but in this case . . . I was wrong." Abraham looked blankly at Desmond.

There was another pause. Then Rebecca said. "Desmond, I think we need to let you in on the rest of the story."

"What's that?" asked Desmond. "Please go ahead."

"Well . . ." said Rebecca.

"Yes?"

"I . . ."

"Go on."

Her voice was faltering. "I was the one who gave the morphine to Mrs. Gurewitz, Mr. Alvarez, Mr. McLeod, and Dr. Vilgis."

"You what?"

"It's true. I couldn't bear to see them suffer and I'd decided that it was the right thing to do. But Margaret . . . the CEO . . . she also kept telling me . . ." She stopped.

Abraham broke in. "Rebecca and I have just been talking about it. She was caught up in the whole pernicious Freedom to Choose process. The CEO singled her out and exerted pressure on her, with both threats and promises. At the same time, Rebecca was disturbed at what she thought was the avoidable suffering of the patients and their families."

"But . . . I agree that we shouldn't prolong life just for the hell of it . . ." responded Desmond, still coming to terms with the new information, "but you can't just go out and kill people!"

Rebecca did not answer. "Rebecca was doing what she thought was right at the time," Abraham added expressionlessly. "It was the wrong thing to do, but her intentions were honorable."

There was another pause. "What about Mrs. Dreyfus? What happened to her?"

"I don't know. That had nothing to do with me. I think she just died unexpectedly of natural causes."

There was a long silence. Abraham was looking vacantly into space, Desmond was shaking his head slowly in disbelief, and Rebecca had buried her face in her hands. After a while Desmond said, simply, "So what do we do now?"

There was another pause. Abraham's mind was awash. There was the CEO, with her cruel obsession, and there was Rebecca, who had committed unspeakable acts out of raw compassion.

"We have to think it through," he said. "We have two problems: the deaths in the ward and my attempted murder. We could go to the police . . . But I'm not sure that would be a good thing to do."

He spoke slowly and deliberately, trying to contain his emotion and to force his mind to examine the issues systematically. "First, regarding the deaths, it wouldn't do any good for Rebecca to be charged." He breathed heavily and avoided looking at her. "It would cause incalculable pain and suffering to everyone concerned—to the families of the deceased patients, to the other doctors and nurses involved, to all patients and families who have anything to do with the Royal Prince John whose trust in us will be shaken, to the whole community . . ." There was a long pause. "On the other hand . . ." He was almost choking on his words. "On the other hand, what's happened . . ." Abraham's voice broke off. "I don't know! I really don't know!"

There was a long silence. Neither Rebecca nor Desmond said anything. After a while Abraham continued, with even greater weariness. "The other problem's about the CEO. Despite all the circumstantial evidence described by Desmond do you think we'd be able to prove anything? Everything's just supposition. Unless someone saw her coming into this room she'll just deny all knowledge. She'll just accuse me publicly of being an alcoholic, and she'll accuse Rebecca in relation to the deaths. It'll be in all the newspapers. The police will have to get involved. It'll be messy. This is not going to produce a good outcome."

He stole a glance at Rebecca. She looked lonely, scared, and lost. He wanted to reach out and take her hand but he knew that would be the wrong thing to do. He felt inside him a curious mixture of revulsion about what had happened, of deep emptiness, and deeper love. He had not known that it was possible to feel such contradictory emotions.

They both waited for Desmond to reply. "It's really complicated," he said gently. "You're right that it's surely not our aim to compound the suffering. There's been too much of it already." Then he expressed himself more decisively. "But we do need to get rid of the CEO. We've got to kill Freedom to Choose." He blanched at his unintended pun. "And we have to restore trust in ourselves and among ourselves."

Still battling with his feelings, Abraham was grateful for the simple wisdom behind Desmond's words and by his evident compassion. He shook his head slowly, just like Desmond had been doing, thinking of how wrong he had been. He burned with humiliation at the extent to which he had misjudged this courageous man who had discreetly maintained his dignity when Abraham was treating him with suspicion and disrespect, who had then saved his life, and who could still speak of restoring trust. Abraham thought he had seen and experienced so much humiliation by now he must be one of the world's experts in it.

"You're quite right. I think we need to signal to Margaret that we know the full story," replied Abraham. "She'll make the same calculation we have. She won't want to be dragged through the mire of police investigation and maybe the courts, even if the chances of a conviction are low. And if any of this gets out—even as an unsubstantiated rumor—her authority within the hospital will be destroyed. She'll have no alternative but to leave. How do you think we should send the signal?"

"Much as I hate to say it, I'm afraid it'll have to come from me," said

Desmond. "You've got too much of a history with her already. If there's any chance that this could be linked to your personal feud she'll just dig her heels in and refuse to go. But if it comes from me she'll know she's lost the support of the nurses as well as the doctors and that there's no alternative." He waited a moment for a reaction and took Abraham's and Rebecca's silence for agreement. "Leave it to me," he said.

Abraham suddenly became aware of his own and Rebecca's partial state of undress, which Desmond had carefully ignored. Embarrassed, he started tidying his clothes, buttoning his shirt and tucking it into his trousers. Rebecca responded to his actions in a similar manner, moving to the corner of the room and turning her back on them while she adjusted her underclothing. She finished by putting on her shoes and running her hand through her hair.

The three walked to the door. Abraham and Desmond stood face to face. Abraham hugged Desmond. "Thank you, my friend," he said simply.

He turned to look at Rebecca, and their eyes met. She was pale, sad, and lonely. They held their gaze briefly. He tried in that moment to express to her his understanding, his gratitude, and his love. It was a lot to put into one silent glance but he knew that the opportunity to tell her all these things would never come again.

"Goodbye, Rebecca," Abraham said.

PART 19

QUIETUS

103.

It had been a long couple of months on the ward. When Abraham had returned from vacation, battered from his personal tragedy, he had been looking forward to the clear, uncomplicated focus of clinical practice. He always expected it to be intense and vivid. In the past few weeks, however, his whole world had been completely devastated.

He had entered the period with calm anticipation. He had had confidence in his own abilities and in the past had always enjoyed the challenges and complexities of clinical work. He had thought he was good at handling meetings with patients and families, at managing the high emotions involved, and responding to the need for careful, delicate adjustments in language and expression. He was an expert, after all. Although confident of his abilities he had also tried to maintain a degree of circumspection and reflectiveness about his limitations. He had avoided entering territory outside his expertise. Despite his reputation for roguishness he'd been measured and abstemious and—admittedly—had not objected to being seen by both patients and colleagues as a pillar of the community.

This comfortable formula had always seemed to work well in the past. But now, in a few short weeks, the whole comfortable equilibrium had been totally annihilated.

In spite of the difficult relationship they had had, in spite of the cruelty and jealousy and pusillanimity, he desperately missed his father. He was overwhelmed by how crucial the very fact of his father's continuing existence had been to him. Even when he had not seen him for weeks at a time, he realized now, he had always been aware that he was there. When they were not arguing in person he was often engaged in silent dialogues with him. He formed part of his intellectual and moral coordinate system. He provided order and stability to Abraham's life, as disordered and chaotic as his own mental state could be. Now, however, he was gone. All the things that Abraham might have said to him, all the arguments they might have had, all the disagreements and jokes and accusations that could have been made—they were now just silence.

He missed Mrs. Timoshenko, too. She had symbolized for him a whole world of meaning and imagination. In a curious way she represented his own ancestry. She was a link with a cultural tradition with which Abraham identified more than he had ever consciously recognized. She, too, was part of his imaginary world. And as in the case of his father, the sad, intricate symphony that had been her life had now been replaced by silence.

He reflected on the students. He recalled how he had shown off in front of them, flaunting his skills at observation and reasoning, and how he had basked in their adoring looks, their wide-eyed openness, and their sense of being overwhelmed by the task they faced. He remembered with pleasure their capacity to be moved by a new experience or discovery, as when Mrs. Newton told them about her illness and her life and admonished them to be true to their passion. He recalled the wonder on their faces and their moist eyes as her tragedy penetrated to their tender, untested souls.

He recalled his own lapses. There were, for example, his overconfident summaries of the medical facts, illuminated by the searing light of reason, that ignored the deep black waters of tragedy that lapped all around. He thought of the man with the heart condition who had loved animals. Who would have known that he harbored such a deep, unfulfilled yearning? How could Abraham, or anyone, armed just with the power of reason, have been able to see that? He had relied too heavily on his own thought processes, on his observations and deductions, and in doing so he had ignored the man's actual pain; to use the words of the students, he had ignored "the person behind the illness."

He had misjudged many people. Not all, but some. He had not understood the significance of Mrs. Dreyfus's relationships with her daughters. His actions had led to the betrayal of Mrs. Simpson. He had not been able to save Quentin Prince. And above all, to his enduring shame, he had tragically misjudged and misunderstood Desmond.

He had always said to whoever would listen that it was necessary to be "values driven"—that is, to be authentic, to avoid, as Marina Bell had chillingly put it, "faking it." He did his best to follow his own dictum. He tried hard. But he was imperfect, and not everything always remained under his control. Despite his precise deployment of logic and reason they were not enough; in fact, they were no more than the bare scaffolding on which the real stuff of illness and caring were built.

Everyday life is a plenitude containing many intense and vivid experiences. He had known that. He had told people about it. He had written it in books and articles. But he had never before actually lived it himself. He had been at the place where life and death decisions had been made many times, but it had never previously been his life; he had never previously been called upon to put himself at risk, to stake his own life and truth. When he was eventually called on to do so it was not at all as he had imagined. The cool scalpel of reason had turned out to be impotent against the unruly forces of imagination and emotions. In the tumultuous ferment, the training and the years of ingrained discipline gave way—to what? To brute feeling, to the tidal wave of sensory passion. Surely, it should not have to be like this.

He had genuinely tried to be driven by values. It was true that he had been pushed to the limit. But he had even gone beyond the limits by which he himself had defined moral probity. In his relationship with Rebecca he had passed into forbidden sexual territory, with who knows what consequences. What he did was wrong, or he had always thought it would have been wrong. But when it happened it had glowed with splendor and joy like nothing he had ever been able to imagine before and, he was sure, like nothing he would ever experience in the future.

He had crossed boundaries. He had been to the far limits of where human beings could go. At these limits he had found that much of what he had previously taken for granted, on which he had relied without question, no longer seemed valid. When he had reached the horizon, what had once appeared firm and solid had turned out to be no more than a mirage.

The phone rang. It was Jenny. "Hello, Abraham. No, don't panic, you're not late! I'm just calling to remind you that you have a clinic this afternoon. It's my new system, to remind you in advance and not to wait until there are ten patients waiting. You start at two. Is that okay?"

"Thanks, Jenny. I don't know what I'd do without you. I'm on my way."

He hung up the phone, put on his tie, and took up his stethoscope. Before he left he looked around his office. It had been his haven in a heartless world; it was now a haven that had seen some truly wild turbulence.

He set out for the clinic. Passing by the cafeteria he spotted Nic and Madeleine, who were sitting having lunch. He greeted them and Nic called him over. "Hello, old boy! Why don't you join us? We haven't seen you for so long. What have you been up to? Probably whiling away quiet hours writing your arcane philosophical texts while the rest of us are up to our elbows in everyday life, I bet!"

"I'd love to join you, Nic and Maddy, but I'm afraid I've got a clinic. Jenny just called to make sure that I'm not late. Perhaps we can meet for coffee a bit later."

"That'd be good," said Nic. "By the way, what do you think of the news?"

"What news?"

"You haven't heard! It's all everyone's talking about. The CEO's gone. She sent an email to all the staff at nine o'clock this morning saying that she was resigning to take up an important senior position with the government. Apparently it's been created especially for her. Fred Tauber's taken over as acting CEO as of this afternoon. The CEO's dead! Long live the CEO!"

Abraham just shook his head sadly. "That's the end of an era for the Royal Prince John."

"I thought you'd be overjoyed," said Nic. "After all, it's what you've worked for tirelessly for months. And it will mean that Freedom to Choose is finished."

"Yes, that's a good thing," said Abraham. "But the cost was high, wasn't it? And the battle was really bruising. I'm really not sure that there have been too many winners out of this difficult episode."

"You're uncharacteristically somber today," said Nic. "I was going to propose a wake at my place tonight. That might brighten you up. Would you come?"

"I'm not sure," said Abraham. "I'll try. I don't know. I'm tired after the months on the ward. You and I do need to talk, though, about the patients. I believe that you're taking over for me on Monday."

"Happy to talk any time!" said Nic. "But I trust you to leave everything shipshape. Of course, I'd expect nothing less. I have every confidence in you."

"Thanks, Nic. I do have to go. I'll see both of you a bit later." He turned to leave.

"Goodbye, Abe," said Madeleine. "Oh, by the way, you do know about Rebecca, don't you?"

Abraham's heart stopped. He spun around. "Rebecca? No. What?" A wave of terror swept over him.

"She's left too. I saw her this morning on her way out. She looked awful . . . odd, harassed. She put in her resignation, effective at nine a.m. today. She said she needs time. She wants to travel, maybe leave medicine altogether."

"Did you talk any more with her?" He did not disguise the ardency of his interest.

"I offered to talk to her if she wants to. She looks like she's not ready to talk yet, though. I'm concerned. She looked so weird. All I could think of was that she seemed . . . haunted. I think we really need to change the system. It's so unforgiving for young doctors. They're called upon to shoulder too much responsibility. It's especially hard for the young women. It'd be a tragedy if we lost a precious jewel like Rebecca because we weren't able to nurture her and give her the protection she needed."

"I suspect that your words are truer than any of us will ever know," said Abraham. He was choking with his own emotion and could barely speak. He knew that Nic and Madeleine could see how affected he was and he wanted to avoid having to explain himself to them. "Thanks for all the updates. I'll see you on Monday."

He turned away again and this time walked off quickly without looking back. His head was throbbing and his body was aching. It was aching for all the pain he had experienced in the last two months, and it was aching for Rebecca, whom he knew he would never see again.

He reached the clinic. Jenny was obviously pleased to see that for once he was on time and allowed him to spend a few minutes by himself in the consulting room before starting to see patients. He shut the door and sat in silence, thinking of nothing.

He went out into the waiting room, took the medical record on top of the pile and looked at the name. He almost smiled.

"Marina Bell," he called.

AFTERWORD

This is a work of fiction. The characters, places, events, predicaments, and dilemmas it describes are products of the imagination. The Royal Prince John Hospital, the Swamp Road Local, Abraham, Desmond, Rebecca, the CEO, and the patients do not exist and have not existed.

This is not to say that the content of the book is completely disconnected from real experiences. On the contrary, it has emerged from contact over many years with patients, nurses, doctors, and others who have shared their stories with me. I want to thank all of these people for the insights they made possible. I thank also the imaginary characters for the often surprising and unexpected lessons they have taught me. They may not have been flesh-and-blood real, but they were able to show me things that I could never otherwise have seen. I thank deeply John Wiltshire, Sally Gardner, Frida Komesaroff, Ilya Komesaroff, Rob Irvine, Victoria Baldwin, Elizabeth Kath, Paul James, Doug White, and Jeanne Thornton, who have commented—rigorously and trenchantly—on the world of the Royal Prince John Hospital as it has taken shape. I should also like to thank all the members of the team at Greenleaf Book Group for their helpful ideas and suggestions. I give particular thanks to Mirranda Burton for her evocative illustrations. The work has a great many faults but would undoubtedly have contained many more without the assistance I have received.

GLOSSARY OF MEDICAL TERMS
AND ABBREVIATIONS

Advance directive: A statement regarding kinds of treatment someone does or does not want in the event that he or she becomes incapacitated.

Amiodarone: A drug to treat irregular heart rhythms and other abnormalities of the heart.

Antibiotic: A drug to treat an infection.

Anticonvulsant: A drug to prevent epileptic seizures.

Aspiration pneumonia: Infection of the lung that results from inhaling food or stomach contents.

Atherosclerosis: Disease of the blood vessels: the most frequent cause of heart attacks.

Atrial fibrillation: An irregular heartbeat that sometimes predisposes to strokes.

Benzos, benzodiazepines: Anti-anxiety agents.

Carcinoma: A kind of cancer.

Cardiac failure (CCF): Congestive cardiac failure, the effects of inadequate or inefficient pumping of the heart.

Cardiology: The study of the heart.

Catheter: A tube that can be placed in a blood vessel, urinary passage, and so on.

Crohn's disease: An inflammatory disease of the bowel.

CT, CAT scan: Computed axial tomography: a sophisticated method of constructing X-ray images.

Cystic fibrosis (CF): An inherited condition that causes early destruction of the lungs and other problems.

Diabetes mellitus: A condition involving inadequate regulation of blood sugar levels, associated with damage to many organs.

ECG: Electrocardiogram a test to assess the electrical rhythms of the heart.

ECMO: Extracorporeal membrane oxygenation: a technology to oxygenate the blood where the lungs are unable to do so naturally.

ED: Emergency Department.

Edema: Swelling in a part of the body as a result of the accumulation of fluid.

EEG: Electroencephalogram: a test to assess the electrical rhythms of the brain.

Glasgow Coma Scale: A scale for assessing levels of consciousness, with fully normal being 15 and the lowest possible being 3.

Hemorrhage: Bleeding.

Heparin: A drug to prevent the blood from clotting.

Hypotension: Low blood pressure.

ICU: Intensive Care Unit.

IV: Intravenous; into the veins.

MRI: Magnetic Resonance Imaging: a sophisticated method of constructing images of the inside of the body using magnetism.

Naso-gastric tube: A tube that passes through the nose into the stomach.

Neurology: The study of the nervous system, including the brain.

Nil orally: Nothing by mouth: a treatment condition imposed in a variety of settings.

Non-steroidals, NSAIDs: A class of drugs used to treat inflammation or pain.

Oncology: The study of cancer.

Palliative care: A branch of medicine that cares for people with terminal illness.

Parieto-occipital region: Part of the brain on the side toward the back.

Prednisone: A drug that treats inflammation or suppresses the body's immune responses, sometimes referred to as a "steroid."

Registrar or reg: Hospital medical staff more experienced than house medical officers but still undergoing training.

Renal: Referring to the kidney.

Rheumatoid arthritis: A condition that involves inflammation and often destruction of the joints.

Staging: The process of determining the extent of spread or advancement of a malignant disease.

Steroids: Hormonal drugs, including prednisone, that reduce inflammation and the body's immune responses.

Subdural: Inside the brain, under the "dura" or outer covering.

Tachycardia: Fast heartbeat.

Thyroid gland: A gland in the neck that controls the rate of the body's metabolism and other functions.

Warfarin: A drug used to prevent the blood from clotting.

ABOUT THE AUTHOR

Paul Komesaroff is a physician and philosopher at Monash University in Melbourne, Australia. Among his other books are *Experiments in Love and Death* (2008), *Objectivity, Science and Society* (2009), *Troubled Bodies* (ed., 1995), and *Pathways to Reconciliation* (ed. with Philipa Rothfield and Cleo Fleming, 2008). This is his first novel.

www.ingramcontent.com/pod-product-compliance
Lightning Source LLC
Chambersburg PA
CBHW061619210726
48287CB00001B/208